CAMP REWIND

Praise for Meghan O'Brien

Thirteen Hours

"Meghan O'Brien's writing style is entertaining. She is creative and her story isn't the typical romance. It was a lovely little story with the elevator being the highlight of the story. If you want a long and very sexy foreplay then this book is for you."—*The Lesbian Review*

"Ms O'Brien has a knack for erotica and she sure isn't shy in showing it off! Goodness, this was a scorcher. I finished it about 24 hours ago and am still blushing, burning, and wanting."—*Prism Book Alliance*

"Meghan O'Brien has given her readers some very steamy scenes in this fast paced novel. *Thirteen Hours* is definitely a walk on the wild side, which may have you looking twice at those with whom you share an elevator."—*Just About Write*

"Boy, if there was ever fiction that a lesbian needs during a bed death rut or simply in need of some juicing up, Thirteen Hours by Meghan O'Brien is the book I'd recommend to my good friends…If you are looking for good ole American instant gratification, simple and not-at all-straight sexy lesbian eroticism, revel in the sexiness that is *Thirteen Hours*."—*Tilted World*

Battle Scars

"[The] main characters were well written and I could feel the pain and hope in each of them. As a former US Marine, I usually have a difficult time with books that try to discuss military concepts, philosophy, and events but I didn't feel that way with this book. There were plenty of things in this book that I could relate to."—*C-Spot Reviews*

The Muse

"Entertaining characters, laugh-out-loud moments, plenty of hot sex, all wrapped up in a really fun story. What more could you ask for?" —*The Lesbian Review*

By the Author

Infinite Loop

The Three

Thirteen Hours

Battle Scars

Wild

The Night Off

The Muse

Delayed Gratification: The Honeymoon

Camp Rewind

Visit us at www.boldstrokesbooks.com

CAMP REWIND

by

Meghan O'Brien

2016

CAMP REWIND

ISBN 13: 978-1-62639-793-4

This Trade Paperback Original Is Published By
Bold Strokes Books, Inc.
P.O. Box 249
Valley Falls, NY 12185

First Edition: October 2016

CREDITS
Editor: Shelley Thrasher
Production Design: Stacia Seaman
Cover Design by Sheri (graphicartist2020@hotmail.com)

Acknowledgments

Thank you to Shelley Thrasher for another wonderful editing experience. I absolutely love working with you. Thanks as well to the entire team at Bold Strokes for doing what they do—and putting up with my sometimes scatterbrained nature!

Thanks also to my wife Angie for being the best.

And finally, a shout-out to all the people I love: I appreciate your friendship and acceptance of a hopeless introvert like myself.

Last but not least, 1) Hi, Kathleen! 2) Sorry, Mom and Dad, this one has sex in it, too…

For the shy ones

CHAPTER ONE

"Camp Rewind?" Alice Wu stared at the cheerful brochure her therapist had just pushed into her hands, instinctively dubious that a sleep-away camp for grown-ups could offer even one answer to her many problems. "This is because I told you I wished my parents had sent me off to camp like a normal kid instead of forcing me to study next year's schoolwork and practice cello in my bedroom all day, every summer. Isn't it?"

Her therapist, a wonderful woman named Dawn Jackson whom she'd located via an online search only thirty minutes after being served divorce papers by her ex-husband, combatted Alice's negative tone with a sunny smile. "Looks like fun, don't you think?"

As usual, Dawn managed to radiate such genuine good cheer that, despite her anxiety, Alice couldn't help but return her smile. "It looks... interesting."

"And *fun*." Dawn clasped her hands together on her lap and established eye contact, a sign that she was trying to make a serious point. "Alice, we've been meeting once a week for almost a year now. Again and again, you've made it clear that you blame the lack of opportunities you had to interact with other kids during your so-called 'non-childhood' for the social anxiety you feel now. I know the idea of a summer camp for grown-ups is intimidating, but you've made real strides over the past few months, even if it doesn't always feel that way. Camp Rewind is an opportunity to interact with your peers in an environment that's not only ideal for making new friends, but which also happens to encompass exactly what you missed growing up. Sounds perfect, doesn't it?"

• 11 •

Alice studied a glossy photo of two women and a man standing next to one another at an archery range, arrows nocked, aiming at targets some distance away. Her stomach churned at the thought of subjecting herself to a week of unfamiliar activities with strange people. According to the brochure, in addition to archery, the camp offered volleyball, arts-and-crafts activities, horseback riding, swimming, boating, nighttime campfires, and what they called a "drunk field day." "Bring your own booze?" She skimmed the rest of the text. "You know I'm not a drinker. I'm not going to *become* a drinker just to fit in."

"Drinking isn't required." Dawn's tone, like always, remained calm and modulated in counterpoint to Alice's rising anxiety. "It's an option, since this *is* a getaway for adults, but I'm confident you wouldn't be the only person to choose not to imbibe. Plenty of people will go simply to bask in the nostalgia, or perhaps to experience a piece of a childhood they never had. Like you." She paused. "Believe me, I know how frightening this sounds. But doesn't *some* part of you want to go?" She pointed at a photo of two women laughing and appearing full of joy while sitting side by side in a paddleboat. "Don't you want this for yourself?"

The image blurred as Alice's eyes filled with tears, which spilled over and ran down her cheeks before she could force away the emotional maelstrom triggered by the pointed question. "Of course I do. I *want* to be happy. To have friends, a boyfriend, or…whatever. You *know* that."

"Yes, I do." Dawn softened her voice. "I know, too, how scary it is to imagine putting yourself out there like I'm suggesting. But, darling, if you want to change your life, you've got to do the work."

"I understand that, really, but this feels like learning to swim by jumping into the Bering Sea." Alice turned the brochure over in her hands before hurriedly passing it back to Dawn. She couldn't *possibly* spend four days and three excruciating nights in the company of total strangers. What if everyone hated her? Or ignored her altogether? "Can't I try something a little less intense at first? Like, an event that lasts only a few hours?"

"You can do whatever you want." Dawn set the brochure on the arm of her chair, still within Alice's line of sight. "I certainly can't force you into anything. You're an adult. You make your own decisions. That said, I believe you're ready for this. I really do."

Dawn's words stirred up a whole lot of complex feelings, likely as intended. At thirty-six years old, Alice didn't have all that much experience making decisions for herself. Her parents—particularly her mother—had dictated her entire life, including her daily schedule, until she was twenty-one years old. That was when her then-college boyfriend, now ex-husband, managed to secure her father's blessing to propose marriage, freeing her from one prison to live in another. John, her ex, was a brilliant engineer, as well as a narcissist and control freak. Though she'd accompanied him to work and family events, and occasionally, in the beginning, out with friends, she'd spent most of her married life alone at home, isolated from the outside world. She read a lot. Tinkered with her own engineering pet projects. Fantasized about being a happier person, more normal, more socially adept. More loved.

It wasn't that John explicitly forbade her from having friends. He simply hadn't cared to include his painfully shy wife in his plans, more often than not, and she felt too socially awkward to even attempt to meet people outside of work on her own. Now that they were divorced, the loneliness had become too much to bear. She was desperate for a social life, but her first few efforts had been near-to-complete disasters: one Internet date with an attractive firefighter who'd reacted to her obvious case of nerves by immediately losing interest, an evening at a social painting event where she'd frozen up and seemingly rebuffed a very nice woman who'd tried to engage her in small talk, and two meetings of a local book club where she'd failed to work up the courage to contribute beyond a mumbled introduction. *That* had been starting small, hadn't it? Why would Camp Rewind be any different for a hopeless dork like her?

"What are you thinking?" Dawn's low, soothing voice interrupted her headfirst plummet into self-flagellation.

The tears started to flow again, which only added to the immense shame Alice already felt. "I've already tried less-intense activities, haven't I? And failed. I don't know how to talk to people. I freeze up, stutter, lose my words…even mix them up or run them together, sometimes. So why would attending a summer camp that will not only force me to interact with a bunch of people I don't know, but also sleep *in their presence*, work out better than what I've already attempted?"

Dawn scooted to the edge of her chair and extended her hands. After a brief hesitation, Alice took them. Squeezing gently, Dawn murmured, "I can't promise it will. What I *can* promise you is that this is exactly the sort of experience you feel would have benefited you as a child. Would have changed your life, I believe you said."

Alice had made that foolish statement two sessions ago. Now she wished she hadn't. She'd been so certain, at the time. *I guarantee that if my mother had let me spend even one summer at camp like a normal kid instead of locking me away in my bedroom to become the perfect student and musician—a daughter she could take pride in—I wouldn't struggle so hard to make friends today. Just one week in the summer having fun with other kids my age…would have changed my entire life.* Scowling, Alice realized that she couldn't deny how much importance she'd arbitrarily placed on the notion of a traditional summer-camp experience. "I was being silly. A few days of arts and crafts and drunken three-legged races has never *really* changed anyone's life."

Dawn clucked her tongue. "I wouldn't be so sure about that."

Alice allowed herself to imagine actually going, for a moment. "But what if…" To her absolute horror, the tears that had recently subsided threatened to return on the back of a single, humiliating thought. "What if I don't make any friends?"

Once again, Dawn squeezed her hands. "I have faith that you can and *will*. You're intelligent, attractive, and quite funny, once you're able to relax. There's plenty for you to talk about and potentially connect with someone on: your robotics career, your garden, music, the trip you took to China last year to meet your father's family for the first time." After a moment of obvious hesitation, she added, "To be perfectly candid, I'm told there are usually plenty of opportunities for casual romance at camp, if you were interested in that sort of thing. I know you're lonely, and you've said you're curious about whether you could enjoy physical intimacy with someone who isn't John. This could be a safe place to explore that area of your life as a single woman. If it's a fling you're after, I can't imagine you won't find a willing partner. Even if you *are* a little quiet in the beginning." Dawn winked.

"Yeah. Maybe I'll meet someone who enjoys their women silent and frozen in fear," Alice muttered. "Which, let's admit, would be astoundingly creepy."

Dawn laughed and let go of Alice's hands. "Oh, I have more faith in you than that. You've learned to talk to me, right? It took you only two sessions to find your voice. First day at camp, you look around, find the friendliest face there, and pretend you're talking to me. Even if you don't come out of the weekend with a real friendship, I highly doubt that anyone will be outright mean to you. It may be called Camp Rewind, but these are adult men and women we're talking about. There might be one or two jerks in the crowd—there always is, right?—but I'm positive most everyone will play nice."

Alice swallowed against the boulder that had lodged in her throat. "I'll probably be the only one who shows up alone."

"I wouldn't be so sure about that, either." Dawn picked up the brochure, drawing Alice's attention to the cover for the umpteenth time. *Ideal for singles, couples, and platonic groups of nostalgia-seekers!* "But even if you *are* the only one who shows up alone, many adults want to go to a camp like this to make new friends the way they did when they were young. The brochure talks about that at length. You're not the only grown-up who hasn't had recent practice in the art of meeting people. For many, it's a real struggle to form new friendships after graduating from school."

Wasn't that the truth? Alice's last friendship, which had been admittedly superficial and largely based on the fact that she and Lin were the only two women in their class following a robotics engineering track, ended when she graduated from college and became John's wife. Since then, she'd yearned for another female friend—a *real* one, like she read about in books or saw on television—but hadn't any clue where to find someone like that. Was it possible Camp Rewind really *could* be the answer?

Maybe I should go.

"If you hate it, you can always leave." Dawn reassured her with a smile. "The cool part about being a grown-up at camp is that you'll have your own car. You can drive yourself right the hell home, whenever you want."

"That's true." Alice flicked her gaze again to the brochure in Dawn's hands. She sighed. "I'm sorry. As much as I *want* to try, I honestly can't see myself going through with this."

"Well, then that's the problem." Dawn handed the brochure back to her, and Alice took it without thinking. "Close your eyes with me."

Having learned to trust Dawn's methods—especially when they didn't involve communal sleeping arrangements or cavorting with groups of attractive strangers—Alice did as instructed. "Now what?"

"Imagine yourself arriving at camp. Parking. Getting out of your car, pulling your suitcase from the trunk, finding the main office where you'll give your name to check in."

Eyes tightly shut, Alice was already struggling not to vomit. "I feel sick."

"Breathe. In, out." Dawn inhaled and exhaled audibly. Alice matched her rhythm, and after a few breaths, as her stomach began to settle, Dawn went on. "Now picture yourself meeting someone—a friend or something more—and having the time of your life. What *that* might feel like, how much confidence you would gain. How happy you would be."

Alice let the fantasy carry her away, but not for long. She'd yearned for true companionship as far back as she could remember, but thinking about the subject stirred up vague, confusing, unsettling desires that she didn't know how to address. Forcing back those thoughts before they could take hold and prey on her emotions, she opened her eyes and pinned Dawn with a hard look. "I don't want to talk about this anymore today."

Dawn's expression faded, ever so slightly, into disappointment. "Like I said, Alice, I can't make you do anything you don't want to."

More than almost anything, Alice hated to disappoint. She blamed her mother for that. Guts twisted, she mumbled, "Sorry."

"There's no need to apologize. But will you do me a favor?"

Alice sniffled. "Maybe."

That earned her a chuckle. "Take the brochure home. Go online and do a search for more information. Think about it, sincerely. Optimistically."

Full of dread, Alice stared again at the brochure that had made its way back to her hands. "All right."

"Nobody will force you to go."

Good. She nodded. "I understand."

"You'll have to make the choice yourself." Dawn caught her gaze, forcing eye contact. "All I can do, Alice, as your therapist and someone who genuinely cares about you, is *strongly advise* that you consider enrolling in the upcoming session. You can't overcome your fears until you confront them. After all the good work you've done during the past year, it's time to take the next step. I have no doubt that you're ready for this. You're ready to be happy."

She *was* ready. Except when she wasn't. Alice cursed under her breath, fighting the urge to rip the Camp Rewind brochure to shreds. It would be better than succumbing to the full-body sobs threatening to take over. If only the happiness she so desperately wanted would simply…happen to her. Unfortunately, as Dawn never hesitated to point out, life didn't work that way. If she wanted to be happy, she had to do her part. She had to *try*.

"Fine," Alice muttered. When she saw the degree to which Dawn's eyes lit up, she clarified her point. "I'll go online. Check it out. Think about it."

Dawn beamed at her as though she'd already signed up. "I'm proud of you."

"I didn't say I was going." Alice frowned. Why did it feel like she had?

Dawn's expression of deep satisfaction never wavered. "You can let me know what you've decided next week. We'll talk about coping mechanisms and the cognitive behavioral tools for dealing with your anxiety in a camp-like setting. We can also role-play introducing ourselves to one another and making small talk."

As much as she hated the way Dawn always managed to push her exactly where she didn't want to go, she was also grateful. A little. Maybe. Stomach aching, Alice heaved a sigh and buried her face in her hands.

"Want to spend our last couple minutes together telling me how much you hate my suggestions? That usually seems to make you feel better." Dawn sounded amused. Good for her.

Alice shook her head. "Not this time."

She did hate the suggestion, of course. A summer camp for grown-ups sounded like the perfect social hell. Unfortunately, it also kind of, sort of, sounded like *fun*.

And it was probably, as much as she hated to admit it, exactly what she needed.

CHAPTER TWO

Rosa Salazar parked her brand-new-to-her-but-used car in an empty spot in the corner of Camp Rewind's gravel parking lot, as far from the main office as she could get. Then, hands shaking, she slipped on her sunglasses and checked her appearance in the mirror. She was still struggling to get used to her recently bobbed haircut, a dramatic change from the long, dark locks she'd treasured since adolescence. She hoped the sacrifice had been worth it and that nobody would recognize her during this first tentative step back into the land of the living after a year and a half in Internet-induced hell.

As was her habit, Rosa glanced at her phone despite the fact that she'd vowed to stop doing so for the next four days, minimum, at least fifty miles ago. An on-screen notification alerted her to the fact that she'd received three emails during her hours-long drive through the redwoods. One from her mother, full of concern, a short, encouraging note from her best friend Trayvon—one of the few people who'd stuck around after the firestorm she'd unleashed with a single, freelance essay picked up by a popular gaming website—and finally, an anonymous, colorfully detailed rape and death threat bearing the subject line, *Die you cunt social justice warrior slut whore*.

"Just another day online." Wearily, Rosa deleted the threatening email and powered down her phone. She was almost numb to such correspondence at this point. *Almost*. "What a perfect time to unplug."

She studied her reflection again, trying to judge the likelihood that someone would recognize her. The woman in the mirror looked nothing like the small photo posted alongside her lengthy critique of the previous year's massively bestselling video game for both its sexist and racist sensibilities, as well as its overreliance on sexually violent imagery to tell a lurid, immature story. She also appeared far older, and less optimistic, than the various snapshots of her younger, carefree, sometimes provocatively posed, college-aged self that her detractors had scraped from every social media account she'd ever created during the ugly, rage-filled aftermath of her essay's publication, when the Internet reacted to her opinions by creating cruel memes and sometimes downright pornographic images mockingly depicting her face and body. Best of all, she bore very little resemblance to the woman whose solo masturbation video—filmed for and texted to an ex-boyfriend years ago, long before she'd realized how easily cloud storage could be hacked by those determined to ruin someone's life— had been disseminated online without her consent, swiftly going viral and doing exactly that.

Some days it felt like everyone in the world had seen her naked. Touching herself. Moaning, saying stupid, *insipid* things. Things she'd never intended for anyone except her ex-boyfriend Marcus to hear. Logically, she knew not *everyone* followed Internet and social media scandals of the month, but living in the Bay Area, it rarely felt that way.

Even her father had seen the stupid video, the first few seconds at least, after some asshole emailed him the file. And it didn't happen only once. Both her parents' inboxes had been so flooded in the beginning that eventually her mother had to change addresses. Her father stopped going online altogether.

Rosa flipped the mirror up, no longer able to stomach the sight of her own face. After the past year and a half, she had a keen understanding of why public shaming persisted as one of the most universal, enduring, devastating forms of punishment known to civilization. It worked. Between her public humiliation and the unrelenting flow of threats promising physical and/or sexual violence, suffering, and even death, she spent most days feeling lower than nothing. Subhuman. A source of endless pain for all the people who cared about her. Those few she had left, at least.

She exhaled. "Enough self-pity." This whole summer-camp experience was supposed to help her escape her life and return to a simpler time when she wasn't an object of ridicule and/or someone who incited violent rage the world over. A time when she wasn't afraid to make a new friend or look a man in the eyes. Camp was about reinventing herself, even if only for a few days.

Here, Rosa Salazar didn't exist. During her stay at Camp Rewind, she would be Lila Sanchez: high school teacher, technology-phobic thus unfamiliar with Internet culture, interested in socializing only with other women. She didn't normally close herself off to any possibility for friendship or romance, having dated across the gender spectrum over the years, but between her almost exclusively male online cult of hate and the ex-boyfriend who'd dumped her right before the vicious comments on her article hit critical mass, she was ready to take a break from guys for a while. Besides, women seemed more unlikely to be familiar with the saga of her gaming-induced infamy. A sexist thought, she knew, but likely also the truth.

With a deep, steadying breath, Rosa got out of her car and trudged to the back of it. She hoisted her duffel bag from the trunk, then stopped and glanced around the lot as wave after wave of doubt rolled over her. Two guys who looked to be in their mid-thirties emerged from the front and passenger seats of a souped-up muscle car parked next to the entrance. They both spared her semi-interested glances as she stood rooted in place behind them, and then one slapped the other on the back of the head and took off running. His buddy whooped and sprinted after his friend, both of them acting like twelve-year-old boys instead of grown men pushing forty.

Maybe this was a mistake. She should have gone to a women-only camp, at least, even if the closest one she'd been able to locate was five states away. After being threatened with sexual assault in all its horrific permutations for more than seventeen months, she had a hard time not feeling skittish about the idea of wild, enthusiastic, alcohol-fueled masculinity.

Even as the worries flew through her head, Rosa rejected them. "No." She slammed the trunk shut and turned to face the office where the men had disappeared. "Fuck everyone. I'm not a victim."

As far as mantras went, it wasn't the most elegant or convincing. But it was hers.

As she took her first, tentative steps away from the security of her car, Rosa noticed that she wasn't the only one experiencing second thoughts. At the other end of the row where she'd parked, a lovely but absolutely petrified-looking woman with dark, shoulder-length hair was white-knuckling her steering wheel while she watched Rosa's slow march toward the main office. What a relief to see someone who appeared even more anxious than she felt. Rosa smiled at the woman but immediately regretted it when she saw the obvious alarm her attempt at encouragement had caused. The woman's arm twitched as though she was going to turn the key she'd no doubt left in the ignition, but instead she stared down at her lap, hard.

Rosa glanced away quickly, happy to afford the woman some privacy to battle her nerves. She, more than anyone, appreciated the exquisite agony of being scrutinized in public. Still, she hoped the woman would manage to gather her courage. Now that they'd shared a few seconds of panic in the parking lot of Camp Rewind, Rosa couldn't help but feel that a kind of bond had been created. Or, at the very least, that she'd identified a promising candidate for a camp friendship. It was impossible to imagine someone so obviously timid passing judgment or making critical, mean-spirited comments to a stranger, though Rosa had certainly been taken by surprise in the past.

Once she reached the camp office, Rosa paused, still tempted to turn around and leave. *And go where?* When home was no longer a sanctuary and death threats were delivered to her purse, did it really matter where she spent the next three nights? She sighed. In the end, only the thought of the shy woman in the parking lot—and how badly she would need a friend if she ever made it out of her car—imbued Rosa with the strength to go check in.

"Stupid," Alice muttered to her thighs, still too afraid to raise her head and check if the woman was gone. She tightened her hands into fists, digging her short fingernails into her palms until it hurt. "Can't even smile back and I'm supposed to spend the next three *nights* here? Yeah, that'll be great. Just perfect."

Frustrated when a fat tear dropped onto one of her balled fists, Alice consciously relaxed her fingers and used the collar of her T-shirt to dab at her face. The only way she could possibly make this situation worse was by giving herself red, crybaby eyes. That's what her mother had called them, on the few occasions when Alice had failed to keep her emotions in check and wept in her presence. Red, crybaby eyes would embarrass everyone, not least of all Alice. They would draw judgment, criticism, perhaps even mockery. Tears were unacceptable. Inappropriate.

Wrong.

Alice finished dabbing her eyes and peered at her face in the mirror. She looked…mediocre. Her mother had raised her to present herself as perfect as possible in front of others. That meant not only her appearance, which ought to be impeccable, but also her mood, attitude, and intellectual abilities. Alice sighed. No wonder she was so intimidated when she interacted with her peers, why she expected everyone she met to critically assess her and then find her lacking. As a child, she'd been told that's what would happen, every time, without fail. Dawn kept assuring her that, by and large, most people didn't care enough to scrutinize strangers for faults, and furthermore, the world was full of kind, open-minded, nonjudgmental people. Rejecting the lessons of her upbringing in favor of a less harsh outlook was a constant struggle, but Alice knew she needed to trust Dawn's wisdom if she ever wanted to grow.

Girding herself, Alice scanned the parking lot but couldn't find the woman who'd smiled at her. Evening was fast approaching, and the lot had filled up since Alice had first arrived two hours ago. She assumed most everyone had already checked in. They were likely in their cabins choosing beds right now, which would leave her no option except whatever was left over. With her luck, probably a terrifyingly tall top bunk in the middle of a crowded room. Tonight the camp was hosting an opening ceremony, some kind of group trivia challenge designed to help introductions, then a bonfire scheduled for after sunset, and every last bit of it sounded almost as fun as being waterboarded. Could she *really* go through with this? She didn't want to disappoint Dawn by leaving, but this was even more terrifying than she'd anticipated.

Alice steadied her breathing and closed her eyes, then visualized herself getting out of the car and walking into the main office. Pictured the woman who'd smiled at her standing in there, also checking in. Maybe if the whole interaction wasn't so unexpected, Alice could manage to smile back. With her eyes still closed, she practiced. Imagined the woman—pretty, seemingly friendly—greeting her with an amiable nod, a flash of her teeth. Fantasy-Alice grinned back while real-life Alice ghosted a smile, in case someone was watching. After a moment, she opened her eyes. As the real world flooded back, so did her doubts.

Exhaling, Alice murmured, "Plan B, then." She opened her glove box and withdrew three hand-rolled cannabis cigarettes she'd brought along in case of emergency. After a lot of research and a little experimentation, she'd discovered that certain strains of the plant helped to calm her anxiety, even enabling her to become more social at times. A toke or two usually had a positive effect, and although she'd had reservations about actually bringing her alternative medication to camp, now it seemed like quite possibly the only thing that would make her brave enough—or at least mellow enough—to walk through that front gate.

She crawled into the backseat and rolled the window halfway down, grateful for the now-deserted parking lot. Lighting up, she took three long drags in slow succession, exhaling each time into a personal air filter so as not to stink up her car or her clothes. When she was done, she carefully extinguished the remainder of the joint and sealed it in a smell-proof container she'd brought along for just that purpose. Once she'd tucked all of her supplies back into her suitcase, she returned to the driver's seat, leaned back, and let out a sigh of relief as both her body and mind began to relax.

"That's better." Alice closed her eyes again, once more picturing the woman who'd smiled at her. She really *had* been attractive, which was a big part of the reason the friendly gesture had been so frightening. Though Alice had never seriously considered dating women, she couldn't deny that they figured prominently in her deepest, darkest sexual fantasies. Warm and euphoric from the cannabis, Alice allowed herself to slip into a brief daydream.

She imagined walking into camp, only to be grabbed by the smiling woman and pushed against a tree for a passionate make-out session. She fantasized gaining the sexual confidence to both give and receive pleasure like she never had before and finally behaving like a normal person, capable of doing and feeling the things normal people did and felt.

Alice opened her eyes, glad when the fear didn't come roaring back. Rather than feel afraid, she felt peaceful yet resolved, albeit frustrated and even a little horny. If she *didn't* go inside, she would end up spending the next three nights alone, as always, wishing for more, stupidly, while refusing to go out and grab the opportunities that presented themselves.

If there was one thing Alice wasn't, it was stupid.

Besides, like Dawn had said, she could simply leave if she didn't like it here. Because she was a grown-up. With a car of her own.

Feeling anything but grown up, Alice opened the driver's-side door and got out. One foot in front of the other. She walked around the car, opened the passenger door. Grabbed her suitcase. Shut the door. Stopped to breathe, to steady her legs. To imagine the smiling woman again, this time as a friend. Someone with whom she could share a paddleboat.

Seduced by the thought, Alice defied her own expectations and went inside.

CHAPTER THREE

Later that night, Rosa scanned the laughing, jovial faces around the roaring campfire in an effort to find Alice, the shy woman from the parking lot. She knew her name only because Marcia, the exceedingly bubbly head counselor, had forced everyone to introduce themselves during a get-to-know-each-other team trivia challenge they'd played following the opening ceremony. Poor Alice had been visibly stricken to be the center of attention for even a few seconds, barely murmuring her name loud enough for Rosa to hear. As the last camper to check in, Alice had joined them shortly after the ceremony began. Unfortunately, Rosa had been seated at the opposite side of the dining hall and so didn't get the chance to introduce herself before they were placed on opposing teams for the trivia challenge. After the challenge ended, she watched Alice literally flee from the dining hall, but by the time she made it out the door behind her, she couldn't see the woman anywhere.

Had she left already? Maybe one forced instance of public speaking had been too much for someone that shy to bear. Rosa's writer mind whirled with possible explanations for where she'd gone and why she was at camp at all when she appeared far too reserved to enjoy the experience. Despite the handful of friendly interactions Rosa had already enjoyed with fellow campers, she was too intrigued by the mystery that was Alice to focus on anyone else.

Her newfound obsession with introverted Alice might simply be a convenient way to avoid throwing herself into camp social life, but she didn't care. As far as she knew, Alice was still at camp, too terrified to speak to anyone unless forced and apparently determined to avoid group activities in favor of hiding out on the periphery. If she really *was* still in the vicinity, Rosa wanted to find and befriend her. Not only to learn her story, but to offer her a boost in confidence, the feeling that she wasn't totally alone.

Truthfully, Rosa ached for her, knowing how unwelcome certain types of solitude could be.

Circling the bonfire, she drifted away from the raucous, tipsy, celebratory crowd as she fanned out her search. Glad for the big, bright full moon above, she made her way to the women's cabin but found it empty. Then she walked to the dining hall, where a lone camp employee was sweeping the floor. After that, she made a tense journey to the parking lot, where she discovered, to her relief, Alice's car still in its spot. So she hadn't left. Not yet.

Back inside the campgrounds, Rosa walked the same path they'd followed during the orientation tour they'd been given after the trivia game. She'd ventured to the far side of the main campus, almost to the lakeshore, when a familiar smell wafted across her path. Pausing to inhale, Rosa suppressed a chuckle and scanned the dark trees surrounding the trail. If that was Alice, she *definitely* wanted to be her friend.

Unsure whether to call out and risk making Alice run or startle her by sneaking up, Rosa searched the moonlit trees for some sign of life. She followed her nose a few steps down the trail, then stepped off the path into the woods. A branch snapped beneath her foot, eliciting a startled gasp from behind a nearby tree. Going still, Rosa cursed under her breath, then said in a loud whisper, "Alice?"

She saw something move behind the tree, and then everything went still. It *had* to be Alice, right? Taking a step closer, Rosa decided to identify herself, only barely remembering to use her fake name. "It's Lila. From the parking lot. I'm coming over there, so if you wouldn't mind at least reassuring me that you're not some B-movie sleep-away camp serial killer…"

"I'm not." The quiet, shaky voice was unmistakably Alice's. She said nothing else.

Approaching Alice's hiding spot like she would a frightened animal, Rosa held up a hand as though preparing to stop her from escaping. "Good. I was hoping to find you. Engaged in my preferred method of social bonding, no less." She came around the tree in time to see Alice's mouth twitch into a reluctant smile. When Alice tentatively offered the better half of a smoldering joint, Rosa accepted with a grateful nod. "Thank you." She attempted to take a hit, but the end had gone cold. Surprised and even a little impressed when Alice smoothly produced a lighter and sparked a flame in front of her face, Rosa grinned as she took a long, deep toke and held it in her lungs until they burned. Exhaling, she said, "Oh, that's nice. I'm not much of a drinker, to be honest, but this hits the spot."

Alice took the joint back with a shy half-smile, tipping her head to stare at the ground as she took her own lingering draw. Rosa sensed that she was trying to stall, unable to work up the courage to enter into full-fledged conversation. That was fine. Somehow, Alice's lack of self-confidence bolstered her own.

"This is nice. Peaceful," Rosa remarked mildly. She hoped Alice could detect the honesty in her words and understand that she wasn't mocking her. Anything but. "No pressure to talk." She took another two hits when Alice gave her the joint again, then a third when Alice waved at her to keep going.

Mid-inhale, Alice briefly caught her eyes and murmured, "You should catch up. Save me from myself."

Rosa blew a lungful of smoke up to float among the branches of the majestic redwoods towering above. "Does that mean you're already baked?"

Alice actually *giggled*. "A little."

"Is it helping?"

For the first time, Alice looked directly into her eyes. "Apparently."

Rosa chuckled and passed the joint. "I was a nervous wreck all last week. Nauseated every time I thought about coming here." She didn't intend to mention her biggest worry: the possibility of being recognized or, worse, harassed, during what was supposed to be a chance to escape her shitty existence for a few days. It didn't really matter, the reason for her fears. Alice's eyes lit up, evidence she'd made a connection. Eager to offer more, Rosa said, "I barely talked myself into checking in. If I hadn't noticed you sitting in your car looking even more terrified than me, I'm not sure I would have. But I figured we might need each other on the inside, you know, for moral support. So...I'm glad I found you."

Alice no longer seemed able to meet her gaze. "I'm glad, too."

"I'm hoping this means I now have someone to sit with in the cafeteria. Because I totally had this nightmare the other day where I was carrying my lunch tray around the dining hall, but all the seats were taken and everyone was staring at me." Rosa left out the part where they'd started to scream that she was a whore, a cunt, a feminist piece of shit who should go back to where she came from. She figured Alice would get the picture without that level of detail. "So…yeah. It would be a real relief to have a friend here. Someone to help me get through the next few days, to enjoy this experience I really *do* want to have."

Alice nodded. "I'd like that."

Rosa waited, wishing that Alice felt comfortable enough to share a little more. For whatever reason, there was so much she wanted to know about her mysterious new friend. Possibly there was nothing at all fascinating about Alice, but the fact that it was so difficult to find out only whetted Rosa's appetite for details. When Alice didn't offer anything, choosing instead to take another pull from the fast-dwindling joint, Rosa asked, "So what inspired you to sign up for camp in the first place? No offense, but you don't seem to be enjoying any bit of this so far. While I'm really impressed that you followed through and actually came, it's hard to imagine you choosing this experience for yourself unless you had a pretty specific reason."

When Alice looked at her, wide-eyed—presumably at the prospect of having to give an answer consisting of multiple sentences—Rosa attempted some damage control. "Or maybe I should mind my own business. Sorry."

Alice handed over the cold roach, which Rosa accepted mostly so it couldn't be used as a further distraction. Then, sighing, Alice shook her head. "No, *I'm* sorry." She took a deep breath and exhaled slowly. Managing only sporadic eye contact, she said, "This was my therapist's idea. I've been seeing her about a year now, and recently she's decided to push me harder to challenge my social anxiety. She's probably right. But I'm extraordinarily bad at this stuff. Like, beyond bad." Sagging, Alice rested against the wide tree trunk and closed her eyes. "So bad that even though all I want is to meet someone this weekend, a friend, you know, or…" She shook her head. "I just want to meet someone and you're really nice, but I still feel *so awkward*, even with you."

Rosa couldn't help but grin at the unexpected torrent of words from Alice's beautiful lips. They *were* beautiful, she decided, around the same time she figured out that she was staring at Alice's mouth. And that Alice was watching her do it. Rosa cleared her throat. "You're not awkward." Alice shot her a look that made it clear she wasn't buying it. Rosa shrugged in concession, then amended, "Well, not *inherently*. You're just…apprehensive. For whatever reason."

"That I am." Alice managed a genuinely friendly smile. "I appreciate you being so kind."

"Same here." Rosa returned the smile, warmed by the knowledge that a tentative friendship had indeed been formed. She couldn't explain why meeting someone so gentle and unassuming meant so much to her right now, but Alice's timid nature felt like a gift after too many fear-tinged, judgment-filled encounters with strangers whose motivations she couldn't discern. "Want to walk back and check out the bonfire together?" When a look of dread passed across Alice's face, she said, "Or we could…stay here awhile."

Sheepish, Alice said, "Here works for me."

"Yeah, me too." A small, dark shape zipped past Rosa's face, some type of nocturnal insect. She flinched and batted it away. The winged beast disappeared into the shadows enveloping them, gone in an instant. Then something buzzed near her ear, making her yelp. "Well, maybe not *here*."

Alice politely hid her laughter behind her hand. "To be honest, my legs are feeling a little wobbly all of a sudden. Maybe we could find somewhere to sit down?"

"Yes!" Rosa leapt out from behind the tree, scurrying back to the relative safety of the path. "Want to check out the lake? We can leave if anyone else has beaten us there."

Alice trailed behind. "Are we allowed to go down to the water at night?"

"Nobody said we couldn't." Feeling somewhat bolder now that they'd established a two-sided conversation, Rosa planted her hands on her hips so she could watch Alice's approach. "And we're adults, right? What's the point of being a grown-up if not to do whatever we want?"

"I've always been more of a follow-the-rules, exercise-caution kind of grown-up."

"I'm most likely here to corrupt you, then." Rosa pretended to curtsey, silly from the joint they'd shared. "Sent by the universe is my guess."

Alice giggled, then promptly stumbled over a tree branch in her path. Rosa moved forward quickly, reaching out to catch Alice's wrist before she could fall. Her hand automatically slid down to entangle with Alice's, like they'd done this hundreds of times before. Rosa held her breath, worried that she'd just blown it, that she'd scared Alice away.

But Alice didn't run. Instead, she tightened her fingers on Rosa's and, chest rising and falling rapidly, whispered, "You lead."

CHAPTER FOUR

They were still holding hands when they reached the lake. Alice wondered whether she should let go—had been wondering from the moment their fingers linked together—but couldn't bring herself to do it. Lila wasn't letting go. Did that mean she liked what they were doing? Alice felt like a sixteen-year-old girl with a crush as she obsessed over every detail of what was happening, desperate to find the meaning in this improbable turn of events.

Perhaps Lila was simply happy to have found a fellow pot-smoker amidst a sea of drinkers. Perhaps tomorrow morning they'd wake up and her new friend would want nothing to do with her in the cold light of day. Or perhaps Lila really was as genuine as she seemed, and as sweet, focused as she was on making Alice feel better about being at camp. That last possibility almost seemed least likely of all, if only because Alice refused to believe that she'd managed to accomplish her one true wish so quickly and easily. That would mean Dawn had been right. She'd made a friend.

"Oh, look!" Lila pointed at three paddleboats tied to a long wooden dock that extended nearly twenty feet into the water. "Let's go sit in one of those—and don't worry. I won't try to talk you into going for a moonlight cruise." She squeezed Alice's hand and tugged her forward. "We can save that for tomorrow night." When Alice faltered, hesitant, Lila laughed. "Kidding. Come on. Let's look out at the water while we talk."

Alice felt drawn along by an invisible force, despite the mild tingle of anxiety still in her belly. The joint had softened the sharp edges of her nerves, allowing her a detached coolness that simply wasn't possible most of the time. For that, she was eminently grateful. Despite her uncertainty over how this experience with Lila would ultimately play out, she'd accomplished more socially in the past fifteen minutes than she had during the previous year of therapy sessions. At this point she was committed to see where this experience led her. She would let the universe take its course.

The dock swayed gently as they stepped onto it, causing Lila to tighten her grip on Alice's hand. Unperturbed by the need to adjust her center of gravity, Alice slipped from Lila's grasp—a move that elicited a low noise of protest—to instead loop their arms together. "I've got you."

Lila pressed closer to her side, cutting the slight chill of the night air. Alice felt her shiver. "Thanks."

Surprised by the quaver in Lila's voice, Alice asked, "Are you cold?"

"No." They walked until they reached the farthest boat from shore, then stopped, still arm in arm. "For being so shy, you're pretty damn smooth." Lila stepped away, but not before giving Alice one last squeeze. "Here, let me get in first."

With surprising grace, Lila climbed into the far seat before offering her hand so Alice could follow. Alice grabbed on without hesitation, already so comfortable in the other woman's presence that she found it impossible to keep second-guessing Lila's motives. She stepped into the boat carefully, pleased when she didn't tumble onto her face. Though with Lila there to break her fall…

Alice shook her head, stunned by where her mind had chosen to wander. She'd found women attractive in the past, certainly. Since the divorce, she'd swapped a real sex life for a secret porn habit, with the girl-on-girl stuff her drug of choice. When she touched herself these days, women almost always played a starring role in her fantasies. Fear of disappointing her parents had kept her from considering such a possibility for herself when she was younger, but now that she was in her thirties, she frankly lacked the capacity to care what her aging parents thought about her romantic choices. She'd already disappointed them with the divorce, her social awkwardness, and her failure to produce grandchildren, among countless other minor failures. So why *not* follow her heart and explore whatever might actually make her happy?

"You okay?" Lila touched her hand. Now seated, she stared up at Alice with open curiosity.

Embarrassed by her thoughts, Alice nodded with a little too much vigor. "Just light-headed."

Lila's fingers caught hers and tugged. "Sit down, then. Relax."

Relax. Alice nearly laughed out loud. That was impossible now that she'd pictured Lila lying beneath her…naked…moaning. She cleared her throat, unsettled by her increasingly dirty thoughts and the unchecked arousal that flooded her veins. At this point, she'd been celibate for nearly two years. That had to be the problem—that, and the fact that she was higher than she'd ever been before. Lowering herself into the boat's seat, she moved with exaggerated care, afraid of revealing her lascivious thoughts through her body language.

Lila launched back into their conversation mid-stream, casual as ever, apparently oblivious to Alice's out-of-control libido. "So, therapy, huh? I actually started going again last year. Same woman I used to see when I was in college. It's nice to have someone objective to talk to about your shit."

"It can be." Unsure what to do with her hands now that she wasn't touching Lila, Alice folded them in her lap. "My mother doesn't believe in therapy. She thinks it's shameful, even crude, to discuss your personal business with strangers." She paused. "With anyone, actually."

"That sounds healthy." Lila's voice was heavy with sarcasm yet tinged with concern. "I'm sorry."

"As you can imagine, she's one of the main topics of conversation during most of my sessions." At the mercy of her upbringing, Alice cringed at the realization that here she was, unloading her personal business onto a complete stranger. What if this *was* inappropriate to discuss? "Anyway, I can't imagine you want to hear me talk about my mother. That's why I have a therapist, right? To spare everyone else."

"I'm happy to talk about whatever you're willing to share." Lila reached across the center console of the boat and touched Alice's arm, tentatively. "I want to get to know you. Overbearing mother and all."

Alice stared at where Lila's warm fingers rested on her skin. She wanted to ask, *Why?* Instead she said, "Careful. You can't imagine how overbearing my mother actually is. I could spend the rest of the night counting the ways and boring you to death."

Lila withdrew her hand, laced her fingers behind her head, and gazed up at the sky. "Go ahead."

Relieved not to have to worry about maintaining eye contact, Alice joined Lila's study of the stars. "How about I give you the short version?"

"All right."

She experienced a moment of worry before speaking, driven by the familiar fear of appearing stupid. *Confront your fears,* she coached herself, focusing on a cluster of stars while imagining her therapist Dawn was seated beside her. "My Irish mother got pregnant by her secret Chinese boyfriend—my father—when she was eighteen years old. Her parents kicked her out of the house, and despite the fact that my father's mother despised her and blamed her for ruining her son's life, they got married and moved into his parents' home. We lived there until I was five, when we moved three houses down the street. My mother embraced the Tiger Mom stereotype wholeheartedly, no doubt because my grandmother constantly judged and criticized her every move. So she put enormous pressure on me to be perfect in everything I did. School, the cello, debate team. I was a reflection of not only her, but of her relationship with my father. If I was anything less than perfect, Grandmother won." Alice stopped talking, feeling as though she'd been speaking forever. "That wasn't very short, was it? My apologies. Apparently that's what a year of therapy gets you."

"No apology necessary." Lila straightened, half turning to stare at Alice's face. "That sounds like a rough childhood."

"Oh, I don't know." Alice hated to claim any kind of disadvantage, particularly without knowing anything about Lila's background. "I had a roof over my head, food on the table, two parents at home, an extended family, a gorgeous cello to play for hours every day." She forced a smile, careful not to sound ignorant about her level of privilege. "Millions of people have rougher childhoods, believe me."

"Very true, but that doesn't make growing up under the expectation of unflinching perfection any less arduous." Lila's hand found hers again, the palm cradling her knuckles. "Don't diminish your experience just because you don't have the most tragic sob story I've ever heard, all right? My mom was always my best friend. I can't imagine growing up any other way. To me, not having that seems rough."

Alice shrugged. "Point taken. And it *was* rough—mostly in that I withdrew socially, too busy chasing my mother's ideals to make any real friends. Or to learn how not to be a total dork."

Lila stroked her thumb over the side of Alice's hand. "Stop that. No more."

"No negative self-talk, as my therapist says." Alice nodded, watching the motion of Lila's thumb. "Right. I'm done."

"Good." Lila ducked her head to catch Alice's attention. "Is your mother still around?"

"Yes. My father, too." Suddenly self-conscious, Alice looked away. "She was brutally disappointed in me when my husband filed for divorce last year. Things have been strained since, to say the least."

"What would she think of Camp Rewind?"

Laughing, Alice glanced over her shoulder at the shore, then grinned at Lila. "Considering that I never went to camp as a kid, I'm guessing she wouldn't be impressed. Luckily, the other benefit of a year in therapy is that I've largely stopped caring what she thinks. Honestly. I'll never make her happy, so I'm no longer trying." Still loopy from the pot, Alice let herself be swept away by her passionate rejection of her mother's judgment. "Now I'm trying to make *me* happy."

"Good for you." Lila sounded wholly sincere, and the praise warmed Alice in ways she could never have anticipated. "Seriously, you need to give yourself a lot of credit. It takes courage to reject a lifelong authority figure and do your own thing. And it *definitely* took courage to come here."

"I don't know." Reluctant to accept the compliment, Alice tried to change the subject. "So what about you? Why are you here?"

Lila's smile seemed to freeze almost imperceptibly. It was the sort of thing that Alice noticed when no one else did. She'd hit a nerve, though she couldn't imagine what. Afraid she'd somehow ruined the easy air between them, she opened her mouth to apologize, but Lila recovered her composure before she could get a word out.

"I just…needed to get away for a few days." Lila's eyes glistened, making Alice's heart beat faster in sympathy. "Recapture a simpler time, maybe. I don't know. I thought it seemed like a good idea, and so far I'd say I was right." She glanced away, then lowered her hand over the side of the boat to test the water. "The lake is still pretty warm."

"I'm not surprised. Temperatures have been unseasonably hot." Alice hesitated, not wanting to trigger any more negative memories in her quest to get to know Lila better. Still, she felt the need to address the tension she'd introduced. "I'm sorry if it felt like I was prying. That wasn't my intention."

Lila gave her a smile that reflected a complex mixture of emotions. "You didn't. Shit." She shook her head, tugging on the ends of her bobbed haircut with what seemed like frustration. "Here you just shared your entire life story—"

"Not the *entire* story." Alice kept her voice mild, all of a sudden worried she was about to chase her only friend away. "I haven't even started talking about my ex-husband yet."

Lila giggled, then fished around before producing the roach she'd passed off earlier. "I'm willing to bet we can get another hit out of this thing. Two, if we're lucky. If you want to talk exes, we probably ought to try."

Alice fumbled in her pocket until she found the lighter. "I'm in."

They erupted into uncontrolled giggles when, during a coordinated lighting of the joint, Lila nearly singed the tip of her nose on the flame Alice held in unsteady hands. The shared laughter felt so good that Alice quickly found herself near tears. She flashed back to the brochure she'd seen in Dawn's office, specifically the way the photo of the two women in the paddleboat had made her feel. After not believing she could ever have a moment like that for herself, here she was only weeks later, having it. Here *they* were.

Lila continued to chuckle as she confiscated the lighter. "Here, let me." She carefully lit the tiny roach, then said, "Want to shotgun this hit?"

Rather than admit she wasn't sure what that meant, Alice said, "Okay."

Lila took a long drag, then leaned across the boat's console to curl her hand around the back of Alice's neck. She pressed her open mouth against Alice's, so gently it made Alice's heart race and her body tremble. Startled by the intimate contact, Alice parted her lips on instinct, despite having no idea what to do. Lila passed the hit to her by exhaling into her mouth, lingering close for long moments after she ran out of smoke. The tip of Alice's tongue poked out automatically and bumped against Lila's top lip, almost as though she were actually bold enough to initiate a real kiss. Panic swept through Alice at the same moment her lungs finally registered the acrid heat of the hit and instantaneously threatened to explode. She jerked away and turned her head to the side, coughing heartily as she tried to recover from everything about the experience Lila had just introduced. A warm hand landed on her back and rubbed soft circles through her T-shirt.

"Easy," Lila murmured. "That was a big one."

It sure was. Alice rested her arms on her thighs and hung her head low as the euphoria of the plant swept over her, grateful for the excuse not to look Lila in the eye. Had Lila felt her tongue? Did she think that had been her attempt at a seduction? If so, was she disgusted? Horrified? *Interested?* Breathing deeply, Alice picked her head up to look out at the reflection of the moon on the water. She had no idea what to say or do next, yet she couldn't help but notice what a beautiful night it was. A night she would no doubt remember for the rest of her life.

Lila's hand ceased its rubbing motion but remained pressed between her shoulder blades. "I'm sorry. I didn't mean to embarrass you."

Alice shook her head, still not sure how to recover their rapport. Finally, desperate to say *something*, *anything* to break the awkwardness of the moment, she observed, "We seem to be apologizing to each other a lot."

"Well, I think it's necessary this time. I never wanted to make you uncomfortable."

Alice shrugged and shook her head again. "You didn't." She didn't expand beyond that. Honestly, she couldn't. "I just didn't want to cough into your mouth."

"I appreciate that." Lila's hand left her back, the spot it had been covering cold with its absence. "That's an old college trick. I was a little wild back in those days."

"I would guess we had pretty different college experiences." Alice chanced a sidelong glance at Lila, relieved yet strangely disappointed to find her once again studying the night sky. "I only started smoking cannabis after the divorce…occasionally, for anxiety. It seems to help."

"I'm glad." Lila shifted her gaze to Alice and met her eyes. "You said your husband was the one who filed. It wasn't a mutual decision?"

"Mutual between him and his girlfriend, perhaps. They didn't consult me."

"Ouch." Lila grimaced, then offered her a half-smile. "His loss, right?"

The cliché rolled over her without connecting. "I doubt he thinks so, but I appreciate the sentiment."

"Have you started dating again?"

Was it her imagination, or did Lila's question hold a note of restrained hope? As difficult as that was to fathom, the evening had already yielded one impossibility after the next. "One date so far, which was a total disaster. I could barely even speak to the guy."

"Why?"

"He was this overly attractive, well-muscled firefighter with a movie-star grin. I froze. Sometimes I think it's my fear of freezing—and by extension looking foolish—that actually makes the social paralysis happen. A self-fulfilling prophecy, I suppose. It's always been like that when I try to interact with people, ever since I was a kid." She could no longer hold eye contact when Lila smiled in a way that lit up her entire face, reminding Alice that she was every bit as attractive as her Internet paramour had been. *More*, even. "Dating…is possibly not for me."

"I hate to repeat myself, but again, give yourself some credit. You're doing really well right now, with me." Lila tapped her arm, rewarding her with a kind expression once Alice gathered the courage to look up into her eyes. "Or am I not overly attractive enough to make you *really* shut down?"

Not for the first time, Alice detected something in Lila's voice that hinted at genuine sexual interest, which wasn't *impossible*, right? It wasn't like she was some hideous monster from the deep. John had been into her, once upon a time. A strange calm came over Alice, no doubt helped along by her unprecedented high. If she made a fool of herself tonight, she could always leave first thing tomorrow morning. Right? Even if that *did* happen, she'd already achieved more than she'd ever dreamed by coming to Camp Rewind. This entire experience had been so surreal, so *wonderful*, that Alice felt moved to trust her instincts and lower her inhibitions ever so slightly.

"I think you're plenty attractive. *Extremely* attractive would be the more accurate way to put it." Alice cringed at the sound of her own voice, yet the words kept tumbling out. "You're exactly the right amount of attractive, I think, so…no, not *overly*. Which is a good thing." Her cheeks warmed, yet she managed not to hide her face, allowing her to witness the obvious pleasure her words elicited. "Maybe I find women less intimidating?"

"You and me both. There's a lot to like about men, but it's easier with other women, isn't it?" Lila moved closer, and for a crazy moment, Alice thought she might actually initiate a full-out kiss. Unsure whether she was ready to take that step, while simultaneously desperate for *something* to happen, Alice felt only marginal relief when Lila gestured at the narrow slice of water visible between her side of the boat and the dock. "Any way I might talk you into a quick swim? The water really does feel nice, if you want to test it with your hand."

Alice's head spun at the sudden change in topic. "Um…"

"You don't have to if you don't want. It's okay, really." Lila pulled back and peered down over the side of the boat, then out at the open expanse of water in the lake beyond. "I just…wouldn't mind cooling off a little."

Alice tried to decide whether she'd done something wrong, but she didn't think that was the problem. Was Lila nervous, too? Or embarrassed? Had Alice not been clear enough about her interest? Or had she misinterpreted Lila's intentions from the start? *Stop. STOP.* The stern admonishment in her head sounded like Dawn, yet it resonated with a righteous dose of her own self-directed anger. *Stop overanalyzing. Go with it. It's the only way to change.*

Lowering her fingers into the water yielded the pleasant surprise that the lake was even warmer than the night air. Alice craned her neck to survey the shore, half-expecting to find that other campers had discovered their hiding spot, but it appeared they were alone. Still, she hesitated. "Won't we be cold after we get out?"

Lila beamed as though Alice had already jumped in headfirst. Before Alice could turn away, she pulled her T-shirt over her head and tossed it onto the dock. Left in what appeared to be a black satin bra, she seemed only mildly bashful as she stood up in the boat and began to unbutton her linen shorts. "I wasn't planning to get my clothes wet."

Alice opened her mouth, but no sound came out. She couldn't tear her eyes away from Lila's belly button or stop herself from imagining what it might be like to put her lips against it, or below it. She watched Lila's hands ease the shorts down over her hips, drawing her attention lower, to black panties with a cut that perfectly emphasized the shapely bottom they concealed. Throwing her shorts onto the dock atop her shirt, Lila turned away from Alice, leaving her little choice but to admire the round butt that was suddenly right in front of her face.

Alice tried not to stare, but there was nowhere else to look. Desperate to speak as if to somehow prove that Lila hadn't rendered her completely tongue-tied, she managed to say, "Yeah, I'm not sure I'm ready to take my clothes off in front of you yet. No matter *how* well I seem to be doing tonight."

Lila looked down over her shoulder, smirking as Alice finally forced her eyes upward. "Like I said, that's totally fine, and I understand." Her gaze slid down Alice's body, a brief assessment. "For the record, though, there's no reason to be self-conscious. I think you're very attractive, too, and nothing about seeing you in your bra and panties could possibly make me like you any less." She cleared her throat and turned back to the lake. "I'm going in. Wish me luck."

Alice started to do exactly that, but Lila launched herself over the side of the boat and into the water before she could utter a single syllable. Crawling over the center console, she scanned the dark water as she waited for Lila to surface. At first she worried that Lila would attempt the classic gag of frightening her by not coming up—which she would have hated—but instead, a dark head and shoulders popped up out of the water about five feet away, and Lila graced Alice with a clearly exhilarated grin.

"It feels amazing!" Lila lay back, arms spread, legs extended, and allowed her body to float on the surface. "So refreshing. We should definitely go swimming when it gets hot tomorrow afternoon. It'll feel divine."

Of course, they'd naturally have to share the lake with their fellow campers during the hottest part of the day. Alice had packed a modest, one-piece bathing suit—and oh, how she wished she'd thought to wear it under her clothes today—but in a crowd, that would feel even more revealing than her cotton bra and panties did now. If she wanted a semi-private swim at camp, she would probably have to do it at night. Maybe even *tonight*. Alice grabbed the hem of her T-shirt in both hands and took a deep breath as she contemplated pulling it over her head.

"Would you prefer I turn around?" There was a splash, and when

Alice checked the source, she saw Lila bobbing in the water, facing away. "I promise not to look."

Silently cursing Lila's keen sense of observation, Alice closed her eyes and tried to decide what she *wanted* to do. Anxiety aside, fears forgotten, did she *want* to swim mostly naked with Lila? The answer was yes. Yes, of course she did. Of *course*. Because that was the kind of thing the woman she wished to be would do, and because this real-life fantasy might get even better if she mustered enough courage to be bold. Go with it, she reminded herself.

Feeling as though someone else was controlling her hands, she tugged her T-shirt over her head and launched it a little too carelessly toward Lila's pile of discarded clothing. Unfortunately, it fell well short of its goal, sliding off the deck and into the water before she could react. "Shit!" Alice fished her shirt out of the lake, feeling both stupid and alarmed by the idea that she had nothing dry to wear back to their sleeping cabin. "Damn it." She squeezed the excess water out of her shirt, then clumsily spread the sodden garment across the dock's surface to let it dry as much as possible without the benefit of sunlight. "*Stupid.*"

"Hey, it's okay." Lila swam up to the boat, waving a hand to get Alice's attention and snap her out of her angry self-recrimination. "You can borrow my shirt. I don't mind, really."

Alice blushed, then folded her arms over her chest when she remembered that she'd stripped down to her bra. "You don't have to do that. It was my mistake."

"I told you, I don't mind. Swimming was my idea in the first place. And plus, that's what friends do." Lila pushed away from the boat to tread water. She smiled, carefully. "Still want to come in? Or are you afraid to risk your jeans?"

Alice managed to chuckle and then, seconds later, to lower her arms from their protective stance in front of her bra. "I'm still coming. Just a little less cavalierly, at least when it comes to casting off my inhibitions."

Lila laughed, not unkindly. "Is it a fair guess you've never said *that* before?"

"Extremely fair." Aware that Lila was still watching, apparently having forgotten her promise not to, Alice overcame the last vestiges of her modesty and stood. Lila's gaze traveled down her body, settling on her hands as she fumbled to undo the button at her waist. She remembered how entranced she'd felt watching Lila do the same thing and marveled at the possibility that her attraction was truly reciprocated.

Lila jerked suddenly and swiveled in place to give Alice privacy. "I'm so sorry. I kind of...spaced out for a minute."

Once she'd managed to thumb the button open, Alice pulled down her jeans before painstakingly placing them, folded, onto a dry patch of dock. "No more apologies. For the rest of the night, at least. Deal?"

Lila nodded without turning around. "You're on."

Though she normally liked to acclimate herself to water slowly—excruciatingly so, according to her ex-husband—the urgency to ensure that her scantily clad body would be submerged before Lila turned around compelled Alice to immediately leap over the side of the boat and into the lake in a less-than-graceful half-dive, half-belly flop. She kicked her feet and rose to the surface upon entry, glad that Lila hadn't witnessed the ridiculous display. After smoothing wet hair away from her face, she cleared her throat and said, "I'm in."

Lila wore a grin when she turned around. "Doesn't it feel incredible?"

Alice had to admit, it *did* feel nice. Every bit of it. She smiled, then kicked her legs to spin in place like a little kid. "Yes." After a few rotations, Alice stopped abruptly at the sight of Lila swimming closer. Her chest expanded, part pleasure, part pain. *All* good. Past the point of self-censoring, she said, "Thank you for talking me into this. No matter what else happens, this will always be a night to remember."

Lila's grin melted into something softer, more melancholy. Her eyes shone brightly under the moonlight, full to the brim with emotion too complex for Alice to interpret. Worried that she'd embarrassed herself with the confession, Alice shook her head to clear it. She felt like she was in a dream state, like she was inhabiting someone else's life. She was probably making a complete fool of herself. Was Lila nearly as caught up in this experience as she was?

As if to answer her question, Lila swam closer. Close enough to touch. Alice kept her hands far below the surface of the water, fisted at her sides, so she wouldn't get herself into trouble like she had earlier, when her tongue had gone rogue during that shotgunned hit. She studied Lila's face, tingling with the anticipation of what might happen next.

Lila's hand brushed against her hip, making her jump. "Sorr—" Lila stopped, perhaps remembering their pact. "I was going to say that I'll always remember tonight, too." As she studied the surface of the water, Alice got the impression she was actively struggling not to swim away.

She's embarrassed, too. At this point, their entire interaction felt so mind-blowingly reciprocal that Alice stopped trying to convince herself that her attraction wasn't returned. It *had* to be. Why else would Lila be so nervous? The question triggered an automatic litany of paranoid thoughts, each more frightening and far-fetched than the last. Alice looked around, peering into the darkness to make sure they were truly alone, that this wasn't just some massive practical joke.

"I was going to hold your hand," Lila blurted out. When Alice met her eyes, she lifted a shoulder and grabbed the back of her neck in one hand, visibly squeezing. "When I touched you just now. I don't want you to think I was trying to grope you or anything like that."

No, Lila's anxiety was 100 percent genuine—and 100 percent unnecessary. "I wasn't offended," Alice explained. "Just startled. Really."

"Okay." Lila exhaled, then forced a fairly unconvincing chuckle. "I have no idea what I'm doing either, as you can tell. Socially."

Alice continued to tread water as she tried to read Lila's face. Did friends usually hold hands? Or had that been Lila's attempt to signal that she was interested in venturing beyond mere platonic friendship? Though Alice had daydreamed about what it might be like to have a casual fling at Camp Rewind, she'd never believed she'd actually get the opportunity. *Especially* not with a woman. But maybe, inexplicably, this was her chance. Clearing her throat, Alice tried not to sound as excited as she felt. "You're fine. And if you want to hold my hand…" Slowly, once again detached from her actions, Alice raised her outstretched fingers to skim across the surface of the water, toward Lila. "I'm okay with that."

"Just okay?" Lila seemed to hold her breath as she awaited the answer.

"*Completely* okay." Alice managed not to react when Lila's fingers carefully entwined with hers. Their bodies drifted closer together, as though compelled by an invisible current. Alice's leg brushed against Lila's, their hips touched, and then suddenly Alice watched her arms loop around Lila's neck—for balance, she thought, preparing an excuse even as she committed the transgression—as they fell into a natural embrace. Frightened by her own lack of timidity, Alice attempted to pull away, but Lila tightened the arms she'd already wrapped around Alice's waist.

"Don't leave," Lila whispered. She rested her chin on Alice's shoulder and placed a hand in the center of her back, holding her so they didn't have to meet each other's eyes. "Please, unless you don't like it."

Alice *more* than liked it. Surrendering to the comfort, she closed her eyes and rested her head against Lila's, enjoying the warmth of another human's skin, the thrum of a second heartbeat echoing through her chest. She hadn't been hugged in years, certainly not by her parents, not since the last time John had bothered to offer her an emotionless squeeze. Being touched felt so good she never wanted it to end. She raised her hands to Lila's back, tracing her fingers over the soft skin, relishing the quiet sigh of contentment she was able to draw out with a simple caress.

They stayed that way for five minutes, perhaps, until Lila began to shiver in her arms. When Alice tried to release her, Lila shook her head and clung tighter. "Wait."

"All right." Alice dropped a hand to rest against Lila's lower back, keeping her close. "But you're cold."

"Getting there," Lila admitted. She kissed Alice's neck, a warm, soft press of her lips, before disentangling herself sheepishly. "So… wow. I know we're not supposed to apologize to each other anymore, but—"

Full of unfamiliar confidence, Alice shook her head. "Don't. We both needed that, obviously. There's no reason to be embarrassed, right? Either one of us."

For the first time, she noticed a shallow dimple in Lila's left cheek. "You're absolutely correct."

"Anyway, that's what friends do." Not that Alice had the first clue *what* friends actually did. It sounded good, though. "Right?"

"Totally." Lila shivered again and nodded toward the dock. "Should we get out?"

Alice emerged from the water before remembering her wet shirt and Lila's offer to let her borrow the dry one. Indeed, despite the fact that her teeth chattered audibly, Lila didn't hesitate to pick up the cold, damp T-shirt. Alice hastily snatched it away. "Thanks, but I'll wear that."

Lila surprised her by swiping it back. "No. I know you're self-conscious, and it's very possible we'll run into other people on the way to our bunks. I meant it when I said I'd wear it for you. Please, let me." Her hands trembled as she pulled the shirt over her head. "Consider it payment for the awesome hug."

Not wanting to start an argument no matter *how* well-intentioned, Alice nodded. "Thanks." She knelt to gather her jeans and Lila's dry shirt, which smelled so good it made Alice dizzy. Dressing as fast as she could, she waited for Lila to button her shorts before extending her arm in invitation. "At least let me help keep you warm?"

With a fairly violent shiver, Lila stripped off the wet shirt. "You know what? I'd rather walk back in my bra. I can carry the damn shirt." When Alice opened her mouth to protest again, her guilt renewed, Lila moved close to her side and cuddled up tight. "I'll happily accept your offer of warmth, though."

Alice curled her hand around a cold, bare shoulder instinctually. The obvious goose bumps beneath her fingers prompted her to tighten the embrace and made her wish she could somehow transfer the heat from her body to Lila's through sheer will alone. Though she'd met the woman less than two hours ago, she already wanted nothing more than to make her happy. As inexplicably happy as Lila had already made her.

They walked to the end of the dock before Lila broke the silence that had risen between them. "That was fun."

Alice smiled at the dark, slightly uneven ground. "It really was."

Lila's cold arm slid behind her back, making the embrace mutual. "And I really haven't made you uncomfortable?"

"Not at all." Alice was glad she didn't have to look Lila in the eyes right then, because she didn't trust herself not to somehow reveal exactly how much she'd enjoyed *everything* they'd just done—and what they were still doing now. She caressed Lila's upper arm with her thumb, betraying at least a little of her true feelings. "Sadly, I'm already more comfortable with you than nearly everyone else I know. Except my therapist."

"That *is* sad, but only because I don't like thinking of you feeling that alone." Lila hugged her around the waist. "On the other hand, hearing you say you feel comfortable with me pretty much wins the goddamn night."

"It'll make sitting together at breakfast less awkward, as well."

Lila's laughter made Alice feel all-powerful, like a bigger and better version of herself. So did the smile Lila directed her way, and the sparkle in what appeared to be a gaze full of affection. "Glad to hear we're still on for that."

"Are you kidding? Of course we are." The combined effect of the cool air, Lila's chilly, still-shivering body pressed tightly against her side, and her own excitement sent a noticeable tremor through Alice, which prompted Lila to draw her nearer. Alice went willingly. "You're stuck with me now."

"Good." As they drew closer to the dwindling bonfire, Lila lowered her voice. "You cold, too? We could go warm ourselves by the fire, if you want."

Alice shook her head. Tonight had been more magical than she could have ever dreamed. No need to ruin it by involving other people. "I think I'll turn in for the night. You go ahead, if you'd like."

"Nah." Lila steered them toward the women's cabin without missing a step. "I'm stuck with you, remember?"

"Yes, but I know you're cold."

Lila released her to climb the cabin steps, leaving Alice bereft in her absence. "True, but I've got dry pajamas inside. Come on."

Alice followed Lila into the canvas-covered structure, blinking rapidly as she tried to adjust to the sudden darkness. Despite two large, screened-in windows on either side of the room, the path between the double rows of bunk beds was only dimly illuminated and wholly perilous to navigate. After stumbling over an object she couldn't identify, Alice whispered, "I can't see anything."

Lila's hand touched her arm, easing anxiety that had only just begun to stir. "Close your eyes and then massage them gently with your fingers for about ten seconds. Supposedly it helps to reset your low-light vision."

Alice gave it a try. When she reopened her eyes, she had no trouble discerning Lila's pretty face only a few tantalizing inches from her own. Something came over her or, more accurately, swept through her. A moment of impossible courage, no doubt inspired by a lifetime of vicarious romantic thrills delivered by Hollywood movies. Unable to detect even a hint of rejection in Lila's expression, Alice moved forward and pressed their lips together in a nearly chaste, somewhat clumsy kiss. Lila gasped audibly the instant their mouths touched, then shot out her hands and gripped Alice's elbows to prevent her from backing away.

As soon as she understood that the kiss was welcome, that she'd only surprised Lila, Alice shut off her brain and let her body take over. Lila's tongue poked out, licking her upper lip, so Alice opened up to let her inside. She moaned at the improbable softness of another woman, so different than anything she'd felt before. Her hands moved on their own, at first resting on Lila's shoulders, then tangling in her hair. Stirred by the incredible passion of this single, first kiss—a kiss more arousing than anything she and her ex-husband had *ever* done—Alice brought her own tongue into play, sliding against Lila's in a dance that left her so hot, so instantly slick, that she couldn't help but blush and pull away.

"Please don't say you're sorry," Lila whispered before Alice could catch her breath. "*Please.*"

"That was the deal, right?" Alice amazed herself by speaking, and coherently at that. But her knees wobbled, threatening to send her to the floor. "I think I need to sit down."

Lila threaded their fingers together, the new familiarity of the gesture making it no less thrilling this time around. "Which bed is yours?"

Alice had only a fuzzy memory of depositing her suitcase on the last available bunk—a top one, naturally—en route to join the opening ceremony-in-progress. "Um…"

Lila pulled her along to the far corner of the room. "No worries, you can use mine. Over here."

Alice's legs melted away when she reached Lila's unmade bed. She sank onto the edge, watching in silence as Lila unzipped a large duffel bag and dug around inside. Though she knew she should probably find her suitcase if only to change out of her wet bra and panties, she didn't yet trust her legs to carry her. Eager to fill the oppressive silence, she murmured, "It's a top bunk, unfortunately. It was the only one that hadn't been taken…I left my suitcase on the mattress."

Lila turned to the side, partially shielding her body from view as she unhooked and discarded her wet bra. "I'll look as soon as I get my pajamas on." Alice tried not to stare at the silhouette of a full, bare breast as Lila rolled a dry tank top on over her head. She adjusted the hem so it hung low over her hips, then swiftly unbuttoned and discarded both her shorts and wet panties in a single, fluid motion, revealing a brief, alluring flash of one plump buttock as she shimmied on a fresh pair of boxer shorts. "Please excuse the half moon."

It took a moment for Alice to understand the playful nature of the comment, but as soon as Lila's meaning registered, any embarrassment she might have felt about sneaking a peek dissolved, along with her, into giggles. "I didn't mean to look."

"It was hard to miss." She could see Lila's flirtatious wink even in the low light, yet somehow managed not to look away. "Anyway, I'm taking it as a compliment."

"Good." In a quieter voice, she added, "You should."

Lila bent to kiss the top of her head, then straightened. "What color is your suitcase?"

"Blue." Alice surveyed the room, growing sheepish as a thought occurred. "It might actually be—"

"Right here?" Smiling, Lila hefted the suitcase down from its place on the bunk directly over Alice's head. "Nice choice."

"I guess so." Alice shivered violently, no longer able to fight off the chill in the air. She sank onto her knees beside her suitcase and unzipped it with shaking hands, searching for an embarrassingly long time before coming up with the long pajama pants and T-shirt she'd brought to sleep in. Glancing over her shoulder, she found Lila with her back already turned. "Thanks."

"Not a problem." Lila shook out a light bedsheet she'd taken from her bag, laying it over the thin mattress as Alice performed the quickest wardrobe change of her life. "I wish I'd realized how chilly it would be at night…or anticipated that I'd do something silly like decide to swim right before bed." She unfolded a second sheet and arranged it on top of the first. "I'd have brought an actual blanket."

Alice hung her wet T-shirt and bra from the corner of the top bunk, then returned to her bag for the quilted nylon blanket she'd packed alongside every other possible supply she'd thought she might need. "Borrow mine." She tossed the drawstring travel bag onto Lila's bunk. "It's my fault you had to walk back pretty much topless."

"Maybe so, but you're cold, too." Lila sank onto her bed and lobbed the blanket back to Alice. "I should have packed smarter."

Exhaustion crept into Alice's bones, sapping her of the energy to argue. Still, she had to try to make amends somehow. She was the reason Lila was suffering. "I'm not sure I'll be able to sleep if I know you're freezing right below me…"

Lila crawled between her sheets and rested her head on the pillow with a quiet, contented sigh. Then she rolled onto her side. "So let's share the blanket. Come on. Get in here next to me before you pass out."

Too tired to argue and not at all eager to attempt a nighttime ascent to the top bunk, Alice found it almost easy to accept Lila's invitation. She withdrew the thermal blanket from its bag, spread it over Lila's body with an air of tenderness she had no idea she possessed, and crawled beneath to stretch out on her side. Perched at the very edge of the mattress, she worried that the bed wasn't big enough for two adults to sleep comfortably until the moment Lila wrapped an arm around her stomach and dragged her backward into a cozy embrace.

Alice relaxed, muscle by muscle, until she no longer had any sense of where Lila ended and she began. A heart beat against her back, mimicking her own. Quiet, even breaths stirred the tiny hairs on her neck, a reminder that tonight, at least, she wasn't alone. Alice relished the heat of Lila's body behind hers, the security she provided. Truly at peace, she gave the arm around her waist a tender caress and then closed her eyes. Within moments, Alice fell into the soundest sleep she'd enjoyed in years.

CHAPTER FIVE

Rosa awoke the next morning to the familiar sensation of a warm body slipping stealthily out of her bed. Without taking the time to remember *who* she'd slept with and what, exactly, she'd done last night, she tightened her arm around her bed partner and murmured, "Leaving without saying good-bye?"

The woman in her bed jerked hard enough to drive an elbow into Rosa's stomach. Inadvertently, she hoped.

"Um…"

Her sleeping partner's sweet-but-mildly-terrified voice elicited an onrush of memories, each one better than the last. Rosa opened her eyes with a smile already on her face. "The deal was no apologies, right?"

Rather than the soft, bashful brown eyes she expected to see staring back, Alice wore an expression of total terror. "I'm…I'm sorry, I…"

Sensing the shift in mood—now that daylight streamed in through the cabin windows and the sound of their rousing bunkmates filled the air—Rosa held up her hand in a silent plea for Alice not to panic. "Alice, it's all right. Really." She sat up and, unsure how to ease her new friend's obvious embarrassment, naturally fell back on good, old dependable humor. "I only drooled on you a little bit. I promise."

Alice's mouth twitched as though she might smile, but instead she rolled out of bed and dug furiously through her suitcase without meeting Rosa's eyes. "I've got to use the bathroom."

"All right." Clearly, Alice needed some space. It made sense. She'd just woken up in another woman's arms, perhaps for the first time in her life. Despite the rapport they'd established the night before—and that goddamn amazing kiss—she was also suddenly sober after a mellow, hazy evening in which she'd obviously exhibited uncharacteristic behavior. She required time to adjust. Rosa understood that, even if all she really wanted to do was go eat breakfast together. "Do you want to meet at the dining hall, or—"

Alice shrugged as she gathered an armful of clean clothes and what looked like a zippered toiletry bag. "You don't have to wait for me."

"Well, I was planning to shower first, anyway, so…"

Alice seemed to pale at the realization that they were headed in the same direction. "Oh."

Rosa sighed. "I'll save a seat for you, in case you make it in time."

Already on her feet, Alice rushed toward the exit with her head down in a blatant walk of shame. "See you later."

She watched through the window as Alice fled the cabin and hurried in a random direction. Studying the retreating form until she'd disappeared from sight, Rosa groaned under her breath, disappointed that waking up together had gone so poorly. "Shit."

"An awkward morning-after already?" A bright, perky voice drew her attention to the next bunk over, where a beautifully dark girl with sparkling brown eyes gathered her own clothing and toiletries. "Damn, you move fast. With the shy one, no less!"

Rosa forced a polite smile. She didn't detect any judgment in her bunkmate's tone but didn't want anyone to get the wrong idea about Alice. "It wasn't like that. We weren't exactly sober when we came back last night, and she was nervous about sleeping in the top bunk… and I didn't pack a warm blanket so she insisted I use hers, and…" She became aware of how ridiculous she must sound. "Anyway, yeah, she's shy. Very, very shy."

"I'll be nice to her, don't worry. I'm Bree, by the way." She stuck out her hand.

For the second time, Rosa only narrowly remembered her cover. Internally, she cringed at the realization that Alice didn't even know her real name. "Lila." She shook Bree's hand, noting the way the other woman's thumb caressed the side of her knuckle. It reminded her, thrillingly, of the way Alice had stroked her arm right before they'd fallen asleep. "It's nice to meet you."

Bree smiled, coyly. "I noticed you at the opening ceremony and had hoped to chat you up at the bonfire last night, but couldn't manage to find you. Guess now I know why."

Rosa surprised herself by blushing. "Guess so."

"Anyway." Bree gave her hand a squeeze, letting go after a more-than-brief hesitation. "I'm not sure how many of the ladies here are interested in each other versus whatever low-hanging fruit can be found in that cabin of Neanderthals next door, but if you find yourself in need of some no-strings-attached company this weekend—"

Rosa took a moment to admire the curves revealed by Bree's thin camisole, particularly the large, dark outlines of her erect nipples. It was an offer she probably shouldn't refuse, but somehow, the lure of getting to know Alice better proved too difficult to resist. "If so, I will *definitely* come see you."

Bree raised a well-manicured eyebrow, soaking up the insinuated praise. "Don't wait *too* long. You're not the only one who moves fast."

Letting her gaze slide down the rest of the curvaceous body, Rosa homed in on the sight of red, silky panties that clung suggestively to Bree's pussy, an enticing vision all but hidden between nearly closed thighs. As she snuck a peek, Bree's knees inched apart to give her a better view. If last night with Alice hadn't been so purely, inexplicably magical, igniting both her libido *and* her imagination, Rosa could have easily lost herself in that warm, inviting space. "I'll bet."

Bree reached across the gap between their bunks, nudging Rosa's attention back to her face with two shapely fingernails under her chin. "Go woo the shy one. Let me know how it goes, either way. You could even bring her along to play with us, if it turns out she's into that kind of thing."

Intrigued by Bree's directness, Rosa nonetheless knew it would be a cold day before Alice consented to a random ménage à trois at Camp Rewind. "I can almost guarantee that won't happen, but I'm filing the image away for a lonely night in the future."

"Do that." Bree winked and stood, picking up her shower sandals. "In the meantime, I'm going to wash up and get something to eat. Find me if you need someone to sit with."

"Thanks," Rosa said. As much as she liked Bree—or more directly, as much fun as it would be to fuck her—she *really* hoped that wouldn't be necessary. Alice had specifically talked about sitting together in the dining hall. Would she really ditch her now, after last night?

After that *kiss*?

Rosa grabbed her toiletries and a change of clothes, then made her way through a gauntlet of curious faces to the cabin door. Outside, the air was crisp and camp life was beginning to stir. A steady trickle of male campers stumbled out of their cabin toward the bathrooms, one of whom stopped, bent at the waist, and puked into a nearby bush. Rosa wrinkled her nose, half-sympathetic, half-disgusted as she considered what it would feel like to nurse a hangover in this place.

"You don't even want to know what he did to wake us all up this morning."

A deep, masculine voice startled her into awareness, so close behind her it made her heart slam into her chest and her body stiffen in alarm. She whirled around to face the stranger, only partially relieved to find a friendly looking man with a receding hairline and black-rimmed glasses that perfectly set off his dark, thick eyebrows. He was an appealing mixture of dreamboat and geek, though the latter gave her pause as she wondered whether he'd ever played the sacred cow of racist, misogynistic video games and, if so, whether he knew about her wildly unpopular opinions and the humiliating payback she'd suffered as a result of publishing them online.

He offered an apologetic smile. "Sorry. I didn't mean to scare you."

"I was distracted by the view." Rosa returned his smile and resumed her walk toward the bathroom. She wasn't surprised when he kept pace at her side. "I hope you didn't get stuck sharing a bunk with him."

"Other side of the room, thankfully. I've never been a big drinker, but I'll tell you, what I witnessed this morning is a cautionary tale every human should hear about. Except you, of course, since I imagine you'd like to eat today."

Rosa chuckled enough to be considered polite. "I appreciate that."

"Believe me, you have no idea how much." As they approached the wooden structure housing two separate bathrooms, her new companion extended his hand across his chest. She took it. "I'm Derek."

"R—Lila." Again, she barely caught herself before slipping out of character. And, again, she struggled with the reality that Alice had no idea who she really was. "It's nice to meet you."

"Likewise." He scanned the length of her body less subtly than she imagined he'd intended. "You planning to do any archery today? Or horseback riding?"

Either Camp Rewind was a veritable meat market or else she gave off an aura of pure desperation, because she was pretty sure she was being hit on for the second time this morning. She hadn't even brushed her teeth yet. "To be honest, I'm not sure." Currently, her only plan was to find Alice and see what *she* wanted to do. Anxiety that Alice might not want her to tag along made her belly churn unpleasantly. "If I need a riding partner, I'll let you know."

Derek coughed, alerting her to where his mind had taken the mild innuendo. "Or else I'm a pretty accomplished archer, if you'd like me to share some pointers with you."

Rosa edged toward the women's bathroom and showers, eager to start searching for the one person she really wanted to spend today getting to know. "Maybe. Me and another woman had talked about hanging out—"

"Bring her along." Derek grinned, openly eager for her to accept his invitation. "The more, the merrier."

"I don't think so. She's pretty shy." Keen to escape Derek's sales pitch, Rosa demurred with a gentle smile. "Thanks anyway."

"All right." Derek didn't hide his disappointment, but she was relieved by the lack of anger beneath it. "I get it. But if you decide you'd like some tips, or a lesson, either archery *or* riding…"

The insinuation hung in the air between them as he laid his intentions bare. "I appreciate the offer." Rosa tried to negotiate a smile warm enough to seem well mannered, but not so friendly as to encourage his sexual interest. "But I've actually got my eye on that other woman I mentioned, so…" She shrugged. "I'm not the droid you're looking for."

Derek slapped his hand over his heart, feigning a grievous wound. "She even quotes *Star Wars*. Why do all the good ones have to be lesbians?"

Suddenly worried—perhaps irrationally—that she was in danger of blowing her cover as a semi-professional geek, Rosa stepped across the threshold of the bathroom door. She didn't bother to correct his precise labeling of her sexuality, though she usually resisted any and all efforts to sort her into any kind of box. This weekend, she planned to remain 100 percent Sapphic, no exceptions, even if Alice wanted nothing more to do with her. Right or wrong, she felt safer and less at risk of exposure that way. "Life isn't fair?"

"Obviously not." Derek tipped his head and backed off. "See you later. Good luck."

"Thanks." Rosa exhaled when she was finally left alone long enough to think. She hoped Alice wouldn't be angry that she'd already disclosed the crush she'd developed to two complete strangers. Derek didn't know *what* woman she liked, at least, though with the way gossip tended to travel, she wouldn't be surprised if the rest of their cabinmates were openly speculating about how she'd ended up sharing a bed with "the shy one." It was only a matter of time before all of Camp Rewind knew she and Alice had slept together, no doubt.

Shit. Would Alice be able to withstand that kind of scrutiny?

Sickened by the thought of exposing her to any type of public speculation, Rosa couldn't help but consider how Alice would feel if she knew how much negative attention she continued to attract on a weekly—if not daily—basis in her real life. Or worse, how much negative attention a new love interest might draw. Her ex-boyfriend had been doxxed almost immediately, his name, address, and other personal information released online for everyone to see. Two days of harassing, threatening messages and he'd been out of there, breaking up with her so fast she barely had time to process the loss. How would Alice handle a relationship like that? It would literally be her worst nightmare.

Disheartened by the fact that her deep interest in Alice simply wasn't realistic—that it couldn't go anywhere, not for real—Rosa took solace that Alice had never indicated she was looking for anything more than casual fun. And barely even that. Though Alice wasn't the type of girl she'd ever envision inviting home for a one-night stand under normal circumstances, this weekend, Rosa would take whatever she could get. Because that *kiss* last night, when Alice had shocked the hell out of her by simply *going for it*, had been truly phenomenal. She wanted more, even if only another brief make-out session. Alice excited her in a way she hadn't felt in a long time.

Maybe ever.

Stomach fluttering, Rosa walked into the bathroom, eager to find Alice and reestablish the camaraderie and flirtation they'd found at the lake. She glanced beneath every bathroom stall, one after the next, but none of the ankles or shower-shoe-clad feet looked familiar, and Alice's distinctive toiletries bag was likewise nowhere to be seen. Uneasy, Rosa paced alongside the shower stalls and listened. When she reached the end of the line, she watched and waited until each one had recycled its occupant and confirmed an unsettling fear.

Alice was gone.

❖

Suspended in a state of nightmare-level awkwardness, Alice hid behind a redwood tree only twenty feet from the women's bathroom, clutching her toiletries bag in both hands as hot tears spilled from her stinging eyes. She'd intended to go in after her great escape from Lila's bed, but managed to time her arrival to perfectly match that of two other women. The prospect of being looked at or spoken to by anyone who might have seen her snoozing in the arms of a woman she barely knew was too terrifying to risk. So into the woods she'd fled, to hide behind a tree like a fool and wish she were anywhere but here.

She *could* simply leave Camp Rewind. That much was still true. Unfortunately, all her things, car keys included, were back at the cabin, inside her suitcase. Though she assumed that most of the other campers had made their way to the showers by now, a few stragglers would surely happen along, especially with the way the alcohol had flowed the night before. She was scared to death to risk any taunts or jeers from her fellow grown-ups, as much as she wanted to believe that wouldn't really happen. Hence, the idea of returning to the scene of the crime was presently too awful to entertain. Also, she needed to pee. Badly. If not for the specter of poison ivy and random voyeurs, she would be tempted to find a private place to squat amongst the trees.

She'd watched Lila disappear into the bathroom almost ten minutes ago and expected her to emerge at any moment. What then? She might return to the cabin to search for Alice or else assume she'd already gone to breakfast and head to the dining hall in the hope they might sit together. Alice battled a twinge of guilt at the thought. Despite her embarrassment upon waking up with her cheek resting on another woman's soft, warm breast, its nipple pebbled against the corner of her mouth, Alice realized that running away had been an overreaction, and leaving camp altogether would be even worse. Last night she'd been utterly convinced of Lila's good intentions and comfortable enough to *fall asleep in her arms*, for goodness sake. It wasn't as though Lila had done anything to deserve being ditched less than twelve hours after they'd vowed to stick together.

Alice exhaled and fell back against the tree, frustrated with herself. Once again. *Like always.*

No, Lila didn't deserve to be ditched, but Alice didn't know how to face her after last night. After that kiss. Crossing that line had been 100 percent her own doing, and although she didn't exactly regret the bold move, she wished she knew how to deal with the aftermath while stone-cold sober. What would Lila expect today? Or tonight, for that matter? Alice's hopes and fears intersected and overlapped and contradicted each other. Was honest-to-God *sex* on the table? No matter how shy she might be, Alice wanted—even *needed*—to get laid. Even if sex with John had never exactly rung her bell, she loved making herself come and held out hope that someone else might one day achieve the same feat. She imagined an orgasm felt different when it wasn't from your own hand. She yearned to find out for sure. Yet the idea of making herself that vulnerable, of attempting to please someone more sexually experienced than herself and potentially failing, left her hoping against hope that Lila wouldn't try to take their physical relationship any farther.

Then again, if she didn't, Alice knew she'd be crushed by the slight. She sighed. Camp life was confusing.

Alice peered around the tree at the sound of feminine voices exiting the bathroom. Not Lila's, which was almost a relief. She'd already witnessed Lila's friendly interaction with the man who'd accompanied her to the restroom and wasn't sure how she'd feel about witnessing yet another bond being formed. She wouldn't normally consider herself the jealous type. But Lila represented a sort of lifeline in this aggressively social environment.

If she is making friends…maybe she doesn't need to sit with me. Maybe I should just leave.

Almost as soon as the thought crossed Alice's mind, Lila walked out of the bathroom alone. She wore an expression of worry mixed with concern that Alice had no trouble seeing even from her distant vantage point and scanned her surroundings with an air of what Alice imagined might actually be longing. Just before Lila's searching gaze turned to her hiding spot, Alice impulsively retreated and tried to make herself as small as possible. Back behind the tree, like a completely maladjusted human being.

Alice closed her eyes. She counted to ten. She tried like hell not to burst into tears. When she opened her eyes and checked again, Lila was gone. Where, Alice didn't know. Which meant she still wasn't sure what to do next.

After another minute or two of standing frozen in an absolute panic, Alice's bladder made the decision for her. She would pee, then hopefully find an open shower stall where she could wash off the previous night's swim while she decided what to do. It wasn't much of a plan, but it was all her brain could manage while also contending with the urgency of her bodily functions.

So there it was: she would pee, she would wash up, and then she would figure out whether to run away from Camp Rewind or summon the absolutely insane amount of courage required to stay.

Good. Anything was better than paralysis.

CHAPTER SIX

Whatever sheepishness Rosa might have felt about her decision to smuggle two pancakes concealed in paper towel, a banana, and a not-so-easily hidden bottle of apple juice out of the cafeteria evaporated in a flash when she finally spotted Alice slinking around the periphery of the dining hall at least ten minutes after the last camper had bused his own table and left. Worried that Alice hadn't yet eaten and wouldn't have a chance before the cafeteria workers finished putting everything away, she'd taken the few items of food with her despite being wholly uncertain about whether Alice was still on the premises.

Though Rosa had wound up accepting Bree's breakfast invitation after all, even engaging in some friendly banter and an innocuous round of girl-watching, the mystery of Alice's whereabouts absolutely consumed her throughout the entire meal. She'd experienced wave after wave of sorrow and regret at the possibility that Alice might have actually left Camp Rewind, and her life, for good.

Now, having caught sight of familiar dark hair and those pretty, lonely eyes lingering behind a towering redwood tree, Rosa exhaled as soul-stirring relief swept through her body. Weak-kneed, she couldn't hold back the joyous grin that exploded across her face.

How ridiculous to feel *any* of this about a potential, casual, summer fling. Unfortunately, her head had a terrible track record when it came to swaying her heart from wherever it decided to scamper.

Afraid that Alice might run away again if she didn't hurry up and acknowledge her presence, Rosa called out, "I missed you at breakfast. Do you like pancakes?"

Alice went completely still, her temptation to flee painfully obvious, painted across her face like a tattoo. But rather than engage in a repeat performance of that morning, she nodded and mumbled something Rosa couldn't hear. Taking that as permission to approach, Rosa closed the distance between them as quickly as she dared, before Alice could disappear. She put on her kindest face, unhappily aware that all the progress they'd made toward a tentative friendship seemed to have vanished now that the sun was up. Cautiously, she offered Alice the pancakes, banana, and juice. When Alice accepted the food with a soft, grateful murmur, Rosa asked, "Did you already eat?"

Alice shook her head. "Thanks." The word came out in a bare whisper. "I'm sorry."

They really were right back where they'd started. "I thought we said no apologies?"

Alice's nose crinkled up like she might cry. "Yes, but I *am*. Sorry."

"All right." Reluctant to overstep, Rosa only barely resisted the urge to touch Alice's arm, or give her a hug, or offer *some* physical comfort to erase the sadness from her eyes. "It really is, Alice. It's all right. You needed time to regroup. That's fair, and I get it. No offense taken."

"I freaked out when I woke up and we…" Alice held her breakfast in her hands, staring down at the food without any real interest or hunger in her expression. "I just…really wasn't myself last night."

"Oh, I don't know. You don't think that was simply 'Alice, relaxed'?" Rosa exhaled, remembering how they'd walked back to the cabin pressed against one another in an effort to share their meager body heat. "Whoever she was, I liked her. A lot."

Alice snorted quietly. "I think that was more like 'Alice, incredibly stoned.'"

"Maybe a little of that, too." Rosa studied Alice's expression, trying to decide whether she was offering a simple apology or if this was some kind of brush-off. Her stomach twisted at the thought that it might be the latter. "Do you regret last night?" She wasn't entirely sure what part of their evening she was asking about. Sharing the joint, holding hands, swimming? The unexpectedly emotional embrace in the lake? That *kiss*? Perhaps Alice only regretted that they'd shared a bed in a place where others could see. "I'll understand if you do."

And it would break her heart.

Alice could no longer meet her eyes. "Not exactly."

"Then…" Rosa ducked her head so that Alice had no choice but to look at her. "Do you want to find somewhere private to sit and chat while you eat?"

Alice, flushed, hesitated a moment before nodding. "All right."

Careful not to allow Alice's uncertainty to infect her, Rosa mustered her most confident grin. "Should we look for a spot near the water or find a secluded little patch of forest for ourselves?"

A group of three women and two men came into view as though summoned by the question, beach towels slung over their shoulders as they sauntered down the path toward the lake. Alice watched them with an expression of dread, then turned back to Rosa, wide-eyed. "Somewhere secluded is good."

Rosa tried to prevent her dirty mind from taking an extremely inappropriate flight of fancy at Alice's words, but it was impossible. She wanted to kiss this woman again, to touch her, to eventually make her comfortable enough to open up, literally and figuratively, and let Rosa inside. Though her instant attraction to Alice's symmetrical, well-proportioned features and oh-so-soft body wasn't at all mysterious, she had no logical explanation for her overall obsession with a woman she barely knew. Especially one who played so hard to get. Perhaps she was intrigued by the challenge Alice presented?

Rosa didn't think that was the real explanation, but it was less dangerous than the other possibilities. Far less.

Alice was staring at her. "Lila? Do you know a place?"

Startled to realize she hadn't been paying attention, then overcome with guilt at the sound of her fake name falling so naturally from Alice's gorgeous lips, Rosa blurted out, "We'll find one." Face hot, she swiveled and took off in a random direction before Alice noticed how flustered she was, hopeful that she'd follow.

They walked past the archery range, caught a glimpse of the horse stables just as a mare was being led out into a small paddock, then eventually reached the edge of the complex of camp buildings. Dense redwood forest stretched out in front of them, swallowing up two well-trod paths that branched off in opposite directions. Alice glanced over her shoulder at the stables as they approached the trail on the left, as though afraid they might never find their way back. Sensing her concern, Rosa said, "We won't go far, and I won't get us lost. Promise."

Alice met and held her eyes for the first time since they'd woken up together. "I trust you."

"I hope so." Rosa prayed she looked and sounded as sincere as she honestly felt. "I really want you to."

They stepped into the woods, Rosa in the lead. Behind her, Alice cleared her throat. "Why?"

"Pardon?" Preoccupied with trying to understand Alice's question, she stumbled over a root that stretched across the forest floor. Rosa cringed, barely recovering her footing before she hit the ground. "Well, that was smooth."

Now beside her, Alice couldn't seem to hide her amusement. "No less smooth than bolting out of bed and into the woods as soon as I woke up this morning."

"Not sure I entirely agree, but I appreciate you trying to make me feel better." She gave Alice a sidelong glance, winking to clarify that she wasn't actually *that* mortified. "It's nice to see you again, by the way. *Really* nice."

Alice's smile grew, seemingly outside her conscious control. "You, too. Really." She paused, then, turning her focus to the careful placement of her steps, repeated, "*Why* do you really want me to trust you?"

Taken aback by the directness of the question—one whose answer seemed both obvious and potentially precarious—Rosa watched her own feet, careful not to misstep. She didn't want to fall on her face, literally *or* figuratively. "As opposed to wanting you to feel freaked out by me?"

Alice chuckled. Then she exhaled and looked over at Rosa, suddenly serious. "No, I mean…why do you care at all?"

Rosa shrugged. Beyond the fact that she was a compassionate human being, she had many answers to that question. She thought Alice was pretty, if not downright beautiful to her eyes. She was fun, when she relaxed. She also seemed like the least threatening person at camp, the one least likely to recognize Rosa for her social media infamy *or* mistreat her even if she did. And they'd bonded silently right from the start over their shared anxiety in the parking lot, at least from Rosa's perspective. Also, *that kiss.*

Discarding her last thought, Rosa said, "I told you, I need a friend on the inside."

Alice nodded slowly, as though trying to understand. "But you don't seem to be having any trouble making friends."

Now it was Rosa's turn to mull over Alice's meaning. Had Alice seen Derek walk with her to the showers? Or spotted her eating breakfast with Bree? With nothing to hide, Rosa said, "I've been hit on twice this morning, if that's what you mean. And yeah, Bree's really nice, but frankly, I felt like you and I had a sort of connection...or something." She paused to chew on her own words, instantly regretting them. By attempting to assuage Alice's anxiety, she had made herself stupidly vulnerable—and come on *way* too strong. She sighed. Time to end simply. "I had fun last night. I like you."

It took Alice a minute to respond, her voice so quiet Rosa nearly missed it. "I like you, too."

Spotting a fallen tree in the distance, Rosa took a deep breath, grabbed the bottle of water from Alice's right hand, and tangled their fingers together as casually as possible. "I see a place to sit. Over here."

"All right," Alice murmured. They kept their hands linked until they reached the massive trunk, only breaking apart so that Rosa could help Alice climb up to perch on top. "Thanks."

Rosa clambered up beside her, grateful for the serene atmosphere and relative quiet of the forest. This was a perfect refuge from the riotously social atmosphere back at the main camp. Here, they could get to know each other better. Maybe even find their way back to where they'd been the night before. She opened her mouth to ask what Alice did for a living, but Alice surprised her by speaking first.

"So, Lila...will you tell me a little more about yourself?" Having unpeeled her banana in two fluid, expert motions, Alice took a dainty nibble before actually managing to look Rosa in the eyes. She smiled, obviously still nervous. "I feel like I did most of the talking yesterday. I didn't mean to."

If she hadn't felt so awful about her continued deception—and the fact that she'd *intentionally* avoided revealing much about herself—Rosa would have laughed at the notion that Alice had done anything close to too much talking. Instead she sighed, pinched the bridge of her nose, and made a quick, gut-based decision she hoped would save her from—rather than cause—further regret. "No, Alice, you were perfect.

Me, on the other hand…" Her fingers drifted to her upper lip to pick at the skin, an unpleasant tic she'd battled since childhood. "To tell you the truth, I actually…have a confession to make."

"What kind of confession?"

Rosa wished she could better predict how Alice would react. Not only to the news that she'd given her a fake name, but also to the details of her unique social predicament. Right now Alice sounded curious, but not overly concerned. Would she take the subterfuge as a betrayal, or would she understand? Beyond that, would the knowledge that Rosa was regularly harassed by complete strangers to the point of sometimes fearing for her life send Alice running for real? *Fuck yes,* Rosa decided too late. *Almost certainly.*

A tentative hand rested against the center of her back. "It's all right. You can tell me, whatever it is. Really."

The kindness in Alice's voice only made her feel worse. Eager to end the charade, Rosa blurted out, "I lied to you…to everyone. About my name, and…" She tried to remember what she had and hadn't told Alice about herself. "Maybe some other stuff."

Alice's reassuring touch disappeared, but she didn't stand up and walk away. "Why?"

It was impossible to read Alice's reaction in a single syllable. Rosa curled in on herself, missing the warmth of the hand on her back. "I didn't want anyone to recognize me."

"*Should* I recognize you?" Alice unwrapped her pancakes and set the paper towel aside, drawing Rosa's attention to the fact that she was still eating. Which was a good sign, she supposed. "I have to admit, I'm not always good with putting names to faces."

"You won't have any idea who I am unless you happen to follow the video-gaming press or Internet-based sex scandals." Rosa's heart thudded. What was she doing? Morning one and she had already violated the single most steadfast rule she'd made for this place. Rosa Salazar wasn't supposed to exist at Camp Rewind. She'd vowed to leave Rosa at home with the rest of her problems. And still, for whatever reason, it felt suddenly, vitally important that Alice know who she really was. Even if the truth scared her away. "Eighteen months ago, I wrote an article for a popular website. A feminist criticism of an almost universally loved video game. Nothing too scathing, believe it or not. I even acknowledged that the game was occasionally fun to play, despite its rampant misogyny and racist clichés."

When she paused to breathe—and also to figure out how much she really planned to confess—Alice held out the bottle of apple juice. "Want a drink?"

Her nonchalance helped Rosa relax enough to accept the offer. The cool liquid slid down her parched throat, easing the way for the rest of her explanation. "Thank you."

Alice studied her features carefully, as though seeing her for the first time. "Before you go on, will you tell me your real name?"

"It's Rosa." She gave the bottle back, admiring the movement of Alice's smooth, elegant throat as she swallowed a few sips of her own. "Rosa Salazar."

"Rosa," Alice repeated in a murmur. "Pretty name."

"Thanks." Unable to believe how well Alice was accepting the news of her dishonesty, Rosa exhaled in a rush. "I'm so sorry I let you call me Lila for so long. I never wanted to deceive *you*, personally. I just…"

"You had your reasons." Alice capped the juice bottle and balanced it on the tree between them, then looked up at Rosa with a sheepish smile. "I haven't heard of you, by the way."

"I'm glad." Too many people had seen her naked, intimately posed body without her consent already. It might have killed her if Alice had been one of them. "Don't hang out much online?"

"Not really. I mean, a *few* sites, but…" Sheepishness swiftly turned into what looked like mortification, as a blush swept across Alice's face and colored her cheeks a deep, lovely pink. "But no gaming or pop culture or gossip sites at all, really."

Extremely curious about the websites Alice favored—and what made them so embarrassing to talk about—Rosa resisted the urge to turn the subject to a lighter topic. Now that she'd gone down this conversational road, she was keen to reach the end of it as quickly as possible. If Alice was going to be horrified or grossed out or simply turned off by who she was, Rosa wanted it to happen sooner rather than later. It would hurt either way, but the more time they spent together, the more agonizing the prospect of rejection inevitably became.

Rosa's throat tightened as she pushed ahead. "Well, if you don't hang out on the Internet, you may not realize how toxic an environment it can be. Especially, sometimes, for women with opinions. In my case, I pissed off a lot of very passionate gamers, most of them grown men old enough to know better. My worst critics spent months drumming up a hate campaign against me. Thousands of nasty comments were left on my article, some of them completely horrific. Death threats, rape threats, you name it. They sent emails to my boyfriend at the time, to my mother, my father, even my brother. Then my personal information got published online. The address of the apartment where I was living, my cell-phone number, every email address I'd ever created." She couldn't bear to glance over at Alice, to see how horrified she was by each additional revelation. "Eventually my cloud storage got hacked. I'd taken a few nude photos years before for an ex-boyfriend and made this video…" She realized that this was the first time she'd had to tell anyone what had happened to her. Everyone in her life at the time had found out simply because they were online and connected to her in various ways. Alice was the only new friend she'd made since the entire nightmare began, which made the thought of driving her away with this ugliness too painful to bear. "They said they wanted to expose my hypocrisy. How dare I criticize their favorite game's sex and nudity while being such a whore myself?"

Alice's hand returned to her back to rub slow circles, causing Rosa's eyes to well up and spill over.

"I'm so sorry," Alice murmured. "That's awful. I can't imagine having something so private shared with the world."

"I was painfully ignorant back then," Rosa muttered. She dried her tears, ashamed she'd ever allowed them to fall. "When I filmed that video, I had no concept that my dirty little secrets would be easily available to anyone who hated me enough to hunt them down."

Alice gave her a consoling pat. "On the plus side, people tend to have short attention spans. Especially online, or so I'm told. Surely the worst of the fallout has blown over by this point?"

Surprised by Alice's calm, level-headed reasoning—not to mention her more-confident-than-ever tone—Rosa finally reestablished tentative eye contact. Alice patted her encouragingly and shot her a sweet smile. Undeniably tickled by their role reversal, Rosa said, "You feel less intimidated by me now, don't you?"

Alice had the grace to at least look apologetic. "Not in a bad way."

"No?"

Alice began to gather her trash. Despite the difficult conversation, she'd eaten her entire breakfast. "Not at all. I feel like I know you better, like you trust me, which makes *me* trust *you*." She flashed a grin that caused Rosa's heart to momentarily pause. "Thank you for being honest. I can see it wasn't easy."

"You're welcome." Rosa took the trash from Alice's hands. It was the least she could do. "Thank you for not getting spooked. Or disgusted."

"Why would I be? It wasn't your fault. All you did was speak your mind."

Rosa shrugged. She didn't want to say, *I was terrified to make you too afraid to be a part of my life.* What did that mean, anyway? Alice almost certainly realized that associating with her for a few days at camp barely constituted a risk. Nothing more than this long weekend was on the table. They were camp friends who might potentially enjoy a casual fling, if Rosa got lucky. That was all. Which meant she should be able to relax, now that her secret was out and Alice had accepted the sordid circumstances of her life. Unfortunately, it wasn't that simple in her head. Before she could stop herself, Rosa said, "My ex-boyfriend dumped me almost as soon as it happened. He couldn't handle it…and that was *before* the photos and video were posted. He couldn't stand the pressure *or* my emotional response to what was happening."

"He didn't deserve you."

"You're right, he didn't." A jolt of self-loathing hit her in the gut, familiar by now, yet always painful. *Nobody deserves what life with me would bring them.* "I couldn't blame him. It was bad. I probably would have left me, too."

"If he'd really loved you, he would have weathered that storm with you. That's the whole point of a relationship, isn't it?"

Rosa's chest ached. She couldn't fathom ever finding someone who loved her *that* much. "Maybe."

"I think it is." Alice went quiet. Then she said, "But things are better for you now?"

"Much. I still get threats, but not every day. And I honestly think it's just a handful of obsessives at this point. My lawyer succeeded in having the photos and videos removed from Google. They're still out there, of course…you can never completely get rid of something like that online. But they're harder to find, and I don't see them posted nearly as many places these days…" Rosa tried to look happier than she felt, summoning a brave face designed to entice Alice into sticking around for the rest of the weekend. "Honestly, it's only recently that I've been able to start rebuilding my life. Coming here is a big part of that. This is supposed to be my chance to escape, maybe even a new beginning."

She happened to look over just in time to see Alice bite her lip to suppress a tiny—and possibly optimistic?—grin. "That's something we have in common, then. The desire for a new beginning and the theory that Camp Rewind might be the place to find it."

"Hear, hear." Rosa straightened, arching her back in a much-needed stretch. Then she exhaled in a rush and sagged with relief. "I'm so glad that didn't scare you away."

"Must seem pretty amazing after how I reacted to waking up in your bed."

Relieved laughter bubbled up in Rosa's chest, boosting her mood. "A little, maybe."

"I'm pretty embarrassed about that." Alice folded her hands in her lap, almost as though she wasn't sure what to do with them. "And maybe also slightly…confused."

Rosa assumed she was referring to her sexuality. Since this was only a weekend fling, she had no problem being a straight woman's experiment. "That's all right."

"No, I mean…" Alice played with her fingernails while studiously avoiding Rosa's gaze. "I know you liked…what happened last night. What I…what I did in the cabin."

"The kiss?" Rosa held back laughter when Alice flinched at her directness. For someone so shy, she showed remarkable courage by even raising the topic. Yet she exuded a unique innocence that set Rosa aflame. "I liked it *very* much."

Alice couldn't hide her pleasure. She nodded for a few seconds before uttering, "Me, too."

"Good." Rosa waited to see if she would say more, but her patience expired almost immediately. "Want to do it again?"

Alice's eyelashes fluttered as her pulse visibly quickened, the creamy, kissable spot at the base of her throat thrumming under Rosa's admiring gaze. "Yes, but…"

She held herself back from edging closer. "But?"

"I guess I was just wondering…not that it matters, really, but…" Alice gripped her knees until her knuckles turned white. "I mean, it sounded like you'd been with women in the past, but you've only mentioned ex-boyfriends. So have you…" She stopped talking, took a steadying breath, then exhaled deliberately, making Rosa wonder whether she was witnessing a therapeutic technique in action. "Have you been with a woman before? Or is this…is this a first for you, too?"

Rosa half-smiled, hoping that the answer wouldn't disappoint Alice. "To be honest, I'm not sure I have very many firsts left at this point. No, I've been with women *and* men. On one occasion, at the same time." She cursed her candor as soon as she made the disclosure. If this was to be Alice's first encounter with a woman, would she really feel at ease with someone as extensively experienced as she was presenting herself? Still, Alice deserved the truth. "If I had to label myself, I would say I'm pansexual, which basically means that I'm potentially attracted to any human. The ex-boyfriend to whom I sent those dirty pictures and that…*video*…well, he was assigned female at birth. I had a serious girlfriend in college. My only one. She broke my heart." Apparently unable to stop the deep dive into her varied history, she decided to conclude with a full accounting. "But I've slept with six women total. I can honestly say that the best sex I've ever had was with other women."

Alice's eyelashes fluttered again. She quickly returned to her study of her fingernails. "Oh, that's…good."

Strange as it seemed, Rosa detected sincerity in Alice's words. "Really?"

"Yes. At least one of us isn't a fumbling amateur."

Rosa laughed out loud, a sunny, buoyant expulsion that lifted her spirits considerably. Careful not to move too fast, she picked up the apple-juice bottle from between them and set it on the trunk at her other side. Then she wrapped her arm around Alice's waist, tugging gently while allowing her plenty of space to refuse. "So you're not revolted by my slutty ways?"

Alice scooted closer until her body pressed tightly against Rosa's side. "No. Intimidated again, *maybe*." Her rapid heartbeat echoed through Rosa's rib cage, confirmation that Alice was indeed nervous, if not aroused. "And…intrigued, to be honest."

"There's no reason to feel intimidated. Really. Truly. You're the catch here."

Alice shocked her silly by releasing a loud guffaw. She clapped her hand over her mouth and stared at Rosa with an expression of abject humiliation. "Sorry."

Rosa gave Alice's hip a playful pinch. "You *are*. And don't be so embarrassed. You're adorable when you laugh."

Alice lowered her hand to reveal a bashful smile. "I still don't understand why you're interested in me."

"Superficially, because I think you're gorgeous and very, *very* sexy. On a deeper level, because I had fun with you last night, and I like you a lot, and I think we have more in common than either of us might have guessed at first sight. Whatever the reason, I want to spend the next few days hanging out with you. I want us to survive Camp Rewind together."

Alice rewarded Rosa with the tentative brush of her warm lips across her temple. "You're so sweet—and fun, and gorgeous, too."

Rosa shivered, tingling from head to toe from that one simple physical gesture. She couldn't remember the last time she'd been this turned on by something so innocent. "I actually haven't been with anyone in a year and a half, so…it's not like I have any *recent* experience." With a shrug, she leaned closer to subtly inhale the scent of Alice's freshly shampooed hair. "For a while I just wasn't in the mood. Lately, it's been difficult to work up enough trust to meet someone. So maybe I'm not terribly intimidating, after all."

Alice trembled against her. "I've got you beat. It's been nearly two years for me."

"I thought you said your husband filed for divorce last year?"

"He did." Alice smiled without humor. "But our marriage had been over for a while."

"Oh." The nature of their conversation emboldened Rosa to take Alice's hand between her own. "Was there anyone before him?"

Alice shook her head. "He was the first. The only."

Staggered by her genuine lack of experience, Rosa wasn't sure if she was ecstatic or petrified by the thought of being only the second person to ever touch Alice intimately. "Oh. Wow."

Alice stiffened almost imperceptibly. "Yes. I'm not only inexperienced with women but also, essentially, with men as well." She searched Rosa's eyes, worry etched across her delicate features. "Hence my feeling intimidated."

"Well, now *I* feel the same way." Rosa rolled her shoulders as the weight of her responsibility toward Alice bore down on her. "Listen, I don't want to pressure you into anything. What I really want is a friend here at camp. If you're also interested in some no-strings-attached fun on the side, all the better. But even if all that happens between us this weekend is a kiss or two, maybe a little hand-holding, please believe that I'll be perfectly happy with that. Even the most innocent camp romance would provide me with enough sweet, wonderful memories to sustain me for the rest of my life."

Alice smiled, but Rosa could detect mild disappointment behind her eyes. "At the moment, kissing and holding hands sound unbelievably exciting, albeit a bit nerve-wracking. While I'm not sure I'm ready for more than that right now, I hope we can keep...other stuff on the table. If I do decide I want more, I mean." She paused, as though wrestling with whether to continue. Finally, she exhaled. "At the risk of sounding blunt, meeting you presents an opportunity I'm not likely to find often, or easily, to explore something I've been curious about for years. That said, if I promise I won't let you pressure me into anything, will you promise to respect whatever decision I make about how far I want to go with you this weekend?"

Translation: if she could work up the nerve, Alice wanted to get laid. Rosa placed a finger under Alice's chin, tilting her head to get better access to her full lips. "All right." She marveled at the dilation of Alice's pupils, the quickening of her breath, as she anticipated Rosa's next move. "May I kiss you now? I'm dying to even the score after last night."

Alice chuckled, and Rosa had to forcibly keep her from lowering her face in a show of modesty. "Yes."

Rosa closed the distance between their mouths inch by inch, releasing Alice's chin at the last second so she could pull away if she wanted. But Alice didn't. Instead, the softness of her lips drew Rosa in, encouraging her to trace the tip of her tongue over the upper, then the lower, in a silent plea for entry. Alice opened her mouth to allow Rosa inside, where her tongue met Rosa's in a playful dance that hinted at none of the anxiety Alice professed to feel. The kiss was perfect. Even better than their first, which had already attained a kind of mythical status in Rosa's admittedly hazy memory. Moaning at the surge of her long-forgotten hormones, Rosa tightened her arm around Alice's waist as she let her other hand drift up to caress the delicate line of her clavicle where it peeked out over the V-neck T-shirt.

Alice inhaled swiftly, her breath hastening. Concerned she'd moved too fast, Rosa returned her hand to her side. Moments later, Alice ended the kiss and left them both panting. She caught her breath first. "Why'd you stop touching me?"

Feeling silly, Rosa lifted one shoulder in a lopsided shrug. "I thought I might be going too fast, so I tapped the brakes." Alice used her thumb and index finger to flick Rosa on the bicep. More surprised than hurt, Rosa yelped. "Ow! What was that for?"

"You *just* said you'd respect my decisions about how far I want to go."

"Touché." Rosa rubbed the spot Alice had targeted, more to generate sympathy than alleviate any pain. "You made a noise. I got concerned that you were worried I was about to put my hand on your breast."

Alice licked her lips. Her nostrils flared. "Were you?"

"Well, I…" No point in being dishonest, was there? "No. I mean, I don't think so. I figured we would stick with basic making out. I'm in no hurry to get past first base."

This time there was no doubt that her caution had caused Alice displeasure. Appearing despondent, she lamented, "I shouldn't have told you I'd slept only with my husband."

Rosa shook her head and held Alice's hands in her own. "Please don't say that. I want you to be honest with me. I'm not trying to punish you for your candor, I swear. I just…don't want to overstep." Thinking back to Alice's disappearance into the woods that morning, she admitted, "I don't want to frighten you away."

Alice's eyes grew shiny. She grabbed a fistful of Rosa's T-shirt collar, pulling her in so that their faces were only inches apart. "You won't, and I'm *so* sorry about this morning. I won't run from you again.

Even if I'm scared." She blinked as her tears threatened to spill over. "*Please* trust me. I know it's my fault you don't, but...*please*. I really do want this. *I'll* stop you if you go too far."

Unable to withstand her sorrowful, imploring tone, Rosa kissed Alice again. Hard. To her astonishment, Alice matched her intensity without hesitation, kissing back with a passion that seemed to erupt from deep within. Emboldened by the response, Rosa once again placed her hand at the base of Alice's throat, then dropped slightly lower to stroke her collarbones. When Alice whimpered this time, Rosa stayed the course. She traced her blunt fingernails along the defined ridge of bone mere inches above the slope of Alice's breast, wondering how it would feel when she finally gave in to the urge to cradle one with her palm.

Alice apparently wondered the same and decided to find out by moving the hand that had been tangled in Rosa's hair to rest lightly against her left breast. Rosa groaned loudly, shocked and thrilled and tickled beyond reason to have found such an excellent way to spend her time at camp. She placed her fingers over Alice's, urging her to squeeze, to feel, to explore. Seemingly unable to concentrate on two tasks at once, Alice broke the kiss and stared at their joined hands.

Rosa removed hers to allow Alice an unimpeded view. Mouth slightly ajar, Alice watched her slim fingers fondle the plump breast, clearly entranced by the sight. "That feels good," Rosa murmured. And it did, even if Alice's current mindset was geared more toward exploration than offering pleasure. "Do you like it?"

Alice's cheeks bloomed rosy pink. "Yes." She pulled back slightly, but rather than withdraw, she captured Rosa's shirt-and-bra-covered nipple between her fingertips and pinched. "Do you?"

A rush of wetness stained Rosa's panties. She shifted, trying to be subtle about the depth and intensity of her arousal. All at once, she was ready to *fuck*. "Very much."

Exhaling harshly, Alice removed her hand and bent at the waist. She took a few deep breaths, no doubt in an attempt to regain her absolutely impressive composure. "That was kind of amazing."

Rosa glanced down at her own chest and grinned. Had *anyone* ever found the simple act of touching her clothed breast amazing before? She didn't think so. She'd lost her virginity in high school by going all the way with her college-aged boyfriend the very first time they'd gotten physical. He'd been with enough girls before she slept with him to have not considered her naked tits much of a novelty at all. Deeply affected by Alice's visceral reaction to that one semi-innocent, breathtakingly intimate touch, Rosa once again wound her arm around Alice's middle to give her a sideways hug. "Yeah, it was."

Alice's heartbeat fluttered against Rosa's side. "After all my bravado, I think I need a little break. To catch my breath."

"Me, too." Rosa kissed Alice's temple as she swelled with affection for the woman in her arms. "Why don't we take a walk? We could go back to camp to check out one of the activities, or else venture farther down this trail."

Alice chuckled. "I'm not sure I was asking for *that* much of a break." As Rosa watched, her expression became determined, like she'd made a decision. "But maybe we *should* check out what's happening back at camp. For a few minutes, at least."

"If it's lame, we'll come back here." Rosa sensed that Alice wanted to take advantage of some of the camp-sponsored extracurricular options, if only to tell her therapist she had. "Or find somewhere else to be alone."

Alice wrung her hands together, the dark cloud of her anxiety creeping back overhead as Rosa watched. "Should we check out the arts-and-crafts building?"

"Sounds like fun." Rosa pushed herself off the fallen tree before taking Alice by the hips and helping her down as well. "If you want to leave, tell me. I won't be upset." She took hold of Alice's hand. "Having you all to myself is hardly a punishment."

Alice beamed so hard she actually showed her teeth. "You're a very nice woman."

"I assure you, my intentions are anything but pure."

"Promise?" Alice adjusted her grip, threading their fingers together with an easy air that Rosa found downright heartening.

Maybe Camp Rewind really will help both of us learn to trust. "Promise."

CHAPTER SEVEN

Hand in hand with the sexiest woman she'd ever worked up the courage to talk to, let alone touch, Alice felt minimal anxiety about their foray into Camp Rewind's daily hustle and bustle. At least, up until the moment they encountered a small group of men walking toward them as they approached the archery range. The tallest of the three, a muscled blond, stared at their entangled fingers with all the subtlety of a five-alarm blaze at a fireworks factory. His eyes lit up as if their affection was the best thing he'd seen all day. One of his companions mirrored his lascivious look, but the other simply waved at them with a bland, friendly smile.

"Morning, ladies," said the personable one.

"*Very* good morning," his tall friend added, like a dope.

Alice nearly yanked her hand from Rosa's grip but managed to stop herself just in time. Not only would she embarrass both of them further by doing so, she would also undoubtedly hurt Rosa with that type of knee-jerk reaction. For someone as worldly as Rosa seemed to be, the idea of being embarrassed about whose hand she held—and what it implied about her sexuality—would undoubtedly come across as pathetically precious. By the same token, a woman who had endured rape and death threats and public humiliation and unrelenting hatred as a result of an organized campaign to destroy her life surely felt fairly unmoved by some poorly disguised lust and mild innuendo. Determined to prove that she could handle being with Rosa this weekend, in *every* respect, Alice clung to her hand even tighter.

"Indeed it is." Rosa practically chirped the cheery reply, leading

Alice past the small group without slowing. "Good luck on the range today, guys. Oh, and if you need any pointers, find Derek. He's apparently quite accomplished."

Good-natured laughter echoed at their backs as they walked away. "Will do!" the friendly camper called out. "Thanks for the advice."

"Any time!" Rosa looked back over her shoulder, grinned, waved, then immediately sought out Alice's eyes. "You okay?"

"I'm fine." It was the truth, for the most part. Considering the absolutely foreign, anxiety-ridden situation she'd landed herself in—stuck in an unfamiliar, inherently social environment while attempting her first same-sex romance—Alice felt astonishingly calm. Which wasn't even close to *entirely* calm, but at least she seemed to have progressed beyond the paralysis stage. "Still nervous, but fine." She rested her head against Rosa's shoulder for just a second before straightening. "Thanks for talking."

"No problem at all. I'm used to talking."

"And writing," Alice said lightly. Though she'd learned a little about Rosa, including her real name, she was eager to find out more. As much as possible. "Is that how you pay the bills? Or do you have another job?"

Rosa's smile was restrained. "I cobbled together a living freelancing for a while. Not so much since everything went down, unfortunately. I sold an article shortly after...that *one*...but hackers took down the site that published it almost immediately. Not before I received an outpouring of hate in the comments section, though." She sighed and lowered her volume as they walked past a female counselor in an official Camp Rewind T-shirt, who waved at them politely. Once the counselor was well out of earshot, Rosa said, "I'm currently working on a book about public shaming in the Internet age, but I'm not sure I'll ever have the guts to publish it."

Alice frowned. The idea that faceless online critics might have succeeded in silencing Rosa's voice bothered her more than she could articulate. It wasn't only because she believed that women should be free to express their opinions even when they ran the risk of upsetting men or otherwise threatening the status quo. On a more personal level, the idea that strangers had managed to steal one of Rosa's passions in life—or two, perhaps, if the ex-boyfriend fell into that same category—made Alice hurt from head to toe. While she silently acknowledged that it was much easier said than done, Alice couldn't help but express a heartfelt desire. "I hope you do. Some day."

Rosa chuckled without humor. "Well, it would certainly help me keep the lights on. Controversy does breed curiosity."

"But I understand why you'd want to wait a while. To let everyone forget."

"Unfortunately, the Internet never forgets."

Rosa's obvious regret tugged at Alice's heart. She could never have imagined wishing so sincerely for some way, *any* way, to ease the pain of a near stranger, but with Rosa that was exactly what she yearned to do. If someone walked up to her right then and told her that giving a speech to a crowd of five hundred people would erase this difficult episode from Rosa's life, she was pretty sure she'd actually take them up on the offer. Somehow, she would find a way to conquer what was perhaps her biggest fear. Anything to eradicate the lost, empty expression Rosa got every time she talked about what had happened.

Regretting her inability to do more, Alice said, "I'd like to read the book whether or not you end up publishing it. Sociology isn't my field, but I do find the subject fascinating, if not slightly disturbing."

This time Rosa sounded genuinely amused. "Social behavior *is* disturbing at times, absolutely."

"Lila!" Standing in the open doorway of the arts-and-crafts building a mere twenty feet in front of them, Bree waved frantically in a bid to catch their attention. "Shy girl! Get your sexy asses over here."

"Oh God," Alice mumbled under her breath, unthinkingly.

Rosa caressed her thumb. "Back to the woods? Or would you be willing to go inside if I asked Bree to tone it down a little?"

Reassured by the subtle contact, Alice took a deep breath, then exhaled evenly. The goals she and Dawn had agreed upon for her time at camp required her to participate in at least one group activity. Now that she had a friend—one goal down—this second task should be much easier to achieve. That was unless Rosa's undeniable magnetism continued to attract additional hangers-on. "We can go inside."

Rosa led Alice to the building wearing an easy smile. "Hey, Bree. Are you coming or going?"

"Not coming yet, unfortunately." She popped an expertly manicured eyebrow and darted her gaze back and forth between Rosa and Alice. "How about you ladies?"

"We're taking it slow this morning. Thought we'd find a creative outlet while we get to know each other better." Rosa let go of Alice's hand to approach Bree, wrapping an arm around her shoulder so she could pull her aside and whisper in a low voice. Bree nodded, offering a barely audible apology before they broke apart and Rosa returned to stand at Alice's side.

Bree shot Alice a conciliatory smile. "My apologies for the overly effusive welcome. I know I come on a little strong."

Alice's face heated. She hoped Bree didn't think she was upset. "It's all right." It wasn't, clearly, but she still felt the need to say so. "I'm just…"

"Reserved. I get it, and I should have known better." Bree gestured through the door. "They've got all kinds of fun stuff in here. Want to check it out?"

Disappointed that she and Rosa wouldn't have the privacy to talk openly, Alice nonetheless nodded in agreement, polite and gracious in every circumstance. Just like her mother raised her. "Sure."

As Bree turned to enter the building, Rosa squeezed Alice's hand. *Is this okay?* she mouthed.

Alice nodded and mustered a brave smile. This was good for her. Interacting with more than one adult woman who wasn't her mother, her therapist, or a colleague, both at the same time, even, was a groundbreaking step to take. If this didn't constitute growth, she didn't know what did.

Inside the building was a bright, spacious room with eight long, wooden tables lined by benches. Only half the tables were occupied, and as Bree led them to an empty one at the far side of the room, Alice gazed around at the various projects and people on display. She spotted a colorful paper-bag jellyfish, two sticky-looking women slaving over a pair of papier-mâché bowls, a pair of grown men who laughed hysterically as they acted out a vicious battle using cartoonish figures they'd fashioned out of pipe cleaners and construction paper, and a lone woman bent intently over a number of thin sticks that she'd painted wildly different colors. Their intended purpose was unclear. They reached their vacant table before Alice could finish her survey of the room and its various wonders.

"I don't know about you ladies, but I feel like getting my construction-paper mosaic on. Anyone else?"

Rosa scanned the tables around them with an expression of mildly overwhelmed indecision that perfectly echoed what Alice felt inside. "I'm not sure yet. I may need to look at all the options before I decide."

Bree pulled out a chair, set down her bag, and turned toward the front of the room. "Going to get supplies. I'll be back."

Alice exhaled as soon as she left. Worried that Rosa would think her rude, she said, "She's nice."

"She really is, if a little single-mindedly focused on getting laid this weekend."

The comment triggered a memory of something Rosa had said during breakfast. "She was one of the people who hit on you this morning?"

Rosa stilled, then carefully met Alice's gaze. "Does that bother you?"

"No." If Rosa had wanted Bree, she could have had her this morning. Instead, she'd tracked Alice down without knowing whether she'd even *wanted* to be found. "I certainly can't blame her."

"Well, as it happens, you've managed to capture my full attention." Rosa pulled out the chair nearest to Alice and gestured for her to sit. "Would you like me to fetch supplies for both of us? What do you want to make?"

A mostly male chorus of voices cheered from a spot near the far wall, in an open area free of tables or supplies. Alice's curiosity overrode her sense of caution—*we can leave if I say the word*—and she took a few steps away from the table, craning to catch a glimpse of what had everyone so excited. As she watched a handsome, deeply tanned man in board shorts and a plain T-shirt demonstrate his crude creation, she couldn't help feeling similarly thrilled by the spectacle. "Miniature siege engines!"

"Huh?" Rosa stood close to her side and joined in her study of the playful competition. "Oh, I get it…they're trying to see how far they can launch a marshmallow? That's cute."

It was more than cute. It looked *fun*, and Alice was suddenly eager to win. "They're building siege engines from Popsicle sticks, wooden blocks, and rubber bands." Upon scanning a smaller table near where the crowd had gathered, Alice spotted a stack of the small plastic cups that were intended to hold the ammunition. "Over there. That's what I'm doing."

"Yeah?" Rosa seemed tickled by her choice, or else her unabashed enthusiasm. "Want me to grab some supplies for us?"

Alice turned to Rosa, grabbing her hands with enthusiasm. "That would be *so* great. Thank you." She started to release Rosa's hands but stopped, their fingertips still linked. "Wait. You don't have to do the same thing as me…if you don't want."

"I know." Rosa pulled away after blowing her a kiss. "I do want. At least to try." She nodded at the group of guys who attempted to launch their marshmallows farther on each successive attempt. "Look what a great time *they're* having."

Giggling, Alice sat in the chair Rosa had pulled out. "I think it'll be a lot of fun."

"Then that's what I want. To have fun, with you." Rosa walked backward a few steps and waved, clearly reluctant to leave her side. "I'll be *right* back. Two shakes."

Alice blushed at the overwhelming wave of affection she felt for Rosa, especially because she'd probably never even see her again once camp had ended. But how could she *not* feel warmly about a grown woman who measured time in terms of a lamb's tail? "I'll be fine. Go." A thought occurred. "Make sure to get lots of Popsicle sticks!"

"Yes, ma'am." Rosa tipped an imaginary hat, then scurried off.

Alice was unsurprised and only vaguely uneasy when Bree returned to their table mere seconds after Rosa left. She dropped a stack of differently colored pieces of construction paper on the table, followed by a larger sheet of white card stock, a pair of scissors, a bottle of glue, and a freshly sharpened pencil. Sliding into the chair across from Alice, Bree exhaled and studied her materials for a few seconds before picking up the pencil and the sheet of card stock with an expression of serious determination. She glanced up at Alice. "I should warn you in advance, I've never made a mosaic before. Or really done a whole lot of arts and crafts like this. This *could* turn out to be a real disaster."

"Me neither," Alice said honestly. "That's why I picked the engineering project."

Bree glanced over her shoulder, scanning the room until her gaze landed on Rosa. "Yeah, too complicated for me." She placed the card stock on the table, then turned it this way and that as she studied its blank surface. "I like art. But my elementary school in Detroit didn't have a lot of money for supplies, and nurturing the creativity of inner-city kids wasn't exactly a top priority for anyone. My mother always encouraged me to draw, though, every chance I got. She tried to give me and my brothers every opportunity possible, but there was never any money to send us to a camp like this one. Not after my father died." Touching pencil to paper, she began to draw using bold, confident strokes. "Lung cancer. He was a big cigarette smoker from the time he was eleven years old. Disgusting habit." As though suddenly realizing that she might have just unthinkingly served Alice an insult, Bree looked up in alarm. "You don't smoke, right?"

The truth came tumbling out. "Not often, and never tobacco."

Bree chortled in delight and went back to her drawing. "Full of surprises, aren't we, Miss Alice?" She paused to offer a warm smile, probably in case Alice had misinterpreted the comment. "How about you? Ever come to a camp like this as a kid?"

"Never." Alice watched as the distinct shape of a gorgeous, strong-boned female face began to take form on Bree's paper. "My parents probably could have afforded it, but my mother in particular didn't value purely social activities. She did send me to an intensive summer music program once, when I was sixteen, to play the cello. They had us practice so much we barely had time to interact with the other campers—and there were no arts and crafts."

"Lame." Bree shot her a sympathetic look. "Your mom's a real hard-ass, huh?"

"Yes." *Hard-ass* was indeed an accurate term to describe Amanda Wu.

Rosa returned to the table with a veritable wealth of Popsicle sticks, an assortment of wooden cubes that had small holes drilled into their faces, some slim wooden dowels, two marshmallows sitting in a stack of plastic cups, a fist full of rubber bands, a few lengths of string, and a cordless hot-glue gun. "I really hope this is enough stuff."

Alice's mouth stretched into a silly grin at the sight of her new friend, and her heart beat a little faster. "I'm sure it is."

"Good." With an exaggerated sigh, Rosa dropped into the chair next to Alice's and folded her arms over her chest. "Now please tell me you know what you're doing, because I looked at what they've got going on over there, and frankly, I'm baffled." Her attention drifted to Bree's paper, and her eyes widened comically. "Holy shit, Bree, that's incredible!"

The visage of a veritable African queen had emerged from Bree's pencil strokes, revealing an absolutely unbelievable level of talent. Bree lifted the pencil from the paper and let it hover near the woman's mouth while she tilted her head and considered her work. "It's not bad," she conceded. Another stroke of her pencil brought further definition to the woman's full lips. "She's my mother." She lifted her eyes to meet Alice's, still sympathetic, but also full of pride for her own maternal influence. "Figured I'd take this home for her. Let her hang it on the fridge."

Alice grinned. "Your first camp project." Her smile faded at the bittersweet certainty that her own mother would never accept such a gift from her without unleashing some type of withering insult or passive-aggressive comment. Not wanting to take away from the significance of Bree's gesture, she forced a happier face. "Your mother will love it."

"Unless I mosaic it to death." Bree turned her attention back to her sketch. "Probably should've started with something simpler."

"I have complete faith in you." Rosa's hand crept over to rest on Alice's knee, squeezing tenderly, but her eyes remained locked on Bree's creation. "You're a true artist."

Bree snorted but visibly soaked in the praise. "Tell that to my boss at the hospital where I work security. My actual career is as fucking unartistic as it gets." She gazed across the table at Rosa, a drawn-out look of admiration that managed to spark a tiny flame of jealousy deep in Alice's stomach. "But I really appreciate you saying that. Thanks."

Eager to impress Rosa even half as much as Bree had, Alice answered her earlier query. "I know what I'm doing." She waited for Rosa to look at her, then grabbed a few Popsicle sticks and began laying them out on the table. "Want me to show you how to build a simple catapult?"

Rosa angled her chair to give Alice her undivided attention. "Sure."

Alice arranged four wooden cubes in a rectangular formation, then placed two Popsicle sticks alongside them to form the long sides of the rectangle. She glanced across the table at Bree's scissors. "Mind if I borrow those for a second?"

"Go wild." Bree giggled, probably at the very idea of Alice doing any such thing.

Resisting the urge to blush, Alice cut another Popsicle stick in half, then laid one of the shorter pieces next to the bottom pairs of cubes so three sides of the catapult's base were outlined. "We'll use hot glue to secure these sticks to the blocks and form the bottom of our base. Like this." She squeezed dollops of hot glue onto the ends of a longer stick, then pressed it against two wooden blocks until the adhesive set. She followed up by gluing another long stick to the opposite set of blocks. "Why don't you do the same thing for the other side?"

Rosa gamely followed her instructions, creating the other half of their mini siege engine's base. "I take it you've done this before?"

"Maybe." Alice grinned as she slid yet another cube onto a wooden dowel, positioning it squarely in the middle of the rod. She squirted glue onto one end, then fitted the stick into a wooden block from each side, joining them. After that, she placed more glue onto the ends of another half Popsicle stick. "I'm actually an engineer."

"Like, professionally?" Rosa watched Alice secure the other end of the two sides together by attaching the half stick to the bottoms of a block from either section. "Oh, I see what you're doing."

Alice held the freshly glued sections together with her fingers. "Good. You can glue the other half stick on top of this one as soon as it's ready." She glanced over at Bree, but their companion looked suddenly preoccupied, cutting out tiny pieces of colorful paper while simultaneously staring at an older, flaxen-haired woman who was bent over her own masterpiece two tables away. Satisfied that she'd recaptured Rosa's interest—and Bree's had turned elsewhere—Alice relaxed slightly as she passed their nearly finished base to Rosa. "Here you are."

"Thanks." Rosa's attention also flicked to Bree, and then she bent to whisper into Alice's ear. "I don't want her. I want *you*."

The unmistakable desire in Rosa's voice, restrained though it seemed to be, caused Alice to quake in anticipation. Struggling to keep her volume low, she murmured, "I want you, too."

Rosa kissed her cheek and backed away. Focused again on the materials in front of her, she cautiously squeezed glue onto her half Popsicle stick and affixed it to the spot Alice had indicated. "So, you're an engineer. As your actual day job?"

"Yes." When Rosa finished her task, Alice added two more long sticks along the outermost edge of the two sides, creating more surface area on the base. "We'll need these to attach the vertical part of the frame."

Rosa rested her chin on the heel of her hand as she watched Alice position yet another pair of long sticks in an upside-down V on one side of the base. "Do you work in an office?"

"I split my time between an office and a lab. Depends on the day and what project I'm working on." She nodded at their shared pile of supplies. "Want to do the other side of the frame?" She released the pieces she'd been holding together. "Again, just do the same thing I did."

Rosa constructed the other half of the frame, carefully. "Is that right?"

Alice reached beneath the table to pat Rosa on the thigh, pleased by how seriously she seemed to be taking their project. "It's perfect."

Rosa danced happily in her seat, pulling Alice's attention to her wondrous chest. Instantly her mind was back at that fallen tree, reliving the weight and heat and suppleness of Rosa's breast in her hand, especially the way she'd been able to feel the hard nipple as it stiffened against her palm, even through the layers of material separating her from Rosa's bare skin. It took Rosa snapping her fingers, loudly, to break Alice out of her lust-induced trance.

Distracted from her cruising, Bree whistled in apparent delight. "Can't blame you for looking, Alice."

Red-cheeked and thoroughly chastened, Alice arranged three Popsicle sticks in a line, end over end, then grabbed the glue gun, desperate to do something with her hands. "Sorry."

"Don't be embarrassed." Rosa pinched Alice's elbow, her voice a bare whisper. "I love the way you look at me."

Alice created two long beams consisting of three sticks apiece, then glued them together using wooden blocks on each end and in the middle, for a total of three points of contact. Wanting to move past the awkward moment, she said, "This is our arm. We'll glue the bucket to one end."

"All right." Rosa's quiet voice soothed her frayed nerves. "That's starting to look really impressive."

"I agree." Bree also spoke gently, seemingly aware that she'd once again made Alice uncomfortable. "None of the other ones I saw over there looked that good."

Alice doubted the veracity of Bree's statement, as this makeshift contraption didn't come close to representing her best work. Still, she accepted that to the layperson, her ability to model even a simple mechanical device might seem laudable. "Thank you."

Returning to their catapult's frame, Alice bridged the gap between the top of her upside-down Vs by using another Popsicle stick cut in half and two smaller wooden cubes. The next, crucial step was to glue one end of her launching arm to the middle cube in the dowel at the front of the base. After that, she used a few rubber bands to secure the center of the arm to the top brace she'd just created. Finally, she adhered an empty plastic dish to the end of the arm, holding both pieces in place until she was convinced the bucket wasn't going anywhere. As a test, she pulled down on the bucket end of the arm, creating tension in the rubber bands she'd wrapped around the catapult's top brace. She let go, and the arm sprang back into place smoothly, ready to launch a marshmallow.

"Wow!" Rosa reached out to touch their creation, then stopped. "May I?"

"Of course." Alice pushed back from the table, giddy that Rosa seemed so pleased. "Want to do the first launch?"

"Yes." Rosa grabbed the catapult and a marshmallow, and found a clear patch of floor behind their table. "We'll test it here, then take it across the room to see if we can beat the standing record."

"What's the record?"

Drawing back the arm, Rosa launched a marshmallow into the air, sending it to bounce off a distant wall. "I think you've beaten it." She picked up the catapult with exaggerated care. "Want to come watch?"

Alice glanced over at the launch area, disappointed to see that the small crowd had only grown. A bearded camp counselor had joined the trio of siege engineers and seemed to be demonstrating a technique that prompted an enthusiastic group discussion. "I don't know."

"You don't have to." Rosa shifted on her feet and glanced across the room, clearly eager to join them. "Do you mind if I leave you for a few?"

"Not at all. Please do." As much as Alice wanted to test her machine's capabilities, she wasn't ready to interact with an entire group of strangers. Not yet. She marveled that Rosa could do it at all, given the harassment and shame she'd suffered at the hands of others. "Let me know how it goes."

"I will." Rosa appeared genuinely excited to compete. "I'll be right back."

Once Rosa walked away, Bree commented, without looking up, "That girl is *into* you."

Permanently flushed by this point, Alice spotted the string Rosa had brought along with the rest of their materials. She'd always felt more comfortable engaging in idle chat when she had a task to focus on, so she immediately set to work on a more advanced design for her second siege engine. If Rosa loved that silly catapult, a Popsicle-stick ballista was bound to be an even bigger hit. Even with her hands busy, Alice's heart pounded as she struggled to respond. "I hope so."

"Oh, she is." Bree reached across the table like she might touch Alice's arm, but stopped before making contact. "Relax, Alice. You're beautiful, you're brilliant, and you've clearly got that woman hooked." Her hand retreated, returning to its own work. The mosaic, still only partially completed, already looked like something that might hang in a museum. "Hell, *I* even like you, and that's despite the fact that you've denied me the chance to get into Lila's panties. You're in, trust me—so enjoy this time with her."

Alice felt like she might literally burst into flames. Her hands moved faster, cutting, arranging, threading, tying. Building. It was the one thing in life that made her feel powerful and in control. Social interaction existed at the extreme other end of the personal-capabilities spectrum, yet she told herself that she could *do* this. Bree was only being friendly and familiar. Nothing she said was meant to embarrass Alice or make her feel bad. In fact, it seemed obvious she intended to do the opposite. Without taking her eyes away from her work, Alice said, "I am, more than I've ever enjoyed anyone or anything in my life."

Bree made a quiet noise. Amusement? "Sounds like the feeling's mutual, then."

Alice realized too late how her comment must have sounded. She enjoyed Rosa more than anything, *ever*? While it wasn't entirely inaccurate, that certainly wasn't something she wanted Bree to know. *Or* Rosa. The last thing she needed was to screw up their time together by being too intense and serious for Rosa's comfort. Scrambling to mitigate the damage, Alice said, "My therapist would be shocked if she knew I was seriously considering a fling with another woman. But I don't know. I've always fantasized about having casual sex, even if I've never felt brave enough to pursue it." She cringed as she listened to herself. In her effort to deny having any deeper feelings for Rosa, she came across like a pathetic, cowardly horn-dog. Also, she was talking about *sex*, with someone she barely knew. Fumbling, Alice said, "Not that I only want her for her body. I like her."

Bree chuckled. "I know."

Alice sighed and cut her firing rails into shape. "I'll stop talking now."

"I told you, relax. You're among friends here."

The tender warmth of Bree's words washed over her like a balm. Alice tore her attention away from construction long enough to make brief eye contact, always a difficult gesture but ultimately rewarding when she saw the sincerity in Bree's amiable gaze. "Thanks. I *really* didn't get out much as a kid. Or an adult, for that matter."

"A weekend of firsts, I imagine." Bree looked down, gluing a small scrap of dark-brown construction paper on her mother's cheekbone. "That'll be exciting. For you *and* Lila."

Grateful for yet another reminder that she was the only one who knew Rosa's real name, Alice smiled. "Indeed."

Rosa came back to their table as Alice put the finishing touches on her ballista. She radiated enthusiasm and good cheer, a jubilant lightness of spirit that infected Alice the moment she laid eyes on her. Securing the feet and back of her newly crafted projectile rail to its accompanying base, Alice greeted Rosa with an uncharacteristically broad smile. It actually made her cheeks ache. "Record broken?"

"Yes!" Rosa took the seat next to Alice with a flourish, pumping her fist into the air. "Jamal loved your design. He was impressed you came up with it on your own."

Alice rolled her eyes. "It was painfully simple. I've built much more complex machines than that." *Like robots*, she added silently, though she didn't dare boast out loud. The specter of her mother hung over her head, urging her to strive for perfection, always, while never showing blatant pride about what she'd actually accomplished.

"I see that." Rosa tilted her head as she examined the second, slightly more complicated siege engine. "What *is* it?"

"A ballista." Alice searched the area for a projectile. "Bree, may I borrow your pencil?"

"Absolutely." Bree continued to glue scraps of construction paper to her drawing as she stared at the ballista with a bewildered expression. "Lila, I hope you're not intimidated by smart women."

Rosa wrapped her arm around Alice's waist. "Nope."

Fingers shaking, Alice loaded the pencil onto the projectile rail, then pulled back the string to demonstrate its firing mechanism. "See?"

"You built that in less than twenty minutes," Rosa said, looking at Alice for confirmation. "Seriously?"

Alice shrugged. "It's really not that amazing." *Not half as amazing as the way your perfect breast felt in my hand.* The thought floated to the surface unbidden, traitorous in its devastation to her composure. Rushing to cover up her lascivious inner monologue, she added, "You haven't even tried it yet."

Rosa scooted so she was facing Alice and, in a now-familiar gesture, caught hold of both her clammy, trembling hands. Embarrassed by her body's reaction to social anxiety, Alice cursed her watering eyes and tried to slip from Rosa's grasp, but Rosa held on as though her sweaty palms didn't matter at all. "Hey," Rosa whispered under her breath. "Are you okay?"

Alice nodded gamely, forcing away tears she refused to allow to fall. *Pull it together, Alice.* "Yeah."

"Do you want to go?"

Alice shook her head. She'd built the ballista for Rosa and certainly didn't want to make them leave before allowing her the fun of shooting it at least once or twice. "No, I'm sorry. I'm fine." She checked Bree in her peripheral vision, glad to see her engrossed in her own work. "I'm trying, but...small talk with someone I barely know isn't easy. Neither is accepting compliments...from anyone. Or having random, inappropriate thoughts at the worst possible moments."

Rosa's lips twitched. "Inappropriate thoughts about me, or Bree?"

"You, of course." Alice cringed at the speed of her response. She exhaled. "I must be the most uncool woman you've ever kissed."

"Not even close." Rosa pecked her cheek and turned back to Alice's newest machine. "This ballista is epic, and there's *no way* something so freaking cool could have been engineered by someone who wasn't equally cool." She winced after the words left her mouth, appearing genuinely contrite. "More compliments. Sorry."

However difficult to accept, Rosa's praise *did* make Alice feel good. Like maybe she was worth something after all. "I'm glad you like it."

Rosa carried the ballista over to their private testing ground behind the table. She lined up her shot, pulled back the string, and launched Bree's pencil across the room. When Rosa glanced back at her, glowing, the air between them turned electric. For whatever reason, Alice's geekiness seemed to excite her. Not only that, but the awkward shyness that repelled most people hadn't yet driven Rosa away. How could she have possibly found someone so perfect at a meat-market summer camp for adults? She wished she'd met Rosa on an Internet date instead, or *anywhere* that would have encouraged the possibility of more than a few-night stand. Despite her mixed messages to Bree, Alice could easily see herself ending up with someone like Rosa.

Even if it *would* put her mother in an early grave.

"Mind if I take this over to show the guys?" Rosa jerked her thumb in the direction of the testing grounds, where only Jamal and one other male camper remained. Two additional men sat across from one another at a table nearby, presumably improving their designs. Having retrieved the projectile during Alice's daydreaming, Rosa had their ballista locked, loaded, and ready to go. "I have a feeling Jamal will get a big kick out of this."

"Sure." Alice experienced a mild tug of desire to join her. Not only to counter any condescending expressions of surprise that she could engineer a simple machine by herself, but also, mostly, to share in Rosa's excitement and enthusiasm—those intoxicating, uplifting emotions *she'd* helped to create. Also, it would save her from another sex-tinged chat with Bree. "Wait!" She stood up. "I'll come with you."

"Yeah?" Rosa extended her hand, tentatively. "I'd like that."

Grateful for the effort to spare her the attention that would come from once again showing affection in front of others, Alice pushed aside her fears and walked to Rosa, threading their fingers together and holding on tight. "I apologize in advance if I embarrass you."

Rosa ran her thumb over Alice's knuckle. "You could never embarrass me." As they walked toward the main launch area, where

Alice's first catapult was at that moment undergoing a thorough examination by one of the aspiring engineers, Rosa whispered into Alice's ear. "Remember, I'm the queen of the shame. Nothing you say or do could ever compare to the humiliation I've brought onto myself. Not even close."

Saddened by the reminder of Rosa's painful burden, Alice lifted their joined hands to her lips so she could kiss Rosa's knuckles. "At least nobody seems to recognize you here."

Rosa chuckled. "I should hope not, or else cutting my hair was a complete waste."

Alice was still trying to imagine how Rosa, so adorable in a bob, used to wear her hair when they reached Jamal and the male camper. The handsome counselor grinned at Rosa, then stepped forward to offer Alice his hand. "You must be Alice. I'm Jamal. Sweet catapult design you've got there."

Alice shook his hand, pretending that she was at work dealing with a colleague. A professional interaction would be marginally easier than this one. "Thank you, but it's pretty rudimentary."

"Unlike this," Rosa said, and held out the ballista for him to inspect. "I got back to the table and she'd nearly finished constructing this puppy."

Jamal's eyes lit up. "A ballista!" He clapped Alice on the back as she tried not to look panicked. "That's excellent. Taking it to the next level, aren't you?"

Alice lifted a shoulder and fidgeted. It still didn't seem like a huge deal in the grand scheme of things, but she accepted that in this environment, such an accomplishment would naturally draw polite praise. "I tried."

Rosa set the ballista down in the launch area, pulled back the strings, and shot the pencil a few inches past the cardboard marker that denoted the current record distance. The male camper standing next to Jamal groaned and tossed his pencil in the air in mock frustration while Rosa leapt to her feet and cheered.

The camper sighed, then winked at Alice. "Great. Back to the drawing board I go."

Alice took a moment to speculate about what else she could build—and how much it would impress Rosa—if only she had more time and materials. It felt good to use her abilities to make Rosa happy. So good she wished she could do it every day. "Nice shot," she called out to Rosa. The smile she received in return made her entire body tingle.

"That was all you, baby." Rosa jogged down the length of the course to grab the pencil, returning before Alice had a chance to miss her.

"Maybe we just make a good team."

Laughing, Rosa scooped up the ballista and walked to her. She set the siege machine on the table beside the first catapult, allowing the trio of interested campers to crowd around and examine its design. "Left to my own devices, I would have probably glued a plastic cup to a Popsicle stick, used it like a lacrosse stick, and called it good." She came to stand beside Alice, while Jamal stepped in to form the point of their conversational triangle. Rosa jerked her thumb at Alice with an air of pride. "She's a professional engineer, but you probably guessed that already."

"Makes sense." Jamal folded his arms over his chest, appearing genuinely interested in her story. "What kind of engineering?"

"Robotics."

Rosa slapped Alice on the arm, lightly, as her face went agog. "*What?* You build freakin' *robots*?"

Alice shifted her weight from foot to foot, regretful that the reality of her work couldn't possibly match whatever Rosa might be picturing. "Yes."

"Like, industrial robots?" Jamal looked every bit as hungry for details as Rosa. "Toy robots?"

"Um…" Alice glanced back and forth between them. All this attention made her antsy. "I started out designing industrial robots for the factory floor, but over the past five years, I've been working with robotics designed to aid in deep-sea exploration…going where people can't, basically." She watched their reactions, amazed by the depth of the respect she could see in their eyes. "I also have a personal project I've been working on for years. A companion robot I call AFFY." Self-conscious about her motivation for building AFFY, not to mention the meaning of the acronym she'd chosen (A Friend For You), Alice trailed off. "Yeah. Different kinds of robots."

"You build robots," Rosa repeated. She glanced at Jamal before turning back to Alice to give her hand a fervent squeeze. "That's *bad-ass*!"

"Really?" Alice had figured that Rosa would be let down by the discovery that she wasn't in charge of creating a cyborg army or a cabal of house-cleaning androids. "I guarantee you it's not as exciting as it sounds."

"No? I saw how much you enjoyed building a catapult out of Popsicle sticks. I'm not buying that you don't get off on building motherfucking *robots*." Rosa took a breath, then exhaled slowly in an apparent effort to calm down. "I'm sorry. I don't want to make you feel self-conscious. You just need to know that what you do is super cool."

"Agreed," Jamal said. "*Way* cool."

"Thanks." Alice shuffled nervously before saying the first thing that came to her mind. "But it's not like I'm building giant fighting robots or anything. Just submersibles and—"

Rosa gasped out loud. "Wait, *could* you? Build a fighting robot, giant or otherwise?"

Programming and mechanics were the only aspects of life in which Alice rarely doubted herself. "Well, yes. If I wanted to."

"Why *wouldn't* you want to?"

Rosa's question was so earnest that Alice couldn't help but laugh. Jamal shared her amusement, vocally and with gusto, and that's when, against all odds, Alice relaxed and began to enjoy the camaraderie. Smiling, she said, "If you wanted me to build you a fighting robot, I totally would."

Jamal snorted. "Keep your voice down or you'll have a line of new best friends out the door."

"I'll say." Rosa looked at Alice as though she wondered what else there was to learn. "I absolutely want a fighting robot. We could enter it in a competition."

Alice's heart pumped harder at the implication that they might continue seeing each other after the weekend was over. "Maybe we will."

"Personally, I'd like to do some research on simple robot designs for a future camp session." Jamal scanned Alice's face, as though gauging her willingness to talk more in depth about the subject. "Maybe you could give me some tips, send me in the right direction?"

One of the male campers approached them with a simple, slightly modified version of her catapult in his hands. "Mind if I give this a whirl?"

Jamal ushered him forward. "Absolutely."

"Why don't you let me think about it for a day or so, and I'll come back with some ideas for you?" Alice wanted to be helpful but could feel that she was about to hit her limit for social interaction in a group setting. "I told Lila we'd take a hike after this, and to be honest, I'm looking forward to the fresh air."

Jamal gave her an easy grin. "Sure thing. I'll let you brainstorm. You can decide whether it's feasible as a camp project."

"Sounds good." Alice turned to Rosa, who stared at her with a mixture of fondness and respect. "Should we go say good-bye to Bree and head out for our hike?"

To her relief, Rosa picked up on her cues immediately. "Let's do that." She shot Jamal a teasing wink. "Shall we leave these here as examples?"

"If you don't mind." Jamal fiddled with one of his own specimens, a simple but well-constructed slingshot on a base. "We need all the inspiration we can get." He sent them off with a friendly wave. "Have fun on your walk, ladies. Be safe."

They said their good-byes and walked back to their table only to discover that the flaxen-haired woman Bree had been admiring earlier had joined her. The two of them had their projects laid out side by side and were clearly engaged in some playful flirtation while they worked. Bree tore her eyes away from her new companion as they approached, seeming surprised but not unhappy to see them again. "Hey, you two. Lilaa, Alice, this is Enid."

Rosa and Alice each said hello, drawing a polite greeting from the woman at Bree's side. "It's nice to meet you both."

"Likewise." Rosa patted Bree on the shoulder. "Can you believe how talented Bree is, Enid?"

Enid nodded in passionate agreement. "That portrait is unbelievable. Absolutely breathtaking."

Bree had no trouble accepting the compliment or escalating whatever they'd interrupted. "You're too sweet, Enid. You know...I could draw *you*, if you'd like." She curled her lips and winked. "Clothing optional."

Enid's cheeks turned pink, but she seemed delighted to have received such a bold proposition. "Check, please!"

"On that note," Rosa interjected, "Alice and I are going to take a walk and have some quiet time."

"*Quiet* time, I gotcha." Bree gave them a thumbs-up. "Go, have fun." She focused again on Enid. "We will, won't we?"

Enid quivered. "*Yes*, we will."

Once Rosa had guided them outside into the fresh air and relative quiet, Alice began the decompression process. The tension in her muscles gradually melted away, leaving her in a state of moderate physical exhaustion from the sheer effort of holding herself together for so long. She sagged against Rosa, appreciating the solid warmth of the body at her side. It left her wanting—no, *needing*—more of what she'd so far only sampled. "Want to go back to that tree where we ate breakfast?"

Rosa changed direction mid-step, pointing them toward their new destination. "Yes."

"Thanks. I need a break from other people for a while. I'd like to just be with you."

Rosa pulled her into a sheltering, one-armed embrace. "I want to be with you, too."

Alice looked around to ensure nobody was within earshot. "Do you think we could make out again?"

"Kiss a woman who builds robots for a living?" Rosa snorted, then laid a loud, wet one on Alice's temple. "Sold."

CHAPTER EIGHT

Cold was an understatement. Though Rosa would never admit it out loud, she was infatuated. Deeply, painfully infatuated. Now that she'd gotten to know Alice better, she found not only her sweetness or her sensuality or even her gentle compassion compelling. She admired her brain, her subtly competitive nature, the courage she showed by pushing against the boundaries of her comfort zone, again and again, because she knew it would help her grow and because she *wanted* to be happy. When Rosa factored in the thrill of bedding a lesbian virgin—a woman who'd only been touched by an ex-husband who likely hadn't satisfied her the way Rosa could—Alice was a wet dream come to life.

She also might actually convince Rosa to fall in love again.

Not that she planned to tell Alice any of that. It was better to keep *that*, along with the rest of her unrealistic, selfish desires, to herself. While Alice had impressed her more than once by summoning a quiet, determined strength to confront situations she found scary, being together in the real world would require more than mere bravery on Alice's part. Though they could take steps to prevent anyone from knowing about their relationship, and keep Alice's personal information offline while counting on the passage of time to diminish the threat of harassment, Rosa's next partner might one day be targeted because of something she'd written. She couldn't let that happen to Alice. She *wouldn't*.

Alice cleared her throat, alerting Rosa that she'd fallen silent for too long. "You all right?"

"I'm excellent." Rosa mustered what she hoped was a convincing smile. She didn't want to dwell on the future today. Camp was supposed to be a vacation from reality, not a way to complicate her life or further depress herself. Vowing to focus instead on having fun with Alice this weekend, and hopefully getting laid, Rosa shoved aside all thoughts that didn't pertain to the here and now. She tightened her arm around Alice, relishing every second of physical contact. "You really *don't* give yourself enough credit. You were great in there. The building part *and* the social part."

Alice gave her a tepid smile. "You're very kind, but I'm not sure I'd go so far as to say I was *great*." She leaned against Rosa, who pulled her closer. "I was adequate. I didn't embarrass myself." She fell quiet, but Rosa could practically hear her brain whirring as it replayed every bit of the experience. "At least I don't think I did."

"You didn't. Not at all." Rosa couldn't hold back a frown as she studied the lingering tension on Alice's face. Was it possible she truly didn't realize how much her designs had impressed everyone? Or how friendly, un-intimidating, and receptive the arts-and-crafts crowd had actually been, to both of them? "Everyone loved you—*and* your siege machines. You held your own with Bree. I'm proud of you."

"You are?"

The depth of emotion she heard in the simple, whispered question startled Rosa. She stopped walking, gazed around to make sure they were alone, then drew Alice into a tender, heartfelt hug. "Yeah, Alice. Extremely proud." Rosa kissed a hot cheek and, reluctantly, returned to Alice's side so they could resume their journey. "I could tell none of that was easy for you, but you did it anyway. Not everyone can overcome their fear and really put themselves out there. You did. That's impressive."

She could sense Alice's embarrassment without even looking at her. "I'm trying."

"And doing remarkably well." Rosa glanced over as Alice cracked a tiny smile at the compliment, which elicited an answering grin from Rosa big enough to make her cheeks ache. "Also, you look absolutely beautiful right now."

Alice's characteristic pink glow deepened. "Thanks. So do you." With effort, she made brief eye contact before returning her attention to the uneven ground. "Looks like Bree may have found someone else for the weekend. Any regrets?"

Rosa snorted. She doubted she'd lost her chance to be with Bree, particularly if Enid was open to a threesome. But no one excited her like Alice. She wasn't sure anyone had *ever* excited her like Alice. "None at all."

"Even if all we do this weekend is kiss and...touch a little more?"

Rosa pressed her nose into Alice's hair, which smelled vaguely of apples. "Even then." She tickled Alice lightly, a gentle admonishment. "Stop being so dubious about my wanting to spend time with you. I'm having fun. Aren't you?"

"The most fun I've ever had." Nothing in Alice's tone cast doubt on the sincerity of her statement. "That's why...It's just...I..." She cleared her throat, obviously embarrassed by her inability to put a thought together. She breathed in. Exhaled slowly. Then said, "Maybe you seem too good to be true?"

Here's a woman with shockingly low standards. More of the self-loathing that had become second nature over the past eighteen months swamped Rosa. Losing the battle with her own insecurities, she said, "I'm not even half of what you deserve."

Alice bumped her shoulder into Rosa's, knocking her slightly off balance. "Don't say that."

Rosa accepted the correction with a nod. "I'm just saying, don't be surprised that someone wants to be your friend. You're attractive, you're smart, you're interesting, you're fun to be around...there are far worse choices for a companion out there, believe me." Worried that she was skirting awfully close to revealing her unexpectedly deep feelings, Rosa pivoted back to the subject of Alice's past. "Did you date in high school?"

"No. My parents forbade it. When I started seeing John in college, we kept the relationship secret for over a year." Alice shrugged self-consciously. "I'm ashamed to admit how much influence I allowed them to have over my life, and for how long."

"Not anymore, though."

"No." Alice straightened, a minor adjustment that made her seem more confident. "But unfortunately, my opportunity to learn how to be normal has long since passed."

"You so sure about that?" Rosa stepped onto the leftmost trail where they split, following the path back to their personal make-out spot. "I mean, granted, you'll never *actually* be sixteen again. But you've already made two friends here at camp—three if you want to count Jamal—and we *are* currently sneaking off to do what teenagers love to do…"

"I suppose you've got a point." Alice rested her head against Rosa's shoulder. "You still seem too good to be true."

"So do you," Rosa said without thinking. The pure pleasure Alice radiated in response nullified her concerns about voicing the truth, despite how vulnerable it made her feel. "In the past, I always wanted to be social. Fearing other people is new for me." She paused, considering what she wanted to articulate, how much she wanted to reveal. "I *hate* it. I hope one day the fear goes away and that I'll regain the confidence I used to feel in crowds or with people I don't know. But for now, the only way I've felt halfway comfortable meeting new people has been to disguise my identity and hide who I really am. Except with you." Overcome by emotion, Rosa lifted their joined hands to kiss the back of Alice's, waiting until after she was sure her voice wouldn't waver to speak again. "I really, truly didn't plan to tell anyone my name this weekend, let alone confess my entire life story. If nothing else, I need you to believe how much I genuinely like *and* trust you. Otherwise you'd still be calling me Lila, like everyone else."

"I believe you," Alice said quietly. "I just…hope my lack of experience isn't a disappointment."

Not wanting Alice to feel pressured to do more than made her comfortable, Rosa said, "You know, it's not like I came to Camp Rewind to get laid."

Alice raised an eyebrow, seemingly more amused than upset about the possibility she was lying. "No?"

Smirking, Rosa said, "I'm not saying the thought didn't cross my mind…but no, that wasn't my primary goal. I wanted to escape. To have fun. Make a friend, maybe share a few kisses with someone if I was very lucky." Again, she pressed her lips against Alice's hand. "You make me feel very lucky. Regardless of what we do, or don't do."

"I feel lucky, too."

"Besides, the whole lack-of-experience thing is sort of…exciting." Rosa lowered the arm she'd wrapped around Alice's back and gave her hip a possessive squeeze. "Hopefully that doesn't sound too creepy, but it's the truth."

"No, it's perfect." Alice opened her mouth to follow up with another comment, but a distant noise drew their attention to a smaller trail off to the right. They were still a couple of minutes away from their breakfast spot, but the nature of the noise, and the slightly louder one that followed, piqued Rosa's interest. Alice's, as well. Coming to a standstill, Alice tilted her head and listened. "Was that…"

An unmistakably feminine moan interrupted her question while confirming its answer. "Sounds like we aren't the only ones who wanted quiet time," Rosa murmured.

Alice took a step away from Rosa and rose onto her tiptoes to search the trees surrounding them. The unseen woman cried out in apparent ecstasy, and at the same moment Alice's mouth dropped open as she locked in on her target. "I can see them."

Rosa watched how the pulse point at the base of Alice's neck began to throb, the way her breathing quickened, and decided that Alice—sweet, shy Alice—was a genuine voyeur. Without hesitating, she took Alice by the hand and walked them closer to the spot she was straining so hard to see. Alice's eyes widened when she realized what Rosa was doing, and she immediately put on the brakes.

"They'll see *us*!" Alice hissed.

Noting that Alice's objection centered around being discovered watching—and *not* the potential violation of privacy she was committing against a couple who had chosen to fool around where they might be seen—Rosa smirked. "You looked like you wanted a better view."

She was stunned when Alice's eyes got teary and her face flushed a deep red. "I'm so sorry. It isn't right for me to watch them. Just like it wasn't right for all those people online to…watch that video of you."

Touched by her concern, Rosa looped her arms around Alice's waist and pulled her closer until their hips were pressed together. They stood just off the trail, and now that Alice had pointed them out, Rosa had no trouble spotting the increasingly noisy couple. The woman lay on her back on a blanket spread across the ground, nude, while her partner—a man, from the sound of his excited groans—rested on his stomach with his head between her spread thighs. Rosa murmured, "I made that video for my boyfriend, sent it only to him, and he respected my request not to share it with anyone else. Our friends here, on the other hand—" She paused to let Alice enjoy a shuddering moan from the woman, punctuated by her fist pounding the ground and a shouted praise to God. Rosa grinned and angled her face to lick, then nip, at Alice's throat. "*They* have chosen to strip naked and get pornographic in a spot where anyone walking on one of the main hiking trails can easily see. And in case we *don't* see them…" A strangled groan pierced the air, perfectly timed to underscore Rosa's point. "They're making damn sure we'll hear them." Rosa took Alice's earlobe between her lips, nibbling. "I'm fairly confident these two are cool with being watched. If you want to look, you should. *We* should."

Alice planted her hands on Rosa's shoulders, then glanced surreptitiously in the direction of the exhibitionist couple. "I don't want them to *know* we're watching, though."

Rosa tugged Alice a few feet closer to the lovers, placing her own back against the massive trunk of a redwood while encouraging Alice to use both arms to cage her against the tree. "If they see us, we'll say we stopped to make out and were too distracted to even realize they were there."

Clearly dying to take another peek, Alice couldn't stop her gaze from drifting to the side of the tree. "Or else run like hell?"

"We could also do that." Rosa brought her hands up to trace Alice's shoulder blades. She whispered, "Last I saw, he was going down on her. Is he still?"

Alice's throat jumped as she swallowed hard. "Uh." She exhaled, then swiftly tilted to the side and peered around the enormous tree trunk. Once again, Rosa saw Alice's pulse accelerate as her arousal deepened, but this time, she was lucky to also be close enough to feel the subtle pump of Alice's hips against her own. "Yes."

Unable to help herself, Rosa ran her nails down the center of Alice's back, then moved lower, to caress her firm ass through her shorts. Alice gasped, tearing her attention away from the amorous couple to stare at her with such urgent desire that Rosa tightened her fingers on instinct.

"That feels good," Alice breathed. Rosa sensed that she only managed to speak the words because she was worried Rosa might take her hand away. "Don't stop."

Rosa captured Alice's mouth in a quick kiss, needing a taste despite being eager to continue their whispered conversation. "I won't." She gave Alice's buttock a gentle squeeze and pulled ever so slightly to the side. Then she curled her fingertips around the plump cheek so the index and middle brushed against the inviting crevice between. "Tell me what you see."

Trembling, Alice leaned out for another long, lingering look. The sounds coming from behind Rosa told much of the story: the woman loved having her pussy eaten, and her friend was willing to indulge that desire with noisy enthusiasm and seemingly never-ending energy. Rosa studied Alice's face and eyes as she observed the action, aware, too, that Alice took immense pleasure from witnessing this particular act. If her labored breathing, dilated pupils, and eager hips hadn't made that obvious enough, the slight dampness Rosa suddenly felt on her hand removed any doubt from her mind.

Desperate to hear Alice's answer, Rosa whispered, "What do you see?"

Under her breath, and without tearing her eyes away from the scene, Alice said, "He's still…going down on her."

Rosa moved her other hand to cup, squeeze, and gently pull apart the other buttock, allowing her fingertips to venture lower, until she was so tantalizingly close to Alice's pussy that she could literally feel its heat on her searching digits. "Tell me what that means. What he's doing." Afraid to push Alice too hard, she amended her request. "Or kiss me again."

Alice returned to her original position and stared shyly at Rosa's chin. "He's licking her."

True to form, Alice seemed determined to challenge herself by engaging in the verbal foreplay Rosa had attempted to initiate. Yet Rosa experienced a wave of doubt, the distinct fear that she had taken things too far and too fast. She struggled momentarily with the temptation to de-escalate their encounter but knew in her heart that doing so would only upset Alice. She'd promised to trust Alice to set her own limits, and that's exactly what she planned to do—particularly when nothing about Alice's body language indicated that she was ready to stop. Despite Alice's shy countenance, her hips thrust firmly against Rosa's, grinding her against the tree in the obvious pursuit of friction.

Rosa placed her lips against Alice's ear, eliminating the need for eye contact. "Licking her pussy?"

Alice jolted against her body. "Yes."

"Licking her *here*?" Rosa pushed her fingers deeper between Alice's thighs, nearly touching where she imagined the opening would be. She groaned at the impossibly sultry heat she could easily feel. "Do *you* like being licked like that?" Flattening her fingers, she stroked Alice through her jeans, simultaneously horrified and thrilled about her own forwardness. "Licked all over your pussy?"

Alice clung to Rosa's shoulders as though she might collapse without additional support. "I…don't know."

Heart rate accelerating, Rosa drew back far enough to look Alice in the eyes. "You don't know because your ex-husband wasn't very good at it, or because he didn't go down on you at all?"

Alice seemed almost ashamed as she shifted her gaze past Rosa's shoulder. "He said he didn't like it. The taste."

"But let me guess. He had no problem putting *his* dick in *your* mouth." When Alice's look of shame deepened, Rosa forced herself to calm down and soften her tone. "I'm sorry, that's just so…so *typical.* And unfair."

Alice managed a bashful smile. "I always thought so."

Raising the hand not currently lodged between Alice's thighs, Rosa caressed her jaw and stared deeply into her eyes. "But…you—"

"Excuse me." A somewhat familiar, feminine voice called out, interrupting her question and sending Alice scrambling to bury her face in Rosa's shoulder. "If you two would like to join us, you're more than welcome. We brought another blanket along."

Her male companion piped up. "We also like to watch."

Certain that Alice wasn't going to reply to the invitation, Rosa carefully stepped away from the tree while nudging Alice out of her embrace and back toward the main trail. "Um…as much as I appreciate the offer, we're going to have to pass." In her peripheral vision, she saw Alice turn and literally run in the opposite direction. "So sorry to interrupt. You two, uh…go back to whatever it was you were doing."

"With pleasure," the woman's companion answered, before very noisily returning his mouth to its former position.

"Maybe next time!" the woman chirped. Then she moaned loudly, which gave Rosa the perfect opportunity to follow Alice's example and bolt.

She caught up to Alice thirty feet down the trail, heading back toward the main camp. "Wait!" she shouted, slowing to a jog as she caught up. "You don't want to go back to our spot?"

Alice shook her head, trembling from head to toe. "I'm sure it makes me a hypocrite, but all of a sudden our fallen tree doesn't feel nearly private enough." Dropping her volume, she muttered, "Not for what I want to do with you."

Unsure whether Alice had intended her to hear that last part, Rosa chose not to acknowledge its implication. Out loud, at least. Inside, her heart leapt. Hoping to lighten Alice's mood, Rosa said, "At least you don't need to feel any guilt about watching. It seems we stumbled right into a carefully laid trap."

Alice broke into a reluctant smile. "Apparently so." After a brief hesitation, Alice grabbed her hand. "I'm not saying I don't want to make out again. Just that I'd like to find somewhere a little more secluded first."

"Understood."

"Also...thanks for letting me run away back there."

"My pleasure." Rosa moved closer to Alice's side. "Consider me your all-purpose social buffer. I live to serve."

Alice laughed. But when she spoke again, there was no mistaking the deep emotion behind her words. "Like I said, too good to be true."

As she had earlier, Rosa fought not to get swept away by her worries about what would happen after camp. So they liked each other. That was hardly news and, with Alice in particular, seemed like a necessary prerequisite before any type of physical encounter. Would it hurt when they had to say good-bye? Yes. It would absolutely torment Rosa and, she assumed, probably Alice as well. But their eventual separation was necessary and inevitable—for Alice's sake, in particular. If a certain level of heartache was unavoidable at this point, the best thing to do was wholeheartedly appreciate the time they had together before it all came crumbling down.

Without slowing their pace, Rosa moved in to steal a quick kiss. "We'll look for a more private spot. All day, if we have to."

"Well, I personally have no higher priority." Alice pulled her back in, stopping in the middle of the trail to share a longer, deeper kiss. When they broke apart, Alice said, as though finishing her previous thought, "Maybe we can take a boat and find somewhere to go ashore on the other side of the lake?"

"That might be easier to pull off under the cover of darkness..." Rosa wasn't positive the counselors would green-light such an operation, day or night. "If we don't want to get caught, that is."

"True." Alice heaved a sigh. "So what now? Keep walking?"

Rosa considered their options. If Alice truly wanted a well-rounded experience, this was probably a good time to persuade her to try another camp-sponsored activity before they turned their sole focus toward fooling around. "Do you like horses?"

"Enough to ride one?" Alice sounded caught between curiosity and panic, as seemed to be the case more often than not. "Maybe."

"I've always wanted to try," Rosa said. She slowed her pace and gestured at the stables up ahead. "Why don't we check it out? It'll give us a chance to settle down a bit, talk some more, maybe figure out other places we could go to be alone. After we're done, we'll take another walk and see what we can find."

Alice's shoulders relaxed slightly. "Sounds like a plan."

Relieved that Alice hadn't protested her suggestion to take a breather, Rosa said, "Thanks." She hesitated. "You got me pretty worked up behind that tree."

"That's not a bad thing." Alice withdrew her hand from Rosa's, leaving her cold, then reignited her by trailing her fingertips down Rosa's spine, over the small of her back, along the curve of her butt, to end with a tentative squeeze of one cheek. "Is it?"

"No." Rosa shivered as goose bumps sprang up from head to toe and her nipples hardened into painful points. Through gritted teeth, she murmured, "But neither is anticipation."

Alice exhaled, removing her hand from Rosa's ass to entangle their fingers once more. "You're right."

Granted, Alice's entire life has been anticipation without any payoff, so I suppose that's easier for me to believe. Taking pity, Rosa decided to leave the rest of their day up to Alice. If she wanted to eschew the rest of what Camp Rewind had to offer and spend more time exploring the pleasures life had denied her so far, who was Rosa to judge? She cleared her throat. "Or we could just go search for a place to be together right now. Even if it's my car."

Alice's eyes lit up for only a second before she shook her head and waved away the suggestion. "No, you're right. It would be good to settle down…*and* get to know each other better. That couple really freaked me out with their invitation to join them, and really, the only thing that sounds better than kissing you is learning more about your life. Not just the past eighteen months, but the other parts…all the parts that made you who you are today."

Unexpectedly warmed by the sentiment, Rosa stopped to pull Alice into another tight embrace. She felt like she never wanted to let go. When Alice hugged her back, desperately, Rosa wasn't sure how she would. Stop thinking about it, she scolded herself internally. Aloud, she whispered, "I'd like that. A lot."

❖

A half hour in the saddle was all Rosa needed to determine that a horse whisperer, she was not. The pretty spotted mare she'd been assigned had absolutely no interest in following her directions and seemed to barely tolerate Rosa's presence on her back. Alice fared better, communicating well with the larger, speckled gray horse she'd gamely hoisted herself onto, but she didn't exactly look *comfortable* straddling the giant animal. Despite her lack of equestrian skills, Rosa enjoyed every second of the brief ride simply because Alice kept asking questions that made it clear how much she actually gave a shit about Rosa as a person, and not just a body.

In all honesty, Rosa hadn't often encountered that attitude during her admittedly sketchy dating history. She'd had a few serious relationships, sure, but after the girlfriend who'd broken her heart in college, she'd never again sought out the same kind of deep, intimate connection she'd once fallen into so easily and with such innocent enthusiasm. It was too frightening, too potentially painful, to willingly risk suffering the loss of another such bond. Right or wrong, that self-protective mindset led her into a string of relationships with people who made her feel more like a body, or a good time, than a person with inherent, nonsexual value. Somehow, meeting Alice not only stirred up all her long-forgotten feelings of self-worth and hope for the future, but also, their friendship made her feel *good* in a way she hadn't in far too long.

Without a doubt, this friendship with Alice was beginning to feel dangerous. Emotionally, Rosa was already in way too deep, and she couldn't fathom a way out—nor did she want to, technically, if that meant not spending the rest of the weekend together.

After their not-so-relaxing adventure on horseback, they grabbed a snack from the canteen to serve as a late lunch during the run-up to the dinner hour. Another bonfire was scheduled for that night, and multiple counselors were already hard at work stacking wood and setting up tables and chairs around the fire pit. Rosa and Alice lingered at the edge of the crowd, watching for a minute or two, before they struck out on another hike into the forest at the opposite edge of camp, conversing nonstop the entire time.

Rosa talked about growing up with an older brother who protected her from the bullies at school while tormenting her mercilessly at home and how much she both loved and despised him as a child, depending on the situation they were in. She shared stories about her mother, like the way they used to sing in the kitchen while preparing dinner together and also the heartbreaking disappointment she'd detected in her voice over the phone when Rosa had warned her about the pictures and video being spread around online. She told Alice how proud her father had been when she'd graduated from UC Berkeley with honors and how much he still loved her now, despite all that had happened. She revealed her list of favorite guilty pleasures, including first-person-shooter video games and cheesy science-fiction films. She even managed to find a way to bring up her newfound vegetarianism and penchant for eating far too many dark-chocolate squares in the hours before bedtime. By the time Rosa finally stopped talking, she couldn't imagine what was left to tell. She felt like she'd just laid her entire life bare.

Nervously, she checked Alice's face. "So…enough about me?"

Alice guffawed before gathering her into a long-awaited hug. After watching the bonfire preparations, they'd explored the woods until discovering an abandoned cabin on the outskirts of the property. Now they sat on a wooden picnic table outside its front door, more isolated from the rest of camp than they'd been all day. They hadn't heard another human voice in over an hour, which had allowed Alice to unwind and therefore come out of her shell like never before. It was a beautiful sight, nearly as beautiful as the sound of Alice's hearty laughter at her expense.

Rosa drew back from their embrace wearing a grin. "I'm pretty sure you know absolutely everything about me at this point. There are no mysteries left, nothing to talk about."

Alice surprised her by initiating a kiss, not their first since they'd sat down, but deeper and more passionate than any they'd shared all day. Or ever, for that matter. Rosa's heart thundered like an innocent schoolgirl's when Alice pressed into her mouth with confidence, her clever tongue chased by an unself-conscious moan. Unsure what to do with her hands, Rosa cupped Alice's face, kissing her back as hard as she dared. She jerked slightly when tentative fingers landed on her breast and cradled her with the utmost tenderness before almost instantly moving away. Alice ended the kiss seconds later.

"I didn't mean to startle you." Contrite, Alice folded her hands in her lap. "Or be too forward."

"You didn't." Rosa shot Alice an apologetic wince even as the half-truth passed over her lips. "Well, you might have caught me by surprise. But you certainly weren't too forward. Not even a little bit." Truthfully, despite the messiness of her growing feelings for Alice, Rosa still hoped they would go all the way this weekend. *All the way*, she repeated in her head and tried not to roll her eyes. *Like we really are a couple of naive kids.* "I want you, Alice. Every inch of you. Don't hesitate to touch me…wherever you'd like."

"I want you, too," Alice whispered. She paused, then pulled Rosa into another kiss. Softer this time, but every bit as intense. Her free hand drifted again to Rosa's breast, settling carefully into place with her palm centered over the tip.

Rosa leaned into the caress with a quiet moan, pleased when Alice whimpered and tightened her fingers in response. Her nipple hardened against Alice's hand, the turgid flesh so sensitized that a simple, timid brush of Alice's thumb over the areola caused Rosa's pussy to contract in a faint echo of the orgasm her body desperately craved. Rosa cried out, a full-throated groan that Alice muffled by deepening their kiss. She dropped her hands to Alice's shoulders, itching to caress the small, seemingly flawless breasts below. She yearned to trace their shape, and tug at the nipples, and try to make Alice as ridiculously wet as she was.

Alice tore her mouth away from Rosa's long enough to whisper, "Touch me. Please."

Thrilled to have been granted permission, Rosa slid the hands that were on Alice's shoulders down to her chest until she held a firm yet impossibly soft breast in each. She exhaled—shakily—at the same time Alice inhaled—swiftly—both of them so affected by this new level of physical intimacy that their kisses stopped and they simply stared at one another in silence as they explored with mutual caresses.

Alice's cautious, surprisingly skilled touch overwhelmed Rosa so much she found it difficult to speak, yet she sensed how vitally important it was that she offer positive feedback. Barely able to put together a coherent thought, Rosa gritted her teeth as Alice pinched her nipple, then twisted it lightly. "That feels *really* nice." To prove it, she mirrored the action on Alice's breasts, finding the erect nipples with ease, pinching, then twisting. "See?"

Alice squeezed her thighs together so overtly that Rosa couldn't help but notice. She shivered beneath Rosa's hands. "Oh…" she whispered, as her quivering intensified. "Keep doing that."

"This?" Rosa tightened her grip on Alice's nipples, tugging them harder. Hard enough to make Alice gasp and tremble uncontrollably. Alice reciprocated by plucking at Rosa's nipples until she did the same. "*Fuck*, you feel good," Rosa whimpered.

"So, *so* good." Alice lowered her hand to Rosa's waist, pushed beneath the hem of her T-shirt, then slid up to touch the slope of the left breast where it rose above the cup of Rosa's bra. "Please don't stop."

Rosa molded her hands to Alice's chest, stroking the peaks lovingly. "I won't." Swept away by Alice's clear enthusiasm—and encouraged by the slim fingers that snuck beneath her bra to graze her bare nipple—Rosa whispered, "May I kiss one?"

Alice barely took a cursory glance around to make sure they were still alone before nodding her consent. "Yes."

"I want to taste your skin." Rosa curled her fingers around the hem of Alice's T-shirt and lifted it a few inches, moving gradually to allow Alice time to change her mind. Her gaze fell to take in the creamy flesh she revealed, first a tiny, soft, oh-so-kissable tummy, then an absolutely mouthwatering breast concealed within a fashionable pink-and-gray-striped bra. Not hearing any protest, Rosa forged ahead, grabbing the top of the silky bra cup and yanking the material down so that Alice's naked flesh spilled over. She took only a second to appreciate its aesthetically perfect form before covering the stiff nipple with her lips and laving it with her tongue.

Both of Alice's hands flew to her hair and wound into the short locks, holding Rosa in place. "Ohhh," she whimpered, far more quietly than Rosa would have assumed her capable. "Please, just like *that*."

Rosa suckled on the nipple, then gently bit down, using her teeth to tug teasingly on the erect nub. Groaning, Alice lowered her hand beneath Rosa's chest to cup one of her heavy breasts. She palmed the flesh roughly, then tweaked the nipple so hard that Rosa nearly came without any clitoral stimulation at all—something that had happened only once or twice in her life. If Alice could bring her to that special place *already,* on her first try—but the awestruck thought ended abruptly when Alice gave her nipple another twist, causing Rosa to instinctively suck harder before taking as much smooth, soft flesh into her mouth as she could. The fingers on her head tightened as Alice arched her back to offer herself up to the worshipful treatment.

"It feels..." Alice gasped, then jolted when Rosa narrowed her suction to the by-now no-doubt painfully erect nipple. "It feels so..."

Excited by Alice's unambiguously ecstatic reaction to finally rounding first base, Rosa kissed over to the other breast, pulling it free from the bra to offer the same treatment she'd given its twin. Her hand drifted up to caress the flesh she'd already covered with wet kisses, loath to neglect any part of Alice's body while her mouth memorized the lay of the land. She savored the audible appreciation for her efforts, unable to remember the last time she'd felt so agonizingly aroused by anyone or anything. Alice's fingers, now tweaking her other breast, drove Rosa even closer to the orgasm it felt like her body had craved since their very first encounter. Or, hell, for the past eighteen months.

She might have come, too, if Alice hadn't chosen that moment to gently push her away. "Wait. Stop."

Rosa flew backward, afraid she'd missed some obvious signal in her excitement. She pulled Alice's bra up and her shirt down, hastily covering the bare skin. "I'm sorry."

"No." Alice caught her by the arms, keeping her close. "Don't be, please. I just..." She gestured at their less-than-clandestine surroundings. "This doesn't feel like the right place. It's not the right time." She frowned. "Though believe me, I wish it was."

Rosa exhaled, relieved that Alice's only objection seemed to be their location. Despite their apparent privacy, someone *could* come along the same trail they had at any time. It was even possible that the cabin they'd discovered wasn't as abandoned as it seemed. "I get it." She angled her body away from Alice's on the picnic table, needing the space to cool her ardor. "You're damn sexy, Alice Wu. Don't doubt that ever again, for as long as you live."

Alice sounded breathless when she finally responded. "You make me feel that way."

"Because you *are* that way." Having regained a marginal amount of control, Rosa met Alice's eyes to underscore the sincerity of her words. "Your ex was a pathetic buffoon not to appreciate what he had, and downright stupid for never tasting the sweetness lying next to him in bed all those years." Despite her need to cool down, Rosa couldn't help but give voice to the raging desire still smoldering inside her. "If you were mine, I'd bury my face between your pretty thighs for hours at a time. *Days*, if it wouldn't kill both of us."

Alice's chest rose and fell rapidly, and for a second, Rosa thought she might eschew modesty and take them both down onto the picnic table for another make-out session. Unfortunately, that's when they heard the voices. At least two of them, their owners far enough away to be out of sight, but still too close for them to engage in any activities they didn't want anyone else to see. Exhaling, Rosa took Alice's hand in both of hers and raised it to her lips, kissing the knuckles. "You're right. This isn't the place, or the time."

"That whole 'in your car' idea is sounding better and better every second."

Rosa laughed at Alice's frustrated muttering, though truthfully, she felt exactly the same way. Her desire to be alone with Alice had become so intense that she briefly considered suggesting they ditch Camp Rewind altogether and drive back to her apartment in Berkeley so they could spend the rest of the weekend in a real bed. Of course, by doing so, it would be a lot more difficult to keep this casual once they stepped back into the real world. The escapist utopia of summer camp was the ideal setting for a fleeting romance, which was exactly what this time with Alice needed to be. Fleeting, even if the notion broke her heart each and every time she tried to reinforce it with her head.

Fleeting, for *Alice's* sake.

With a heavy sigh, Alice hopped off the picnic table and faintly tugged Rosa's hand. "At least the sun is about to set. Want to return to camp and wait for the bonfire to start?" She paused while Rosa stood, then welcomed her with a light, mostly innocent kiss. Backing away, Alice whispered, "I wouldn't mind taking another shower. Before tonight."

Rosa's entire body tingled at the implication. Alice wanted to be clean. For tonight. After a day of necking and heavy petting in the summer heat, her panties thoroughly soaked as a result, Rosa thought that was probably a fine idea. "Me, too."

"All right." Alice exhaled through her nose, bit her lip in an effort to suppress what looked like an eager smile, and set off toward the main camp at an unexpectedly fast pace. "Let's go."

Powerless to resist despite the emotional devastation she feared awaited her at the end of the weekend, Rosa followed.

CHAPTER NINE

Two hours later, Alice stood well back from the roaring bonfire and the raucous crowd gathered in a circle around the tall flames. Freshly showered, trimmed, and shaved, she was ready for anything that might happen once she and Rosa managed to find a suitably remote spot away from the party. Wanting to be prepared for any eventuality, she'd tucked one of her remaining joints into the pocket of her thin cotton hoodie, along with a lighter, in case she needed a relaxation aid. Despite feeling remarkably comfortable with Rosa only twenty-four hours after their first meeting, actually *having* full-blown lesbian sex would likely induce plenty of performance anxiety. She wanted to be *good* at this. Good enough to blow Rosa's mind, possibly even to make her consider the possibility of continuing to see one another, even casually, after camp ended.

Alice had no idea if such a thing was even realistic. Rosa's life was complicated, to say the least, which should frighten her far more than it actually did. Perhaps because she had only an abstract notion of what Internet-enabled harassment might be like? That might explain part of her lack of concern about Rosa's baggage, but honestly, it was more that she'd come to care for Rosa so much, and so very fast, that it seemed impossible to imagine anything scary enough to persuade her not to seize any opportunity she could to stay in her life. Even though she was too often afraid of the world in general, with Rosa, nothing felt too intimidating to confront.

With Rosa, she felt truly powerful for the first time.

The object of her desire slid an arm around her waist and whispered into her ear. "Ready to borrow a boat?"

Alice nodded, determined to go through with their plan despite having to break a few rules. Thirty-six wasn't too pathetically old for her first stab at teenage rebellion, was it? "I've got a sleeping bag ready at my bunk. And a flashlight, a first-aid kit, a compass, and fire-starting supplies, just in case. Oh, also some snacks and bottles of water to stay hydrated. And a GPS beacon in case we get lost."

Rosa chuckled, presumably at her overpreparedness. She murmured, "I'll bring my fingers, my tongue, my lips and teeth...and an eager body for you to explore to your heart's content."

Alice found it suddenly hard to breathe amidst the smoke and noise of the bonfire party. "We should go."

"Before you ruin another pair of panties?" Rosa licked her earlobe before moving away.

"Too late for that," Alice mumbled. As Rosa led them from the crowd, Alice waved distractedly at Jamal the counselor, who paused in the midst of what looked like an amusing conversation to shout a greeting as they passed by. After walking a short distance, she sighed in relief when the bustle of the party atmosphere finally subsided and she could once again hear herself think. "Well, that's a blessing."

Again, Rosa laughed, but as always, her amusement never came across as being at Alice's expense. Instead it felt warm, affectionate, even loving. "I have a feeling things will only get crazier as the night goes on."

"Which is exactly why I really love our plan to get as far away from everyone as possible while they're drunk and distracted." Alice lowered her volume when they reached their sleeping cabin, in case some other equally antisocial souls had decided to retire early. "Among other, totally obvious reasons, of course."

"Of course." Rosa palmed her ass as soon as Alice stepped forward to enter the cabin. "Like being able to find out how it feels when another woman makes you come?"

Alice paused inside the doorway when her knees weakened at the risqué comment. Rosa seemed to be an expert at destroying her composure with only a few simple words, having managed it countless times already since they'd met. She supposed it made sense. The woman *was* a writer, after all, and Alice was so fiercely attracted to her it literally made her clit hurt. She'd never anticipated feeling so strongly about another human being, sexually or otherwise. The sensation was intoxicating and brought her to a long-awaited understanding of why the rest of the world had always seemed so obsessed by an aspect of adult life she'd never truly connected with before.

Because it was *fun,* Alice decided. Because, with the right person, it felt *good.*

Quiet giggles from somewhere within the spacious sleeping quarters alerted Alice to the fact that they had interrupted another couple. Instinctively, she realized who had been missing from the bonfire: Bree and Enid. Rather than feel embarrassed, Alice battled a wave of envy at the thought that at least *they* had found an acceptable place to connect. As horny as their day full of playful touching and heated kissing had left her, she nearly considered pushing aside her modesty to embrace the exhibitionist that lurked within. *That's* how badly she wanted Rosa. Enough to do just about anything.

Like steal a boat.

Rosa took hold of Alice's hand and guided her between the rows of beds. As they passed Bree's clearly occupied bottom bunk, Rosa whispered, "Don't mind us."

Alice tried to ignore the sound of giggles that dissolved into quiet moans. Never having experienced a wild youth of her own, she found the act of watching real, live people unself-consciously fool around in semi-public places utterly disconcerting, even a bit unsettling. It also happened to turn her on like crazy, and she was pretty sure Rosa knew that. Eager hands smoothed over her back, her ass, her stomach, her breasts, all while she tried to stand on her tiptoes to reach the supplies she'd left on the top bunk. "Lila," she whispered at last, seconds from tumbling onto the hard floor from sheer, clumsy desire. "*Help* me, will you?"

"I thought I was." But the hands disappeared, and seconds later, Rosa reached past her to grab the rolled-up sleeping bag off the bed. "Sorry," she said, more genuinely. "I'm extremely excited."

Alice grinned as hard as she pleased, confident that Rosa couldn't see her goofy joy in the dark. "Me, too." She retrieved the backpack that held the rest of the supplies, and then they tiptoed past Bree and Enid again before escaping the cabin, and the main campground, in search of their secret getaway. Only the night before, Alice would have never dreamed of agreeing to borrow a paddleboat for an unauthorized nighttime cruise. Now she was not only on board with the idea but also, secretly, hoped that their clever choice of transport would allow them to steal away for most of the night. She wanted to spend hours, days—years, if she could—exploring every last delight Rosa Salazar had to offer. There would never be enough time to get her fill, to sate the hunger she felt for this woman. The day and a half they had left at camp wouldn't even come close.

That ticking clock left her desperate, and desperation made her brave. Boosting a boat was the least she would do to be with Rosa before the weekend ended. She'd never been so motivated to attain any goal in her entire, overachieving life. She'd wanted to have sex with another woman for so long but hadn't anticipated ever being attracted to anyone who could also make her feel comfortable enough to disrobe in her presence. Though her anxiety rose as they built up to the moment of truth, she was almost positive she could do this with Rosa.

She *had* to, or she'd never forgive herself. Of that, she was certain.

Alice exhaled in relief when they reached the lake and found the area deserted. They barely spoke as they hurried down the wooden dock and climbed into the paddleboat tied up farthest from the shore. Rosa set the sleeping bag in a sunken storage cubby in the rear of the boat, then took Alice's backpack and stowed it alongside. Gingerly, Rosa hopped in, climbed over the center console, and offered Alice a hand to help her step down into the other seat.

"Careful," Rosa whispered as Alice sat. "I need to lean over you for a second…" She did exactly that, brushing her breasts against Alice's arm, then her cheek, as she strained to untie the boat from the dock. After a few moments of increasingly frantic fumbling, Rosa muttered, "Probably should've had you get in first."

Alice turned her face to kiss the pliant flesh now pressed against her lips. "No, this is good," she mumbled.

Rosa's body shook with poorly suppressed laughter. "Now *you're* the one who's not helping."

Feeling uncharacteristically saucy, especially for a struggling boat thief, Alice craned her neck, opened her mouth, and sucked on the tip of Rosa's breast through her T-shirt. Rosa startled noticeably, then moaned, sagging against Alice as she surrendered to whatever naval knot had vexed her. Tickled to have gotten revenge for Rosa's antics back at their bunk, Alice released the nipple from between her teeth. Then she put her hands on Rosa's shoulders and carefully guided her down into her seat. "Why don't you let me do this?"

Visibly shaken, Rosa exhaled in a rush and collapsed against her headrest. She closed her eyes. "Maybe that's a good idea."

It was hard to imagine someone like Rosa battling the same nervousness Alice felt every time they stopped touching and her brain had a chance to return to the question of what would happen once they reached their final destination, yet, that's how Rosa suddenly looked. *Seriously* freaked. Concerned, Alice put a hand on Rosa's knee, unsure whether they should go through with their minor heist. "Are you okay?"

Rosa opened wide, dark eyes that glittered under the bright moon. "Yeah, I'm just…" She bent forward, wrists on her knees, and exhaled. "I really want this to be perfect for you. I wish…" Another rueful sigh. "I guess I wish there was a real bed around here somewhere…with some rose petals…maybe candles." Rosa lifted a shoulder, seemingly embarrassed by her fantasy scenario. "I want this to be *right* for you."

A real bed would be nice. *Very* nice. But the lack of one wasn't even close to a deal breaker. Not when they were *this* close.

"All I need for tonight to be right, *and* perfect, is you." Alice squeezed Rosa's thigh before turning to untie the simple knot connecting them to the dock. She coiled the loose rope and stowed it under her seat, then gestured for Rosa to place her feet on the pedals in front of her. That accomplished, she pushed off from the dock and sent them floating out into the water. "I have no expectations. Really. As long as we're together, doing whatever comes naturally, I'll be happy."

Rosa pumped her legs to turn the boat away from the dock and out toward the far side of the lake. "I think I'm a little…nervous." She fell silent, then mumbled, "Sorry."

Alice reached across the console between them to first pinch Rosa's bicep, then grab her hand and hold tight. "I'm sure you realize I'm not exactly full of confidence, either. Don't apologize."

"But I'm *supposed* to be the confident one."

"Who says?" Alice increased her speed, straightening the boat's trajectory so they pointed clear across the lake. "Because you've had more sex than me?"

"Well…yeah." Rosa stroked her thumb over the side of Alice's hand. The touch sent thrilling electricity through her body. "It's not like I don't know what I'm doing."

The bold statement, delivered so casually and without pretense, triggered yet another flood of wetness to stain the replacement panties Alice had swapped for the ones Rosa had ruined over the course of their afternoon together. Alice suppressed a disappointed whimper. She'd hoped not to be a total mess by the time they got to wherever they were going, in case Rosa offered to make good on her earlier intimations and introduce Alice to the pleasures of receiving oral sex. At this point, it was difficult to imagine allowing Rosa to put her mouth anywhere near that area when her pussy was already coated in her slick, copious juices and surely fragrant with her desire.

Rosa lifted Alice's hand to her lips and traced the tip of her tongue along the edge of her index finger. Then she pulled the finger inside her hot mouth, sucking until Alice swore under her breath at the realization that now she was even wetter than before. Struggling to regain her composure, she croaked, "I'll say."

Rosa released Alice's finger with a suggestive flick of her tongue. "It's important to me that you enjoy whatever we do. I want to make you feel *good*. Better than you ever have."

A tendril of worry unfurled in Alice's gut, the niggling concern that she wouldn't meet Rosa's needs. She recalled Rosa's earlier comment about showing her how it felt to have another woman make her climax—and that worry multiplied by ten. "You will. You already have. Even if I'm unable to reach orgasm, that's my fault, *not* yours. Each time you've touched me it's been incredible. More incredible than I knew I could ever feel. So I'll enjoy whatever we do tonight, absolutely, even if I can't…you know…"

Rosa's pedaling faltered, sending the boat slightly off course. Alice slowed her pace to match Rosa, until they stopped moving altogether. Slowly, Rosa turned in her seat and gathered Alice's hand to her chest. She pressed the knuckles against her heart and stared into Alice's eyes. "Sweetheart, did your ex…did John ever make you come?"

Alice wished she could crawl under her seat and hide. "I'm not sure that was his fault, either."

"Well, have you ever given *yourself* an orgasm?"

She glanced over the edge of the boat into the dark water, tempted to jump overboard to avoid admitting how frequently she masturbated and how skilled she'd become at the art of self-pleasure. Yet she couldn't lie. "Yes." She cleared her throat, face on fire. "Many times."

Rosa breathed out. "Okay, so I submit that it probably *was* his fault." She lifted Alice's hand to her lips again, pressing soft kisses against the knuckles this time. "Alice, I would *love* to try to be the first person to give you an orgasm."

Alice's worry exploded into full-blown dread. What if she couldn't deliver? She'd make Rosa feel bad, which would, in turn, make *her* feel terrible. She wanted nothing more than to experience true sexual pleasure from another person's hand—or mouth—but her sudden fear of failure threatened to decimate the courage she needed to go through with the very thing she wanted more than life itself. "I want that, too. But if it doesn't happen—"

Rosa silenced Alice with a kiss. "I won't be offended. I won't be upset. I'll ask you to show me how you like to be touched and lie there next to you—kissing you, stroking you—while I listen to the sound of you getting yourself off."

Unable to sit still anymore, Alice resumed pedaling. Was Rosa's suggestion supposed to make her feel *less* anxious? "I...don't know about that."

Rosa matched Alice's speed. She looked over her shoulder, back toward the dock they'd left, and exhaled. "Maybe the best idea is to let this evening follow its natural course, wherever that happens to lead us." She gave Alice's thigh an encouraging pat. "And not worry so much about what will or won't happen. Whether I make you come tonight or not, my only goal is that you feel worshipped, and adored, and every bit as desired as you are. By me."

Alice's chest tightened, constricting her heart in a not entirely unpleasant way. "That sounds like a plan."

"And if you have any questions or, uh, concerns...you know, about how two women, or..." Rosa winced. "Whatever." She shook her head, openly disdainful of the words coming out of her mouth. "Please don't hesitate to ask. Sometimes talking about it first...helps."

Though the idea of talking openly about lesbian sex with the woman she was about to fuck made Alice woozy, she had to admit, it also made her feel both excited and reassured. "Well, I *have* watched porn." She checked Rosa's face, gauging her level of surprise and/or disgust. Not seeing any judgment in Rosa's amused expression, Alice eased into an entirely new realm of disclosure. "A lot of porn, actually, since the divorce." Heat crawled up her neck and settled across her face. "I'm sure it's not always a very realistic depiction, but...I think I know what to do."

"Do you watch only lesbian porn?" Rosa sounded genuinely curious, like her answer would solve a mystery she'd long yearned to unravel. "Or all different kinds?"

"Different kinds, I guess, but lately..." Despite Alice's mild discomfort, she couldn't help but marvel at the wonder of having someone to confide in about her most private desires. She hadn't yet explored this topic in therapy, and therefore it was the biggest secret in her life. "Mostly the lesbian stuff." She paused, then admitted, "Honestly, for the past eight months or so...*only* the lesbian stuff."

She could hear Rosa smile. "You really *have* been thinking about this, haven't you?"

"*Thinking* may be too mild a word for it." Alice had become downright obsessive about the idea of satisfying this long-simmering curiosity, desperate to discover whether the gender identity of her partner would influence her ability to derive true satisfaction from physical intimacy. She'd simply lacked the courage to take the first step and tick the *women* checkbox on her Internet dating profile's *Interested In* section. If Rosa hadn't approached her the night before, it might have taken her months, even years, to work up enough nerve to take the initiative and actively seek out a female lover. To find not only a genuine friend at Camp Rewind, but also the chance to explore her most compelling fantasy, felt to Alice like a breathtaking stroke of luck. In some ways, it still didn't seem real. "Rosa, I'm getting ready to sleep with you one day after meeting you. *Me.* I've already done more with you than anyone except my ex-husband. That must tell you how badly I want this."

Rosa sounded more self-assured the next time she spoke. Clearly, her uncertainty had eased. "What's your favorite kind of porn scene?"

"Oh. The, uh..." Neither of them had reintroduced graphic language into the conversation since getting into the boat, and Alice wasn't sure she could start. Grateful she didn't have to look Rosa in the eyes, she managed a clipped reply. "Cunnilingus."

Rosa snorted quietly. "You're so cute."

Alice scowled while feeling secretly warmed by the affectionate taunt. "Stop it."

"No, you are." Rosa's voice lowered an octave. "So you love to watch pussy-licking. Earlier in the woods must have been a real treat."

"Well, it would have been better if it had been two women…"

Rosa chuckled. "I'll give Bree and Enid a heads up."

Alice whipped her head around, only to be greeted by Rosa's moonlit smirk. "Don't you dare."

Rosa managed to kiss her again while mostly maintaining the rhythm of her still-pumping legs. "So, do you touch yourself when you watch those scenes?" Staying close, she kissed Alice's jaw, then her shoulder. "With your hand? A vibrator?"

And…there went her panties for good. Shuddering, Alice whispered, "My hand."

"I like that." Rosa traced the tip of her tongue along the edge of Alice's ear and nibbled on the lobe. "It means you already know how to touch a woman. It means you know what *you* like." Rosa's hand landed on her thigh, delivering a visceral surge of pleasure to Alice's clit. She gasped for air. "Do you have a favorite fantasy, Alice?"

"Just…" Heavy with desire, blood pumping, Alice lobbed the equivalent of a verbal grenade, knowing exactly how it would land. "For a woman to eat me out."

Rosa rested her forehead against Alice's temple, no longer pedaling. Alice stopped, too, allowing their boat to continue drifting forward. Rosa's steamy breath came out in quick puffs against Alice's flushed cheek, which only made Alice burn hotter. "Then that's exactly what I'm going to do." Without backing away, she gestured toward the dark shoreline now only twenty feet in front of them. Also unwilling to separate, Alice tilted her head to take in a promisingly sandy beach with what appeared to be a signed trail at one end, barely visible in the moonlight.

"After we go ashore and find a safe place to roll out your sleeping bag, sweetheart, I'm going to kiss you *everywhere*. I'll slide my tongue over all the places you touch when you're in bed alone, and I'll lick your clit and suck on your pussy so gently your thighs will tremble like crazy and you won't be able to *stand* it." Rosa's fingers tightened on Alice's knee before sliding higher up her thigh, nearly to the juncture. "Whether you come in my mouth or simply take satisfaction from knowing how much *I* love going down on you, I promise, Alice, it will feel *incredible*. No reciprocation necessary, no strings attached. I can't think of anything I'd rather do tonight than turn your favorite fantasy into reality."

Nearly all of the hesitation Alice had felt earlier, along with her concern about reaching a distinct end goal, almost vanished. She believed that Rosa wouldn't take a lack of orgasmic response as an indictment of her abilities *or* Alice's attraction toward her, and she further believed that Rosa enjoyed performing cunnilingus enough to do so willingly and without any expectations or the need for reciprocity. But it wasn't the idea of putting her own mouth between Rosa's legs that posed the last remaining—and potentially insurmountable—issue. The *issue*, as she was reminded while entertaining the thought of how Rosa might taste, was her panties. How wet they were…how wet *Alice* was.

Heartbroken, Alice admitted, "I'd love that, really, but I'm not sure I'm…" She searched for a way to explain that wouldn't make her want to shrivel up and die. "Prepared for such an up-close visitor to that area."

Rosa pulled well back, studying Alice's face with a clear look of confusion. "Alice, we both spent forty-five minutes showering and grooming in the bathroom before the bonfire. I find it hard to believe you could possibly be that unpresentable…ever, actually. Is something wrong?"

Wishing that Rosa wouldn't make her spell it out, Alice hid her eyes behind her hand. "Yeah, I'm clean, I'm groomed…but I'm also *soaking wet.* You're killing me, woman, with your verbal foreplay."

Rosa laughed so heartily that Alice dropped her hands and glared. With a bright grin, Rosa shook her head and eased across the boat's center console yet again. "Alice, I *love* the taste of a woman's juices. On my lips, my tongue, my chin…all over my face, ideally, if I do my job right…" She drew the tip of her tongue along the indentation over Alice's top lip, a promise of things to come. "I *need* you to be wet so I can feel how badly you want what I'm doing to you." She drew away and looked toward the shore. "There's no such thing as too wet." She pumped her legs a couple times and nodded at Alice. "So let's go."

Alice went.

CHAPTER TEN

It took them less than five minutes to find the perfect spot.

Well, perfect *might be overstating it,* Alice decided as she surveyed their surroundings. The boathouse had a roof, an even surface to lie on, and four sturdy walls, but the center of the cavernous space was vast and open, full of dark lake water dimly lit by the moonlight streaming in through the small windows. Alice eyed the rippling surface warily after walking through the back entrance Rosa had simply unlatched, reluctant to take her attention away for even a second lest a murderous aquatic creature emerge from the depths. She allowed the beam of her flashlight to play over the center of the black lagoon only briefly before losing her nerve and again shining it onto the floor in front of her. "This is…a little creepy, don't you think?"

Rosa tossed a casual glance over her shoulder as she walked ahead toward the flight of stairs at the other end of the boathouse. Then she slowed and turned to Alice without a hint of reproach in her expression. Instead, there was only concern. Yet another way she differed from John. "Would you rather find somewhere else?"

Alice shook her head, skirting the edge of the pool as she made a beeline for the staircase leading to the second floor. This place was likely as good as it would get, creepiness aside. "I just hope the door at the top is unlocked."

Rosa beat her up the stairs and made a triumphant noise when she successfully turned the knob that granted them access to a large, window-filled storage room. Alice turned off her flashlight when she reached the top of the stairs, pleased by how well the nearly full moon illuminated the space. She closed the door behind them, relieved to leave the menacing water below. In another stroke of luck, she realized the door had a lock, which she engaged without hesitation.

"This works," Rosa said softly, turning in a circle as she looked around the sparsely occupied space. Cardboard boxes and life preservers and oars and even a couple of small kayaks lay scattered in haphazard piles around the room, but there was a large patch of open floor next to one of the massive windows, and more importantly, nobody would interrupt them here. "Don't you think?"

"I never imagined we'd find someplace this *nice*." Alice walked to the open area and unshouldered her backpack, ready to unburden herself of its weight. She unzipped her hoodie and tossed it onto the floor. That's when her legs weakened suddenly in anticipation of what was about to happen. *She's going to go down on me. A* woman *is going to go down on me.* Another rush of wetness poured from her, and she groaned, sinking onto the floor as she contended with a surge of emotion and arousal that left her momentarily breathless. "I'm really happy we did."

"Tell me about it." Rosa unzipped and unrolled the sleeping bag near the window. She seemed lighter than when they'd first gotten into the boat, and more confident. "There may not be rose petals or candlelight, but I dare say this isn't a bad setting for a first time."

Even if she wasn't technically a virgin, Alice marveled at how much tonight really *did* feel like the first time. With John, she hadn't wanted the sex nearly this badly, yet still managed to walk away distinctly unsatisfied. Everything about tonight—this place, her partner—hinted at a very different outcome. "It's perfect." Not an overstatement. Not anymore.

Rosa's smile grew at her bold praise. "*Perfect?* Not too creepy?"

Alice flashed back on the image of the dark water below and shuddered. "Don't remind me."

Cooing, Rosa offered Alice a hand to help to her feet. "I'm sorry. Let me take your mind off it?"

"All right." Caught between uncertainty and desire, Alice allowed herself to be pulled to her feet, and then she collapsed into Rosa's arms when invited to do so. Her proximity to the moment when she'd actually have to remove her clothing and reveal her naked body had slowly eroded the bravado she'd felt on the boat. Though Rosa had already seen her bare stomach and breasts, the thought of how much trust it would require to allow someone to come face-to-face with her most private spot, and how vulnerable such an examination would surely make her feel, left Alice shaking within the embrace. Worried that Rosa would misread her hesitation, she said, "This is the part where I get nervous, but please don't think that means I don't want this. I do."

Even if I can't imagine taking off my pants for you.

"I know you do." Rosa spoke in a soft voice and ran the backs of her fingers across Alice's cheek as she looked into her eyes. "Relax. It's just me." She kissed Alice, a deliberate reminder of all the other kisses they'd shared over the past twenty-four hours. She murmured another reminder against Alice's swollen lips. "The chocolate addict who thinks you're an engineering genius because you built me a ballista out of Popsicle sticks." She shot Alice an impish smile. "We've had so much fun today already. This is us having a little more fun. *Grown-up* fun." She punctuated the thought by moving a hand down to cup Alice's ass. "But it's still you and me, like before. Shall we lie down?"

"Please." Alice allowed Rosa to lead her to the sleeping bag, then melted onto it, resting on her back in the center in what she hoped was a subtle invitation for Rosa to climb on top of her. She'd imagined how it would feel to be pinned beneath that curvaceous, womanly body more than once, and her desire to find out for certain far outweighed her nervousness about what might happen after that. "Hold me for a minute?"

"Definitely." Rosa sank onto her knees, then stretched out alongside Alice while simultaneously slipping a thigh between hers. She gathered Alice into an intimate embrace that fell slightly short of what she'd secretly desired. "How's this?"

"Wonderful," Alice said truthfully. She pressed her mouth to the base of Rosa's throat, enjoying the way her pulse thrummed strongly beneath her lips. "But…you could lie on top of me, if you want."

Rosa raised an eyebrow, apparently tickled by her reluctance to simply ask. "Could I?"

"If you want," Alice whispered. She kissed Rosa's throat again, then nudged her knee deeper between Rosa's thighs until she could feel the heat of her arousal through her jeans.

Rosa's hips sought out hers, luring her into an instinctive dance Alice's body couldn't help but join. "What do *you* want?"

Alice bit her lower lip as Rosa's thigh pressed into her throbbing, sensitized flesh. "I want you on top of me."

Rosa flipped them so Alice lay flat on her back, then climbed over Alice so they were breast-to-breast, hip-to-hip, aligned from head to toe. She worked her thigh between Alice's, briefly, before Alice allowed her legs to fall open and accepted the sensual weight of Rosa's lower body resting against hers. Rosa ground into her pussy and pulled Alice's hands up to pin them against the sleeping bag over her head. Hips undulating, she stared into Alice's eyes as she first bent to nibble her lips, then briefly tangle with her tongue. When Rosa lifted her head again, fierce hunger burned in her gaze. "If you want something from me, ask. The worst that I'll do is I say no…but honestly, that's not usually what happens."

Alice gulped for air, no longer able to breathe normally. Her head swam with delightful anticipation while her body screamed at the nearly painful arousal blooming between her thighs. "Kiss me again," she whispered, desperate for something to ground her, to keep her from flying apart. "Please."

Rosa captured her mouth in a surprisingly restrained kiss. Passionate as ever, and sincere, but also strangely calm. Alice detected a tender undercurrent in this union of their lips and tongues, an unspoken reinforcement of the bond they'd forged over the course of a single, intensely emotional day. Without speaking a word, Rosa reminded Alice not only of the intimate friendship they'd built so quickly, but also the genuine trust she felt for this woman she'd only just met. When they finally broke apart to recover, Alice closed her eyes and exhaled, relieved to have recovered her composure at least slightly.

Rosa flexed the fingers on Alice's wrists before loosening her grip. "Is it all right to hold you like this?"

Alice craned to take in the sight of Rosa pinning her hands to the floor. "Very." She scraped together her courage and looked into Rosa's face, ready to embrace the honesty that had sprung up between them. "As long as you *really* don't mind a ridiculous amount of wetness."

Rosa drew the tip of her tongue along Alice's top lip, then bit the bottom one, pelvis surging. "I *really* don't." She lowered her face to whisper in Alice's ear. "I *really* can't wait to find out how your pussy tastes."

Alice's heart crashed against her chest wall, again and again, threatening to send her off into another round of hyperventilation. The only coherent thought she managed to hold on to was that she didn't want to be the only one who was naked. Nor did she want to be the first to take off her clothes. Heeding Rosa's advice to give voice to her needs, Alice said, "Will you...can I see you first?"

Rosa let go of her wrists and sat back on her heels, leaving Alice temporarily adrift without that intoxicating weight to anchor her in place. She barely had time to mourn the loss before Rosa pulled her T-shirt over head to reveal a black bra with lace trim, thereby rendering her disappointment moot. Rosa wore a knowing smile as she reached behind her back to unhook the clasp. She peeled the bra away slowly, uncovering bare skin inch by tantalizing inch. By the time she dropped her bra onto the floor beside them, Alice could only stare helplessly with her mouth ajar, struck dumb by her first real look at Rosa's naked breasts.

"You're beautiful." Alice startled at the sound of her own ragged voice. She hadn't intended to say that aloud, but judging from the beaming grin that immediately overtook Rosa's gorgeous mouth, it was clear she'd done the right thing. She let her gaze wander over Rosa's full, wonderfully proportioned breasts, the dark, pebbled nipples, the rise and fall of her heaving, flushed chest and hesitantly raised a hand into the air. Yearning to cradle the bare flesh with her palm, she asked, "May I?"

Rather than answer, Rosa guided Alice's hand to her breast and pressed the center over a diamond-hard nipple. "Whatever you want."

A delicious shiver ran through the length of Alice's overheated body, from the top of her head to the very tips of her toes. *I can't believe I'm actually touching a half-naked woman.* Her other hand floated up to join its twin so that she held a plump tit in each. She massaged the pliant mounds, plucked at their tips, and then finally pushed them together so she could sit up and run her tongue across both erect nipples with one long swipe. Rosa grunted and shuddered beneath her touch, clinging to Alice's shoulders when she nearly lost her balance.

"*Fuck*," Rosa groaned. Her breath quickened when Alice seized one nipple between her thumb and forefinger while testing the other with her teeth. "You're not the only one who's insanely wet right now."

Alice smiled around Rosa's nipple, eager to believe she wasn't alone in her over-the-top arousal. "No?"

"Pinkie swear." Rosa combed her fingers through Alice's hair in a gesture that felt very much like nonverbal praise. "Would you like to see?"

Alice swallowed hard. She'd never wanted anything so badly in her entire life, yet amidst all that need, part of her still quaked with fear. "Yes. Please."

Rosa stood and unbuttoned her shorts slowly, deliberately peeling the denim away from her hips like she was performing a striptease. "Do *you* mind that you've gotten me so excited?"

Rapt, Alice stared as Rosa kicked her shorts away before slipping her fingers down the front of her black briefs with a contented whimper. Alice shook her head and moved nearer, not wanting to miss even a single second of the show Rosa was putting on. She would surely revisit this night in her head for years to come, so she tried to memorize every detail. The style and cut of Rosa's panties, the conspicuous movement of her searching fingers, the faint, unfamiliar scent of another woman's arousal that hung in the air like the sweetest perfume. Rosa removed the hand from her briefs and showed Alice shiny fingers coated with slick, clear fluid. Then Alice watched, entranced, as Rosa gave the fingers a sensual tongue bath while humming in appreciation of her own flavor.

Rosa lowered her hand from her mouth and smiled, a bit coy, completely sexy. "Told you I like how it tastes."

Alice's breathing hitched. She pushed herself into a sitting position and reached for Rosa's hand. "Come back down here with me."

"First let me do one more thing." Rosa hooked her thumbs around the waistband of her panties and lowered them to the floor. She pushed them aside with her foot and turned to face Alice with her hands on her hips. Her confidence wavered and dissolved within the span of a single, heartrending second, and Alice watched her plummet into a palpable bout of self-consciousness. The hands came off her hips, and Rosa carefully lowered herself onto the sleeping bag, no longer able to meet Alice's eyes. Despite her obvious discomfort, she sat facing Alice and let her legs fall open to reveal what lay between her shaking thighs. "See?" she whispered. "Soaking wet."

Alice didn't look. She couldn't. Not yet, not until she'd assured

Rosa she was safe. Despite being wrapped up in her own anxiety, she immediately recognized what had just happened. After all of Rosa's comments about the shame she felt over that stupid viral video, and about the thrill she'd once derived from showing off her body and performing under the cold, watchful eye of a camera lens, Alice understood the current situation plainly. Rosa hadn't shared her body with *anyone* consensually in well over a year, yet during that time, she'd been told again and again—by strangers, acquaintances, even friends and family—that by behaving like a brazen slut, she'd gotten exactly what she deserved. With those damning indictments ringing in her head, who could blame Rosa for faltering when it came time to reveal her body to someone new? What struck Alice as extraordinary was Rosa's sheer determination to stoically push through her discomfort, presumably for Alice's sake. Simply so *Alice* would feel more comfortable.

Overcome by a hurricane of emotion—affection, compassion, gratitude, sorrow, anger, even love—Alice murmured, "Rosa, look at me." Rosa tore her attention away from the window, eyes shiny with unshed tears. Alice smiled and scooted closer until their faces were only inches apart. "Rosa, you're *beautiful*."

Just as Rosa had calmed her earlier with a single, heartfelt kiss, now Alice gave it a shot. She pecked Rosa's lips and then, encouraged by the way they parted slightly, slipped her tongue inside the hot, welcoming mouth. She immediately registered a new flavor, similar to the scent she'd caught in the air. *That's Rosa.* Afraid to escalate the kiss before verifying that everything was okay, Alice broke off with a shaky exhalation. "I can taste you," she said without thinking.

Rosa's mouth stretched into a slow smile. "And what do you think?"

"That I want more." When Rosa groaned and dove in for another kiss, clearly affected by her answer, Alice moved away with a quiet noise of regret. "But wait…first…" She studied Rosa's face, considering how best to approach this subject without upsetting her further. "I know you want to give me whatever I ask for, but it can't be at your expense. If something makes you feel too exposed, or too vulnerable, or too embarrassed, don't do it. Please. Tonight needs to be every bit as good for you as it is for me. That's the only way this will feel right."

Rosa's chin wobbled briefly at her words, her expression so raw it shook Alice to her core. She sensed that Rosa's lovers didn't treat her so kindly, and not just because Rosa had hinted as much during various conversations throughout the day. It was obvious by the way she seemed genuinely stunned by Alice's request, and shaken, like she wasn't sure how to react. "Thank you," Rosa whispered after a long span of mutual silence. "But I've never been self-conscious before, and I don't want to be now. Not because of what happened, not because of some *stupid* article I wrote about an even *stupider* video game."

"Then...do you want me to look?" Alice used the backs of her index and middle fingers to dry a tear that had spilled onto Rosa's cheek. Earlier, she'd pleaded with Rosa to trust her enough to honor her stated desires despite whatever outward signs of fear she displayed, so it only seemed fair to extend that same courtesy to Rosa. If Rosa wanted to push through this apprehension about allowing a new lover unrestricted visual access to her body, Alice would help her do that. "And see how ridiculously wet you are?"

Rosa laughed, a genuine exultation. "How is it that this suddenly feels like *my* first time?"

"Because it's *our* first time." Alice returned to Rosa's lips for a gentle nibble, having missed their pliant warmth against her own. "And we both want this to be really good."

Chuckling, Rosa spoke between peppered kisses. "That's true." One last kiss and she broke away, planting her palms on the sleeping bag beside her hips so she could ease back and meet Alice's eyes. "Personally, I think we're off to an excellent start."

Alice felt a bare thigh land against her clothed knee, alerting her to the fact that Rosa's legs had once again fallen open. "Me, too." She licked her lips and tried to work up some saliva in her suddenly dry mouth. Apparently all the moisture in her body had decided to relocate between her thighs. "So..." She fought not to drop her gaze, waiting for more explicit permission to take a peek.

"Look at me," Rosa whispered. She took Alice's chin to direct her attention lower and, at the same time, spread her legs while lifting her pelvis to better display her shiny, swollen, ridiculously *magnificent* pussy. "See how wet I am?"

"Rosa," she breathed, unable to come up with anything more clever to say.

"You did this." Rosa released Alice's chin and used both hands to hold herself open, exposing glorious, pink folds and the hint of an engorged clit whose shape Alice could barely discern under the glow of the moonlight illuminating their makeshift bed. She wished for a flashlight, fascinated by her first real-life encounter with another woman's pussy, yet kept quiet, reluctant to put Rosa under a literal spotlight or risk turning their encounter into a mere gynecological examination. Despite her sense of caution, she found herself angling to see better, shifting forward to improve her line of sight. Rosa reclined further and even tilted her hips to give Alice a better view. Submitting to the unflinching scrutiny, she rearranged the position of her fingers to pull her inner labia apart, revealing her dark opening and impossibly more wetness.

The act of bravery inspired one of Alice's own. Not wanting Rosa to feel isolated in her nudity, she quickly stripped off her T-shirt and bra without tearing her eyes away from the vision in front of her. "God, Rosa, you're breathtaking."

"So are you." Rosa's eyes darkened as she indulged in her first real opportunity to stare openly at Alice's bare breasts. "Why don't you go ahead and take off your jeans, while you're at it? You can leave your panties on." Her expression turned wolfish, hungry. "For now."

Oddly, Alice barely felt nervous at this point. Though she wasn't entirely sure why, she was more than happy to ride this newfound wave of confidence. "All right." She stripped off her pants, glad to be free of the constricting denim. Left only in panties, she settled back at Rosa's side. Still holding herself open with one hand, Rosa took a breath before moving two fingers of the other one down to rub small, tight circles around her clit. Cognizant of the mental hurdle Rosa almost certainly had to overcome to even consider masturbating in front of someone she'd met only the day before, Alice wrapped her in her arms and held her close as she watched Rosa's continued efforts to coax the erect clit farther out of its hood. Alice kissed Rosa's shoulder and murmured, "Is that how you like to be touched?"

"Yes." Rosa panted, nostrils flaring, and trembled against Alice's chest. "Would you..." She bit her lip and shivered under her own ministrations. "Would you like to try?"

"Touching you?" While Alice didn't think she was ready for mutual masturbation—not yet—she was more than game to slide a finger into Rosa's inviting depths. Every lesbian porn film she'd ever watched streamed through her mind, a veritable montage of hand jobs and acts of digital penetration she now drew upon for heroic inspiration. She knew what to do. Right? "Yes."

Rosa used the hand that had been playing with her clit to catch Alice around the wrist. "Want me to show you?"

Alice nodded, unable to put together a coherent verbal response. *Yes!*

"I'll probably feel like you, but different." Rosa guided Alice's outstretched fingers to rest upon her scorching folds before covering them with her own damp hand. "You told me you know what you like, so use that knowledge to learn how I react to your touch." Separating Alice's index and middle fingers from the rest, she helped her apply light pressure while moving the tips in tiny circles over the impressively hard ridge of her clit. "I'm really sensitive, so I usually like a gentle hand. That is, unless—" Whimpering, she finished in a rush, "I'm in the mood for something rougher." She paused to gasp as Alice caressed the length of her shaft, having strayed from Rosa's guidance in a moment of improvisation. "That's so, *so* good, Alice." Rosa lifted the hand she'd been using to hold herself open and combed through Alice's hair, reinforcing the praise, while her thighs quavered wildly. "Keep doing that and you'll make me come."

Alice's breathing stuttered at the mere suggestion. "Really?"

"*Definitely.*" Rosa dropped her hand from Alice's and grabbed a fistful of the sleeping bag beside her hip. "Unless you'd rather let me go down on you first."

Alice grunted her refusal, content to give before she received. It was better this way. If Rosa actually managed to make her come, Alice would probably appreciate the opportunity to simply pass out afterward. If she didn't, at least the awkward silence that was sure to follow wouldn't rob Rosa of whatever pleasure Alice might be able to provide. "May I keep touching you for now?"

"Yes, my sweet girl." Rosa looked sheepish about the uttered endearment, like she hadn't actually intended to say it aloud. Abruptly, she shifted to lie flat on her back and exhaled. "So much for no reciprocation necessary."

Alice stretched out next to Rosa and massaged her clit delicately. "Did you really think I would pass up the chance to do this?" Swirling her fingers through the thick, copious wetness, she relished the hyper-responsiveness of Rosa's bowstring-taut body to even the lightest brush against her sensitive flesh. "To learn how to make a woman come?"

Rosa moaned, again appearing to take overt pleasure from the idea of Alice's relative inexperience. "I'm not convinced you need a teacher, baby. You feel so fucking *incredible*." She let out what sounded like a low growl, arching her back to push insistently against Alice's hand. "Want to put your fingers inside? It would be so nice to have you in my pussy."

Alice couldn't believe how fast they were moving. Prior to yesterday evening, she'd never even kissed a woman. Now she was on the verge of fucking one. "Yeah." She paused to take a breath, slow her heart rate, and try not to pass out. Carefully, she slid her index finger lower and searched through slippery folds before finding the slick circle of Rosa's opening. She traced the entrance with a feather-soft touch, trying to imagine how it would feel to sink into a willing, open vagina that wasn't her own. "You'll tell me if I hurt you?"

"You won't." But, assuaging her fears, Rosa reached between her spread legs, positioned two of Alice's fingers at her entrance, and helped push her inside. Her pussy was snug and blistering hot, pulsing around Alice as she began to move. Out, in, out, in, again and again until Rosa's hips were rolling to meet each thrust. "See?" Rosa gasped, easily matching her rhythm. "Doesn't hurt at all."

Overcome by the sight of her slim digits disappearing into Rosa's body, Alice got onto her knees and raised her butt high in the air, desperate for even the tiniest bit of friction against her own heated flesh. Rosa released a loud groan, perhaps at the wanton sight of her lewd pose, then moaned breathily when Alice remembered the proper technique and brought her thumb up to circle the distended clit that now stood proudly at attention. Like a puppet, Rosa's entire body jerked at each stroke, an obviously involuntary reaction that made Alice giggle with pure glee.

Awestruck, Alice whispered, "You like it." Not a question. A fact. "Rosa, you're so warm, so *soft*, so tight around my fingers." She twisted her wrist, exploring everywhere she could reach. "I could stay inside you like this all night long."

Rosa's chest moved rapidly, her nostrils flared. "I'm not sure I'd survive that."

A tremendous energy swept through Alice, born of her certainty that Rosa was deriving honest pleasure from her touch. Even though John had obviously enjoyed fucking her during the beginning of their relationship, the satisfaction he'd taken from her body never left her feeling powerful. Instead, she'd felt dirty, compromised, and, perhaps worst of all, unfulfilled. With Rosa, *everything* was different. Every pass of her thumb over Rosa's throbbing clit elicited a breathless moan that bolstered her self-confidence to heights unknown, making Alice feel, for once, like she could take on the whole world if needed.

She pressed her lips to Rosa's ear and whispered hotly, "I wouldn't let anything happen to you."

Rosa stiffened, and shook, and threw an arm around Alice's shoulders. "Oh, Alice," she groaned, clinging tightly as intermittent spasms wracked her already trembling frame. "Oh fuck…how are you…this…on the first…time, my *ass*."

Alice grinned at the implication of Rosa's jumbled accusation. "A good imagination, the Internet, and lots of quality time with myself," she said, translating the question Rosa had tried to ask. She slipped her fingers out of Rosa's pussy, painted her clit and labia with a renewed layer of hot juices, then stuck them back in. "But really, I'm doing whatever feels good."

A loud cry slipped past Rosa's tightly compressed lips and echoed off the walls, making Alice glad they'd found a place where Rosa could give full voice to her pleasure. She'd never heard a sweeter sound, especially because *she* was the one who'd caused that desperate, ecstatic wail. Emboldened, Alice started to tell Rosa exactly how much she enjoyed listening to her get fingered, but Rosa cut her off with an even louder shout that was quickly followed by a high-pitched, girlish moan and then, thrillingly, a gush of hot juices that spilled onto Alice's palm. Strong muscles contracted around Alice's fingers for what felt like whole minutes while Rosa whimpered and clutched at her arm, likely to ensure that she wouldn't withdraw until her climax had burnt itself out.

"Not yet," Rosa whispered, still fluttering inside. "Stay."

Shushing her, Alice rested her cheek on Rosa's breast and listened to the rapid thrum of her heartbeat. "I'm not going anywhere."

Rosa placed her hand over the fingers still embedded within her body. "Holy *shit*, Alice. Where the hell did you learn to do that?"

Alice rolled her eyes. She assumed Rosa was playing up her success in an attempt to boost her confidence. "I'm glad it was all right."

"*All right?* Alice—" Rosa's hips surged, and she groaned as she dragged Alice's fingers out until only the first inch or so remained. She guided Alice back inside, setting off another round of involuntary contractions. "I promise…I'm not just…being nice." Rosa's nostrils flared, and in her peripheral vision, Alice saw her toes literally curl. "You're a freakin' natural."

"Yeah?" Alice took Rosa's nipple into her mouth, sucking lightly as she dragged her fingers from their cozy home to perform another slow, deliberate insertion. The tremors that hadn't yet subsided swiftly intensified, causing Rosa's thighs to quake violently as she sobbed with what sounded a little too much like distress. Alice stilled her fingers. "Do you need a break?"

Rosa gave a vigorous nod, tears streaming down her cheeks. "I think so, yeah."

Somewhat concerned, Alice withdrew as carefully as she could, slightly guilt-stricken about savoring each and every aftershock caused by the friction against Rosa's sensitive pussy. "Please tell me the truth. *Did* I hurt you?" She laid her sticky fingers over Rosa's soaked labia, hating to sever their intimate connection already. "I'm *so* sorry if I did."

Rosa laughed and rubbed her watery eyes with the heels of her hands. "Oh no, baby…not at all."

Vaguely unconvinced, Alice sat up to watch Rosa recover. Her face and chest were visibly flushed, even in the low light, and she wore a goofy smile that belied the tears she'd shed only moments ago. Quietly, Alice murmured, "I didn't mean to push you too far."

Rosa's hand landed on Alice's thigh, up high near the juncture, reminding her that she was naked except for a pair of drenched panties. "You didn't. It's…there are only so many times I can come before my body forces me to stop and recover. And…it's been a while. And that was *intense.*"

Alice returned her gaze to Rosa's pussy, elated that she no longer seemed self-conscious at all. "You…really had more than one orgasm?"

"Didn't you feel me?"

She had, yet it seemed too incredible to believe. "Yes."

"You made me come, Alice Wu, *multiple* times." Rosa took the hand Alice had used to fuck her and placed it back onto flesh that continued to throb and leak hot juices, evidence to support her claim. "It was obvious you did your homework. Go forth into the world with renewed sexual confidence, young Padawan, because I'm not sure there's anything left to teach you."

Except one thing. Now more excited than nervous despite being messier than ever, Alice swiped her fingers through Rosa's sodden folds and raised her hand to her mouth. She hesitated only briefly before slipping the wet digits between her lips. Rosa's sweet flavor exploded onto her taste buds, ratcheting her hunger to greater heights. Mumbling her approval, she licked her fingers one by one, exhilarated to be so happy with the taste. She'd hoped she would be.

Once she'd cleaned herself thoroughly under Rosa's watchful gaze, Alice snuck her hand into her own panties. As expected, she was as wet as the mythical great flood. She sighed, a mixture of pleasure caused by the light touch of her fingers and disappointment at the thick, almost ropy strands of fluid that clung to them. "Fingering you didn't exactly help my wetness problem."

"Except I told you, it's not a problem."

Skeptical, Alice pulled her hand from her panties and spread her fingers to show how the viscous fluid connected them. "Seriously?"

Rosa sat up, approaching as though she might take Alice's saturated fingers between her lips. "You smell yummy."

Blushing, Alice stuck the fingers into her own mouth, determined to check the flavor before she allowed Rosa a turn. She tasted less sweet than Rosa did. Surprisingly mild, in fact. Alice went back for seconds, faltering only when she finally noticed Rosa staring at her with a ravenous expression. She pulled the fingers from her mouth with a bashful shrug. "Just checking."

"May I have a turn?"

Alice's stomach fluttered as she once again dipped into the pool of arousal between her thighs. Playing with herself for only a moment, an over-too-quickly tease, she held her breath and offered Rosa three glistening fingers. "All right."

Without breaking eye contact, Rosa bent to take Alice's fingers into her mouth. Her eyes closed as soon as her tongue hit Alice's skin, and a low noise of grateful appreciation bubbled up from deep within her chest. Locking her hand around Alice's wrist, Rosa opened her eyes to stare directly into Alice's soul—or at least that's how it felt—as she sucked every last drop of wetness from the digits. By the time Rosa released her from the hot suction of her mouth, Alice had lost any desire to be demure about the offer of fantasy fulfillment.

Rosa closed the distance between them to take Alice down onto her back in the center of the sleeping bag. She climbed on top and nudged her leg between Alice's, smearing Alice's bare thigh with her hot cum in the process, before once again wrenching her hands above her head to pin her down. As if in slow motion, she bent to kiss Alice's throat and then her nipples—punctuating each teasing peck of her lips with a light nip of her teeth—before at last moving up to whisper into Alice's ear. "You're my new favorite flavor. May I please take off your panties and have some more?"

Alice nodded, unsure she could speak, then gasped, "My heart's beating like crazy."

Rosa rested her hand between Alice's breasts and rubbed, soothing her instantly, if not completely. "Mine, too. You're excited, just like I am. Doesn't it feel good?"

Alice was only used to feeling this level of anticipation as a byproduct of her anxiety. Strange, then, that it *did* feel kind of good… in this context. "Yes."

"Shh." Rosa stroked her chest and then, after Alice's labored breathing began to slow, glanced down the length of her body. "Alice, tell me what you want. Should I slip your panties off? Or would you rather I put my hand inside them and play with your clit a little?" She waited a beat. Then when Alice failed to catch her breath long enough to answer, she added, "Or you could touch yourself while I kiss your breasts."

Alice had already experienced having her breasts kissed. Masturbating herself was old hat. As much as she'd adore watching Rosa's hand work within her panties while she jerked Alice off, that wasn't what she wanted right now, either. Because what she'd never done—what she wanted more than anything—was to feel the sensation of another person's tongue on her clit. *Be brave, Alice.* She inhaled deeply, then exhaled through her nose. "Take them off."

Rosa hesitated long enough to make Alice worry that she'd been spooked by her case of nerves, but then Rosa launched into action, shifting to sit beside her hips, fingers curled beneath the elastic waistband of her panties. She checked Alice's face before lowering the sheer fabric at a glacial pace in a long, drawn-out reveal, bit by torturous bit. Rosa swallowed, seemingly rapt at the sight of Alice's hip bones, her neat triangle of dark pubic hair, her naked thighs. Hoarsely, she whispered, "Alice, I've never wanted anyone as much as I want you. That's the truth."

Somehow Alice believed her, and that imbued her with all the confidence she needed to open her legs. "Same."

Rosa laughed, and Alice took a moment to study her features in the soft, bluish light that filled the room. She was as stunning as ever, if a bit mussed, but what made her truly ethereal was the kindness and compassion lighting her up from within. Rosa took Alice's hand and kissed the knuckles softly, then grinned at Alice until she couldn't help but grin back.

"What?" Alice murmured. The air felt suddenly charged, crackling with possibility.

Rosa seemed to sense the change, too, and broke eye contact while visibly struggling to regain her composure. Alice sensed that Rosa's emotions were running every bit as high as hers, most likely sending some of the same intense, confusing messages to her heart that Alice was also struggling to process. Afraid to move, afraid to even breathe, Alice said nothing, waiting for Rosa to take the lead. She didn't want to speak and ruin this moment between them or bring their transcendental evening to a crashing halt.

After countless shared breaths, Rosa looked into Alice's eyes again, still full to the brim with passion but with a noticeably tighter hold on her emotional state. "I'm going to lie on my belly between your legs." She began to move down the length of Alice's body on the first word, acting out her intentions as she spoke. "And press your smooth, sweet thighs apart." Her hands landed high up on Alice's inner thighs—mere inches from her swollen labia—and gently nudged her legs open until they were wide enough to accommodate Rosa's torso. "And admire how pretty your mouthwatering pussy looks up close."

Rosa's searing breath washed over Alice's overheated labia, and her heart hammered at the realization that Rosa was right *there,* in the place John had been too disgusted to put his mouth, even after she'd once broken down and begged him to try. Her breathing faltered as fear crawled up her spine, the growing certainty that she wasn't *right* down there, that *nobody* would enjoy feasting on her like that.

All those thoughts—*every* thought—evaporated at the warm press of Rosa's lips against her labia. Alice inhaled sharply at the ecstatic pleasure of the intimate kiss, stunned by the discovery that reality, in this case, surpassed every fantasy she'd ever had. She opened her mouth to speak, to ask Rosa if she looked okay, if she tasted all right, but could only moan when Rosa drew the flat of her tongue along her labia, from right above Alice's opening on up to flick the hard point of her erect clit. Afterward, Rosa lifted her head and gazed up at her, lips wet, chin already shiny with Alice's juices. "You taste even better than you look."

Rosa kept her eyes locked on Alice's as she licked the length of her pussy again, then very gently sucked on one side of her labia in a way that turned Alice's muscles to water. Paralyzed by the unimaginable bliss of it all, unable to move or even to *look* at what was happening to her, Alice balled her hands into fists and tried to commit everything about the way Rosa was making her feel to memory. She groaned loudly, unashamed by the disappointment that crashed over her at the sudden, momentary loss of Rosa's sultry mouth. "Please," she whispered, sounding so pitiful she cringed. "Please don't stop."

Rosa kissed her labia, then rubbed her face back and forth in an apparent effort to cover her chin, nose, and cheeks in Alice's wetness. She drew away, checked to make sure Alice was watching, then pulled open her outer lips while deliberately touching her tongue to the rigid clit she'd exposed. Once again, Alice wished for a flashlight, in love with the vision of her pussy being licked and sucked by a graceful, feminine mouth. It looked and felt so heavenly, in fact, that a familiar pressure swiftly bloomed between Alice's thighs, signaling the beginning of the end.

"No," Alice whispered. She didn't want this to be over. Not yet. Not so *soon*. "No, *no*."

Rosa backed off slightly, still connected to her by a thin line of saliva and cum. "Stop?"

"No!" As much as she wanted to draw this out, Alice couldn't imagine asking Rosa to slow down, let alone stop altogether. "Don't stop. I just…" She gasped when Rosa's tongue returned to her opening and pressed slightly inside. "Oh, fuck." Her voice came out low and gravelly, unrecognizable to her ears. "I *like* that."

Rosa worked a hand beneath her to grab one of her butt cheeks while wrapping her other arm around Alice's shaking thigh. Raising her face after a firm suck on Alice's labia, she bared her teeth in a feral growl. "You like being licked?" Going back in, Rosa batted Alice's clit with her tongue, then slurped noisily. "Getting your pussy eaten out?"

This was worlds better than any porn movie she'd ever seen, and even while watching those, Alice rarely made it to the end of the video. Defying her expectations of failure, her body surged to the finish line before she could shout a warning or do anything at all to try to forestall the inevitable. As she convulsed with wave after wave of orgasmic pleasure, Alice flung her hands into Rosa's hair in an effort to force her tongue more firmly against her pulsing clit. When she realized how easily this new handhold would allow her to fuck Rosa's talented mouth, she did exactly that until the last of her contractions had faded away. It took a few seconds after her climax had ended to come back to herself, and longer still to loosen her grip on Rosa's head.

"I'm sorry, I didn't—" Alice gasped when Rosa's tongue very gently traced a path from her clit down to her opening, triggering multiple aftershocks. "Hurt you, did I?"

Rosa snorted, lifted her head to wink at Alice, then continued to casually lap at her labia. "I'm not nearly as delicate as you think I am," she said in a teasing manner. Eyes twinkling, she pulled Alice into her mouth and uttered a low, drawn-out hum to deliver delicious vibrations straight to her clit. Rosa pulled back, waited a few seconds for Alice's whimpers to quiet, then broke into a triumphant, beaming smirk. "By the way, you came *fast*."

"Tell me about it," Alice lamented, though she couldn't help but smile in relief at their accomplishment. She *wasn't* broken. She *could* feel the same excitement and pleasure with a lover that she saw in films and read about in stories. "So I guess it *was* John's fault, after all."

Rosa wrinkled her nose and covered Alice's whole pussy with her mouth, sliding her tongue in wide circles over the slippery, heated flesh. She licked and nibbled and sucked until Alice teetered on the edge of an improbable *second* orgasm, then pulled away to let her calm down. "Clearly."

Alice felt around for Rosa's hand, grabbing it as a wave of deep gratitude crashed over her. Apparently they *weren't* done here yet. Rosa seemed both ready and willing to make her come again, to draw out this once-in-a-lifetime experience a little while longer. Even as she marveled at Rosa's generosity, a warm stream of air blew over her hyper-aroused clit, raising goose bumps across every inch of Alice's sweat-dampened skin. Feeling it needed to be said, Alice caressed Rosa's cheek and murmured, "You know, you don't have to…uh, do that again." She stopped talking briefly when Rosa gave her labia a sensuous slurp in an apparent act of defiance. "If you don't want to."

"I know that." Rosa let go of her hand so she could use her fingers to spread Alice open, until her hard clit jutted out far enough to allow Rosa to take it between her full, supple lips. She bobbed her head up and down, sucking Alice off theatrically, then swirled the tip of her tongue in fast circles until Alice lifted her hips in a silent plea for more. Rosa drew back with a self-satisfied grin. "But you seem to *really* enjoy it… and since the first time went by a little too quickly for my liking…" She nuzzled into Alice, inhaling. "I want to make you come in my mouth again." Her tongue snaked out to toy with Alice's clit in an infuriatingly abrupt tease. "As long as you don't mind."

Alice cradled Rosa's face in her hands, pulling her forward. She ran her fingertips along the strong line of Rosa's jaw when it resumed working against her. "I love how this feels *so much*." She planted her feet and lifted her hips, thrilled by the suggestiveness of the image they created, one woman feeding her eager cunt to another. "You're very, *very* good at that." She stroked Rosa's hair, recalling how much she'd enjoyed that comforting touch coupled with verbal praise. "The best I can imagine."

Rosa smiled around her clit. "Thank you." She turned and nipped Alice's inner thigh. "Do you want me to put a finger inside you this time?"

With her pleasure already approaching an excruciating zenith, even the slightest amount of penetration was sure to send Alice over the top. Yet despite her certainty that Rosa's hand would lead to her eventual undoing, Alice was powerless to resist the offer. She wanted to experience all of Rosa, every bit, before this ended. "Yes, please." She hesitated, then decided to try matching Rosa's effortlessly filthy mouth with a little risqué dialogue of her own. "Fuck me." She paused, feeling silly. "In my pussy."

An amused grin crawled across Rosa's face, but before Alice could get too embarrassed by her fumbling attempt at dirty talk, Rosa crawled up to capture her mouth in an amorous, Alice-flavored kiss. She broke away after a brief dance of their tongues, murmuring, "I'll fuck you, baby, so good you'll feel it in every step you take tomorrow."

Alice was positive she would die—literally *expire*—when Rosa once again descended the length of her body and fit her shoulders between her widely spread thighs. The return of the fiery tongue nestled against her swollen labia caused Alice to gasp, then sob in anticipation as Rosa finally brought a finger up to circle her opening in a deliberately gentle tease. Alice rocked against Rosa's face and squirmed wildly on the fingertip that kept dipping shallowly into her entrance without offering any real satisfaction. Frustrated, Alice angled her pelvis down in an attempt to impale herself on the taunting digit.

In response, Rosa pinned one of Alice's thighs to the sleeping bag using her free hand and lifted her mouth from between Alice's legs to rasp, "Yes?"

"Yes!" She'd never burned to be possessed by *anyone* before that moment, yet now she felt as though she'd fly apart if Rosa didn't fill up the vast emptiness inside her. *Immediately.* "Put your finger in."

Rosa released a quiet, strangled whimper as she sank the tip no more than an inch past Alice's entrance. She bent to keep lapping at Alice's clit, cautiously twisting this way and that as she worked her surprisingly thick-feeling finger inside until she could go no deeper. Alice vocalized her approval through a continuous stream of breathy moans and high-pitched whimpers, not bothering to feel self-conscious about sharing the unthinking, mewling noises of pleasure John had once mimicked during a particularly cruel afterglow session. She knew by the way Rosa's free hand tightened on her thigh that she was getting off on Alice's loud enjoyment of her efforts, and besides, Rosa would never intentionally make her feel bad.

Rosa had only ever made her feel good. *Inconceivably* good.

As though determined to prove that point, Rosa withdrew slowly before pushing all the way back in, so that her knuckles bumped against Alice's ass and the entire length of her finger was firmly embedded within her vagina. Alice's inner muscles contracted around Rosa before she could pull out again, her body already well on its way to another shattering climax without very much effort at all.

"Shit," Alice swore as tears leaked from her eyes. "Rosa, I'm…"

She bit her bottom lip, unable to withstand the urge to pump against the tongue now fluttering rapidly against her clit. "You're gonna make me…"

The finger inside her angled upward, brushing over a reactive, ecstasy-inducing spot deep inside. At the same time, Rosa gave her clit a noisy slurp while smoothly increasing the speed of her thrusts without changing the amount of force behind them. Ready to burst, Alice made a frantic grab for a handful of their discarded clothing so she could ball it up and stuff it beneath her head, readjusting her position until she had a clear line of sight to watch Rosa's mouth on her labia. She wanted to take one last, long look before this was over, in case it never happened again.

Giving her exactly what she needed, Rosa picked her head up far enough to grant a perfect view of her sinuous tongue playing over Alice's painfully swollen clit. Alice held her breath as she watched the performance, enthralled by the sight of a woman she'd already come to care about offering her unselfish pleasure in the most intimate way possible. A ragged whimper escaped her throat, causing her to tense her thighs and try to hold on just a *little* longer.

Rosa brought her free hand up to frame Alice's pussy, using her thumb and forefinger to spread her open to a point barely shy of mild discomfort. Feeling powerfully exposed yet wildly turned on, Alice fought not to close her eyes and instead maintained a laser focus on Rosa's skillful technique, the milky fluids that coated her new lover's face, and the mind-blowing vision of her own hyper-aroused pussy looking so objectively *sexy* in Rosa's mouth. When Rosa pulled back farther so that only the tip of her tongue continued to roll against the throbbing clit, Alice finally caught a glimpse of the long finger sliding in and out of her body. That image tore the last of her self-control to shreds.

Alice came—*again*. Loud and long, chased by a renewed flood of juices, the biggest orgasm of her life soaked Rosa Salazar's beautiful face. Alice's back arched off the sleeping bag as her entire body went momentarily rigid, and Rosa took that opportunity to grab her butt and drag her closer, grinding her face between Alice's legs until she finally had to beg Rosa to stop.

"Rosa." Alice panted, placing a reluctant hand on the top of her still-moving head. "Please, I can't…" She tried to decide whether she *could.* A single, direct lick across her clit convinced her that as much as she wanted to keep going, her body was finished. Pushing against Rosa firmly, she gasped, "Stop. I can't take any more."

Rosa surged up the length of Alice's body and captured her lips in a wet, impassioned kiss while very gingerly withdrawing from her tender pussy. Alice moaned at the aftershocks set off by the careful extraction and then, not wanting Rosa to leave, threw both arms around her shoulders and pulled her down into a desperate hug. Although perfectly aware that Rosa would feel how fast her heart was beating with their chests pressed together like they were, she no longer cared about playing it cool. Not anymore.

"*Multi*-orgasmic," Rosa whispered in a low, sensual tone that brought forth yet another wave of happiness. "That settles it: John was mediocre, and *you* are absolutely perfect." She kissed Alice's earlobe, then her throat, then shifted to lie at her side without leaving their close embrace. Rosa wore a smile that Alice couldn't help but return, full of pride and affection and joy, yet a sliver of uncertainty shone through in Rosa's gaze. "So was that everything you hoped it would be?"

Alice tightened her arms around Rosa, unable to get close enough. "It was more than I even knew was possible."

A gentle hand stroked down Alice's spine, lulling her into closing her eyes. For just a minute. Rosa pressed butterfly kisses over her cheeks, and in that instant—wrapped up in Rosa's arms—Alice felt cared for in a way she never had before. In a way she'd never *imagined* feeling cared for.

Or loved.

"Thanks for sneaking out with me," Rosa whispered, sleepily.

"Of course." Alice squeezed her as tight as her exhausted muscles allowed. "I like you," she whispered in reply. *I think I'm falling in love with you.* But she kept her musing silent, too afraid to say so in case the feeling wasn't mutual. Searching for a way to vocalize the intensity of her emotions without scaring Rosa, she mumbled, "You're my person." When she felt Rosa's body tense against hers, ever so slightly, she added, "At camp. My camp person."

After a moment of shared silence, Rosa gathered her closer for a brief, heartfelt bear hug. "You're my person, too."

"Good." Eyes still closed, Alice brushed her lips against Rosa's chin, then her mouth, and then cuddled against her chest. "Can we rest for a minute? Not long. I know we need to get back, but…I don't want to move yet."

"I don't, either."

If Alice wasn't so sleepy, she might have wondered more at the waver in Rosa's voice. She might have asked her to talk about what she was thinking or feeling in the aftermath of such an intensely intimate experience. She might have panicked about what would happen after camp was over. But because it was all she could do to stay conscious, she lay her head on Rosa's breast and listened to her heartbeat, reliving everything her new best friend had just made her feel as she drifted off to the soundest, most peaceful sleep of her life.

CHAPTER ELEVEN

Rosa awoke to an odd sensation. A soft, cool pressure slithered across her ankles, then tickled the bottoms of her feet. She frowned without opening her eyes, stretching one leg to nudge at the nuisance— probably the sleeping bag, she decided, having gotten wound around her legs while she slept—before unmistakable *movement* against the top of her foot convinced her that whatever had woken her up was *alive*. Her eyes shot open and she bolted upright, dumping a still-unconscious Alice onto the sleeping bag beside her as she yanked her feet up in sheer panic. At the sight of the freakishly long black-and-white snake that had been cuddling with her toes only seconds before, she let out a mighty, high-pitched scream.

Alice jolted awake with a start and looked around the sunlit room with wide, unfocused eyes. "Rosa? What's wrong?"

Rosa grabbed Alice's arm and pointed. "*Snake!*"

All the tension drained out of Alice's body when her gaze landed on their unwelcome visitor. "Oh, dear." Still naked from the night before, she crawled down and carefully grabbed the snake around the middle of its horrifically slithery length. Using both hands, she gripped it carefully in a position that kept his head well away from her body. Then she stood and took a few steps away from the sleeping bag before turning to face Rosa. "It's only a California king snake. He's harmless, I promise."

"How the *fuck* did he get up here?" Rosa shuddered as she reached for her discarded shirt and bra and pulled on her clothing as hastily as possible. "We're indoors! And upstairs!"

"Hard to say." Alice examined the snake carefully, turning him this way and that, almost in admiration. "He could have hitched a ride with us—maybe he came from the boat?—or it's possible he made his way up here on his own. Snakes can be excellent climbers, given the right surface."

Rosa shuddered even harder as revulsion rolled through her body. "I *hate* snakes."

Alice turned away, blocking Rosa's view of the reptile, and glanced over her shoulder with a sympathetic smile. "I gathered." She scanned the storage area, apparently trying to decide what to do with her scaly charge. "I'd take him outside, but I would want to put some clothes on first…" Her eyes appeared to widen in alarm as her attention drifted to the window. "Rosa, the sun is up!"

"Yes." Eager to speed up their escape from the snake pit, Rosa finished dressing and began to collect Alice's clothes. "I noticed that when I traumatized myself by seeing every detail of that creature molesting my ankles."

"I mean it's *all the way up*." Alice paced nervously back and forth a few steps, still holding the unhappy-looking snake in her outstretched hands. "Everyone is probably awake by now. What if they've already noticed the boat is missing?"

Cursing under her breath, Rosa knelt to roll the sleeping bag while she took multiple nervous peeks out the closest window to study the sky. Alice was right. Somehow, they'd managed to sleep in until well past sunrise, something Rosa really hadn't anticipated needing to worry about. Between her small bladder, occasionally aching back, and lifelong tendency to wake up at least once before the sun, she'd assumed she would be conscious long before it was necessary to return to camp. In all honesty, she'd hoped to initiate a second round of sex before they left, once she'd had the chance to recover for an hour or two. For over a decade now, that had been her modus operandi with a new lover—fuck, pass out, rinse, repeat. *How* had she managed to sleep so peacefully, and for so long, in such unlikely conditions?

"Alice, I'm really sorry." Rosa shouldered the backpack, grabbed the rolled sleeping bag, and hurried to give Alice her clothing. "You're right. I overslept. It's my fault."

"We *both* overslept." Alice's self-consciousness about being the only naked one seemed to catch up with her. Blushing, she gestured toward the door without making eye contact. "Leave my clothes on the floor and go downstairs. I'm going to have put this little guy down before I can dress, so I'll meet you there in a minute." Her gaze darted out the window again. "*Less* than a minute."

It wasn't difficult to detect the extreme stress in Alice's voice. She was *really* worried about returning the boat so late. Not wanting to worsen her anxiety, Rosa did exactly as requested, without comment. She dropped Alice's clothes on the floor at her feet, then hefted the backpack one more time and rushed to the door. "I'll pack up the boat and wait for you there?"

"Perfect." Alice jogged to an empty kayak and bent to set the snake inside. "Go."

Rosa ran downstairs two steps at a time, having no interest in being in the room once her morning visitor again slithered free. Heart hammering, she exhaled in relief when she verified that the lower floor of the boathouse was every bit as empty as it had been the night before. With the sun streaming through the windows, it also didn't look nearly as ominous. Despite the seriousness of their situation, Rosa couldn't help but smile as she thought about Alice and all her beautiful contradictions: afraid of social settings, breaking the rules, and dark, watery garages, yet courageous enough to pick up a random snake *and* conquer a host of anxieties in service of fulfilling her deepest fantasies. All that, and she was in possession of a legitimately brilliant mind like no one Rosa had ever dated before—along with a pussy that tasted like liquid joy.

Rosa's cheer faded as she reached the paddleboat and loaded their supplies. Two years ago, she and Alice might have made a real go of things. Though Rosa had always been the opposite of shy, dating someone with Alice's challenges wouldn't have seemed outside the realm of possibility. In fact, she wagered she would have been good for Alice—maybe even as good as she suspected Alice would be for her. She could have nudged Alice out into the wider world, helped her make new friends, all while loving her the way she had deserved to be loved from the beginning. Perhaps she might have even healed the primal wounds caused by Alice's parents, especially her mother, along with John, who'd clearly never even *tried* to make her feel good. Two years ago, Rosa might have been the best thing to ever happen to Alice, just as Alice was indisputably one of the best things to ever happen to her.

But not now. Today, post-backlash—post-*shame*—Rosa had nothing to offer anyone except stress, misery, humiliation, and heartache. She didn't even want to imagine how Alice would react to some of the threats she'd received in the past, or how she'd feel if she was ever the target of similar promises of brutal rape and murder. How, precisely, that style of harassment and intimidation would worsen the anxiety Alice already struggled so hard to overcome. Rosa didn't want to imagine and refused to find out for sure. She *never* wanted to cause Alice that special brand of pain.

Rosa wasn't only concerned that Alice might be terrorized if they dated. Alice would surely feel embarrassed about being with her. Ashamed. How could Alice—or *anyone*—stand to date someone whose naked body had been subjected to millions of nonconsensual views? Worse than simply witnessing her nudity, strangers around the world had watched a private act in which she'd intentionally performed for the camera, exposing herself in the lewdest ways possible...after she'd railed against the video-game industry for objectifying and oversexualizing their female characters. Consequently, she was a woman whose face, name, and body had been worked into countless hurtful memes. A punchline. Reviled by thousands, exposed to millions, no longer a private citizen but an unwilling laughingstock.

No. She could never drag Alice into that mess.

A soft touch on her back caused Rosa to yelp in shock. She whirled around before relaxing at the sight of Alice standing right behind her.

Alice wore a thin-lipped smile. "Ready?"

"Yes." Rosa walked to the back of the boat and braced her hands against the edge. "Get in. I'll push."

Alice helped her start the forward motion, then hopped over the side and into her seat. As soon as the sandy ground fell away and the boat was afloat, Rosa joined her. They both fit their feet to the pedals and started pumping their legs in silence, neither one saying a word until they were at least twenty feet away from shore.

Finally, chest aching with regret over the way their morning-after had begun, Rosa gave Alice a sidelong glance and a weak smile. "You okay?"

"Yes." Alice's tone was apologetic, but her expression remained tense in spite of the weak grin she managed to direct Rosa's way. "I'm sorry. Just worried about getting caught."

Rosa placed a careful hand on Alice's shoulder. "It'll be all right, Alice. Even if we do get into trouble, I'll take the blame and tell them it was all my idea. You can even slip away and hide. I won't mind, really."

Alice's eyes immediately welled up, and for a moment, Rosa worried that she'd said something wrong. But then Alice looked at her with more love than anyone she'd ever slept with before—more, even, than the girl who'd broken her heart in college—and she realized that what she'd said had been exactly right. And oh-so-treacherous, if they truly intended to part on casual terms the next day. Without slowing her pedaling, Alice touched Rosa's face, a loving caress that made it momentarily difficult to breathe.

Afraid of what she might say, Rosa rushed to cut Alice off before she could speak. "Hopefully everyone will still be at breakfast and we'll be able to slip right in undetected."

"Like you slipped into me last night?" Alice murmured, uncharacteristically sexual in both tone and demeanor. It seemed that Rosa's reassurance had flipped a switch, allowing her to reflect on the reason they'd snuck away in the first place. Alice bit her lip, clearly savoring her memory of the moment of penetration despite their current predicament. "Although, believe me, you were *far* from undetected."

Abandoning caution in the wake of Alice's bold show of desire, Rosa said, "You were so tight." She allowed herself to revisit Alice's flavor, hints of which surely remained all over her face. "And your pussy tasted *so good*."

Predictably, Alice blushed at her blunt language, and *fuck*, Rosa adored that pretty, red-cheeked face. "Really?"

"Absolutely delicious." Rosa slowed her feet to allow the boat to rotate until it pointed directly at the distant docks, then sped up again. "I'd go down on you again in a heartbeat. In fact, I'd drop to my knees right now if we weren't in such a hurry."

For a second Alice's pace faltered, but she recovered quickly. "Stop tempting me to get into even bigger trouble."

Rosa smiled wistfully. "That's how I roll."

They settled into an easy silence as they crawled their way across the lake. As they drew nearer to the opposite shore, Rosa's heart sank at the sight of an indistinct form standing on the boat docks, watching their approach. It appeared that Alice was right. They *were* in trouble. A niggle of dread slithered and twisted in Rosa's stomach like a boathouse snake. It wasn't that she was worried for herself—she could handle being scolded—but she hated to think of Alice having to endure any amount of discomfort because of something she did.

Rosa swallowed thickly. "I'm so sorry about whatever happens next."

"No apologies." Alice's hand landed on hers, gripping tight. "It was *my* choice to take the boat. I desperately wanted last night to happen, so I took a risk. Then I overslept, just like you did. If you hadn't woken us up, I might have slept another hour or more." Her voice softened. "Last night really wore me out."

Rosa squinted as the form on the dock began to take shape: a blond counselor whose arms appeared to be folded across her chest. "I shouldn't have fallen asleep." She hadn't intended to, but the peace and sanctuary of Alice's embrace had lulled her into blissful slumber against her will. "I should have been more careful."

The fingers covering her knuckles tensed. "Don't, please." Alice tried to sound lighthearted, but the quaver in her voice gave away her rising anxiety. "You said everything would be all right."

Aware that her self-recrimination was only making Alice feel worse, Rosa exhaled at length. "It will. I'll handle it." Compared to everything she'd been through over the past eighteen months, the thought of dealing with an angry camp counselor—Marcia, she realized, the exceedingly bubbly one—didn't even make her break a sweat. What bothered her, and what she simply couldn't handle, was to see Alice suffer and know she was the cause. "When we reach the dock, get out of the boat and walk away. I'll take the verbal beat-down and meet you at breakfast."

"No, I'll..." Even without looking, Rosa could hear Alice summoning all the bravery she possessed. "I'll stay with you. I won't abandon you like that."

"But I can handle it." Rosa lowered her voice as they got closer to the dock, not wanting Marcia, who now looked exceedingly *impatient*, to overhear their argument. "You can't."

Alice scoffed and released her hand. "Don't tell me what I *can't* handle."

Rosa cringed at the hurt beneath Alice's words, the very emotion she'd never wanted to inflict. "I'm sorry, I just..."

"You want to protect me," Alice murmured. She smiled at Rosa, eyes sparkling with a mixture of fear and elation. "But I can take care of myself. Honestly."

The angry lilt of Marcia's normally sunny voice silenced any reply Rose might have offered. "Good morning, ladies."

Rosa waited for a reprimand, but when none came, she replied with a simple, "Good morning to you."

Marcia wore a tight-lipped smile as they pedaled up alongside her, and she dropped to her knees to help moor the boat to the dock. "Funny, but I remember seeing both of you at the opening ceremony on Thursday evening when I went over the rules here at Camp Rewind."

Rosa snuck a sidelong glance at Alice, who sat in silence, her face bright red and her eyes cast down in shame. It was clear that despite Alice's determination to remain at her side for this tongue-lashing, Rosa would be speaking for both of them. "I'm so sorry. I never intended to stay out overnight—"

"All the paddleboats were accounted for at sunset yesterday evening before the bonfire." Marcia tightened the capable knot she'd fashioned, then offered Alice a hand to help her out of the boat. "Which means you must have taken this one *after* dark. Since you both attended the opening ceremony and therefore heard me read the rules, I can only assume you realized you were breaking more than one of them by doing so."

"I apologize." Rosa had no plans to offer a defense, only to take her punishment in whatever form it came. "It was my idea, completely, and I never meant—"

"To get caught," Marcia said, snippily. "I'm sure that's true." She reached into the boat's storage area and retrieved the rolled-up sleeping bag and the backpack full of supplies. "Well, you girls certainly *packed* for an overnight excursion."

Rosa frowned, fed up with both the interrogation and Marcia's condescending tone. Alice looked ready to jump into the lake to escape the reprimand, making Rosa wish she'd taken the advice to simply run away. Sighing, she climbed out of the boat and onto the dock so she was on more even footing with the counselor. "I wanted to take my friend stargazing away from the drinking and the noise. The sleeping bag was a place to lie on the hard ground while we looked up at the sky. We'd intended to bring the boat back right away, but after an hour or so out there, we fell asleep by accident. That's all."

"Uh-huh. Stargazing, really?" Marcia looked them both up and down as though trying to judge their true intentions. "Can you ladies appreciate what it's like to wake up to the news that not only are two of my campers missing, but one of my boats, as well?"

Alice hung her head so low that her dark hair curtained her face and hid her rosy cheeks. The sight tore into Rosa, bringing her protective instincts to the front. Rather than be intimidated, Rosa threw back her shoulders and, in an even tone, said, "Look, Marcia, we're all adults here. I took a boat when I shouldn't have, stayed out longer than I should have, and now I'm trying to take responsibility and apologize so we can all move on. Give me my demerits or hard labor or whatever punishment you think is appropriate, but please, stop berating us. A little shame goes a long way, don't you think?" Willing Marcia to show some compassion, she gestured subtly at Alice, who trembled, her narrow shoulders bowed. "This was *my* fault. If you want to kick me out of camp, I'll leave. Just *tell me* what you want."

Marcia seemed taken aback by her directness. Her mouth opened, but no sound came out. After a moment, she cleared her throat and her features lost their harsh edge. "It's a liability issue. Do you understand?"

"Completely." Rosa made eye contact so that Marcia would both see and hear her sincerity. "I swear that nothing like this will happen again…if I'm allowed to stay."

She didn't miss the alarm that flashed across Alice's partially obscured face in response to the suggestion that Rosa might be expelled from Camp Rewind. Rosa shared her anguish at the thought. Once she left camp, their time together was over. Best-case scenario, Rosa stayed and they had thirty or so hours more to savor their connection before it faded into the realm of bittersweet memory. But if Marcia made her leave now, they would be trading good-byes within the hour—which felt *far* too soon after all they'd shared the night before.

Sadly, that probably meant their separation was already long overdue.

Guts churning, Rosa refused to break eye contact with Marcia while she awaited the verdict. If she got expelled from camp, at least she wouldn't have another magical night of falling for Alice Wu to sharpen the agony of the inevitable. Yet she knew that Alice would be disappointed, if not devastated, by the type of swift, decisive break she would most likely have to deliver in the parking lot after she'd packed her car. Rosa didn't want that, either. Granted, both of them would eventually experience the pain of saying good-bye, one way or the other. It was simply a question of when. None of the options in front of her seemed appealing in any way, except for the fantasy where she continued to see Alice despite her fucked-up life and nobody suffered any terrible consequences.

"You can stay," Marcia said, looking back and forth between her and Alice. "Both of you. But no more boating privileges, either of you, for the rest of the weekend."

"That's fair," Alice replied in a whisper Rosa suspected only her ears had detected.

"Very fair," Rosa echoed. "Thank you."

"Oh, I'm not done yet." Marcia gave them a syrupy smile, and Rosa had to force her nose not to wrinkle in response. "As I'm sure you both know, today is field day—'drunk field day,' as some of the campers like to call it, for obvious reasons—and we could use some help manning the refreshments booth. Since you two enjoy being away from the drinking and noise, anyway, I'm sure you wouldn't mind taking the first shift. All you have to do is hand out bottles of water, distribute towels to people participating in the water-balloon toss or the watermelon-eating contest, and take care of any trash you see in the area."

"All right." Rosa's stomach sank at the knowledge that such a socially involved punishment would be sheer torture for Alice, and not terribly fun for herself, either. The task would put her into contact with almost the entire camp population, vastly increasing her risk of being recognized by an Internet-savvy gamer type. The very last thing she wanted was for Alice to be right there next to her if the worst came to pass. "I can do that, but please…taking the boat *was* all my idea, and Alice is super shy. Maybe she could sit this one out?"

"No, it's all right." Alice spoke so softly Rosa had to strain to hear. "I'll work the booth with Lila."

"Great!" Marcia clapped her hands together, then shooed them toward the shore. "Breakfast will be over in thirty minutes, so I suggest you trot along and grab something to nibble. You'll report to Counselor Sandy by the main athletic field at ten forty-five, in the clearing behind the archery range. Do you know where that is?"

"Yes, ma'am." At this point Rosa was finding it hard to keep her sour mood out of her tone. She continued to try solely for Alice's sake. "I'll be there."

"Excellent. Run along now, my little delinquents." Marcia winked at Alice, patronizing till the end. "You've got a busy day ahead of you."

Rosa's empathy urged her not to keep Alice there one second longer. Taking her by the hand, Rosa led them away from Marcia as fast as their feet could carry them. With visible effort, Alice lifted her head and pushed her hair out of her face with her free hand, taking slow, deliberate breaths in a clear effort to calm her nerves. Once they were out of Marcia's line of sight and alone among the trees, Rosa tugged Alice to a stop. She took Alice by the shoulders and stared into her eyes, trying to determine exactly how badly she'd screwed things up. That had been exactly the sort of interaction Alice normally followed the rules to avoid. If not for Rosa, she wouldn't have had to withstand Marcia's pointed remarks or receive a punishment seemingly designed to torment her. Even here at camp, Rosa had managed to inject unnecessary drama and turmoil into Alice's quiet existence.

Proof that she really *was* poisonous to those she cared about.

"Are you all right?" Alice asked, stealing the question from Rosa's lips. "You seem really upset."

Rosa barked helpless laughter, her mind spinning at the role reversal and her tumultuous emotional state. "I was going to say the same thing to you."

"I'm fine." Alice stared at her, naked concern painted across her face. "Getting yelled at wasn't exactly *fun*, but I survived."

Rosa caressed Alice's cheek tenderly. The lingering heat of the shame Marcia had so effortlessly induced scorched Rosa's fingers, burning at her conscience with a fury that left her nauseated. "I wish you'd just let me handle it. You should have walked away, like I told you to."

"First of all, I'm not sure Marcia would have gone for that. She was scolding both of us, and if I'd simply walked away during her lecture, I'm certain it would have turned out much worse. For me *and* you."

She was right, of course, but Rosa couldn't let go of her guilt over having put Alice in the position to be dressed down like that in the first place. Angry at herself, at Marcia, even at Alice, Rosa said, "We should never have taken the boat. It was a stupid idea." She turned to storm off toward the cafeteria, but Alice caught her wrist before she could leave.

"Rosa, wait." When Rosa refused to turn around, Alice stepped in front of her, angling her head to force eye contact. "You remember that taking the boat was actually *my* idea, right? *I* was the one who made the initial suggestion, at least. I'm not saying it wasn't stupid, but... seriously, stop beating yourself up." Alice hesitated and then, after a beat, added, "As far as I'm concerned, it was all worth it. Last night was the greatest experience of my life—by far—and *completely* worth getting in trouble over. All right?"

Rosa nodded, surprised by how difficult it was not to look away from Alice's piercing gaze. "I'm glad you feel that way."

"How do *you* feel?" Alice asked, and for a second Rosa's heart dropped at the blunt question, until Alice said, "About having to work the refreshments booth this afternoon. I saw the look on your face when Marcia suggested it. Given your worries about being recognized, I assume you're concerned about being right in the middle of the action like that."

"It's no big deal," Rosa lied. "Even if someone *does* think they know me, chances are they'd never bring it up to my face. In case they were wrong, I mean." She managed a halfhearted chuckle as she envisioned reliving a mortifying scenario she'd actually encountered before. More than once. "That would be kind of awkward, don't you think? 'Hey, aren't you the whore who fingered herself in that viral video?'" She tried to ignore the shock that briefly passed over Alice's face, not wanting to feel tempted to interpret its meaning. "Anyway, I'm sure everything will be fine. Even if someone *does* say something, I'm a big girl. I can handle it."

Alice's chin wobbled for the briefest moment, long enough for Rosa to see. "Rosa, honestly, why don't you let me...I can do the punishment myself. I'll say you got sick and had to go lie down for a while."

"Don't be ridiculous."

Alice blinked, clearly hurt by Rosa's sharp reply. "I'm *serious*."

Rosa closed her eyes, both touched and frustrated by the offer. She'd rather die than allow Alice to take on any of her burden, but it meant everything that she would even consider setting aside her own fears in order to protect Rosa from harm. "No, sweetheart," she murmured, the endearment falling from her lips without thought. "I could never ask you to do that."

"You're not asking. I'm offering."

Rosa was afraid to open her eyes, certain they would spill the tears elicited by Alice's earnest tone. "I know. I still can't let you suffer through that alone." Sniffing, she wiped a hand over her face and looked at Alice with a sober expression. "What upset me most about Marcia's choice of punishment was knowing how much you would hate being forced to interact with other people all afternoon. That's why I asked her to let you off the hook. So truly, as much as I appreciate the sweet offer…"

"Understood." Alice took a tentative step forward and opened her arms. "For the record, I didn't want to be let off the hook because that would have meant less time to spend with you."

Rosa's chest swelled until her heart felt like it might burst. She was heartened by the comment, especially the way it seemed to acknowledge the limited lifespan of their friendship, and felt the wall she'd spent the morning trying to erect crumble a bit. Caught between enjoying their last full day together and preparing her heart for the impending split, she nonetheless found it impossible not to pull Alice into a tight, emotional embrace. Defeated for the time being, she mumbled, "I would have missed you, too."

Alice relaxed noticeably and rested against Rosa's chest as she trailed soft kisses up the line of her jaw to a spot just behind her ear. She paused to breathe, "As long as you're with me, I'll be fine."

Rosa cringed, unwilling to see herself as some kind of savior. Not when she was anything but. "It's *because* you're with me that you're in trouble at all."

Alice sighed, then murmured, "You know, we *could* simply leave camp. No one is forcing us to stay."

Frightened by the implication of Alice's suggestion, Rosa shut down her vocal discontent about their afternoon plans. She wasn't yet ready to have a hard conversation about why they couldn't leave camp together, particularly because she feared cheating herself out of the rest of the only morning-after—not to mention the only *Saturday*—they would ever share. Calling up a smile she hoped appeared far calmer than she felt, Rosa pulled back so she could see Alice's face. "No, we should stay. I'm not ready to go home yet." When Alice opened her mouth to respond, Rosa grabbed her hand and entangled their fingers, leading her in the direction of the cafeteria. "Come on. I don't want to miss breakfast. I worked up a crazy appetite last night."

Alice squeezed Rosa's hand, matching her pace to stay close by her side. "Funny, when from where I was lying, it looked like you had plenty to eat."

Rosa groaned, unprepared yet again for Alice's newly wicked sense of humor. "You've turned into quite the saucy little minx, haven't you?"

"Because of you." Alice swung their joined hands in a spontaneous burst of jubilation. She seemed to have recovered from their encounter with Marcia already, which was more than a little surprising. *Shocking* might be the better word. Only two nights ago, Alice could barely utter a full sentence in Rosa's presence. The morning after that, she'd run away to hide for over an hour before only reluctantly re-engaging in conversation. Now, after one night of admittedly tremendous sex, Alice had somehow transformed into a bouncy, vivacious flirt. Even if this new and improved Alice was on display for Rosa's eyes only, her playful attitude represented a tremendous breakthrough.

Because of me. Rosa tried not to dwell on how Alice would feel when they parted ways, while at the same time wondering how, exactly, Alice felt about the fact that their weekend together was more than half over. It was possible that Alice didn't actually want anything to do with her at all after tomorrow, even if her words and actions seemed to hint otherwise. In reality, Rosa couldn't fathom that Alice was totally zen about the prospect of trading abrupt good-byes with the first real friend she'd ever made, let alone the woman who'd taken her lesbian virginity—and, in the process, given her the first non-self-induced orgasms she'd ever experienced.

Rosa's long-simmering apprehension exploded into full-blown dread when she realized how terribly, painfully selfish she'd been in her handling of Alice Wu. In her eagerness to recapture a happier, simpler time for herself, she'd toyed with the emotions of a woman who seemed all but guaranteed to want more than she could currently offer. Even if Alice hadn't yet asked for anything beyond a single weekend of fun, Rosa was suddenly, horrifyingly certain that a request for *more*— whatever form that might take—was practically inevitable. Had she really expected Alice to be satisfied with an abruptly terminated four-day friendship after a lifetime of unhappy solitude? With a speedy, transcendent fling, then a voluntary return to celibacy? Alice seemed overjoyed this morning, despite their misadventure, almost like she was a different person.

Rosa tried to imagine whether Alice's newfound confidence would persist even after she was forced to reject a hypothetical request to carry their relationship into the real world. She imagined that would be a huge blow for Alice, to be discarded after a weekend of physical intimacy and close friendship. Hell, it would be a huge blow for *Rosa*, and she was used to being treated that way.

Shit. Rosa tried not to let her inner despair show on her face. *What have I done?*

Left squarely in the center of a mess of her own making, she hadn't the slightest idea how to engineer a clean getaway. Part of her didn't even *want* to get away. But after the terrible guilt she'd felt back at the dock at the sight of Alice's mortification, it seemed clearer than ever that making a definitive break was the right thing to do, even if she crushed Alice in the process. Becoming a part of Rosa's tragic existence would mean certain humiliation and terror for who-knew-how-many years, and she simply wasn't willing to put anyone through that—*especially* Alice. Ending their association cleanly was the only solution, if she cared for this woman at all. It was deeply unfortunate that her own selfish stupidity had created a situation in which causing Alice tremendous pain was unavoidable, but tomorrow would be better than later. Better than after they'd fallen in love.

It *had* to be.

CHAPTER TWELVE

In a way, Alice was relieved that she now had a built-in excuse to skip the physical hijinks and hilarity of drunk field day. Passing out water and towels to the so far only mildly intoxicated campers was nerve-wracking enough, but to actually participate in a tipsy three-legged race or water-balloon toss would have been so much worse. Embarrassed by the boorishness of a pair of male campers who stood nearby catcalling a trio of women whose tank tops had been soaked through by errant balloons, Alice doggedly narrowed her focus to the stack of dry towels she'd just refolded, then to Rosa's unusually silent presence at her side. She sensed that something was bothering Rosa, but every attempt she'd made to inquire about her state of mind had been shut down immediately. By now, Alice detected a constant, low-level tension between the two of them that hadn't existed prior to that morning, though she wasn't entirely sure what had happened to set it off.

Maybe she's simply had her fill of me. Alice was worried, and not for the first time. *She got what she wanted, right? Perhaps she's too polite to tell me that she wishes I'd leave her alone so she could try hooking up with someone else before the weekend is over.* As much as she didn't want to believe that could be true—*didn't*, in fact, believe it at all—the increasingly awkward silences coupled with Rosa's apparent reluctance to touch her were beginning to feel meaningful in a way that left Alice thoroughly disturbed. At first she'd hoped Rosa's fear of being unmasked at the refreshments booth had caused her strange mood, but Alice could no longer convince herself that the risk of exposure was

Rosa's only problem. *Alice* was the problem. She could feel it—even if she wasn't sure what she'd done wrong.

Logically, she knew that even if Rosa didn't want to see her again after tomorrow—or even after this morning—it didn't necessarily mean she had misstepped in any way. Rosa had never presented their fling as anything other than a casual, short-term hookup, most likely because that's exactly what she wanted it to be. *But what if that's* not *what Rosa wants?* A tiny, hopeful voice piped up from deep down inside, where Alice filed away all her impossible hopes and dreams. *What if she's behaving so oddly because she hates the thought of saying good-bye every bit as much as I do?*

Unfortunately, Alice wasn't sure that was the correct explanation, either. Not after the way Rosa had been so hard on herself since the moment they'd woken up in the boathouse. Secretly, she suspected that Rosa was still beating herself up over their botched heist and the consequences it had produced. Not only that, but she'd seemingly convinced herself that she was bad for Alice. In spite of multiple attempts to argue otherwise, Rosa had apparently drawn the conclusion that her net effect on Alice's life was negative. But over one stolen boat? A single, albeit humiliating, reprimand? Alice wanted to confront her about the topic directly, but not while surrounded by the laughter and revelry of their peers. Checking the wristwatch she'd purchased especially for camp, Alice grumbled under her breath at the realization that they were only thirty minutes into a three-hour punishment.

"If you need to take a break, please feel free." Rosa never looked away from the cup of water she was pouring for a sweaty, appreciative man who continued to shout loud encouragement at the two remaining balloon-toss teams. "I've got this."

Alice frowned at what was beginning to feel like a pattern of Rosa encouraging her to leave. Either Rosa was over their friendship and wanted her to fuck off now, or she didn't want Alice around to watch if someone *did* happen to confront her about her Internet fame, or, most innocently, she simply wanted to spare Alice from a task she admittedly wasn't enjoying in the least. No matter Rosa's motivation, Alice didn't want to go. She hated the thought of missing even a single moment of what time they had left at Camp Rewind, because more and more, it felt like the next twenty-seven hours were all she would get of Rosa. "No, I'm good."

"Okay." When her customer left with his water, still shouting, Rosa flashed Alice a brief smile. "Hanging in there?"

"Totally." Alice forced a big grin. When a cheer arose from the crowd surrounding the water-balloon tossers, she resisted the urge to look at the hectic scene, not wanting to sharpen the unease she already felt about her and Rosa's stiffer-than-normal interaction. Something was off, definitely. "Lila," she said, mindful of their surroundings. "May I ask you something?"

Rosa darted her gaze this way and that before finally, reluctantly, meeting her eyes. "Sure."

Alice bit her lip, suddenly convinced that she'd misread absolutely everything about their relationship. *When someone tries to get rid of you, isn't the polite thing to go?* Taking a deep breath, she girded her heart for a crushing blow. "Am I bothering you? I mean…do you *want* me to leave you alone?"

Rosa's features softened, and for a moment, she was once again the woman Alice had started to consider her one true friend. Which was *not* a smart way to feel about someone she'd met at a hookup camp, admittedly, but their time together had liberated Alice's heart in every way. She'd undeniably grown to care about Rosa. Alice didn't even want—or know how—to try to change that.

Smiling kindly, Rosa murmured, "No, Alice. I don't want you to leave." One side of her mouth lifted in what looked like reluctant amusement. "You're my camp person. Remember?"

Alice wanted to tell Rosa that she wouldn't mind being *more* than her camp person, but it wasn't a good idea, and definitely not the right time. Honestly, it might *never* be the right time to make that sort of proclamation, but Alice figured it was better to take the risk tomorrow while they said their good-byes than to do it when they still had the entire night ahead of them. Maybe she'd have an opportunity to be alone with Rosa again, even if she wasn't certain where they'd find enough privacy to do everything she wanted to do. Perhaps she would eschew the need for privacy altogether, she mused, if the alternative was to never experience the taste and feel of Rosa's body again.

She started to tell Rosa that, hoping to entice her with the promise of more pleasure if only she'd stick around a while longer, when their next patrons arrived. Enid beamed happily within Bree's one-armed embrace, waving as they approached the booth. "Hey, ladies."

Alice returned her smile easily, less intimidated by the gregarious older woman than most of the other campers. "Hello, Enid." She flicked her attention to Bree as an instinctive blush rose on her cheeks. "Bree."

"Shy Alice, Ms. Lila, what's up?" Bree dropped her hand to pat Enid on the ass, a move that seemed to delight Enid. "Me and my girl here just dominated the water-balloon toss. It turns out Enid has a deceptively strong arm, among her many other compelling skills."

"Congratulations," Rosa said, handing each woman a cold cup of water. "On both accounts."

"Why, thank you." Bree knocked back the contents of her cup as a man Alice recognized as Derek—whom Rosa had previously pointed out as her would-be suitor from their first morning at camp—walked up to the booth, soaking wet above the waist. At the sight of him, Bree's face lit up. "Hey, look. Here comes second place."

"Ha ha." Derek gave the entire group a good-natured grin as he shook water out of his short, dark hair. "You two were tough competition, I'll give you that."

Rosa reached across Alice to hand Derek a dry, neatly folded towel. "Better at riding than tossing, I see."

Bree chortled at what Alice assumed was a naughty innuendo, even if she didn't entirely understand its meaning. "Put *that* on your online-dating profile."

As Enid hid a giggle behind her hand, Derek gave Rosa a cocky, self-assured bow. "To tell you the truth, I've never fielded a single complaint about *any* part of my repertoire."

"I'll bet." Rosa winked at him, but rather than be jealous in any way, Alice felt only admiration for Rosa's easy manner with people and pride for having managed to catch the attention of such an extraordinary soul despite her own awkward nature. "But I'm guessing water balloons aren't a normal part of that repertoire?"

The group laughed when Derek agreed with an exaggerated sigh. "A new skill to hone, obviously."

"Only if you want to win the hearts of easily impressed women everywhere," Bree said.

Seeing an opportunity to contribute, Alice supplied a fun fact. "In ancient Greece, young, marriageable women were occasionally offered as prizes for all types of competitions. A terrible practice, for obvious reasons, which probably only rarely called for the skill set required to both toss a water balloon with precision and catch it with the appropriate care."

She stopped talking abruptly, aware of how many words she'd just said and how ridiculous each one had sounded. Still on a natural high from the past twelve hours—even with the joint she'd taken along with them the night before yet unlit—Alice subverted her usual instincts and kept talking on the off chance something worthwhile would come out. "But anyway, I wouldn't bother to hone your tossing skills. There's something to be said for the appeal of a wet male torso when it comes to winning a woman's heart, easily impressed or otherwise."

Derek broke into a toothy grin before striking a bodybuilder's pose in his soaked T-shirt, the thin cotton plastered to his vaguely defined pectoral muscles. "Right on, sister." He conducted a less-than-subtle inspection, scanning Alice up and down, and dissolved into a softer smile as they finally locked eyes. "I like you. What's your name? And do you happen to enjoy a good toss every now and again?"

Rosa moved to Alice's side, wrapping an arm around her waist to pull her close. "I like her, too. A lot."

Warmed by the show of possessiveness only because it proved that Rosa still cared, Alice tried not to let too much of her satisfaction infect the conciliatory smile she gave Derek. "My name is Alice. And yeah, sorry, I'm taken." She hesitated, paranoid that she'd just spooked Rosa with the bold declaration. Scrambling to mitigate any damage she might have caused, she added, "At least for the rest of the weekend."

Rosa tensed almost imperceptibly when Derek gave Alice a friendly, hope-tinged grin. "Well, since that doesn't sound like a *total* brush-off..." He backed away from the booth, still rubbing the towel over his damp hair. "I think I'll quit while I'm ahead. Catch you later, ladies." He directed a parting smile in Alice's direction. "Alice, it was a pleasure meeting you."

Alice could only tip her head, too shy to manage a verbal response while Bree and Enid stared at her. Once Derek was out of earshot, Alice turned to Rosa and said, "You're right, Lila. He's a total flirt."

"I'm pretty sure *you're* the one who started the flirting." Rosa's tone was difficult to read. She was either impressed with Alice, or annoyed, or possibly some combination of both. "Clearly you've got more game than you let on."

Bree and Enid exchanged bemused looks, and then Bree grabbed

Enid's hand to tug her toward the raucous activity on the field. "Come on, darling. The three-legged race awaits." As they walked away, she pinned Enid with a lascivious stare that made Alice long for the time, mere hours ago, when Rosa had gazed at her the same way. "Win or lose, I plan to enjoy my first experience having a sexy woman tied to my leg."

When they were gone, Alice turned to Rosa with an apologetic frown. "I'm sorry if I upset you by flirting with Derek. I wasn't trying to hurt you, just...fit in. It was something to say, not an intentional come-on. I would *never* hit on someone else right in front of you. I couldn't stand to hurt you like that."

Rosa shook her head, guilt tightening her beautiful features. "No, sweetheart, *I'm* sorry. I had no right to act like a jealous dick. It's not like I have any claim on you. Even if I did, you have every right to flirt with whoever you want." She exhaled, forcing an easy smile. "Honestly, I'm proud of you. Dawn will be, too. I know it's only been a couple days, but you've really blossomed here at camp. You've *grown*." She hesitated, then said, "Maybe you *should* get Derek's number. He seems like a nice enough guy."

Though it was obvious from the expression on her face that Rosa hadn't enjoyed making it, the suggestion still hit Alice like a punch to the stomach. "I don't want to date Derek." Sure of at least one thing after last night, Alice clarified her comment. "For one thing, I'm a lesbian."

Warmth bloomed in Rosa's gaze, a look of genuine pride. "Congratulations, Alice." Winking, she momentarily regained her light mood. "I can't say I didn't see that one coming."

"All credit to you." Alice didn't miss the way Rosa cringed at her words, as though she literally couldn't stand to hear any praise. Lowering her voice, Alice said, "Look...if I hadn't met you, I'd probably still be hiding behind a tree somewhere. And that's only if I hadn't left camp already. Everything I've accomplished this weekend, all that I've experienced, is thanks to my time with you. That includes being able to confirm what I'd suspected for a while now." She drew Rosa into a tight hug, beyond caring that everyone around them could see. Let them look. If there was any way to convince Rosa that their friendship made Alice's life objectively *better*, she had to try. "I'm not entirely sure why the incident this morning with Marcia has shaken you so badly, or why you've been quiet and ruminating all afternoon, or even why you've apparently decided you're bad for me despite all the times I've told you otherwise, but *please*, believe me, the world is brighter with you in it. *My* world is brighter."

Rosa stiffened against her a full second before the catcalling duo turned their vocal attentions toward them.

"Check it out, motherfuckers. We got some lesbo action happening right over here!" The louder of the two men, already soused, hooted as Alice quickly backed out of their embrace. "No, don't stop, girls! Give us a little titty action next."

His friend doubled over laughing at the fierce glare Rosa directed their way. "Yeah, rub your boobs together! Or whatever it is you ladies do when there's no man around to take care of you."

"Like actually enjoy ourselves?" Rosa called out, anger seeping into her tone. "Here's a better idea. Why don't you and your BFF go tie your legs together so you can give us a little douches-hitting-the-ground action?"

Already shaken by the men's crude comments, Alice shrank back at the unambiguous challenge in Rosa's jibe. When the men scowled at each other before advancing on their booth, she put a shaking hand on Rosa's back and rubbed it in a timid attempt to calm her down. "Ignore them," she whispered. "Please."

"Relax, bitch," the first man said as he sauntered up to the counter. "And fetch me some water."

Glowering, Rosa thrust an already-filled cup at him with so much force that liquid sloshed over the edges and onto his hand. "Enjoy."

The man chugged the remainder of the water in two gulps, then tossed the empty cup onto the ground behind Alice. Without thinking, she bent to retrieve it, eliciting a wolf whistle from both him and his friend. "*Thoroughly* enjoyed that, as a matter of fact." The drunken cad blew Alice a kiss when she rose to her feet and whirled to face them. "Thanks for the view, sweet cheeks."

Alice gasped when Rosa lunged over the counter and grabbed a handful of the man's shirt, yanking him close to snarl into his face. "Get the fuck out of here before I report you for harassment. Don't think I won't."

As Rosa held the clearly startled lout in her grasp, his friend's eyes shimmered with sudden, hazy recognition. "Holy fucking shit.

Aren't you that chick from the Internet?" When Rosa released the first man's shirt, openly shaken by the accusation, his buddy's mouth dropped open while simultaneously widening with glee. "The feminazi with that solo-masturbation video I used to jerk off to last year! Rose something-or-another."

It felt like the world was crumbling around them as Alice watched all the color drain from Rosa's face. This was Rosa's worst-case scenario come to life. The very idea that this could happen had nearly prevented her from getting past Camp Rewind's front entrance two days ago, and now here she was, living out her nightmare with Alice here to witness every excruciating second. Though her heart thudded more violently than she'd realized was possible and her entire body quivered with adrenaline, all of Alice's normal self-preservation instincts faded away, leaving behind only the urgent need to defend Rosa.

In as steady and clear a voice as she could manage, Alice said, "My girlfriend's name is Lila, we've been together since college, and she's too shy to let me take pictures of her at the beach, let alone make naked videos." Alice narrowed her eyes at the men and stepped in front of Rosa to block her from their view. At a loss about what to do next, she brightened when she spotted Sandy, the no-nonsense, crew-cut counselor who'd helped set them up at the refreshments booth, watching from a short distance away. Alice waved her over, eager to summon an authority figure onto the scene. Then, buoyed by her unexpected show of strength under pressure, she added, "I'm sure both of you paid the same exorbitant registration fee we did for the privilege of spending the weekend here. It would be a shame not to get your money's worth because you just *had* to get drunk and run your mouths. I've already had the misfortune of seeing Marcia, the head counselor, get really pissed off. You don't want to make the same mistake."

The guy who'd recognized Rosa continued to crane in an effort to look around Alice so he could see her face, but the other man elbowed him sharply when Sandy made her entrance. The imposing counselor put her hands on her narrow hips and stared down the two jerks. "Problem, gentlemen?"

"No, sir," snarked the man as he yanked his buddy away from the booth. "Just a misunderstanding."

"Fair enough. Keep your misunderstandings far away from these two for the rest of your stay. Got it?"

"Yup." Rosa's "fan" leered at them over Sandy's shoulder as he and his friend stumbled away. "Not her, my ass. I'd recognize that dimple on her cheek anywhere."

"Which cheek?" The friend guffawed.

"At any rate, I got bored with that vid at least eight months ago. Didn't get me hard anymore," he said loudly enough for everyone to hear. "Though you'd better believe I'm watching it again when I get home. For confirmation."

Rosa wilted as soon as the men were far enough away that their voices no longer carried. Concerned for her, and shaken—yet still riding a wave of elation over the fact that she'd been able to rise to the occasion and protect her friend—Alice turned as Rosa gave Sandy a weary nod. "Thanks."

"If they bother either of you again, let me know and I'll take care of it." Sandy granted them each a gentle smile. "You two make a really cute couple. I want all the memories you take home from Camp Rewind to be happy ones."

Alice blushed at the realization that Sandy probably assumed they were in a real relationship. Before she could correct the mistake, Rosa said, "We appreciate that, truly."

Sandy lingered by the booth for another few minutes, and when it appeared that the bullies had indeed moved on, bid them good-bye with an apologetic nod. "I need to go make my rounds, ladies. Make sure nobody's fallen where they can't get up or puked anywhere someone might step in it."

Alice wrinkled her nose while Rosa summed up her unspoken disgust. "Drunk field day is gross."

Sandy smiled sympathetically. "It sure can be." She waved as she wandered away to search for a situation in need of her expertise. "Stay out of trouble, you two. One more hour and I'll let you go a little early, okay?"

Alice sighed as gratitude swept over her. "I can't wait." Taking advantage of their relative privacy, she caught Rosa's hand and laced their fingers together like they really *had* been doing this for years. "You all right?"

Rosa looked down at the ground. "I'm so sorry you had to deal with that. But…it meant a lot that you said what you did."

"I'm sorry *you* had to deal with it." Alice squeezed Rosa's hand mildly. "Those guys sucked, but I survived. How about you?"

With a listless shrug, Rosa mumbled, "I've been better."

Worried about Rosa's state of mind, Alice decided that a change of scenery was in order. That, and social isolation. Kissing, too. Intentionally brightening her tone, Alice said, "Want to take a walk into the woods after Sandy lets us go? I'm almost positive my bar for privacy has been lowered substantially since yesterday."

Rosa stunned her by tearing up, biting her lip, then finally pressing the back of Alice's hand against her mouth. She exhaled shakily and closed her eyes. When she finally spoke, it sounded as though the effort caused her physical pain. "Alice…" Alice dreaded what she would hear once Rosa managed to utter the rest of what she had to say, certain that nothing capable of putting that much sadness into her soulful brown eyes could possibly feel good to hear.

She was right—it didn't feel good, at all, when Rosa suddenly delivered both a perfect cliché and the kiss of death in four succinct words. "We need to talk."

CHAPTER THIRTEEN

Unfortunately, they couldn't *really* talk until after Sandy had released them from duty. Rosa knew that even before she blurted out the dreaded phrase, but the large, laughing group of men and women who stumbled up to their booth while the statement still hung in the air—while Alice stood there, mouth agape, undoubtedly struggling to parse its meaning—made it excruciatingly obvious that she'd chosen the most inopportune moment possible to drop that kind of bomb. Avoiding Alice's gaze, Rosa silently poured cups of water for the crowd. After a beat, Alice joined her. When their steady stream of customers finally thinned out, then vanished altogether, Rosa spent an awkward minute tidying up without speaking. She was afraid to return to the topic she'd foolishly introduced too soon.

Finally, Alice broke the silence. "That sounded ominous."

Rosa tried not to wince. She *really* shouldn't have said anything until they were alone. Then again, she'd been worried all afternoon that once they *were*, she'd simply lose the nerve to initiate the difficult conversation they needed to have. As much as she wanted to let go of all her hang-ups and enjoy one last day with Alice—maybe even sneak off and fuck her again—after the morning they'd had, Rosa couldn't help but feel like the most selfish asshole in the world for even considering the idea. It was clear that she meant a great deal to Alice and, with each passing minute, increasingly apparent that Alice would be more than happy to see their fling extend beyond the weekend. Despite the obvious caution she'd shown with her words, Alice had hinted at her desire for an impossible future in a dozen subtle ways. Unfortunately, even *Rosa* had slipped a couple times, dropping casual comments as though they might actually have a shared "after camp" to look forward to.

Stupid. She'd been so *stupid.*

It had to stop. *Now.*

Unable to look Alice in the face, Rosa said, "I know."

When Alice spoke again, her voice sounded thick. "Have I done something wrong?"

"No, Alice." Chest burning, Rosa poured water into a handful of cups she'd arranged in a circle, almost wishing for more campers to interrupt them. "You haven't done anything wrong. I promise." She swallowed thickly, hating herself for what she was about to say. "It's me." Another cliché.

"Is this because Marcia caught us?" Alice sounded so sad, so beseeching. "Or because of what that jerk just said to you?" After a beat, she touched Rosa's shoulder. Tenderly, she said, "You know that doesn't matter to me, right?"

Rosa shrugged away without thinking, too ashamed to accept her kindness. She didn't turn around, not wanting to see the hurt she knew must be etched across Alice's beautiful face. "I know, but it matters to *me.*"

"So…" Even without looking, Rosa could hear exactly how much pain she'd inflicted. Alice whispered, "You *don't* want to hang out with me anymore?"

Closing her eyes, Rosa pulled back from the situation and, in a moment of sickening clarity, viscerally *understood* exactly how callous she must seem. She'd taken Alice's lesbian virginity not much more than thirteen hours ago, becoming only the second person her new friend had ever slept with. Now, the very next afternoon, she was fumbling her way through a half-assed breakup speech—a full day before their time together would have reached its natural end. She'd never intended to cut Alice loose before the end of camp, but then again, she hadn't realized how being with Alice would make her feel. How frightening it would all become, and how *fast.* Nor had she allowed herself to appreciate how *Alice* would almost certainly feel after such a formative experience as the one they'd shared in that boathouse. Not until too late.

She was a real piece of shit. Even more justification for keeping Alice away from her messy, painful, chaotic existence.

"It's not that I don't *want* to hang out with you." Rosa knew she owed Alice an explanation, yet she wasn't entirely sure how to present her reasoning in a way that wouldn't trigger an argument or, alternately, make her seem like a calculating asshole who'd simply used Alice for sex. "I love spending time with you, Alice. But that's the problem. I'm pretty sure I love it too much, and I think maybe so do you. And I...I told you I was just looking for a friend here at camp. Some casual fun for a few days, nothing more."

Another trio of women approached the booth seeking water, interrupting her stilted speech. Rosa pushed already-filled cups into their hands, glad when they scooped them up and scampered off to watch whatever activity currently had the crowd roaring. No longer able to stand not knowing how Alice was reacting to her shittiness, Rosa turned to face her.

Alice's eyes swam with tears. "We can't hang out today because we *like* each other too much?"

Rosa couldn't imagine feeling any lower. "When I signed up for camp, I never expected to meet someone like you. My goal for this weekend was to *maybe* have a no-strings-attached fling, if I could work up the nerve, but that was it. I mean...I wasn't even going to tell whoever I hooked up with my real *name*. At this point in my life, with the way things have been—the way they *are*—even a casual hookup feels like a huge, scary step to take, but this thing with you...I *know* it's more than a meaningless fling. For both of us."

Alice inhaled to speak but quieted when Sandy reappeared at their booth as though conjured by their shared distress. "Hello again, ladies." She gestured to a tree about twenty feet behind her back, where the more sober of Rosa's harassers stood with his arms folded over his chest. "Jason is going to relieve you of your duties a little earlier than planned. You're free to go enjoy the rest of your afternoon."

Rosa couldn't help but smile at the idea that justice, however minor, was being served. "Where's his friend?"

"In the main office speaking with Marcia." Sandy smirked. "No doubt *wishing* he could sling cups of water instead."

"I warned him," Alice mumbled. Then, louder, "Thanks, Sandy."

"Yes, thank you." Rosa stepped out from behind the booth, grateful for the opportunity to continue their difficult talk in private. She felt a sick certainty this conversation would end with both of them in tears. "Good luck dealing with that asshole."

"I can handle him." Sandy flexed her impressive arm muscles. "Go, have fun. Stay away from the boats!"

Reddening at the playful admonishment, Alice nodded fervently. "We will."

They left in silence. Once they were well away from the field and the noise of the other campers, Alice picked up right where they'd left off. "So I'm more than just a meaningless fling?"

Rosa gave Alice a sidelong glance. How honest should she be? If she confessed the true depth of her feelings—the fact that she was freaking out precisely *because* of how badly she wanted to keep seeing Alice after camp was over—it would only make what she had to do that much harder. Not wanting to lie, she tried to downplay her emotion. "I care about you deeply, Alice. I *like* you. I'm afraid that if we keep doing what we've been doing…" All they'd really done was enjoy the other's company, no strings attached. She was simply *assuming* that tomorrow Alice would ask for more—and knew herself well enough to realize she would want the same. "I guess I don't want saying good-bye to hurt any more than it already will. For both of us."

Alice held onto her upper arms, as though she'd caught a chill despite the eighty-five-degree summer weather. Her eyes had gone watery again, and despite the fact that her knuckles had turned white with the force of her grip on herself, Rosa could see she was trembling.

Alice took a deep breath, then said, "But if we both like each other—if, maybe…we're both developing real feelings—do we really *have* to say good-bye?"

This was exactly what Rosa had feared would happen. Being candid about her feelings had been a calculated risk; she hadn't wanted Alice to believe their entire friendship was a farce or that her only aim had been to get into an ostensibly straight woman's panties, but her admission of real, albeit conflicted, emotion had clearly opened the door to a fantasy Rosa couldn't possibly fulfill. "Yes," Rosa said firmly. "*Definitely*, we have to say good-bye."

"Why?"

Rosa exhaled in frustration. Hadn't Alice been listening when she'd laid out her life story? Hadn't she already *lived* a single hellish morning in Rosa's world? "You know why."

"Because of the article?" Alice very tentatively slipped her hand into Rosa's. This time Rosa didn't pull away. "I told you, I don't care about that. Any of it."

Rosa barked laughter, a harsh sound that echoed through the trees surrounding them. "That's because you have no idea what it even means!" When Alice flinched, Rosa softened her tone. "Look, you admitted you're not online much. You have no idea what it's like to be ridiculed and shamed on a global scale. To have your family and friends be harassed because of *you*. Yes, the worst of it has died down by now, but you saw what happened back there with those guys. I probably still have at least one incident a week like that. Sometimes more. Some of them *far* worse." She battled a wave of grief, depressed that a bunch of Internet trolls had effectively ruined her first chance in years to have a legitimately fulfilling relationship. "I can't guarantee the whole controversy won't get stirred up again, and *again*. On the Internet, information—including photos and video—is eternal. This whole situation…it's something I'll always live with." She swallowed. "I can't have you live with it, too."

"So…what? Your plan is to be alone for the rest of your life?" Alice sounded so heartsick that Rosa had to blink away the tears that suddenly clouded her vision. "Rosa, that's tragic. Seriously, seriously awful."

Disturbed by Alice's conclusion, Rosa frowned. "I didn't say that." She hesitated. "No, that's not the plan."

"I see." Alice bit her lip, loosening her hold on Rosa's hand. "So you *do* think someone out there could potentially handle being with Rosa Salazar…just not me."

Pain flared behind Rosa's temples, making it hard to think. "Alice—"

"You never promised me a damn thing except a friend here at camp, with fun on the side," Alice said. "I *do* know that."

"Good." Rosa cleared her throat, wishing that Alice's concession actually made her feel better. "Listen, it's only *because* I care so much that I don't want to drag you into my bullshit. I've only recently started to put the pieces of my life back together. Right now, dating, even casually…would be hard. *Too* hard."

"For me?" Alice stared straight ahead at the ground some distance in front of them. "Or for you?"

"Both." Rosa lifted Alice's hand to her mouth, kissing each knuckle in turn. "Sweetheart, I can't watch you suffer because of me. I just *can't*. So please, don't ask me to."

It was Alice's turn to laugh without humor. "What do you think you're doing right now?" She dropped Rosa's hand and stepped to the side, out of reach.

A spark of anger flickered in Rosa's chest. "You said it yourself. I never promised you *anything*. Even after last night…I promised you *nothing* beyond this weekend."

"You're right, you didn't." Alice swiped the back of her hand over her eyes. "I guess I never imagined you'd drop me right after fucking me. Or abandon me before we could spend one final night together."

Rosa's anger turned into nausea. "This isn't about abandoning you."

"Maybe not, but that's what it feels like." Alice stopped walking not far from the edge of the main camp, right before they hit the thick of the surrounding redwood forest. She turned to face Rosa, arms folded over her breasts. "You know, I never asked to keep seeing you after camp until *you* brought it up. I never asked you for *anything*." Her exasperation was plain to see. "I'm not saying I wouldn't have tested the waters tomorrow when we were actually saying good-bye, but you could've just let me down easy then. Why do this *now*?" Her voice broke, and twin tears rolled down her cheeks. "When I can still feel you *inside me*?" She whispered the last two words.

"Because I can't keep going like this *without* saying anything. I already feel like enough of an asshole, so the last thing I want to do is string you along in any way." Rosa's teeth chattered briefly as she battled the urge to succumb to her sorrow and regret. "Alice, it's obvious how much you care about me—so much that you'll subject yourself to situations that terrify you, or even just make you uncomfortable, for my sake. As much as I appreciate that—God, as much as it *staggers* me that you think I'm worth *any* amount of discomfort—I can't stand to see you deal with any of the shit I regularly endure. Not *you*. Now, or in the future." She tensed her jaw and gathered her resolve. "All I can say is…I'm sorry. I was selfish, and…last night probably shouldn't have happened. It was my mistake."

Alice nodded for a few seconds, worrying her trembling lower lip between her teeth, before she managed to speak. "So basically, you're saying that my anxiety is the deal-breaker for you. Because I get awkward and scared and turn red on a regular basis...*that's* what makes me unsuitable dating material. If not for that, who knows?" With a shrug, she smiled as the tears began to flow in earnest. "Well, I guess I can't blame you." She sniffled and turned away, using the hem of her T-shirt to dab at her face while Rosa tried not to steal a peek at the luscious bare stomach she'd just exposed. "You're right. I don't know what I was thinking."

Rosa read the subtext of Alice's tremulous statement. *Nobody would want someone like me.* Devastated to have caused Alice such a swift, heartbreaking descent from ecstasy to agony, Rosa pulled her into a cautious embrace. To her immense relief, Alice came willingly, allowing herself to be held while her arms hung stiffly at her sides. Rosa cradled the back of her head, memorizing the sensation of her silky hair and the warm body against hers. She expected this would be the last time she'd have the chance. "Alice, this really isn't about you at all. *I'm* not suitable dating material. You deserve to be happy, not to live in fear of whatever humiliation lies around the next corner. Not to be pulled into a situation much bigger and so much worse than you have the context to properly imagine. I'm bad for you. Period." She tightened her arms, pulling Alice as close to her chest as she could, savoring the heart beating against her own. "You're an amazing person. Probably the most special woman I've ever met, truly. Certainly that I've ever kissed. I'd love nothing more than to take you out on a date next weekend and see where this goes. You *have* to understand that I'm saying good-bye now only because I care so much. Nobody in their right mind would willingly attach themselves to a life ruined by the Internet. *Especially* in the manner mine was."

Slowly, Alice's hands came up to rest on Rosa's back. "My therapist says that the worst thing for an anxious person to do is avoid the objects and situations that trigger their anxiety. That's why I *came* to Camp Rewind. I don't want to be too afraid to enjoy life. I challenge myself every day to overcome my fears because I want to be happier. The more I do the things that scare me, the easier it all becomes. That's a lesson *you* helped reinforce for me this weekend." She brushed her lips over Rosa's jaw, hesitantly. "I may not seem like it, Rosa, but I'm a strong person. I had to be, to grow up with my mother. I could be strong for you, too."

Rosa felt Alice's tears against her neck and struggled for a moment with the overwhelming urge to abandon her breakup plan. Maybe they *could* do this. Maybe Alice *could* handle her shit. She mumbled, "I know you're strong."

Alice trailed a line of kisses up to Rosa's ear and whispered, "Then trust me. Let me prove it." She exhaled and sank a hand into Rosa's thick hair, pressing their foreheads together. "Hang out with me some more."

Rosa surprised herself by weeping, the hot tears spilling from her eyes in an unending torrent of anger and despair. It would be so easy to say yes to Alice. She *wanted* to say yes. Blocking out the rest of the world was simple here at camp, and for the next twenty-four hours at least, she didn't doubt that they'd have a blissful time together.

But then what? Alice might *think* she could handle Rosa's baggage, but she couldn't. Luis hadn't lasted three weeks before he'd bailed. Granted, Alice was a far superior human being than her most recent ex-boyfriend, but honestly, *Rosa* would bail on her own life if she could. There was a reason she'd once investigated the feasibility of assuming a new identity altogether. In the end, only the prospect of leaving her parents behind had stopped her. Even though she actively caused them pain on an ongoing basis, Rosa remained too selfish to cut herself out of her family's lives entirely. What made Alice so scary was her ability to tempt Rosa to act just as selfishly with someone new, even if it would ultimately break both their hearts and harm Alice in the process.

Hanging on to Alice so she couldn't back out of her arms, Rosa said, "The magic of camp is that the experience is fleeting, and therefore better than reality. Who I am here at Camp Rewind—Lila Sanchez—she's a lot more fun than Rosa Salazar will ever be. If we part now, you'll always have these incredible memories of my best self to hold on to. If we attempt to keep this going...I don't see a happy ending there, for either of us. Let's not ruin what we've shared this weekend by trying and failing to take it into the real world. *Please*."

"*My* real world is one without friends, without a lover, where I have to pay for the privilege to talk to the only person I ever confide in." Tension rippled through Alice's frame, and rising frustration. "I'm willing to risk a few happy memories for even the slightest chance of finding *real* joy." Her voice caught. "Especially since the memories we made together already taste bittersweet to me, after this."

Rosa released Alice and backed away. She had no counter-argument. Alice wasn't wrong. Rosa simply...couldn't. "I'm sorry."

"So that's it?" Alice's chin wobbled. "We can't even spend one last day together?"

How? With as much agony as this, Rosa couldn't imagine ever touching Alice again. Not when she was so damn *undeserving.* "I'm sorry," Rosa repeated, like a dumbass. She wished for something better to say, for some way to fix the mess she'd created.

Alice's face screwed up into an expression of pure grief, for just an instant, before she whirled around and rushed off. "Me, too." Her poorly restrained sobs made the words come out funny, and even from ten feet away, Rosa could see Alice cringe at the sound of her own anguish. "Have a nice life, I guess."

Rosa's heart felt like it had been snapped in two. She was doing the right thing, she was sure of it, so why did everything about what had just happened feel so wrong? Not wanting to separate on such shaky ground, she called out, "Alice..."

Alice slowed, perhaps waiting for her to acknowledge that she'd been a fool, but when Rosa trailed off, unsure what to offer as a balm for her actions, Alice resumed her steadfast march back to the main camp. Without a word. Without looking back.

Shattered, Rosa crumpled to the ground, dropped her face into her hands, and cried for both of them.

Rosa didn't know how long she sat there on the forest floor with tears and snot running down her face, yanking on fistfuls of her stupid, short hair in a twisted version of penance for her stupid, *selfish* part in causing Alice so much pain. All she knew was that when the sound of a lively conversation reached her ears some time later, the act of clambering to her feet made her instantly aware that her entire body ached, as though she'd been sitting in place for hours. Her puffy eyes blurred and stung when she tried to dry them with her shirt. Self-conscious about being caught falling apart, Rosa scanned her immediate surroundings to locate the source of the voices, along with the best tree to hide behind.

Identifying both within seconds of each other, she ducked behind the thick trunk of a nearby redwood and held her breath as a man and woman strolled by. She listened until their conversation about genealogical research, of all things, faded away, then closed her eyes and rested her head against the tree. *What if I just made the biggest mistake of my life?*

No, she reminded herself. Dating you would be the biggest mistake of Alice's life. That was the whole point.

Her contrarian inner voice persisted. *What life? According to her, she doesn't have much of one for you to ruin.*

Rosa lifted her head off the trunk and let it fall, delivering a satisfyingly painful *smack* to the back of her skull. Then she dried her tears one more time and cleared her throat. She'd known from almost the beginning that leaving Alice would hurt, even if she hadn't anticipated how mutual the feeling would become. Or how shitty she would feel about the way it all unfolded. Still, she'd done the right thing—or at the very least, what she'd spent all weekend convincing herself was right. She took a deep breath, then let it out. *What now?*

It was difficult to imagine staying at Camp Rewind until checkout tomorrow afternoon. In fact, it seemed impossible to think about spending even one more night. With Alice in the bunk above hers? Either Rosa's resolve would disappear or else they'd be in for the most awkward sleepover ever.

Maybe Alice will leave.

Rosa's stomach turned over at the thought that she could be gone already. If Alice had walked straight from the scene of their breakup to the cabin to get her stuff, then directly to her car, she could have driven to the highway by now. Erased from her life in a flash, just like Rosa had claimed to want. Yet the very thought filled her with stark, miserable terror and keen regret so agonizing it nearly brought her to her knees again.

Shit, she thought for the second time that day. *What have I done?*

CHAPTER FOURTEEN

After leaving Rosa in the woods, Alice went directly to the women's cabin intending to pack her bag and get the hell away from Camp Rewind for good. She ran out of steam once she reached her bunk, stopping short at the sight of her travel blanket lying, still rumpled, atop Rosa's mattress. It hadn't been moved since she'd woken up yesterday morning to run off and hide, the pivotal incident that had no doubt caused Rosa to deduce, perhaps correctly, that Alice wasn't skilled at handling the unexpected. For a woman whose life was defined by unexpected—and often painful or frightening—interactions with malevolent men, Alice's skittishness would have served as a giant red flag: this chick isn't ready for prime time.

Not wanting to sit on Rosa's bed, but no longer ready to leave, Alice steeled her nerves and then ascended the metal ladder to the top bunk she'd claimed by default. She climbed onto the mattress with exaggerated caution before peering down over the edge once she'd finally settled in. Despite her unease about the distance separating her from the hardwood floor, she celebrated a moment of silent triumph for once again conquering a fear. Regardless of what happened with Rosa, the weekend had been full of such minor victories, and she was proud of herself for each one.

Alice had been lying there for only a few minutes before the cabin door opened and slammed shut. A familiar, hushed whisper caught her attention as the new arrivals made their way deeper into the room. "Give me five minutes. That's all I need."

"Confident, aren't we?" Enid giggled quietly. When they reached

Bree's lower bunk, one bed over, they climbed in together. "I'm more than happy to let you try."

The distinct rustle of clothing being shed launched Alice into a split-second decision to speak up. "Fair warning. You two aren't alone."

Bree rolled off the mattress and stood up between their bunks, peering at Alice in concern. "Hey, girl. You all right?"

Alice knew she couldn't possibly look all right. Ignoring her upbringing, and the natural shame she felt about sharing her problems with others, she answered. "Not really."

Bree frowned. "Yeah, Lila didn't seem all right, either."

Alice tried not to care. "You saw her?"

"In passing." Enid appeared at Bree's side, brows drawn. "We wondered where you were."

"Oh." Alice stared up at the ceiling and debated whether to say anything more. She really shouldn't involve other people in her business. Then again, she didn't want their mutual friends to think she'd broken *Rosa's* heart. "She decided we shouldn't hang out anymore. She doesn't want to see me again after tomorrow and felt like any more time spent together would only make saying good-bye that much harder." Her face screwed up as a fresh wave of pain rolled over her at the reminder of Rosa's lame reasoning. "I don't know. Whatever."

"Alice." Bree's tender recitation of her name did nothing to quell the tide of her resurgent tears. "Want me to beat some sense into her?"

Alice laughed helplessly and hid her face behind her arms. "Tempting."

Enid stroked her calf with so much affection that Alice nearly fell apart entirely. "I'm sorry, honey. That's rough."

"She could have at least waited until tomorrow," Bree said. "I wouldn't have expected Lila to be so heartless."

"That's what I said." Alice lowered her arms and looked at Bree and Enid. *My friends.* Warmed by their presence, she decided to see if talking through the pain would diminish it in any way. "Lila felt like she already cared about me too much, and she could tell how strongly I feel about her. She has…complications in her life that have absolutely convinced her that she's no good for anyone. Particularly someone as shy and prone to anxiety as me. These complications are so…complicated…that she refuses to even consider maintaining a friendship, let alone go out on a real date. She doesn't want me involved in her problems in any way, even though I keep telling her I don't care and that I can handle it. If it means she stays in my life, I'd pretty much handle anything."

Bree grumbled under her breath, apparently affronted on Alice's behalf, while Enid nodded thoughtfully and said, "So she's trying to protect you from whatever's going on in her life, as well as the possibility of experiencing additional heartache by getting more attached than both of you already are, before your inevitable split."

"That's her argument." Rising, Alice sat cross-legged on the top bunk. "I just want her to give me a chance to prove that I can handle her baggage. *Only* because she admitted she has real feelings for me. If I thought she didn't also want to see where our friendship might eventually lead, I wouldn't have pushed back even if I *did* think her timing was terrible. But she implied that in a perfect world, she'd take me out to dinner next weekend. If she hadn't said that, I'd accept this like a big girl and walk away. Honestly. I would never impose myself where I'm not wanted."

Bree and Enid exchanged a look. "Based on how upset she seemed when we saw her, I don't believe you're unwanted," Bree said. "Not for a second." She glanced over her shoulder as though actively resisting the desire to storm out, find the source of Alice's distress, and drag her back there to talk things through. "I understand being scared, but I really wish she'd treated you with more care."

Alice managed a weak chuckle as her sore eyes watered anew. "Me, too."

Enid laid her hand over Alice's with a reassuring squeeze. "Give her a little time to regret what happened. Maybe she'll rethink her opposition to involving you in her complicated life."

"Well, I say make a grand gesture. Show her that you're more capable of dealing with shit than she realizes." Bree shrugged, apparently unable to suggest what form such a gesture might take. "Or else do something so epically romantic that she has no choice but to take a chance on you."

Alice suddenly felt like she'd been dropped into the plot of a romantic comedy for which she had no script. She was wholly unprepared to play her role. "I have no idea how to do that."

Enid patted her hand. "Give her some time, and talk to her in a few hours. Until then, you're free to spend the day with us."

Bree seemed mildly surprised by Enid's offer but accepted the gesture in stride. "Totally."

Alice blushed, perfectly aware of what they'd come in here to do. Just because her sex life had once again gone dormant didn't mean theirs should as well. "Actually, I should probably go talk to Jamal in arts and crafts. I told him I'd give him some advice on doing a simple robotics lesson for a future camp session. He seemed pretty excited about that, so…" She noted the way Bree lit up at the implication that she'd soon have Enid alone. "But…maybe we can hang out tonight at the dance?"

She *really* didn't want to go stag.

"Sure thing." Bree eased into a broad smile. "Escort two beautiful women to an event? Go ahead, twist my arm."

Enid shot her lover an amused wink. To Alice, she said, "Careful, or she'll invite you to spend *all* night with us."

"I certainly would," Bree said seriously, "if I thought Alice were into that kind of thing."

Somehow managing not to wither and die of embarrassment, Alice bit back a grin while she fanned the flames that rose in her cheeks. "*Also* tempting," she admitted. Experiencing an instant of out-of-body awareness, she registered what she'd just said. *I'm flirting. With someone who* isn't *Rosa!* Maybe she really had grown. Still, even if she *could* summon the confidence to participate in a threesome, her heart wouldn't be in it. Not tonight. "Unfortunately, I'm too hung up on the first woman I ever slept with to even consider adding a second and third to the list."

Bree and Enid's eyes both widened at her revelation. "Oh. Wow." Bree hesitated. "Well, maybe that's the problem?"

Enid elbowed Bree hard enough to elicit a yelp. "I think Bree meant to ask, 'Did she ever imply that your relative inexperience was one of the reasons she's reluctant to get more serious?'"

Alice shook her head, then shrugged. "I'm pretty sure that's not it, but…" She searched Bree and Enid's faces. "You guys think that's an issue?"

"Not so long as you don't treat her like an experiment." Enid patted her again. "Given how devastated both of you look about the idea of losing touch with someone you met only forty-eight hours ago, I don't believe that's your intention at all."

Alice shook her head vigorously. "It's not. I got married too young, mostly to get away from my parents, but now…" She took a breath to steady her voice. "I know who I am."

Bree and Enid grinned in unison, like proud mothers. "You sure you don't want me to beat some sense into her?" Bree asked.

Alice shook her head, then very gingerly crawled to her bunk's metal ladder. She lowered her feet to rest on the second rung before turning around to tackle the treacherous descent. "No. I'm going to talk to Jamal, which should give Lila time to reflect while I brainstorm a grand gesture of some sort." She lowered her foot onto the next rung down. "I'll also try not to let this experience ruin the rest of my time here."

"Good plan," Enid said.

"Beautiful plan," Bree agreed, close to Alice's back. "But before all that: want some help getting down from there?"

Alice stilled the foot she'd been sweeping through the air in a fruitless search for the next rung. "If you insist."

Strong hands gripped her around the waist, carefully lifting and then placing her onto the ground. Momentarily shaken by the intimate contact with someone she barely knew, Alice managed to calm her disquiet with a single, steadying breath. She smiled at Bree, face hot. "Thanks."

"No problem." Bree surprised her by pulling her into a warm, lengthy hug. "Don't hesitate to come find us if you need us, okay? We've got your back."

Alice relaxed into the embrace. When Enid joined in seconds later, rather than feel suffocated, Alice breathed easier than she had since leaving Rosa in the woods.

The theory she'd held since childhood seemed to bear out. Friendship really *did* make life better.

❖

Jamal lit up with palpable excitement when Alice entered the arts-and-crafts building. The crowd was sparse compared to the afternoon before, presumably because field day was still in full swing. Relieved to see the counselor unencumbered by other campers, Alice approached his worktable with a rapidly beating heart. She assumed it would take many years of practice to master her physiological reactions while engaged in this type of social interaction, but realistically, it couldn't happen too soon. Battling her unrelenting paranoia about sounding foolish was difficult enough. Having to simultaneously deal with flop sweat, red cheeks, and shaking hands made moments like this particularly excruciating.

"Alice!" Jamal stood and offered her his hand. "I was really hoping you'd come by." His warm brown eyes twinkled as she gave him her firmest, most confident handshake. "Taking a break from stealing boats?"

Fiery humiliation burned through Alice, scorching everything in its wake, but rather than surrender to her instinctive shame, she challenged the thought distortion that made his comment seem cruel, even mocking. Jamal wore a friendly grin, which now wavered at her obvious embarrassment, and he'd never been anything but perfectly nice to her. *He's teasing you. Tease back.* "Yes, for the moment."

It wasn't the wittiest rejoinder in the history of verbal repartee, but it was *something*.

Jamal chuckled, then pointed at a cardboard box full of random, interesting bits and pieces that he'd partially unpacked onto the table. "Okay, so you got me *really* pumped yesterday. I ended up driving an hour to an electronics store last night…" He paused to pull a self-deprecating face. "I know, I know. But I thought *maybe* if you were into it, you could show me how to build a super-simple robot. Any kind at all." He put his hands on the box and shook it lightly. "The salesman told me I had everything I would need…"

Alice peered into the box, relieved to have a technical challenge on which to focus her energies. She let her gaze dart over the contents, along with the items already on the table, as she tallied a mental inventory. There were different-sized motors, batteries and battery holders, LEDs of various colors, resistors, timers, receivers, capacitors, circuits, and on and on…truly a dizzying assortment of electronic odds and ends. "And then some. How much money did you *spend*?"

Jamal flashed her a toothy grin. "Marcia loved the idea. She's looking for ways to attract campers who are interested in activities other than drinking. She approved a pilot program on the spot, seed money included."

"Nice." Alice further unpacked the box, sorting parts into piles arranged by category. "Well, without a computer to program a micro-controller, our options are somewhat limited. However, we *could* build a simple obstacle-avoiding robot with what you've got here."

"Yeah?" Jamal slapped his hands on the tabletop, so obviously pumped that Alice couldn't help but be swept along by his enthusiasm. "Let's do it!"

"All right." Alice pulled out a chair and sat, picking and choosing the components they would need. "Grab some paper if you want to take notes."

"Good call." He jogged to another table and returned with a notebook and pen. Dropping into the chair beside her, he watched quietly as she continued to sort parts, then said, "You really should come back and teach a beginner robotics course with me at some point. I'm sure Marcia would waive your registration fee."

Alice snorted. "That's if I'm not expelled for general mischief first."

Jamal laughed, kindly. "Tell me the truth. Borrowing the boat: *your* idea or Lila's?" When she looked up, sheepishly, he raised an eyebrow. "*Really.* Didn't expect that."

"That makes two of us."

"So where *is* your partner in crime?" Jamal glanced around as though he might spot her lurking on the periphery. Alice couldn't help but scan the room with him. "I hope I'm not keeping you from her."

"Not at all." Alice attempted to sound casual. "Maybe we'll hook up later, but right now I'm all about building this robot with you. Once I locate a few more bits, we'll start going over the basics."

"Excellent." Jamal propped his chin on his hand, watchful, before brightening as a thought visibly occurred to him. "You know what? You should give the robot we make today to Lila. Sort of an apology for stealing you away like this." He tentatively bumped her shoulder with his, a gesture of camaraderie that still felt thrillingly novel. "Marcia's treat."

She wasn't certain whether building Rosa a simplistic robot fit the definition of a grand gesture, but given what she knew of the woman who'd managed to make her begin to fall in love after less than two days, such a gift *might* be epically romantic enough to make her reconsider letting Alice go. Even if this token wouldn't change anything at all, the memory of Rosa's joy at her silly siege engines allowed Alice to accept Jamal's generous offer without hesitation. "Thanks. She'll like that."

"Well, she's lucky to have you. You're pretty cool."

Unaccustomed to thinking so kindly of herself, Alice couldn't help but nonetheless silently agree with Jamal's assessment—the first part, at least. Rosa *would* be lucky to have her. She had her flaws, absolutely, and she'd never thrive on being the center of attention or choose to actively pursue a busy social life, but given the opportunity, she would love Rosa like the woman had never been loved before. Indeed, if they somehow managed to successfully transition their connection to the real world, they would *both* be lucky, because both their lives would improve. They were good for each other, complications be damned. Alice *knew* that had to be true, because the alternative was too painful to accept.

Now all she had to do was make Rosa believe it, too.

CHAPTER FIFTEEN

Rosa yearned for a charged cell phone so she could call her best friend Trayvon and yell at him for sending her the link to Camp Rewind's website all those months ago. As stressful as her life had been then, at least she'd finally reached a place where she wasn't always in agony the way she was today. Somehow, the pain of breaking up with Alice—a woman she'd known only *two days*—felt somehow worse than anything else she could remember experiencing over the past year and a half. This weekend was to have been her chance to recapture the frivolity of a time before she'd published that article, back when she'd had fun and slept around and naively believed that the universe naturally bent in favor of her safety and happiness. Instead, camp had turned into yet another nightmare reminder of how one simple post on the Internet could ruin a person's whole life in every way possible.

She didn't *want* to break Alice's heart—but nor did she want her own to break. She also didn't want Alice to get mixed up with her detractors or bear witness to the shame Rosa was forced to endure on an almost daily basis. No matter how quickly Alice had won her trust, that seemed like too personal a violation to share with anyone. Too embarrassing. Even if she'd felt comfortable enough to disclose the sordid truth to Alice out loud, it was one thing to describe the harassment she received, and another altogether to experience it up close. Maybe she was a coward, but Rosa wasn't sure she'd survive that. How would she be able to look Alice in the face every day, knowing that her own poor decisions were the source of all their shared misery?

Despite her inner turmoil, Rosa didn't get in her car and leave. She *couldn't*. After confirming that both Alice's bags and her car were still exactly where she'd last seen them, Rosa found it impossible to simply pack her things and go, even though she *should*. If she were serious about ending things with Alice, the smart move would be to drive as far and as fast from this place as her reasonably priced sedan could take her.

Except she wasn't smart. Obviously.

More to the point, Rosa no longer trusted her ability to differentiate between right and wrong. Not with this. Leaving now meant she'd most likely never see Alice again, and despite what she'd said earlier, she wasn't ready for that.

Not even close.

Unfortunately, she also wasn't ready to *see* Alice face-to-face. Her will was too weak, her emotions too volatile. She hated herself for what she'd done, completely, yet wished for nothing more than the privilege of being allowed to love Alice Wu. Turned inside out like this, she didn't know how she'd react if they ran into each other. If Alice opened her arms, she just might fall into them, only to reset the clock on the broken heart that would follow the inevitable end of their relationship. Was it better to feel this way now, or even worse in six months? Rosa thought she knew the answer to that question, but the certainty of future pain did nothing to erase the agony of her present heartache. She had no idea what to do.

Rosa flashed back to the expression on Alice's face right before she'd turned and walked away, the plaintive mask of pure sadness Rosa had glimpsed for only an instant. Alice's primal reaction to brutal trauma—trauma inflicted by *her*—had been so visceral that the memory would haunt Rosa for the rest of her days. As she relived the moment for the hundredth time, nausea bloomed in Rosa's stomach, slowing her rapid, aimless meandering only twenty yards from the path that led to the archery range. Not wanting to linger too long where Alice might see her, Rosa resumed her walk at a more moderate pace, stopping to read the sign posted at the head of the short trail. SOBER ACTIVITY!

Rosa smiled. Perfect. No drunk jerks and, presumably, no Alice. She'd demurred at Rosa's halfhearted attempt to get her to try shooting a bow and arrow the day before, protesting that she would be too self-conscious to learn a new skill around so many strangers. Granted, drunk field day had disqualified most of the other campers from participating in target practice for the next few hours, at the very least, but Alice probably wouldn't think of that.

At least Rosa hoped she wouldn't.

She approached the range tentatively, at first unsure whether anyone had remained behind to accommodate the nondrinkers and those averse to three-legged races. After a quick scan, she spotted the lone counselor on duty, a broad-shouldered, tattooed twenty-something man who sat on a stool with a portable game console in his hands. Wholly intent on the action onscreen, he moved his thumbs rapidly over the buttons in a manner that outed him as a veteran gamer. Exactly the demographic Rosa wanted to avoid. Quietly, she took a step backward and swiveled to make a rapid getaway.

"Hey, wait! I'm sorry. I didn't mean to ignore you. Just let me—" The counselor was fumbling with the controls when Rosa turned around, still staring at the screen, but with a different sort of urgency. "And...done!" He slipped the game system into a hard plastic case and set it aside, then jumped off the stool to shake her hand. "Hi, I'm Nick. The guy who stopped expecting to see sober fans of the bow and arrow at least forty-five minutes ago."

Rosa put on her most practiced, confident facade. Inside, she quaked. *He plays games. He'll recognize me.* Aiming for nonchalance, she said, "I'm Lila. The woman who avoids hangovers at all costs."

Nick rewarded her with laughter and an empathetic nod. "Smart."

"I do what I can." She glanced around, wishing for a graceful exit. What could she say? She'd changed her mind? Or, surprise, she really *wasn't* sober? Choosing the path of least resistance, she said, "You know what? I'm not feeling very well all of a sudden. I should probably go lie down."

Nick frowned slightly, face etched with concern. "I'm really sorry to hear that. I was looking forward to doing something other than failing miserably at this level of Stealth Inc. for the thousandth time."

Rosa relaxed marginally, ridiculous as it sounded, at the revelation of Nick's relatively innocuous taste in games. "That one's brutal," she replied on autopilot, awash in memories of her own time having her ass handed to her again and again by the indie puzzle-platform title. Realizing, belatedly, that she'd just identified herself as a gamer, too, Rosa quickly backpedaled. "Or so I've heard."

Nick gave her a kind smile, then pulled a bow off the wall and offered it to her. "You sure you don't want to shoot an arrow or two? I promise it's easier than Stealth Inc."

Unsure where she'd even go upon leaving the range, Rosa acceded with a reluctant nod. "All right."

"Great." Rubbing his hands together in exaggerated delight, Nick handed her a brown leather cuff from the nearby counter. "Go ahead and slip on this arm guard. It'll prevent the bowstring from snapping your skin."

Rosa slid her forearm into the cuff and fastened it in place, praying she wasn't making a mistake by giving Nick time to look past her new haircut and fake name to discover a genuine gaming antiheroine in his midst. "It's on."

"Don't be nervous." He retrieved an arrow and demonstrated how to nock it on the string, then pull back to aim. "One fluid motion, see? Now…you're right-handed?"

"Yeah." Rosa took the bow and arrow when he offered them, mimicking his technique for positioning the projectile on the string. "Like this?"

"Exactly." Nick grabbed a second bow off the wall, and another arrow, so he could stand next to her and demonstrate the proper stance. "While holding the bow with your left hand, point your left shoulder toward the target. Your feet should be placed a shoulder's width apart, perpendicular to the target. Like so."

Rosa pantomimed his movements, settling in as she aimed at a brightly colored bull's-eye pinned to a hay bale some distance away. "All right."

"Use three fingers to hold your arrow. Good," he said when she followed his example. "Now show me how you raise and draw."

Rosa attempted to duplicate his earlier example but immediately recognized that her form wasn't quite right. "What am I doing wrong?"

"You just need to tweak a couple things." Nick demonstrated raising his bow again. "Hold your bow arm outward toward the target. Your inner elbow needs to stay parallel to the ground, and the bow should remain vertical. So you can literally look straight down the spine of the arrow."

Rosa adjusted her shooting position. "Got it."

"Now when you draw, move your string hand toward your face to an anchor point. Usually that'll be somewhere around your chin, cheek, ear, or even the corner of your mouth. Think of that as a reference point that needs to remain consistent from shot to shot. Try not to relax too much or keep pulling once you reach that anchor point, if you want to achieve maximum power and control."

Rosa watched Nick raise and draw the bow a few more times, using his example to gradually improve her own form. Finally, upon receiving his approval, she asked, "How do I aim?"

"Why don't you follow your instincts? Let the arrow go and see what happens." Warmth crept into his tone. "Pretend it's a video game."

Cringing, Rosa considered feigning ignorance on the subject before immediately discarding the idea. The only thing worse than being the target of crude comments and death threats was having to deny this essential part of who she was. She and her brother had grown up playing games together. He'd never had to lie or feel sheepish about his hobbies, and she didn't want to, either. Rather than answer Nick at all, she looked down the length of the arrow, tried pointing the tip toward the center of the target, and released the taut string. The arrow flew away swiftly, impacting a couple inches below and to the right of the bull's-eye.

At the *thwack* of her successful hit, Nick hooted and cheered. "Right on! Way to make me look like a badass instructor."

Rosa shrugged. "You're not terrible." They traded friendly smiles. "May I try another?"

"Of course." Nick grabbed a handful of arrows and set them on the counter next to her. "Knock yourself out."

Rosa fired three more times, adjusting her stance and aim until, finally, she delivered an arrow millimeters below the top edge of the bull's-eye. A little embarrassed by Nick's enthusiastic reaction, she nonetheless returned his high five with a light chuckle. "Way to make *me* feel like a badass student."

"You're great. Seriously." He leaned closer like he was preparing to share a big secret. "You should see all the shenanigans amateur archers get into, sober or not. It's rare for any of my students to hit the target on their first try."

"I'll have to take your word for it." Pleased to have learned a new skill that suited her better than horseback riding, Rosa lined up another shot and landed it in the bottom corner of the tiny black circle. "This is fun."

"You should think about joining your local archery club. They'll be able to offer you further instruction and practice time. You could even get into competitions, if you wanted." He shrugged as though suddenly worried he sounded like a dork. "I belong to a club in the East Bay. It's a good time."

Rosa questioned the wisdom of getting involved in another potentially male-dominated hobby even as she hated herself for thinking that way. She smiled politely at Nick, appreciating his belief in her natural ability if nothing else. "Maybe I will."

"Everyone at my club is really cool. I don't think anyone would, you know…Give you a hard time. Or anything."

Nick's precision in addressing the source of her concern alerted her that she had, potentially, just been recognized. *Again.* Heart pounding, she was too frightened to simply drop the charade. "Why would anyone give me a hard time?"

Nick blinked, then looked down. "*Lila.* Right. Sorry." He shook his head.

Shaken, Rosa set her bow on the counter and turned to leave. "I should go."

"Wait," Nick called to her back. "Please. You *are* Rosa Salazar, aren't you?"

Still raw from her earlier encounter with the two drunks, Rosa's roiling anxiety morphed into swift, sudden anger. "Leave me alone!"

"I didn't watch it!" Nick sounded panicked, probably worried that she was marching off to report him to Marcia. "The video, I mean. I didn't look at the pictures, either. I wouldn't. It was wrong for them to steal that stuff, wrong to post it, wrong for *anyone* to look. Besides, I *liked* your article." He lowered his voice when Rosa froze in place and finished by muttering, "Even if that game *was* pretty fun. At times."

Uncertain whether he was being sincere, Rosa glanced over her shoulder to gauge the likelihood that she'd actually encountered the rarest of creatures: a random young male supporter in the wild. Steeling her nerve, she decided that her cover was already blown. *Might as well see what happens.* "You're right. It had its moments. Shame they had to ruin it with all that misogyny."

"I agree with you. I wouldn't want my sister in the room with me while I played, that's for sure. I also don't want my baby daughter exposed to games like that, once she's old enough to start playing with Daddy." Apparently picking up that his mention of a child had lowered Rosa's guard slightly, Nick pulled his phone from his jeans and called up a snapshot of a cherubic, dark-haired infant with her father's eyes. "I'll admit, I didn't recognize that shit when I was a teenager, but now I do. The way games portray women sometimes, the actions they might allow you to take...well, it can be really immature. And probably unhealthy." He tucked his phone back into his pocket. "Anyway, I wanted to tell you that you deserve a lot of credit for saying what you did—and...not any of the bullshit I know they've put you through."

Touched, Rosa whispered, "Thanks. I..." She forced back the tears that blurred her vision. "Honestly, I don't hear that a whole lot. Online, yeah, but in real life...for whatever reason, usually only men who hate me recognize me. Or the ones who enjoyed that stupid video."

"Shit, you're brave as hell. I can't imagine being the object of that much scrutiny, online or otherwise. I'd probably hide under my bed and never leave the house again."

Rosa laughed, a mirthless sound that rang hollow in her ears. "Trust me, there were days in the beginning when I pretty much did exactly that. It's still a struggle not to completely isolate myself, believe me."

"Well, you came here." Nick lifted his hands to gesture at their surroundings. "That took balls." He winced, most likely remembering her feminist credentials. "Pardon the expression."

"Sure, I came here, but under a fake name, and with a haircut it killed me to get." Rosa touched her bob in a show of mourning for her previously long, wavy locks. "Not that my pathetic attempt at a disguise ended up working. At all." For someone who wasn't well-known enough to get recognized on a daily basis in the bustling Bay Area, her current track record at Camp Rewind was nothing short of disastrous. "You're the second person to recognize me today."

Nick's forehead creased. "The other guy wasn't a dick, was he?"

"Just a little one," Rosa answered, cracking a smile at her pointed innuendo. "Tiny, I'm sure."

Nick snorted, then laughed heartily, clearly relieved to have gotten on her good side. "Nice."

"Well, he was obviously overcompensating for *something*."

"Pretty sure that's true of most trolls." Nick shrugged and smiled shyly. "You know, the problem isn't your haircut. You just…have a uniquely pretty face. It's your eyes, I think—and the dimple." He cleared his throat and backed away a step, as though to demonstrate that he wasn't trying to get creepy. "They're distinctive."

"Lucky me." But Rosa couldn't help but grin, genuinely warmed by the compliment. "Sadly, it's not practical to wear sunglasses everywhere I go."

"Ah, well. Screw the haters and stand proud. You said your opinion and made your case. People are free to agree or disagree, and that should be the end of it."

How Rosa wished that were true. "In theory."

"I can't be the only one who appreciates the crap women like you suffer through to try to make my favorite hobby more inclusive for my little girl. Just think of all the female gamers out there. Even if they never know your name, they'll benefit because you had the guts to speak up on their behalf." Nick extended his fist in an invitation to bump. "Don't forget about them, all right? Next time some asshole gives you grief, remember my daughter. I hope I can raise her to one day speak her mind with as much courage and conviction as you have." He lifted one shoulder in a sheepish shrug. "Just…don't let those douchebags win. Be strong."

Rosa knocked her fist against Nick's, grateful for the praise even if it fell a bit flat in the immediate aftermath of her ultimate act of cowardice. "I'm trying. Thanks."

"So other than being recognized, are you having a nice time here at camp?" Nick propped his hip against the counter, smoothly transitioning them to a less-charged topic. "Obviously the archery lesson has been the highlight so far…"

"Obviously." Taken aback by how liberating it felt to be out to someone besides Alice, Rosa mustered a genuine smile. "Camp's been quite the experience."

"A good experience, or a bad one?"

Rosa's composure wavered as they skirted the edge of the topic that felt too painful to discuss, no matter how friendly Nick might be. "A little of both?" Hoping to gloss over the subject, she said, "Mostly good. I made some new friends, engaged in rollicking, old-fashioned, camp-style fun. I even got scolded by a counselor."

"Marcia?"

Rosa laughed. "Nice guess."

Nick snorted and rolled his eyes. "Think you'll come back for another session?"

Rosa couldn't imagine ever returning to the scene of her greatest crime. "Maybe."

"If you do, I've got your back." Nick held up his counselor ID badge by the lanyard cord that encircled his neck. "You have no idea how much power and influence these credentials impart."

"Sounds impressive."

"Indeed." Nick dissolved into a goofy smile, returning to his place of rest on the counter. "You going to the dance tonight?"

Afraid she was being hit on, Rosa stayed noncommittal. "Yeah, I don't know about that."

"If you do, come find me. My fiancée is working as a counselor this weekend, too. We'd be happy to hang out in your vicinity, you know, to keep an eye on everything. You're actually, like, one of her heroes. She's a gamer, too."

Genuinely overwhelmed to have scored such an unexpectedly staunch ally, Rosa extended her hand to give Nick's a firm shake. "Thank you, Nick. I really…" Rosa paused, momentarily thrown by her volatile emotional state, until she was sure she wouldn't dissolve into tears. "*Really* appreciate that. More than you can possibly imagine."

"And think about that archery-club idea, all right?" Nick let go of her hand with a wink. "You really do have a knack for this."

Rosa laughed if only to keep herself from crying. She'd love to pursue archery—Alice, too. Why couldn't her life be just that simple? "It's fun. I'll look up the club's website, at least. I promise."

"If you live nearby, I belong to an organization in Berkeley. We'd love to see you there."

Rosa backed away, not prepared to make any decisions until she had her head together. "I'll think about it." She pointed at where Nick had stashed his portable game console. "For now, I'll let you get back to Stealth Inc."

He heaved a sigh. "Great. Back to feeling like a slow, uncoordinated dullard."

"I believe in you."

That earned her a chuckle. "Gee, thanks."

Rosa left the archery range feeling both better and worse than when she'd arrived. Better, naturally, for having had a positive encounter with a young man who knew all about her unfortunate claim to fame. Worse, because although Nick had clearly intended for his compliments about her strength and courage to lift her spirits, the past twenty-four hours had left her feeling the polar opposite of *brave*. As passionately as she'd once believed—and perhaps still believed—that Alice would be better off without her, the act of cutting her loose no longer felt altruistic, but cowardly. Yes, she *was* genuinely afraid to see Alice suffer because of her past, but her own fear of losing someone else she cared about to the nightmare of Internet trolling overrode everything else. Particularly because, unlike with Luis, this time she wasn't risking the loss of someone she simply *liked*. Although they'd only just met, when it came to Alice, Rosa knew she would end up losing someone she *loved*.

She had focused every moment of her romantic life since college on doing everything possible to avoid the same agony she'd experienced after losing her first real girlfriend. Even *before* she'd published that article. To finally go ahead and open her heart to someone—to *Alice*—at a time when she had no reason to believe any relationship could ever work out, because her life was basically in shambles…would that be valor, or stupidity?

Lacking clear direction, Rosa had walked only a short distance past the stables when the wet, awful sound of someone retching into the bushes ahead brought her up short. She squinted, then experienced a jolt of amusement mixed with alarm when she realized that her chief nemesis from earlier—Jason, former fan of her amateur video—stood just off the trail, looking very sick indeed. He glanced up at her approach, warily, then turned without speaking to puke some more.

"Loser," Rosa muttered under her breath. She spun around to head back toward the main camp, thoroughly revolted by the undignified display. That's *the sort of asshat I'm allowing to dictate the terms of my life? Pathetic.* She didn't normally get the opportunity to see the worst of her tormenters face-to-face. Usually she dealt with anonymous threats over the Internet, as well as mean tweets, nasty emails, and venomous blog entries devoted to tearing her down. At one point she'd received a stream of unmarked, vividly handwritten letters in her post-office box, before she'd changed her address. Even if the degrading, mean-spirited, oftentimes threatening words frightened her when they seemed to come from faceless, shadowy enemies, she suspected that the vast majority of the men who had vowed to rape and/or murder her were every bit as impotent as Jason. They posed no real threat to her safety *or* that of a potential love interest.

But all it would take is one maniac. Rosa swallowed, still no closer to finding her inner peace on the subject. *Or if not that, how about six months' worth of sexually violent imagery and threats delivered to Alice's inbox? She'd leave. How many women would willingly submit to being terrorized, let alone sweet, anxious Alice?*

Still at a loss, she'd nearly circled back to the dining hall when an angry voice brought her to a stumbling halt. "Lila, get your scrawny ass over here right *now!*"

Stopping dead, Rosa inhaled sharply at the sight of a visibly angry Bree storming in her direction. The reason for her dark mood seemed obvious. "You talked to Alice?"

"Yeah, you think?" Bree reached Rosa and grabbed hold of her arm to pull her deeper into the trees. "What the hell, girl? You know, I get it if you don't want to keep things going with Alice after tomorrow, but why say you'd keep seeing her if only your life weren't so complicated? That doesn't *help.*"

"Because it's the truth." Losing the battle with her emotions, Rosa felt her tenuous control shatter at the disappointment written across Bree's face. "I don't expect you to understand."

"Good, because I don't. Why dump her *today?*" Bree smacked her own forehead to imply that Rosa was boneheaded, she supposed, before huffing a dramatic sigh. "If you like the woman so much, why not enjoy one more night with her before you go?"

"Because that would've been wrong." When Bree started to protest, Rosa lost patience and shouted her down. "I didn't want either of us to feel any worse than we already do! And I couldn't go on acting like everything was cool when I knew it wasn't! She was falling for me. I couldn't let her do that."

"You're a real hero." Bree crinkled her nose in disapproval.

"What's so messy about your life, anyway? What are you so sure Alice isn't woman enough to handle?"

"It's not about Alice being *woman* enough." Rosa sighed, searching for a way to make Bree understand. Would it really hurt for one more person to know her story? At this point, she no longer cared about keeping secrets. At least not from Bree. "Okay. Where to start? Let's see, my real name isn't Lila. It's Rosa, so…nice to meet you, I guess. Although there's an excellent chance you've never heard of me before, I'm actually widely known on the Internet for all the wrong reasons." She exhaled and covered her face with her hand, too embarrassed to offer a deeper explanation. "Without getting into details…the experience of being mocked, loathed, and threatened by what sometimes feels like the entire world isn't something I'd wish on my worst enemy, let alone a woman I *really*, genuinely care about."

"But Alice knows the details?"

Rosa nodded. "I told her the first morning, after we woke up together and she freaked out. It didn't feel right to hide it."

"Then she's perfectly aware of what she's getting into." Bree popped her eyebrows. "So what's the problem? Believe me, shy Alice is willing to go to all sorts of lengths to show you that you're worth it. She wants you to let her *try*."

"I know." Angrily, Rosa pressed her forehead against the trunk of the nearest tree, then reared back to give herself a firm *clunk* to the front of her skull. "But I'm *scared*," she whispered, and brought her arms up to hide her face against the rough bark. "All right?"

"I know you are." Bree's voice softened as she stepped behind Rosa and wrapped her in a surprisingly gentle hug. "But I truly think you should give her a chance. There are no guarantees, of course, but she *seriously* likes you. I mean…a lot. If you like her, too…"

"I do." Rosa tried to cling to Bree's words, desperate for a ray of hope to dispel the darkness she'd fallen into. "But I've only ever loved one person for real before, and losing her hurt so bad that I've basically spent my entire adult life until now avoiding serious relationships with women just so I wouldn't ever have to feel that way again. I was so young then." She paused. "I don't think I could stand to lose Alice, too. And there's so much standing against us, even beyond my bullshit." Heart heavy, she mentally cataloged the list of reasons a relationship probably wouldn't work. "She's not out to her parents. Her mother is this domineering shrew—"

"I know, it's not easy to trust." Bree stepped back and patted her shoulder. "Alice seems to deserve a little of yours, though, from what I've seen of her. Shit, what if you just gave it a week? Even two. Call it a trial period and end things if it doesn't feel right. Will you really feel any more heartbroken in two weeks, knowing you and Alice really *can't* work, than you do right now?" She helped Rosa off the tree and led them to a nearby bench to sit down. "For all you know, she could be the love of your life. Or maybe not. It's possible you'll go out on a few dates and realize you're better off as friends. Call me crazy, but it seems worth it to find out for sure."

Rosa could no longer remember why that would be impossible. Maybe it wasn't? Then she recalled the worst of the threats she'd received, the ones that kept her up at night and sometimes led her to sleep with a knife under her pillow. "You have no idea how badly certain people despise me. So much that even my friends have been targeted in the past. Let's say things *do* go great between me and Alice and my enemies *don't* drive her away...her life will be ruined. All because she fell in love with me. I don't know if I could live with that."

"Let her life be ruined." Bree held Rosa's hand in both hers, more serious than Rosa had yet seen her. "Alice is a grown-ass woman. You don't get to decide whether she's allowed to fall in love with you. That's her choice—and she's making it."

"But she doesn't know—"

"She knows she wants to give you a shot." Bree squeezed her hand, then released Rosa from her grip. "Let her. If you feel anything for Alice at all, don't treat her like just another fuck-and-run."

Rosa bristled. "I wouldn't do that."

"No?" Bree sat back and folded her arms over her generous breasts. "Is that why Enid and I found her hiding in her bunk earlier, *crying*? Dumped the day after you popped her lesbian cherry? Like that's all you were after?"

Rosa was almost positive she couldn't possibly feel any lower. "You're right. I fucked up."

"Damn straight."

"That said, I'm still scared." Rosa sighed, sick with indecision. "For her, and for me."

"Welcome to life." Bree clapped her on the back. "Sometimes it's terrifying. Other times, transcendent. The trick is not to let the fear keep you from the joy."

Rosa blinked silently at Bree, then slowly extended her middle finger to shoot her the bird. "Fuck you for being so smart. Did you seriously just come up with that?"

Bree shrugged, feigning nonchalance. "Whatever."

"Shit." Rosa exhaled and wound her hair around her fists, pulling until her vision blurred. "Maybe you're right."

"*Maybe?*" Bree poked her in the side. "Go fix this. Now."

"What if I can't?"

Bree snorted, muttering, "Trust me, you can."

Bree hadn't seen the pain Rosa had inflicted earlier. She hadn't watched the light be extinguished from Alice's eyes. "I mean, I *really* fucked up."

"Then you'd better *really* apologize." Bree's sober facade cracked as she wiggled her tongue suggestively. "I'm sure you'll think of something."

The memory of Alice's mouthwatering flavor fractured the last of Rosa's stubborn will. Bree was right. To never know for sure might very well be every bit as devastating as the possible discovery that their relationship wasn't strong enough to survive the transition into the real world. Because what if it *could*? What if she was able to taste Alice whenever she wanted, to share every milestone along the way? Rosa's hands trembled as she clasped her knees. "I never expected to meet someone this weekend."

"But you did."

"Yeah." Rosa blew out a noisy breath. "I'm so not ready for this."

"Like I said, welcome to life. In case you haven't noticed, the universe rarely gives a shit how you feel."

"I *have* noticed that, actually." Rosa offered Bree a grateful nod. "What do I owe you, doc?"

"Bring back Alice's smile, at least for tonight, and we'll call it even."

Rosa stuck out her hand so they could shake on it. "I'll do my best."

"Tell her you're a goddamn fool. Always works for me." After a beat, Bree dissolved into laughter. "In your case, it also happens to be true."

"Maybe." Despite having just chosen to put her faith in Alice and their growing bond, Rosa wondered whether she was even capable of making intelligent decisions anymore. How was it possible to feel this mixed-up about a woman who made her so unambiguously happy? "Call me in a year and we'll decide how foolish I am."

"Give me your number and I will. Fifty bucks says Alice answers the phone."

Rosa scoffed, though the idea that Alice might someday be that comfortably ensconced in her life made her heart flutter. "You're on."

"Great. Maybe I'll buy a new video game with my winnings."

Narrowing her gaze, Rosa searched Bree's face for any sign that she'd misunderstood the meaning of her comment. When Bree simply smiled, Rosa said, flatly, "You *do* know who I am."

"Not until you told me your first name and that people hate you on the Internet…I swear." Bree held up her fingers to indicate scout's honor. "Otherwise I never would've guessed in a million years."

"Fantastic." Rosa sagged in dismay that her infamy was even more widespread than she'd dared to imagine. "I'm starting to feel like I shouldn't have cut my hair."

"Your hair is adorable." Bree clucked her tongue. "Now go, find Alice. She was headed for the arts-and-crafts building, last I saw."

"All right." Rosa briefly considered asking Bree whether she'd ever clicked the link to watch her video but decided she didn't want to know. "Thanks, Bree. This helped."

"And I didn't even have to smack you." When Rosa laughed, Bree simply stared, stone-faced. "I offered. Alice said no."

Maybe it wasn't too late to fix things after all. "I'll be sure to let her know how much I appreciate her lack of vengeance."

Bree cracked a grin. "She's a keeper, all right." Insistent, she nudged Rosa off the bench. "Don't let those guys win. What you said about that game was valid, and you're a beautiful girl with absolutely no reason to feel ashamed—about anything. Go, get your woman. Make this weekend count."

Sufficiently pumped up, Rosa stood and shook out her arms as though preparing for battle. "Right."

Bree stared at her with gruff affection. "Just know that if you hurt her again, I'll kick your ass." In response, Rosa held out her fist. Bree accompanied her answering bump with a dramatic rolling of her eyes and a muttered, "*Dork.*"

"I'm still scared," Rosa said, forcing a smile.

"So is she." Bree tapped her shoe against Rosa's calf, urging her along. "Be scared together."

❖

Rosa went to the arts-and-crafts building first but didn't see Alice anywhere. She spotted Jamal tinkering with a table full of shiny odds and ends, and managed to get his attention long enough to learn that Alice had already come and gone. In fact, Rosa had missed her by minutes. As it was now well past lunchtime, her stomach let out a predictable growl. Maybe Alice had gotten hungry, too? Rosa followed her stomach, and her intuition, to the dining hall, but apart from the peanut-butter sandwich she hastily made herself, she found nothing there. Finally, she went to check the most obvious remaining location: their cabin. Afraid to discover Alice curled up on her top bunk, awash in tears, Rosa walked slowly, taking the time to thoroughly chew and swallow her food.

Coward. Her inner voice suddenly sounded an awful lot like Bree's and made her feel just as bad. *You don't want Alice to suffer because of you? Then end her suffering.* She quickened her steps as she approached the cabin. *If you can.*

But Alice wasn't inside. Rosa walked to their shared bunk bed and stood on her tiptoes to peek into the top, in disbelief that she'd once again come up empty. She'd really expected to find Alice here. Where else was there to look? She pictured Alice hiding out alone in the woods somewhere, too timid to participate in the festivities building up to their last night at camp and the big dance. Right back to where she'd started, except worse—because now her heart was freshly savaged. The pathetic image took Rosa's legs out from under her, forcing her to seek out the edge of her mattress with her hand so she could sit down.

Fuck. She had to find Alice. She *had* to make this right.

Resolved yet no less afraid, Rosa took a moment to collect her thoughts and then went to push herself to her feet. She froze when her pinkie finger brushed against a cold, metallic object. Startled, she jerked her hand away and turned to see what had been left on her bunk.

At first she wasn't sure what she was staring at. Wires and circuitry and batteries and plastic housing…along with a note. For an instant, her heart stuttered at the thought that someone had planted a homemade bomb for her to find. But then she noticed the vaguely humanoid shape of the object, complete with LED lights carefully arranged to form eyes and a smiling mouth. She picked up the note, reading the fuzzy words through watery eyes.

I would fight for you.—Alice

"I apologize for the less-than-impressive design. I didn't have much to work with…only the components Jamal thought to buy, which didn't include a micro-controller. So all that robot can really do is avoid obstacles. Not fight, to be honest." Alice stepped out from behind Bree's bunk, cautiously. "It would actually take a fair amount of effort to make him combat-ready."

Initially surprised by the sound of Alice's low, determined voice, by the end of the slightly awkward speech, Rosa had to wipe away the tears rolling down her face. "I love him."

"I'm glad." Alice's anxiety seemed to ease, yet her eyes still swam with turbulent emotion. "Listen, you don't need to make me any promises. You don't have to say anything at all. Just…can we spend one last night together? No strings attached?"

Rosa wanted many more nights—and days—with Alice than that, but she was happy to seize the chance to reconcile without having to commit to anything aloud. She was still working up to that. Rather than reply, she stood, closed the distance between them, and gathered Alice into a tight hug.

Alice's arms flew around her. "Oh," she breathed, then shuddered.

Her obvious relief brought fresh tears to Rosa's eyes. "I know we said no more apologies, but I owe you a big one. So…I'm sorry I was a goddamn fool."

Alice returned the desperate embrace, clinging to her so tightly Rosa squeaked at the sudden lack of air. "You were scared. I understand being scared, *very* well." She placed her lips against Rosa's ear and whispered, "I forgive you."

Choked with emotion, Rosa said, "Thank you." She kissed Alice's cheek, unsurprised when her lips found salty tears. "You may understand being scared, but you're also really amazing at being brave." She stopped, took a breath, then plunged ahead. "Maybe you can teach me?"

It was vague, and not nearly the bold declaration of her intention to commit to…*something*…that she'd hoped to summon enough courage to offer, but it was a start. And boy, did Alice seem to approve.

Soft yet demanding lips landed on Rosa's, drawing her into a kiss that sent them both stumbling for her bunk. Right before their bodies crashed onto the mattress, Rosa held Alice back with a protective arm. "Wait!" She took a moment to carefully place Alice's robotic creation in her duffel bag, then pulled Alice down on top of her so they could entangle their limbs and reconnect with their whole bodies. "I really *do* love that little guy."

Alice blushed, visibly trying—and adorably failing—to suppress a goofy smile. "I hoped you would."

"And…" Rosa swallowed, tracing Alice's rosy cheek with the backs of her fingers. "I really like *you*. A lot."

"I know." Despite the profession of certainty, Rosa's words were making Alice positively *glow*. "Rosa, I like you more than I've ever liked anyone. I know that must be terrifying for you to hear, but it's true." Grinning, she bent to brush their lips together. "First lesson in courage: face your fears. Don't run away from them."

Having somehow lucked her way back into Alice's arms, Rosa was in no hurry to go anywhere. "Yes, ma'am."

Alice's hips pressed into her, urgently, as she plundered Rosa's mouth in a passionate kiss. When they broke apart, some time later, Alice whispered, "Let's talk about tomorrow, tomorrow. Tonight, the real world doesn't exist. Tonight, all we have is our magically fleeting summer-camp romance. Deal?"

Rosa slid a hand down the length of her back, then curled her fingers around a firm ass cheek, letting her fingertips graze Alice's warm pussy. "Deal." She squeezed the pliant flesh that filled her palm and rubbed at the damp heat emanating from the crotch of Alice's linen shorts. "We should find somewhere to go."

Alice groaned and rocked against her touch. "Right here feels good."

That's when the universe, apparently feeling the need to intervene, sent what sounded like five thousand loud, giggly, chatty women into the cabin with them to get dressed for the farewell dance. Alice swore under her breath, rolled off to the side, and buried her face in Rosa's chest. But what she didn't do was get out of bed. She didn't pull away. She didn't leave.

Rosa held Alice close, mentally shifting gears from lust to rapidly growing love.

"We'll find somewhere," Alice muttered against Rosa's breast, making the nipple harden. "We *have* to."

CHAPTER SIXTEEN

Three hours later, Alice and Rosa stood behind a redwood tree far enough away from the dance raging inside the dining hall that Alice could barely make out the lyrics of whatever mid-90s hit was playing. They were passing the joint they hadn't ended up lighting the night before, trading kisses between hits, while, from Alice's perspective, thoroughly frittering away their remaining time together on idle conversation about nothing that mattered. Although grateful the pungent smoke mellowed the edges of her rampant horniness, she knew it would take more than medical-grade cannabis to ease the throbbing ache between her legs.

Earlier, she'd decided not to push Rosa to define the terms of their relationship beyond Camp Rewind—lest she risk their chance to spend one last night together in relative happiness—so while Alice was *pretty sure* that Rosa's return indicated a willingness to pursue whatever they were building at least until camp ended, part of her couldn't help but wonder whether tonight might still be their last opportunity to be *together*, together. Unfortunately, that line of speculation made it difficult to focus on Rosa's admittedly amusing anecdote about the time she'd taken two dates to her eighth-grade dance.

Even if tonight *wasn't* the end for them, Alice yearned for Rosa's touch. Not only so she could prove what a quick study she tended to be, but also to show Rosa how very *good* she could make her feel if only she were allowed to try. They'd lain in Rosa's bunk for over an hour before the dance began as their camp mates changed and primped and made themselves up around them, and while she would have been embarrassed to let anyone see her snuggled up in another woman's arms at the beginning of the weekend, tonight Alice had found herself, incredibly, not concerned at all. On the contrary, she was proud of her connection with Rosa, proud to have captured the attention of someone so beautiful, so funny, so kind. She was *so proud*, and so enraptured, that she almost felt ready to suggest they go back to Rosa's bed, lingering cabin mates be damned, to celebrate their reunion.

Rosa pulled Alice out of her daydream when she curled a hand around the back of her neck, pressed their mouths together, and breathed out, sending the generous hit she'd just taken from her lungs to Alice's. Without missing a beat, Alice inhaled deeply and wrapped her arm around Rosa's waist to grind their pelvises together. She turned her head to blow out the cloud of smoke, grinned at the blissful, euphoric head rush, and went back to Rosa's mouth for another lazy kiss.

Rosa braced her hands on the tree next to Alice's head, rotating her hips until she hit an angle that made Alice gasp. "I want to be inside you," Rosa rumbled into her ear. "Should we go to your car?"

Alice shook her head, disappointed that Rosa hadn't hit upon a better idea. "I'm not sure that'll work. Earlier, Jamal told me that Marcia busted a couple having sex in the parking lot last night. Knocked on the guy's car window, shone a flashlight in their eyes…then sent them back to their cabins after an undoubtedly embarrassing lecture. I have a feeling she'll be on patrol again tonight."

"Let me guess…liability issue?" Rosa backed away slightly to take a final draw from their dwindling roach.

"I'm sure. I don't know about you, but I'm really not up for having that woman catch us *in flagrante*." Alice moved forward when Rosa flipped the joint around to offer her the end, holding it close to the burning tip with her pinched fingers so that Alice could inhale one last hit. Alice nodded in gratitude as she exhaled and watched as Rosa thoroughly extinguished the meager remnants against the tree. Once Rosa's hands were free, she wrapped both arms around Alice and cradled her close. Since making up, Rosa hadn't seemed to want to stop touching. That had to be a good sign. Right? Reminded of her craven need, Alice murmured, "And stealing another boat is out…"

Rosa trailed her fingers along Alice's ribs, stroking her stomach, grazing the underside of her breast. "Even if I wasn't afraid of Marcia's wrath, I'm sure as hell terrified of snakes, which means that boathouse is dead to me." Her hands suddenly froze in place, and she eased back to scan the area around their feet with a mildly panicked look. "Also, maybe, the great outdoors in the dark."

Alice exhaled, trying to remain calm. She was embarrassed to admit how upset the thought of *not* having sex tonight made her feel. If she didn't think it would cause unnecessary drama, she'd be tempted to suggest they simply choose one of their apartments and go there together *immediately*. Sadly, such a proposal hardly seemed prudent when she still wasn't certain how Rosa felt about the idea of moving their relationship outside camp boundaries in general, let alone right then. Racking her brain, Alice worried her lip with her teeth and reclined against the tree as she reviewed the possibilities, frustrated by how often the specter of Marcia appeared to shoot each one down.

"*Fuck*, you're sexy." Hot lips and sharp teeth sought out Alice's throat as Rosa abandoned her paranoia for desire, once again pressing their bodies together for another feverish round of dry humping. "Maybe I can deal with the snakes. We could walk a mile or so into the woods…I'll press you up against a tree and slip my hand into your shorts…" Rosa kissed along her jaw, pushed her hand between their stomachs, and ran her fingernails along Alice's waistband. She paused to toy with the button and scratched the zipper playfully. "Want to do that?"

Yes, but *no*. Alice wanted more than a quick hand job in the middle of the dark, scary woods. She wanted to lie in a real bed with Rosa, to feel her naked skin, to explore her body without worrying about errant reptiles *or* Hollywood-style serial killers lurking nearby. She wanted to make tonight *count*. Alice surprised herself by abandoning her shyness altogether. "What if we just went back to the cabin? We could be quiet…"

Rosa hesitated before lowering her hand to cup Alice between the legs and gently massage the sensitive mound with her palm. "Could we?"

Alice gasped, grabbing onto Rosa's shoulders so she wouldn't fall down. It still felt oddly foreign to be caressed so blatantly, and with such deliberate care, in a way that was clearly intended to make *her* feel good. The indescribable pleasure of Rosa's fingers emboldened Alice in a way she'd never dreamed possible. "To be honest, I'm not sure I care anymore."

"Really?" Rosa snuck her hand beneath the leg of Alice's shorts to fondle her through her panties. Alice moaned, pushing herself against the searching fingers. When Rosa rubbed her clit through the sodden material, causing Alice to grip more tightly to her shoulders, she could feel whatever argument Rosa might have offered vanish in a surge of arousal. Rosa pressed their foreheads together and gave Alice's pussy a firm squeeze. "You know…maybe I don't care, either."

"We'll never see these people again, right?" Alice didn't want to pressure her into anything that made her uncomfortable, but poised as she was to shed her own inhibitions, she found it helpful to rationalize aloud. "We could stay under the blanket. We don't even have to take our clothes off." She frowned, not particularly liking *that* idea. "Well, maybe we could take *most* of our clothes off."

Rosa shifted her hand, angling her finger beneath the soaked crotch of Alice's panties to brush her bare labia. "All right."

In an instant of startling lucidity, Alice reconsidered their plan in light of Rosa's history—the forced exhibitionism, the shame that accompanied it, her unwanted notoriety—and wondered if she wasn't being insensitive. "We don't have to. If it's going to freak you out…"

"The only thing that freaks me out is the thought of not making you come tonight." Rosa removed her hand from Alice's shorts. "Besides, I owe you an apology, and I intend to deliver." She lifted her hand to her face, inhaling Alice's scent with a wolfish smile. "However you're willing to let me."

Yes, Alice decided, absolutely nothing could keep her from taking Rosa to bed tonight. Not even her anxious brain.

CHAPTER SEVENTEEN

Still unsure what to make of Alice's stunning turnaround on the subject of public displays of affection, let alone full-blown exhibitionistic sex, Rosa had to check in one last time before they entered the cabin. "You're *sure*?"

Alice stopped, exuding a remarkable amount of patience for a woman so obviously in need of a quick, dirty fuck. "Positive. Are *you* sure?"

Frankly, and perhaps surprisingly, Rosa wasn't all that concerned for her own reputation. After all, that had been ruined long ago. The only thing giving her pause was her memory of the Alice Wu she'd met two nights ago, who'd barely responded to her attempts at making small talk, as well as Alice from yesterday, who'd nearly dropped Rosa's hand under scrutiny...who'd been so opposed to the idea of getting caught having sex that she'd agreed to break the rules and *steal a boat*. It was difficult to reconcile this newly uninhibited creature in front of her with the Alice Wu who almost hadn't gotten out of the car at the beginning of the weekend. Stoned or not, getting down around other people was an unquestionably audacious step for someone so naturally timid.

A little high herself, Rosa struggled to explain her hesitation. "I'm fine with this. Honestly. I just..." She shrugged. "Don't want you to get embarrassed if someone hears...or decides to tease us."

Alice held both of Rosa's hands against her chest and stepped closer to stare directly into her eyes. "Some things are worth a little potential embarrassment." She smiled, kissing one set of knuckles, then the other. "Another lesson from Camp Rewind."

"Dawn will be so proud of you." Rosa cracked a grin, but she meant the compliment sincerely. She couldn't imagine how surprised Alice's therapist would be when she heard the recap of this weekend. Mindful that she'd already been scolded about trusting Alice to set her own limits, Rosa exhaled. Maybe it wasn't an entirely bad idea to test exactly how much potential embarrassment Alice could handle, anyway. She would need a thick skin to date the infamous Rosa Salazar, masturbating hypocrite. "Okay. But, before we go inside…top bunk, or bottom? Top would be more private—"

"Yet also more dangerous." Alice chewed on her bottom lip, no doubt calculating the logistics and probability of a fall.

"Agreed. The bottom is safer, but if anyone is already in bed, or comes in while we're…" Rosa wiggled her hand in an unspoken effort to convey all the filthy, wonderful things she wanted to do to Alice tonight. "There's a better chance they'll notice us fooling around."

Alice grabbed Rosa's hand and pulled her up the cabin steps. "Bottom. Safety first. Modesty…some other time."

Rosa dropped her volume to a whisper as Alice opened the door to reveal the dark, seemingly silent interior of the large room. "Squeeze my hand twice if you want to leave and find somewhere else to go. You know…if anyone's in there."

Alice tugged her inside. "All right. Now come on."

Rosa quieted as they stepped into the dark room, attuning her senses to detect signs of life within the apparently empty space. Apart from a single, motionless form that snored evenly in the top bunk nearest the door, everyone else seemed to have vacated the premises to attend the dance. Or at least that's what she thought until they reached Bree's bunk, where a dark arm shot out from beneath an unzipped sleeping bag to brace its owner against the bed frame as she shook with pleasure. Rosa stopped walking instinctively, certain that Alice would give her the signal to leave. *Surely* Alice wouldn't want to offer a free show to a perv like Bree.

But Alice pulled her along past Bree and Enid's blatant fucking, leading them to the opposite side of their shared bunk bed so they weren't standing right beside the other couple. She unzipped her light hoodie while leaning to whisper in Rosa's ear. "I don't think they'll mind, and besides…that's kind of *hot*."

Convinced by Alice's carefree attitude, Rosa pulled her own tank top over her head, followed by her bra. She stopped to kiss Alice lightly and stroke her bare arms. "We'll be more discreet."

A whimper from the bed next to them, followed by a moaned "*Harder*," triggered an audible hitch in Alice's breathing. "Maybe," she murmured back. With impressive speed and efficiency, she stripped down to her bra and panties, then dove beneath the blanket she'd lent Rosa on their first night together.

Not wanting to be left behind, Rosa followed suit and shed her jeans and socks, but kept her panties on…for the sake of propriety? Giggling at the thought, she slipped into bed beside Alice, burrowing beneath the covers as she pulled the woman she wanted to take home into her arms. She smoothed her hand down Alice's chest, over her stomach, beneath the waistband of her panties. Then she placed her mouth against Alice's earlobe and whispered, "Listen to them."

Alice inhaled swiftly when Rosa rubbed three fingers across her labia. Rosa closed her eyes as she tried to memorize the shape and feel of the delicate folds and coated the scorching flesh with the wet heat of Alice's desire. Next to them, Bree and Enid changed positions. Almost immediately, the air was filled with the lewd, distinct soundtrack of oral sex, enthusiastically performed.

"Oh, *shit*," Enid groaned. Apologetically, she added in a slightly louder voice, "Don't mind us. I'll, um—" She broke off with a squawk. "Try to keep it down! Sorry!"

"No worries." Rosa kept her voice hushed as she continued to stroke Alice's drenched pussy. "It sets a mood, you know?"

Alice arched her back, mouth falling open when Rosa's fingertips finally tracked up to circle her engorged clit. She released a quiet sigh, not so loud as to be heard over Bree's noisy efforts or Enid's appreciative moans, but audible enough to make it clear that she was definitely getting off on the semi-public nature of their encounter. Intrigued, Rosa pressed harder against Alice's clit and drew out a breathless, high-pitched whimper. Enid followed up with a cry of disappointment when Bree stopped, mid-slurp, to remark, "I trust you're showing Alice how *incredibly* sorry you are?"

Rosa smirked as she coaxed out an even louder moan from Alice, accompanied by a flood of hot juices she quickly redistributed across the swollen clit and labia. She was almost positive that Bree and

Enid had heard Alice's vocalization that time around and was equally positive that Alice both knew *and* approved of her audience. "Working on it as we speak."

"Good." Bree returned to Enid with a loud suck, then paused to share one last thought. "Get that sweet little pussy one time for us, will you?"

Alice brought her hands up to hide her face, but Rosa sensed the conflicted arousal behind her obvious bashfulness. She seized Alice's labia and tugged lightly before moving down to toy with her opening. Watching Alice's face, she said to Bree, "Enid lets you kiss her clit with that mouth?"

"I sure do." In her peripheral vision, Rosa made out Enid's shadowy form pushing Bree's head back down. "Now fucking *get back to it* already."

Alice's hips bumped against Rosa's hand, searching for more than she could easily give with her panties in the way. After pausing to kiss one of the satin cups covering Alice's delicious breasts, Rosa whispered into her ear while simultaneously teasing her with a brief hint of penetration, sinking the tip of her thumb less than a centimeter inside. "May I take your panties off?"

"Yes." Alice's response was so soft that Rosa could barely make out her consent. As though realizing as much, Alice spoke louder, repeating herself. "*Yes.*"

Rosa arranged the blanket around Alice's body and ducked beneath, not wanting her to feel any more exposed than necessary. She maneuvered Alice's panties down her hips, to her knees, where Alice took the lead and used her feet to push them off the rest of the way. Rosa crawled back up to lie at Alice's side, kissing her gently while returning her hand to its favorite spot between her trembling thighs. Delighted to find her already open and waiting, Rosa skimmed her fingertips across Alice's swollen clit on her way down to the slippery entrance. She kissed Alice's neck, then her mouth, while tracing her opening. "Still okay with this?"

Nodding, Alice hooked her arm around Rosa's neck and returned her kisses. "I'm so glad you're here with me," she whispered, sounding close to tears. "You feel *amazing.*"

Rosa's eyelids fluttered shut as she pushed a single finger inside Alice. She listened to the quiet exhalation the action elicited, felt a shudder of pleasure roll through Alice's body, and smiled at the lifting of needy hips in a silent plea for more. Ignoring the sounds from the neighboring bunk, she rested her forehead on the pillow next to Alice and spoke so she wouldn't be overheard. *"You* feel amazing, Al." The nickname tripped off her tongue like the most natural thing in the world. She prayed Alice didn't hate it. "Warm and tight and beautiful and…" Her throat closed up, but she forced out what she'd intended to say. *"Mine."*

Alice's arm tightened around her shoulders. "Rosa." Her free hand found Rosa's bare breast and tugged at the tip. "Please…"

Rosa didn't know exactly what Alice wanted, so she simply slipped another finger inside and continued to murmur into her ear. "You make me feel things I haven't felt…" She searched her soul, then said, "That I've *never* felt." Bringing her thumb to Alice's clit, she triggered an immediate, audible moan when she rubbed fast, focused circles over the swollen nub. "Thank you for not giving up on me…for letting me touch you like this again."

"Oh!" Alice sucked in a tremulous breath, thighs quivering next to Rosa's arm. She gasped, then said, more loudly than Rosa was expecting, "Slow down or I'll—" Her speech cut off abruptly as she wriggled away from Rosa's thumb but farther onto the thrusting fingers, in a frantic attempt to escape her impending climax. "I'm gonna—*Wait.*"

"You heard her. *Slow down.*" Bree sat up in her bunk so she and Enid could once again shift positions. "Draw it out a little, for fuck's sake!"

Rosa shook with laughter when Alice slammed her thighs shut on her hand and whined, gratefully, *"Yeah.* What she said."

Rosa withdrew from Alice and pressed her thighs apart so she could climb between them, pausing to shed her own panties to allow their lower bodies to touch skin-to-skin. She settled in with a contented groan, which only grew louder when Alice wrapped her legs around Rosa's hips to paint her abdomen with her searing juices. Rocking into Alice, Rosa touched their foreheads together and stared down into her eyes. "Nice and slow, then," she said, loud enough for Bree to hear. Then she lowered her voice to a bare whisper meant for Alice's ears alone. "Not so shy anymore, are we? You *dirty, dirty* girl."

Alice pushed up against her, sliding her wet folds across Rosa's pelvic bone. "There are few things more frustrating than being shy *and* dirty," she breathed. "Therefore, I'm trying to rise to the occasion."

"I'll say." Rosa repositioned herself to ride Alice's thigh while pressing her own against Alice's fiery pussy, grinding hard into the heated flesh. "You *do* seem to be enjoying this."

"Yes," Alice half-moaned, half-whispered as their bodies fell into a natural rhythm.

"Even better than porn?" Rosa nibbled on Alice's earlobe, loving the blatant effect her words had on the woman beneath her. "You've fantasized about this type of thing before, haven't you? Listening to other people fuck, letting them hear *you* get fucked?" She knew she'd hit her intended mark when Alice's movements became more urgent and she coated Rosa in a renewed surge of slick cum. "You like it when I talk to you like this." That one wasn't a question.

Alice clutched her shoulders. "I...yes."

Rosa plunged her tongue into Alice's searching mouth, then threaded her fingers through her dark hair, pulling lightly until Alice moaned again. Someone else joined in with her own cry of pleasure, either Bree or Enid, but Rosa's attention remained locked on the woman beneath her. She broke their kiss and dropped a hand to grab Alice's butt, helping her to ride the firm pressure of the thigh sliding across her pussy. Alice bucked against her, wild and untamed, so much freer than the woman cowering in Camp Rewind's parking lot that it made Rosa's eyes sting with barely suppressed emotion. How much Alice had grown, and so *quickly*. Regardless of whether she acted painfully withdrawn at times and overly anxious at others, Alice hadn't yet failed to surprise and impress again and again. With Rosa by her side to provide loving encouragement, what other hidden layers might they eventually discover?

Humbled by the startling realization that she actually *didn't* know Alice well enough to accurately gauge her ability to weather the shit-storm that was her life, Rosa broke away from their kiss to gaze down at Alice's gorgeous face and trace her jaw with her fingers. She hated to interrupt their heated reunion with her stupid regret but nonetheless whispered, "I really am sorry, Al. *So* sorry. I was wrong to make my cowardice about you, to imply that you couldn't handle my shit. *I'm* the one who couldn't handle it."

Nostrils flaring, Alice stared up at her with an expression of concern contorted by pleasure. "Rosa, it's okay. I understand."

"It's not okay. And no, you don't. Not really." Rosa shook her head as moisture welled in her eyes. *Damn it, this is* not *the time for this discussion.* And it wasn't, mostly, yet there was suddenly so much she burned to say. Earlier, Alice had excused her actions without any hesitation at all, and Rosa couldn't help but feel that had been a mistake. She shouldn't have been forgiven so easily, not without offering a real apology first—an honest one, from her heart. Until that happened, Rosa didn't feel worthy of being with Alice this way.

"What I did *wasn't* okay. Yes, I was scared. I really, *really* like you, and the sex is so good…I could feel myself wanting more, but I'm so afraid to get hurt again…to even let someone get close enough *to* hurt me…and then to ruin your life in the process…" Despite the tears now rolling down her cheeks, she never stopped moving, never slowed her gliding motions against Alice's prominent clit. "None of that excuses what I did. You deserved better." She hesitated, then whispered, brokenly, "You *deserve* better."

A shiny tear tracked its way down Alice's cheek, barely visible in the darkness. Her hips slowed. "But I want *you*."

"I want you, too." Rosa wiped away the tear, then shifted so she could ease her hand between their bodies. She touched Alice's clit, a mere brush of her fingertips that caused Alice to inhale sharply and grab Rosa's shoulders. "I want to feel worthy of this."

"You are." Alice opened her legs so wide her knees hovered over the sides of the narrow mattress and tilted her hips to encourage a firmer touch. Her hand found the back of Rosa's head, winding in her hair, and she pulled Rosa's face down against her chest so she could hear the excited thrum of her staccato heartbeat. "Rosa, your friendship is worth *everything* to me. Even if you screwed up today. *Everyone* screws up. I…unh!" She cried out when Rosa pressed the pads of two fingers on either side of her clit and rubbed harder. "You…deserve…a second… chance."

A second chance. What Rosa wouldn't have given for a real-life do-over eighteen months ago, when it might have saved her from creating the mess she still felt reluctant to drag Alice into. But that tumultuous period of her life had eventually led her to the place she was now, wrapped up in Alice Wu's warm embrace, so perhaps, as the old adage claimed, sometimes things *did* happen for a reason. Besides, if she only ever got one opportunity to right a wrong, she'd rather use it to repair her friendship with Alice. The sometimes-overwhelming nostalgia she felt for her old, uncomplicated existence suddenly seemed so much less immediate than her desire to remain in Alice's life. At this point she *had to*, if only so she could continue to watch her new friend grow. "Thanks for giving me one."

"I only hope you won't require a third," Alice whispered, half-jokingly, in a quavering voice. "*Please.*"

Rosa lifted her head and further shifted her weight to allow her hand better access to Alice's soaked pussy. "Whatever else happens, Alice, I'll *never* treat you that way again. *Ever.* Like you're disposable." She pushed a finger inside, trying to ignore the emotional pain that flitted across Alice's face at her words before the physical pleasure of penetration washed it away. "Because you're *not*. No matter what, you're my friend. Tomorrow, and beyond."

"Rosa…" Alice whispered her name, pleading. "I…" She caught her lower lip between her teeth with a gasp. "I *forgive* you."

A weight lifted from Rosa's soul, a burden she hadn't even realized she'd carried so heavily until Alice relieved it with her absolution. Lighter in its absence, Rosa crushed her mouth to Alice's in a heartfelt kiss, swept away by the need to follow her apology with action. She fingered Alice with care, not as fast or as hard as she wanted to, still trying to draw things out so Alice wouldn't feel cheated. Yet the noises Alice made, those quiet, mewling whimpers, drove her absolutely fucking crazy. When Alice's body jerked, a telltale sign that she was climbing the peak again—*may not be able to orgasm with another person, my ass*—Rosa broke their kiss to beg, "Let me make you come, baby. It won't be the last time, I promise. *Not* the last time."

"Okay." Alice dragged her fingernails down Rosa's bare back to her ass. "Okay." She moved against Rosa's hand, impaling herself over and over, mouth set in a determined line. "Okay."

Rosa smiled at her whispered mantra and withdrew so she could press another finger into Alice's eager vagina. Upon finding that Alice was able to accommodate the addition with ease, Rosa snuck in a third. The snug fit made Alice whimper breathlessly and sent another rush of wetness to slick Rosa's palm. She brought her thumb up to press the engorged clit while at the same time easing her free arm beneath Alice's back to drag her closer to her chest, until she could feel Alice's thundering heartbeat echoing her own. She brought their faces close together and rumbled, "You feel so good wrapped around my fingers."

"Yes," Alice whispered, her breath burning Rosa's cheek. "Like that."

Rosa maintained the speed and pressure of her thumb exactly as Alice requested, pressing open-mouthed kisses to her throat while she steadily increased the force of her thrusts. "Like this?"

Alice dug her heels into the mattress and nodded emphatically, like she was afraid to open her mouth lest she scream out loud. Her eyes screwed shut, her nostrils flared, and her entire body trembled. A few seconds later, she went completely silent, and rigid, as her mouth dropped open in a silent scream. "That's right, love, let go," Rosa murmured, and angled her mouth over Alice's, plunging her tongue inside to taste the euphoria of her release.

Both Alice's arms came up around Rosa's shoulders, holding fast as she rode the crescendo of her orgasm for long, thrilling moments that seemed to stretch into minutes. Her vaginal muscles clutched at Rosa's fingers, repeatedly, contracting with wave after wave of orgasmic bliss while the rest of her body convulsed in a sympathetic loss of control. Rosa kept her fingers moving, kept rubbing with her thumb, until Alice dug her nails into her shoulder blades and whimpered, "Stop."

Rosa stilled instantly. "Out?"

She could see how badly Alice wanted to say no despite her body's clear need for rest. "Slowly."

Rosa eased out of her tight opening a millimeter at a time, watching Alice experience the friction via the subtle expressions that flashed across her beautiful face. "Definitely not our last time together," Rosa whispered, already wishing she could go back for more. "Not by a long shot."

Alice released a slow breath and gazed up into Rosa's eyes. "That was *incredible*."

Remembering their friends, Rosa glanced at the neighboring bunk. The bed was empty. Apparently Bree and Enid had slipped away at some point without their noticing. "I think we're alone now."

The distant honk of a particularly loud snore made Alice giggle, a thoroughly enchanting noise that caused Rosa's chest to tighten. "Well, *almost.*"

"Alone enough," Rosa murmured. She traced a finger between Alice's breasts, then lower to swirl through her short, sodden curls. "Want to come again?"

Alice surprised her by shaking her head. "I want *you* to come."

Rosa wanted the same thing, of course, yet couldn't help but feel that she hadn't yet earned that right. "People could start coming back here at any minute. We may not have much time—"

"Which is exactly why I want to…" Alice hesitated, and Rosa was almost certain she could see her cheeks turn pink even in the semi-darkness. "Lick you."

Despite all they'd just done, Rosa was bowled over by Alice's daring plan. "Really?"

"I didn't get to last night." Alice ran her fingers up and down Rosa's arm, tickled her shoulder, caressed her upper chest. "And I so *badly* want to try."

Rosa swallowed. Nothing sounded more righteous than Alice's tongue on her pussy—except, perhaps, the tickle of her soft hair against Rosa's bare inner thighs—but she hesitated to allow Alice to get that adventurous when they were so likely to be caught. "You're *sure*? If someone sees us, it'll be pretty difficult to come up with a cover story to explain why your head was between my legs."

Alice's eyes drifted shut and she shivered, likely at the imagery evoked by Rosa's graphic concern. "I don't care."

"We could always do that another time—"

"I said I don't care. Do you?"

She says that now… Rosa recalled how Alice also hadn't cared about taking the boat, only to succumb to tension and anxiety the second she'd realized they were busted. Then again, Alice had survived the humiliation. She was still here, still pushing herself to try new things, to face her demons. *Trust her. Trust her, and be brave.* "No, I'd love for you to use your mouth."

Alice's sunny smile was worth any risk, Rosa decided, as she watched gratitude mixed with hunger play over her gorgeous features. "Thank you," Alice whispered. She maneuvered their bodies so that she was on top. Placing a hand between Rosa's breasts, Alice encouraged her flat onto her back in the center of the mattress. "Now just…lie there and enjoy this." She pressed their mouths together, dipped in with her tongue, then forged a trail down Rosa's neck to her breasts, over her stomach, disappearing beneath the blanket as she kissed her way toward her ultimate goal.

Absolutely, Rosa would enjoy this. She couldn't remember ever feeling so excited for a sexual experience. Having Alice go down on her was every bit as thrilling as losing her virginity as a teenager. More, actually, since she already knew it would feel a thousand times better. She allowed her legs to fall open when Alice pressed them apart on the mattress, then battled a powerful wave of self-consciousness much like Alice had the night before. It was one thing for Rosa to dive into an over-the-top messy pussy, but Alice was still new at this. Sheepishly, Rosa whispered, "I'm sorry. You got me really—" A strangled moan burst out of her throat, girlish and louder than intended, when Alice's tongue slid along her sopping labia with unexpected confidence. "*Fuck.*"

"Tastes good," Alice mumbled, and licked her again. Then, "Show me how quiet you can be. Okay?"

Rosa opened her mouth to agree, but the toe-curling pleasure of that surprisingly talented tongue swirling through her wetness coaxed out another, louder moan instead. Alice paused to slap her inner thigh, a light, corrective tap that nearly made Rosa whimper again. Nodding solely for her own benefit, Rosa whispered, "Okay."

The tongue returned to her labia and caressed slowly, carefully, just as she'd demonstrated for Alice the previous evening. There was no haste in her deliberate ministrations, no sense of urgency at all. It didn't matter that up to twenty other women would pour into the cabin as soon as the dance wound down, whenever that might be, or that they could be interrupted at any second, by anyone. Alice was clearly determined to offer her the very same worshipful treatment she'd received the night before, to drive Rosa mad with tentative nibbles, licks, and moments of gentle suction during her first oral exploration of another woman.

The persistent thought that hers was the only pussy Alice had ever tasted made remaining silent a legitimately taxing ordeal. For long, agonizing moments, Rosa resorted to jamming her knuckles against her mouth to keep from crying out, only removing them when she was sure she wouldn't scream. She wanted to praise Alice, to tell her how well she was doing, to ask how she liked it, to talk dirty and try to make her blush, but all she could do was reach beneath the blanket and tangle her fingers in Alice's hair while caressing her face with the other hand. Alice's jaw muscles worked hard as her skillful, determined tongue danced across Rosa's clit, not like an amateur, but a woman who knew exactly what she was doing.

Rosa's control fractured and she whimpered, then moaned, "*So good.*"

"Shh." Alice barely paused to issue the reprimand and instead tightened her fingers on Rosa's sensitive inner thighs in a clear, unspoken warning. She drew the tip of her tongue down between Rosa's labia, waggling it from side to side before pressing against Rosa's opening. The hands on Rosa's thighs moved lower, and a single finger joined Alice's tongue to impishly tease her with the promise of more.

Feeling the urge to beg, *loudly*, Rosa released Alice's jaw and quickly stuffed her fist into her own mouth, biting down. At pretty much that exact moment, the cabin door swung open and closed with an audible *click*, alerting Rosa to the fact that they were no longer alone. *Fuck*, Rosa mouthed silently around her hand. When Alice's tongue pushed inside her, followed by the finger, she swore again, without sound. *Shit!*

Hushed voices grew louder as the newcomers walked nearer to them. Rosa forced her eyes open, straining to make out the two dark silhouettes as she held her breath. All at once—rather unexpectedly—she found herself on the verge of a climax she feared would cause her to shout her praises to the heavens.

"Grab a couple condoms for me, too." An unfamiliar whisper a few bunks over caused Rosa to freeze in place even as Alice continued to torment her with the uniquely satisfying act of dual penetration. "Just in case."

"Slut," her friend accused her. They both dissolved into tipsy giggles. "Gonna fuck Derek tonight?"

"Not sure yet, but I want to be prepared for any eventuality."

"Then here, take three."

Rosa squawked in surprise when the tongue withdrew from her vagina, leaving the finger behind so Alice's lips could latch onto her clit instead. Alice treated her to a firm suck, inducing pulse after pulse of shattering, stomach-clenching ecstasy that forced a helpless whimper from between Rosa's tightly clenched lips. She closed her eyes and writhed against Alice's mouth, not wanting to witness the reactions to her sudden, uncontrollable orgasm.

"Well damn, *that's* sort of hot."

The slut who wanted to fuck Derek gave a drunken whoop of approval. "*Fuckin'* hot! You go, ladies!" Then she and her friend left as quickly as they came, leaving Rosa to ride out the rest of her climax in relative solitude.

That was *hot*, Rosa decided, and beamed up at the ceiling as her body continued to jerk against Alice's enthusiastic finger and tongue. Her relationship with sex and her body had been strained for a while now, to say the least, but somehow, simply by hooking up like an inexperienced kid trying to sneak around, she felt like she'd finally achieved what she'd come to Camp Rewind to do: recapture a simpler time, an optimistic time, with all the requisite fun and mild danger and blissful innocence regarding the harsh realities of the outside world that had once characterized her younger, naive days. In this moment, at least, she and Alice were all that existed in the world, along with the unreal pleasure they'd just given each other, the fun adventure they'd embarked upon in one another's arms.

We can *keep doing this. Even if not forever, then maybe for a while.* Rosa found Alice's face under the blanket with her hands, stroking the defined cheekbones while Alice slowly brought her down from the pinnacle with a series of increasingly tender kisses on her clit. *We could try, at least, so long as I'm brave.* Overcome by the thought, Rosa tugged lightly on Alice's shoulder, encouraging her to crawl back up the length of her body. "Come here, please."

Alice kissed her hard, lips slippery with Rosa's juices and swollen from her heroic efforts. "Was that all right?" she whispered after she'd pulled back. "I'm really sorry I made you come with those women standing right there…it was just all so exciting, and you were *so* yummy…I was only planning to suck on your clit a *little* bit…you know, to torment you. But nicely."

"Nicely?" Chuckling, Rosa tightened her arms and rolled them to the side. She pinned Alice down and tickled her ribs. "A *little* bit? My head almost exploded."

Alice shook with laughter and tried to squirm away from her fingers. "I didn't mean to!" When Rosa stopped the lively assault, she sobered immediately and placed a hand on her cheek. "I hope you weren't too embarrassed."

"Some things are worth a little embarrassment." Rosa winked as she parroted Alice's earlier words of wisdom. "You were right."

Alice's expression turned smug. "I have a feeling you'd better get used to saying that."

Rosa had a feeling Alice was right about that, too, not that she planned to admit it. "Yeah, whatever."

Alice curled an arm and a leg around Rosa and snuggled closer. She laid her head on Rosa's breast, cupping the other in the palm of her hand. She was silent for a minute or so, simply breathing in a manner that Rosa found frankly hypnotic. Then she asked, "Is lesbian sex *always* this good?"

"No, not always." Rosa smiled, and sighed. "This…is kind of special."

"Really?"

Rosa frowned at Alice's mildly skeptical tone. "You want me to trust you, you've gotta trust me. You're an uncommonly talented lover."

Alice nodded. Hesitantly, she said, "It's just that John—"

"Was a fuck-head. Plain and simple."

Alice pressed her smile against Rosa's arm. "Yeah," she said after a while. "He kind of was."

Rosa kissed a lock of fragrant hair that tickled her chin. "He *absolutely* was, to let you go." *To treat you like you were disposable,* she realized, enduring another wave of sorrow as she reflected on the callousness of her earlier actions from a brand-new angle. "Hence my newfound resolution *not* to follow in his fuck-head footsteps."

The cabin door opened yet again, but this time a familiar voice called out softly from across the room. "Is it safe for us to come back yet?"

Rosa and Alice shared a smile at Enid's teasing question. Rosa answered for both of them. "Yeah. As long as you don't mind watching me scramble around in the dark to find our underwear."

Bree approached their bed with a smile so bright that Rosa easily spotted it in the dark. "Allow me." She bent to the floor before Rosa could protest, making her way around their bunk as she collected their carelessly discarded clothing. "Whose are these?" she asked slyly, holding aloft Rosa's matching bra and panty set.

"Mine." Rosa snatched the articles away from Bree and stuck out her tongue. "Brat."

"And these?" Bree twirled Alice's gray cotton panties on her finger, close enough to her face that Rosa suspected she was subtly hunting for a scent. "Shy Alice?"

Simultaneously bashful and coy, Alice smiled at Bree and held out her hand. "Thank you, Bree."

"My pleasure." Bree handed the panties over with a bow before conducting another quick search of the floor. "No bra, Alice?"

"Never managed to get it off," Rosa admitted with faux regret.

"Maybe next time." Bree gave Rosa a solid smack on the thigh, her message plain.

"*Definitely* next time." Rosa tugged Alice back into her arms once she'd pulled on her panties and refastened her bra. Alice rested her head on Rosa's bare shoulder, still wearing that ebullient smile. She wrapped her arm around Rosa's waist and squeezed, vibrating with an internal joy Rosa could both sense and feel. Rosa turned to watch Bree and Enid wrap themselves into a similar embrace. "So what about you two? Do you plan to see each other again after camp is over?"

"From time to time, yes, I imagine we'll get together." Enid released a contented sigh and curled into Bree's side. "Neither of us is looking for a relationship, so it'll be more of a—"

"Fuck-buddy thing," Bree said, with a wet kiss on Enid's lips. "Which works for me. A girl can't have too many special friends."

Alice's fingers flexed against her stomach, making Rosa wonder if she was trying to decide whether their relationship would progress under similar terms. Not wanting to conduct any negotiations in front of an audience, Rosa promised herself that she'd tackle the topic head-on when they had more privacy. "You live close to each other?"

"Six-hour drive," Bree said. "Not too bad."

Rosa lived in Berkeley. Alice, San Francisco. Although bridge traffic might sometimes make the drive feel like six hours, they were lucky not to have a massive obstacle like long distance to overcome. "Worth it, certainly, for great sex with a friend."

"I'll say." Enid hummed a few jolly notes. "This weekend ended a five-year dry spell for me, believe it or not."

"*Five* years," Bree lamented, like it was the worst thing she'd ever heard. "You see why I had to help her make up for lost time."

"A truly noble act," Rosa said, teasing her.

Alice piped up, quietly. "It had been about two years for me. And that was with my ex-husband, who never once managed to make me come in all the years we were married. The first time Rosa touched me...*twice*."

Bree and Enid offered restrained cheers and whistles in response to the disclosure. "*Nice,*" Bree said. "No wonder you've fallen so hard, so fast, Alice."

Rosa heard Enid smack Bree to silence her, felt Alice's face redden against her breast, yet somehow managed to remain perfectly calm in the face of the blatant insinuation. Worried that Alice would believe it necessary to deny her growing feelings for Rosa's sake, she replied, "Alice isn't the only one who fell this weekend." She waited a beat, savoring the subtle jolt of the body pressed against hers when her meaning registered. "I guess all we can do now is wait and see where this goes."

Alice cuddled closer, hugging her so tight that, for a moment, Rosa lost her breath. She pressed a loving kiss into Alice's hair and inhaled deeply to savor the scent. How was it possible she hadn't even known this woman a week ago? In some crazy way, it felt like they'd always been friends. Or, at the very least, like they were meant to be.

"You guys make an adorable couple," Bree said, perhaps sensing that the mild tension caused by her last comment had already dissipated. "In my opinion."

"Well, thanks." Rosa traded shy grins with Alice when she picked up her head to gaze fondly into Rosa's eyes. "All credit to the adorable one."

"And if you guys decide that 'next time' needs to happen tonight, right there beside us, while I lie here pretending to sleep, I want you to know that I'm totally fine with that." Bree rolled Enid so they both faced Rosa's bunk and flashed a semi-maniacal grin. "'Cause I like those sexy little noises Alice makes."

"So do I." Rosa kissed Alice's hair and whispered into her ear, "A *lot*."

"She helped get *me* off," Enid said, eyes glittering in the dark.

"Wait," Bree said with mock indignation. "You're saying Alice and I have to *share* credit for that gusher?"

"Indeed I am."

Bree snorted and, as Alice buried her burning face in Rosa's neck, said, "Way to go, shy Alice. Now you've made *two* women come. Not bad for your first weekend of pussy."

Alice's cheeks grew hotter at the graphic compliment, but her smile also grew wider, which made Rosa feel somehow certain, for the first time, that things *might* absolutely work out. Unless, of course, they didn't.

Either way, she was finally ready to try.

CHAPTER EIGHTEEN

The third time Alice woke up in Rosa Salazar's arms was the best. There was no embarrassment, no alarm, not even a rogue snake to disrupt her peaceful reentry into consciousness. Toasty warm beneath their shared blanket, and thoroughly entangled in Rosa's heavy limbs, she felt safe and content and optimistic in a way that made it seem as though she was seeing the world through new eyes. She sighed, listening to the sounds their cabin mates made in slumber, and tried to decide whether to rouse Rosa or let her sleep longer. Though she wasn't nearly daring enough to initiate early morning, public sex in a crowded cabin while daylight streamed in through the windows, Alice craved a return to the intimacy they'd shared the night before. Particularly because so long as Rosa slept, she had no way of knowing where her head was.

No matter what they'd said before drifting off to their individual dreams, today was their last at Camp Rewind. In a few hours they would reach the pivotal moment when they either kept going, or didn't. As much as Alice didn't want to believe that Rosa would undergo a sudden change of heart—not after their intense lovemaking the night before, surely—she still found it necessary to brace for the possibility.

She tensed her grip on Rosa subconsciously, afraid to wake her and terrified by the thought that she might soon have the miracle of their friendship torn away for a second time. Alice closed her eyes, breathing rapidly as she began to spiral into the sort of catastrophic thinking that always earned her a quick reproach from her therapist. Before she could drown in her anxious thoughts, a warm caress on her bare shoulder coaxed her back from the edge of panic, and Rosa's whispered "You're okay, sweetheart" brought an unthinking smile to her lips. Opening her eyes, Alice melted at the unabashed affection shining back at her from within Rosa's tender gaze. Rosa frowned, not bothering to hide her concern. "Bad dream?"

Alice shook her head but remained silent, afraid to admit what had really spooked her. "Did you sleep well?"

"Like the dead." Rosa studied Alice's face, uneasily. "You?"

Alice nodded, then tucked her head beneath Rosa's chin and tightened her one-armed embrace. "We should go shower before everyone else wakes up."

"All right." The low purr of Rosa's sleep-roughened voice rumbled against Alice's ear, widening her smile. "But first tell me what you were thinking about before."

Alice's smile faded. She considered denying that anything had been wrong but sensed that, without honesty, she would never win Rosa's trust. *Here goes, then.* "I was trying to decide whether to wake you."

"So you could make sure I wasn't planning to pull another dick move?"

Alice shrugged, then shook her head. "I wouldn't put it like *that*."

"Well, I would." Rosa tugged Alice up onto her chest and craned to capture her lips in a heartfelt kiss. "Listen, I made you a promise last night," Rosa mumbled when she pulled away. "You're not disposable, and I'll never do anything to make you feel that way, ever again."

The tiny seed of doubt that had started to take root in the pit of Alice's stomach shriveled and died when she heard the sincerity of Rosa's words. Sighing, Alice rested her head on Rosa's shoulder, too overwhelmed with relief and gratitude and fast-growing love to continue staring into those soulful brown eyes. Not unless she was prepared to burst into ugly tears. She held her hand over Rosa's heart, relishing the steady yet mildly elevated rhythm. "And *you* are worthy, no matter what you've been through, or are going through right now, or *will* go through one day." Stretching to kiss Rosa's neck, she whispered, "Despite all of that, you deserve to be loved. Unconditionally."

Rosa rolled them so that she hovered above Alice, staring down with so much intensity that Alice eventually had to look away. *Did I say* loved?

Rosa stroked the side of her face until Alice worked up the courage to reestablish eye contact, smiling when she did. "Alice Wu," she murmured. "Thanks for hanging out with me this weekend. I know I didn't always make it easy."

Alice looped her arms around Rosa's neck, keeping her voice low so as not to wake their sleeping neighbors. "You too, *Lila*. It may not have been a hundred percent easy, but I wouldn't trade this time with you for anything."

Sheepishly, Rosa kissed the corner of her mouth, then the other side. "I hope you know I wasn't kidding about Lila being a lot more fun than the real me…"

Alice heard the lingering insecurity in the warning and kissed Rosa back, with purpose. Afterward, she whispered, "I'm not interested in the fleeting magic of summer camp. I'm interested in *you*, with all the messiness that entails."

"You still have no idea what you're getting into." Rosa smiled bravely, but Alice detected stubborn fear shimmering in her gaze. "*How* messy…and how *frightening* life with me can actually be."

"I look forward to finding out." Alice couldn't deny that she had some concerns about the negative impact Rosa's enemies could have on her life, but not nearly enough to warrant a return to a Rosa-free existence. Life would always be full of anxieties. For her, friends were a much rarer occurrence. She'd literally never had one like Rosa before. Now that she did, she'd walk through fire for her. Indeed, it was all but impossible to imagine an obstacle too great to overcome if it meant keeping Rosa Salazar in her life. "Besides, like you said…no matter what else happens, we're friends. Right?"

Rosa nodded, eyes watering, and dipped down for a more sensuous kiss. "Right." She smiled against Alice's mouth, triggering the same. "*Very* special friends."

Though they'd put on T-shirts and pajama pants before falling asleep, the slide of Rosa's thigh against her still-sensitive labia triggered a hot jolt of lust. Alice writhed against the mild pressure without thinking, then blushed and forced herself to refocus on the symphony of snoring, mumbling women who occupied the bunks around them. *My kingdom for a private room.* Keeping her voice below a whisper, she asked, "Are we the type of friends who take showers together?"

"In fact, yes. We are." Rosa's hungry eyes darkened, further soaking Alice's already damp panties. "I would be happy to help you get clean."

Alice breathed out slowly, a measured exhalation intended to prevent her from getting carried away and doing something to embarrass both of them. "Because that's what friends do?"

"Because of that, and because I want to touch you," Rosa whispered back, then kissed her throat. "And care for you." Her lips trailed up Alice's jaw, then nipped sharply at her earlobe, causing Alice to gasp. "And make you feel *good. Only* good, from now on."

Alice put her hands on Rosa's shoulders and nudged her away in an attempt to cool down. They needed to take this conversation to a private shower stall, *stat*, before everyone else woke up. With effort, she wriggled out from beneath Rosa and knelt by her suitcase. After a hasty search that yielded one last change of clothing and her toiletries bag, Alice stood and pressed a saucy kiss against Rosa's lips, amused by how dazed she looked about her sudden departure. Under her breath, Alice murmured, "I'm taking you up on that. Come on."

Rosa followed without hesitation, confident and seemingly unafraid.

❖

Under the hot spray of the less-than-luxurious campground showerhead, concealed behind an opaque curtain that rippled gently in the breeze blowing in through the bathroom's open windows, Rosa Salazar fell a little more for Alice Wu during an extended shampooing session that started with her hands tangled in Alice's long, dark hair and ended with three of Alice's demanding fingers lodged deep inside Rosa's pussy. Rosa clung to the shower wall as Alice fucked her from behind, shocked by the strength and confidence with which her body was being claimed and shaken by the knowledge that she'd nearly let a truly prodigious sexual talent go.

Alice's slippery tits glided across her back, the nipples a hard, brilliant contrast to the softness of her supple flesh. She whispered against Rosa's cheek, too quietly, surely, to be heard over the hiss of the shower, yet the words landed with deafening clarity in Rosa's ears. "You're so beautiful like this." Alice's lips pressed against her temple, her tongue tasting the damp skin. "Beautiful with my fingers inside you."

Rosa groaned and set her feet farther apart, purposefully ignoring the ridiculous shower sandals she had on—a last-minute purchase, neon green and one size too large—as she marveled over Alice's exploding sexual confidence. Two nights ago, Alice could barely manage to say the word "pussy" without blushing. Now she was making Rosa blush, and more. Turning her head to give Alice a brutal, needy kiss, Rosa moaned, "Don't stop."

"I won't," Alice promised in a silky murmur. "Not until you come on my hand."

Rosa contracted at the sheer shock value of hearing Alice talk dirty. She was close, *so close*, and Alice drove her determinedly forward without offering a single second of respite. "Oh…"

Scraping her teeth across Rosa's shoulder, Alice held the back of her neck with one hand while the other increased the force of its pounding between her legs. "See what happens when you teach a sexually repressed woman to fuck?"

A sharp cry of pleasure cut Rosa's laughter short. "Unchained…a… beast?"

The hand on the back of Rosa's neck strengthened its grip, urging her to bend at the waist so the fingers inside her could force themselves impossibly deeper, to stroke a spot that made Rosa's knees turn to jelly and nearly sent her crashing down onto the questionably hygienic floor. She held onto the edge of the shower so desperately her knuckles went pale, determined to stay on her feet so Alice could exorcise years of mediocre sex through her pussy. Eager to help usher in the inevitable, Rosa rebalanced herself on one hand and held the other under the hot spray for a minute before lowering it between her thighs so she could touch her clit.

"*Yes*," Alice hissed, and fucked her even harder. The force of her thrusts propelled Rosa forward, sending wet strands of hair into her eyes again and again as she withstood the furious assault. "Rub it for me."

Rosa bit the inside of her cheek so she wouldn't scream. She loved being taken like this, hard and fast and rough, and that shy Alice was the one doing it, in a public shower no less, elevated the experience to an unbearably earth-shattering height. Her fingers hastened on her clit, mindlessly jerking the sensitive ridge of flesh as she engaged in a desperate sprint toward nirvana. Legs wobbling, she rose on her tiptoes when Alice sank all the way into her, knuckles pressed firmly against her labia, to rub the place that made Rosa's entire body quake. Rosa's forehead touched the shower wall as she beat herself off unashamedly, her entire focus narrowed to the singular goal of reaching a much-needed resolution for the nearly painful ecstasy created by their joint efforts. In a moment of divine inspiration, their hands achieved perfect synchrony, triggering simultaneous clitoral and vaginal orgasms that *would* have sent Rosa to the concrete floor if not for Alice's sudden, strong grip around her waist.

"I've got you," Alice cooed, kissing Rosa's shoulder blade as she rode the waves of her multiple climaxes to their bittersweet ends. "I won't let you fall."

Eventually, Rosa brought her arms up and turned in one clumsy motion. More light-headed than she'd anticipated, she promptly stumbled into Alice's waiting embrace with a muttered curse. Alice grunted at the unexpected impact but managed to keep her feet and shook with laughter as she gathered Rosa close to kiss her flushed cheeks. "Even when you try to throw us both onto the floor," Alice joked, grinning.

Rosa smiled at the lighthearted comment, yet couldn't resist the desire to linger on the darker subtext she couldn't help but see. "Told you I'd only bring you down. If not this time…"

Alice's body stiffened against hers. "That needs to stop." Pulling back, she glared at Rosa with unexpected ferocity. "No more self-hatred, all right? Not around me. I don't like it, I don't agree with it, and I'm not going to listen to it anymore. Got it?"

Having never seen Alice so upset, not like *that*, Rosa held her hands up in supplication and nodded obediently. "I apologize. It's a bad habit."

"A *terrible* one."

"I'll try to quit." Rosa hung her head low, vowing to treat herself more kindly if only to avoid pissing Alice off this much in the future. "I know it's not an attractive quality."

"More than that, it's just not *true*." Alice pulled her close again, folding her into a loving embrace. "Whatever happens, I'm going into this relationship with my eyes wide open. If my life somehow gets totally ruined by our association, it'll be *their* fault, or mine, but never yours." She tightened her arms around Rosa and shook her gently for emphasis. "*Never* yours."

We'll see how she feels about that a year from now. The sullen inner voice she'd become well-acquainted with still remained close to the surface—and would likely be a demon she battled for some time to come—but today, Rosa chose to ignore what it was telling her. Rather than allow her self-loathing to throw cold water on her hopes, dreams, and feelings of worth yet again, she listened to Alice instead. She could only do that because she trusted Alice more than the voice, somehow, improbable as it was to feel that way about a woman she'd known for only a few days. Her gut didn't exactly have the best track record on these matters, but as Bree had pointed out, she couldn't let fear destroy her chance at transcendence, no matter how slim that chance might be. If she wanted to be happy one day, she had to *try*.

So that's what she would do. Try—and hope.

"Careful, Alice," Rosa warned in a murmur once she trusted herself to speak. "Or you'll make me fall in love with you."

Alice's breathing hitched. "I hope so," she whispered, so earnestly Rosa nearly wept.

She encircled Alice's waist and hugged as fiercely as she dared, filled with something akin to dread. *I don't want to let her go.* Throat dry, Rosa swallowed past her thick tongue to commit her first act of genuine courage for the day. "Alice, would…would you like to follow me home to Berkeley? We could spend the evening at my place…" She wished she could watch Alice's face for a reaction. *She probably has to work. You just spent three days together. Give the poor woman a break.* "Or we could make plans to see each other next weekend," she said lamely. "Whatever's best for you."

Alice took a step back and searched Rosa's face. Her eyes sparkled with genuine excitement, proof that she hadn't been wrong to extend the invitation. "I'd love to go back to your apartment. I assume you have a real bed…and privacy!" Clapping her hands, Alice wiggled in an unself-conscious, jubilant, celebratory dance, all while gloriously naked. "Yes, let's do that!"

"You're a changed woman," Rosa remarked as she watched the

astonishing show, then raised an eyebrow after Alice froze, lowered her face, and stared at the floor. "You realize that, right? It's legitimately extraordinary."

"Well, you get most of the credit for my weekend transformation." Alice's mouth quirked into a smile as she glanced up and met Rosa's eyes. "After me, of course."

"Of course." Not for the first time, Rosa's brain went haywire as she considered the woman Alice was fast becoming. Her timid, impressive, courageous friend had so much untapped potential, so many layers Rosa could help uncover. Distracted by the direction her thoughts were taking, Rosa reached between their chests and plucked at Alice's erect nipple with her fingertips. "You know, I have some toys at home that I'd love to show you, if you were interested in that sort of—"

"Yes!" Alice said. "*Sold.* You have no idea how many things I want to try."

"Well, that works out, because there are *so* many dirty, nasty things I want to do to you."

Alice groaned but quickly fell silent when the distant sound of feminine voices filtered into the building, signaling that their final moment of solitude at camp had just ended. She listened for a few seconds, then whispered into Rosa's ear. "We should go eat breakfast, say our good-byes, and get the hell out of here so you can hurry up and thank me properly for the dirty, nasty way I just treated *you.*"

Rosa snorted, tickled by Alice's emerging sense of humor. It was so easy to talk to her, to simply *be* with her. Everything just flowed. If their relationship survived the transition to the real world, it would likely bring Rosa the greatest happiness she'd ever known. *Or else the greatest heartbreak.* Disgusted with herself, Rosa delivered a symbolic uppercut to her inner voice's stupid face and instead thought about what toy she wanted to introduce Alice to first. She had a wide assortment to choose from, as well as endless ideas about the many games they could play and positions they could try. Resolving to initiate a serious discussion about fantasies, limits, and safe words over breakfast, for now, Rosa said only, "Don't worry, darling, I promise you'll get yours." She smacked Alice sharply on the butt a couple times, counting on the noise of the showerhead and the not-terribly-animated conversations that bounced off the concrete walls to disguise the sound of her impromptu burst of discipline. "And I'll get mine."

Alice's throat worked convulsively. She stared up at the ceiling, clearly trying to deal with the confusing mixture of anxiety and arousal that almost certainly coursed through her veins. Taking pity, Rosa cut off the flow of water and pushed past the curtain to grab Alice's towel. She wrapped Alice's heaving body in its fluffy depths, then pulled her in for a tight hug. Rosa kissed her cheek and murmured, "The part with all the other people is almost over."

Alice released a strangled, impatient noise. "You swear?"

Rosa chuckled and held Alice at arm's length, hands curled around her slim shoulders. She tipped her head, seriously, before breaking into a full-blown grin. "Then the real fun begins."

And oh, how Rosa hoped that was true.

CHAPTER NINETEEN

G iven her eagerness to see Rosa's apartment *and* her toy collection, the last thing Alice expected to feel while trading good-bye hugs with Bree and Enid was sad. Yet she did, and really, it shouldn't have come as a surprise. Rosa wasn't the only friend she'd made at Camp Rewind. However, Alice wasn't sure when or even if she would see Bree or Enid again. Despite her reticence to socialize at the beginning of the weekend, she'd enjoyed getting to know the two kind yet good-naturedly crass women.

As though sensing her melancholy, Bree rocked Alice back and forth in a bear hug and kissed her cheek. "Rosa has my number. Text me sometime. Or, you know, send a naked selfie. If you want."

"Easy, player," Rosa said, shooting Bree a lightheartedly stern expression while she gave Enid one last squeeze. "Look all you want, but hear this: I'm planting my flag."

Enid raised an eyebrow and smirked at Alice. "I'm thinking your reaction to that could go one of two ways…"

Alice's heart fluttered pleasantly at Rosa's unambiguous declaration of intent. "I have no objection to being claimed by this woman. She can stick her flagpole in me anytime."

Rosa fought against an amused grin that ended up taking over her entire face. "*Wow.*"

"Shy Alice!" Bree raised her hand in an invitation to high-five. "That was *excellent.*"

Pleased, but blushing, Alice dutifully slapped Bree's palm. "I try."

"You know, I like you better and better every day." Bree's eyes revealed a deep, affectionate warmth that Alice found more touching than she would have ever anticipated. "Take care of Rosa, all right? Be good to her. Help her give the middle finger to all those assholes."

Alice nodded seriously. "I will." Upon realizing how much she would honestly miss her foul-mouthed, flirtatious friend, Alice went back in for another quick hug. "Thank you, for everything. Especially yesterday."

Bree lifted Alice off her feet, spun her, then set her free with a kiss on the forehead. "I'm just glad you crazy kids were able to work things out."

Rosa turned to Bree and pulled her into a brief hug. "Yeah, thanks for talking sense into me."

Alice smiled and walked into Enid's outstretched arms, surprised by the new, higher tolerance for physical contact she'd acquired over the past twenty-four hours. In the past, she'd hated for people to touch her in social situations, but it was different with these women. She knew Bree and Enid cared about her, even if they'd only just met, and the memories they'd created together this weekend would stay with Alice for a lifetime. It was difficult to express the level of esteem she felt for them out loud, so, instead of eloquence, a physical gesture seemed like the best way for her to demonstrate how much of an impact they'd truly made. "Take care, Enid. I'm sorry you got caught up in our drama, but I *really* appreciated your friendship and advice yesterday. It meant a lot."

Enid held her for a long time before letting go. "Like Bree said, I'm glad it all worked out." She waited until Alice stepped out of her arms to wink. "Thank *you* for the entertainment last night. To be honest, that was total fantasy fulfillment. I hope I didn't embarrass you too badly."

Alice somehow managed not to hide her face behind her hands. She'd sort of hoped they wouldn't bring up what had happened. "Likewise. I still can't believe I did that."

"To be fair, you *were* pretty high," Rosa offered.

Bree elbowed Rosa in the side, wide-eyed at the revelation. "Holding out on us?"

Rosa gestured at Alice with a grin. "It was hers."

Bree and Enid looked equally surprised as they turned to regard Alice, seemingly in a new light. "Shy Alice," Bree exclaimed, "will you never stop delighting me?"

Alice shifted her weight nervously, unsettled to be the center of attention. "It's medicinal," she said. "For anxiety." She looked to Rosa for help. "Plus, I don't like to drink?"

"I can't blame you there." Enid's face pinched as she turned away, disgusted, from a sight behind Alice's back. "After this weekend, they may need to change the name of this place to Camp Regurgitate."

Unable to help herself, Alice looked over to where Enid's attention had drifted. Bent over a garbage can, flirtatious Derek, Rosa's admirer from their first morning at camp—and the apparent suitor of Ms. Three Condoms last night—barfed his guts out in an exceedingly unsexy manner. Her nose wrinkled as she returned her focus to their circle of friends. "I'm so glad I'm not hung over."

"I'll drink to that." Rosa shuddered. "I'm also *seriously* glad I didn't take that guy up on his offer of a riding lesson."

"Me, too," Alice said, then rolled her eyes and scoffed. "*Riding lesson?* Did he really think that would work on you?"

"Indeed." Rosa smirked at Bree, then asked Alice, "You know, if *you* were interested in riding, I do have the appropriate toys and accessories to make that happen, back at my place. I could teach you how to ride *me*, or maybe show you how it feels to be ridden. Do you think you'd like that? A *riding lesson?*"

Alice's face burned at how easily the lame overture affected her, when delivered by Rosa. "Well…yeah."

Bree guffawed loudly, drawing the attention of a few nearby campers gathered in similar clusters, all bidding their farewells. Alice scurried to Rosa's side, ducked under her arm, and huddled against her solid form. Her growing self-consciousness eased in the warmth of Rosa's presence, allowing her to answer Bree's laughter with a chuckle of her own.

"It all depends on who's doing the asking, I guess." Bree winked, then tapped Enid on the elbow and gestured toward the parking lot. "Why don't we go say good-bye in my car for a few minutes? It's probably time to let these two go home so they can fuck each other's brains out anyway."

Rosa hugged Alice closer. "That'll take quite a bit of dedicated effort on my part. My girl's got a big brain."

Alice was absolutely positive she'd never felt happier. Afraid she was about to get choked up in front of an audience, she locked her attention on her shoes as they traded one last round of good-byes. When Bree and Enid walked away hand-in-hand toward the parking lot, Alice lifted her face and smiled tearily at Rosa. "This really was the best weekend."

"The *best*." Rosa's eyes shimmered with equally intense emotion. "Even though I nearly ruined it."

"No. You just turned it into a better story." Alice took a chance and spoke to the future she hoped they'd have. "You know, for us to tell people when they ask how we met."

Rosa winced. "Unfortunately, I'm pretty much the bad guy in this story."

"Or the hero." Alice took Rosa by the hand and led her toward their cars. They'd loaded their bags before breakfast and planned for Alice to follow Rosa home. "Depending on how you look at it."

"Depending on how it all turns out," Rosa muttered, not quite under her breath.

Alice stopped and stared at Rosa. She blinked.

Rosa kissed the corner of Alice's mouth, then nibbled on her lips. "I'm sorry," she breathed. "You're right, it *is* a good story. Especially the sex parts."

Alice snorted and pulled away. "I'm not sure we'll tell those parts."

"Not to our *parents*, maybe, but—"

"Alice!" Jamal's deep baritone sliced through the chatter surrounding them. Alice turned on instinct with a warm smile. She'd gotten to know Jamal a little more during their robot-building exercise the day before, and she really did like the guy. He was bright, and personable, and adequately geeky to render him relatively easy to be around. "Wait up!"

Alice stuck out her hand awkwardly as he drew near, unsure how to approach this particular good-bye. "Thanks again for letting me keep the robot we built yesterday. And remember, you have my email address if you have any questions about your curriculum."

Jamal gave her a friendly handshake, then a tentative pat on the back. "You'll definitely be hearing from me. I wanted to say good-bye before you left and ask you again to think about coming back to teach a session in the future. Marcia said she'd even pay you a little, on top of waiving the registration fee."

Alice's throat closed at the mere thought of standing in front of a classroom of students and teaching anything, even a subject she knew cold. Careful to remain vague, she hedged. "I'll think about it. For now, I'll send you instructions for a few suitable projects to get you started."

"I'd appreciate that." Jamal grinned toothily as he turned to Rosa. "Lila, it was a pleasure to meet you. I hope to see you at camp again."

"If Alice decides to take you up on that teaching offer, you might." Rosa shook his hand, then put her arm around Alice's shoulders and gave her a squeeze. "For the record, I hope she does. That would be super cool."

"I totally agree." Jamal stuck out his hand and gave them both another amiable shake. "Anyway, drive safe, both of you. Don't steal any boats on your way home."

Rosa laughed. "I'll keep her out of trouble, don't worry."

Alice followed Rosa, hands linked, as they resumed the short walk to their cars. Once in front of Rosa's ride, they stopped to face each other. Alice looped her arms around Rosa's neck; Rosa encircled Alice's waist and drew her into a close embrace. When Rosa tried to gather her even nearer, Alice rested her head upon her strong shoulder and closed her eyes, reveling in the sound of the distant heartbeat thumping in her ear. "I wish we didn't have to take separate cars."

"Tell me about it." Rosa kissed her hair, then placed her hand on Alice's lower back to bring their hips together. "If you've got hands-free capabilities in your car, you could call my cell. We can talk during the drive, assuming the reception holds out."

"I'll do that." Alice eased away, worried that if she didn't stop touching Rosa soon, she'd never convince herself to make the three-hour trek back to the East Bay. "What will we talk about? Riding lessons? Toys?"

Rosa offered an apologetic smile. "That might distract you too much. Your safety is my top priority."

Fair point. Alice smiled back. "Then what?"

Rosa shrugged, her expression as shy as Alice usually felt. "Everything?" Refusing to look away despite an obvious bout of nerves, she gazed steadfastly into Alice's eyes with adoration bordering on love. "I want to know *everything* about you, Alice Wu."

"I'm not sure there's much to tell." The steady confidence Alice had maintained since their reunion wavered as she considered whether she would prove interesting enough to hold Rosa's attention for longer than a weekend. Compared to Rosa, Alice led a painfully dull life. Most of her anecdotes fell into the category of sad or awkward, but rarely amusing, and never charming. She didn't go many places or do all that many things, outside family and professional obligations. Her lonely, isolated childhood had left her with little basis to relate to others. What did she have to talk about? Her newfound predilection for porn and lesbian romance novels, and her desire to recreate the scenes that had kept her company on far too many lonely nights? A wave of doubt about their ability to successfully transition from a weekend fling to a real-world relationship struck Alice squarely for the first time, delivering a devastating blow to her heart. "Honestly, I'm pretty...boring."

"Not to me." Rosa initiated a lingering kiss. Without pulling away, she whispered against Alice's lips, "Anyway, my life could stand to be a little more boring. Boring sounds *wonderful*, to tell you the truth."

Alice had to smile. She knew Rosa was wholly sincere about that sentiment, at least for now. "Well, I could tell you about my cat. I'm not really a 'tell people about my cat' person, to be honest, but Schrödinger *is* quite sweet. He's a polydactyl, or as my neighbor's toddler calls him, a 'pterodactyl.'"

Rosa almost knocked the wind out of her with the swiftness and suddenness of her enthusiastic hug. "*Schrödinger?* I *am* falling in love."

Alice hugged back, fiercely, more than a little stunned by Rosa's sincere appreciation for the geeky reference. Reaching for the obvious joke, she said, "I'm worried I forgot to fill his food dish before I left. Until I get home to check, I postulate that he's simultaneously alive *and* dead, and not simply in my anxious mind."

Rosa quaked with laughter and nearly cut off Alice's air supply by crushing her to her chest. "Alice, you're *so* not boring." After more laughter, she drew back and wiped the tears from her eyes. "Did you really forget to feed Schrodie?"

Alice bit her lip and shook her head. "No. I just wanted to make you laugh."

Rosa grinned and kissed her again, slower this time. "I *really* like you, Al. Never doubt that."

Alice shivered at the nickname, both the way it sounded on Rosa's lips and the memories it evoked of their lovemaking the night before. She *loved* it. "I like you, too."

"Then come on." Rosa gave her one last hug before urging her toward her car. "Let's go be brave in the real world, together."

"And have sex?"

Rosa called out to her as she backed away. "*Lots* of sex."

Alice mustered a playful leer, then, face on fire, walked to her car. As she passed the sedan parked next to hers, the question of when she would see Bree or Enid again was answered in a blinding flash of naked skin, tantalizing curves, and half-fogged windows. She tore her gaze away immediately and scurried into the driver's seat of her car. She had her cell phone in her hand and Rosa on the line within seconds. "Bree and Enid are fucking in the car next to me."

Rosa's chuckle floated over the slightly fuzzy reception of the call. Alice watched as she backed out of her parking spot and steered down the driveway toward the road that would lead them back to their normal lives. "So much for not having you drive distracted."

Alice started her car and pulled up behind Rosa, casting one last glance into the rearview mirror as they drove away from Camp Rewind. "So…may I ask you a question?"

"Anything."

Alice opened her mouth to say one thing, only to have another spill out. "If this works out, will I be, like, your girlfriend?" The instant she put the query out there, she rushed to clarify its meaning, faltering as she strained to recall Bree's terminology from the night before. "Or just…a special friend?"

"I don't want to be your fuck-buddy, Alice. I want to be your *person*." Rosa paused. Her voice sounded startlingly vulnerable and young, tinged with uncharacteristic optimism. "Your *life* person, not just your camp person."

With that type of potential reward on the line, Alice found it shockingly easy to move forward with bravery. "Good. Me, too."

"Now, talk geeky to me while we drive," Rosa said. "Consider it foreplay."

Having never before felt at ease chatting over the phone, Alice couldn't believe how easy it was to sit back, relax, and do exactly that. As she regaled Rosa with the mundanities of her life, holding back no part of her true self, Alice gradually came to an unquestionable, somewhat uncomfortable conclusion.

Her therapist Dawn had known exactly what she was doing. She'd actually been *right*. Most likely, she usually was.

Well, damn it, Alice thought. *Thank goodness.*

CHAPTER TWENTY

One year later

Rosa pushed play on a video she'd downloaded to her cell phone in preparation for exactly the situation in which she and Alice now found themselves. Reclining in the driver's seat of her car, parked in the distantly familiar lot outside Camp Rewind, she angled the screen toward the passenger seat where Alice Wu fought not to succumb to her visibly growing panic. "Here, watch these baby goats."

Alice inhaled and exhaled slowly, and deeply, her mouth eventually quirking as she stared at the screen. "Awww," she cooed, in a voice that still made Rosa's tummy flip-flop even now, one year in. "They're so *fuzzy*."

"Right?" Rosa paused, anticipating the moment the video would become epic enough to break through Alice's unprecedented case of nerves. "Wait for it…" On cue, a tiny pink pig trotted with clumsy enthusiasm into the center of the trio of baby goats who danced around in play, where she was instantly, cheerfully accepted into the fold. "Huh?" She raised an eyebrow at Alice as the delicate features she'd come to know by heart dissolved under the onslaught of cute overload. "How can you feel anything but happy in a world where that pig and those goats are best friends forever?"

Alice giggled and wiped the gathering tears from her eyes. "Okay, you win. I think that actually helped a little."

"Mission accomplished." Rosa smiled and handed over the phone so Alice could cradle it in her hands while she watched the video until the end. When the picture froze, Rosa said, "Listen, baby, you're gonna be—"

Soft yet firm lips pressed against hers, cutting off the verbal reassurance she'd planned to offer. Rosa relaxed into the kiss and pulled Alice closer to her over the center console.

After everything they'd been through since their last go-around at camp, she had no reason to doubt Alice's ability to successfully teach a small classroom of semi-sober campers how to assemble and program basic robotic devices. Over the past twelve months, Alice had endured a volatile coming out to her parents, two months of markedly increased online threats—and, on occasion, in-person comments—directed at Rosa after her infamous article and the backlash it had spawned were the subject of a widely read essay about feminism and gaming, and countless other daily challenges she'd largely met with remarkable grace. Occasionally, Alice endured bouts of anxiety so acute she suffered physical symptoms. Once, a series of particularly graphic threats of sexual torture against Rosa—messages Rosa had tried and failed to hide on social media—had caused Alice to descend into a weeklong battle with unrelenting nausea so severe it forced her to call in sick to work, which had made Rosa sick as well, with guilt. Yet as bad as that had been, this, the two-week run-up to Alice's first teaching experience, was the worst Rosa had ever seen from her. Stomachaches, insomnia, irritability, the works.

It was agonizing to watch Alice struggle to do things so many others found natural and easy, but Rosa had learned that her best move was to simply be there to provide support, and listen, and never judge. Even when the worst came to pass and it was *her* crap that triggered Alice's distress, running away was no longer an option. Alice's pain belonged to Rosa, and vice versa.

They were together now, with all that entailed.

The sound of a throat clearing in the backseat pulled them apart right as Rosa's hand dropped to brush the side of Alice's breast. "All right. Enough encouragement." Trayvon's deep voice was an unwelcome reminder that their weekend of little to no solitude had already begun. "At least while I'm in the car. You guys want me to leave?"

"Yes," Rosa said, at the same time Alice insisted, "No." Rosa frowned at Alice, then glanced over her shoulder into the back. "He could go check himself in." When Trayvon shrugged to indicate his willingness to follow orders, Rosa returned her attention to Alice. "He doesn't mind."

"*I* mind." Alice kissed Rosa's cheek before smiling fondly at him. "Tray is a big part of my moral-support team. I don't want to lose him to the debauchery of Camp Rewind just yet."

Trayvon scooted forward and rested a hand on Alice's shoulder. "I've got you, Al. Don't worry. Besides, I'm too excited about taking your robotics class to abandon you for the first hot guy I find."

Rosa snorted and gestured at Alice with a fond look. "You never know. I did meet the love of my life in this very place…"

Alice practically swooned, then moved in for another soft kiss, breaking away only when Trayvon cleared his throat for a second time. Alice shot him an apologetic grin. "Sorry. Camp does crazy things to me."

Rosa nearly swooned also at the memory of their first weekend together, when painfully shy Alice had both captured her heart and set off on the sometimes arduous journey to become the woman she was today. A woman Rosa loved more than life itself. They'd had countless great times since that weekend, and a staggering amount of phenomenal sex, but their first few days together would always hold a special place in Rosa's heart. That was when Rosa had finally chosen to heal, to move forward, to live her life again. Lifting Alice's hand to her lips, she kissed the knuckles and winked. "I can vouch for that. *Crazy* things."

"Well, I can't wait to find out." Trayvon shifted closer to the passenger side door, fingers on the handle. "Just remember, Al. You've done the camp thing before, and look how well it turned out. This time, you'll have plenty of friends here with you, so it'll be even better."

Better is pretty much guaranteed, Rosa thought privately. *This time, I won't break her heart.*

"We'll have a blast," Rosa murmured, keeping her tone calm and steady in an effort to engender the same in Alice. "Maybe Marcia will even let us use the paddleboat again."

Alice giggled at the memory, and the reference, like Rosa knew she would. "All right, let's go in. The anticipation is the worst part. I'll feel better once I get inside."

"That's my girl." Trayvon opened the car door and slipped out into the fresh afternoon air. "Pop the trunk, Rosa, and I'll unload our bags."

Rosa did as requested but put her hand on Alice's arm to stop her from leaving quite yet. She wanted to make sure to finish what she'd planned to say earlier. "Alice, you're gonna be great. You showed me how to build our fighting bot and taught me to make all kinds of repairs. If you can teach me, you can teach *anyone*. I promise."

Alice snorted softly, yet seemed pleased by her comments. "Well, you're a geek and an enthusiastic student. You also enjoy your all-access pass to my body far too much to give me a hard time about my teaching methods. Plus, I'm comfortable with you. It's different."

"Maybe so, but I'll be there with you tomorrow. You know me and Trayvon won't let anyone give you a hard time, right?"

Alice's nostrils flared as she nodded. "I know."

"You're brilliant, and when you talk about the subjects you love, you're so passionate and exciting to listen to. You know how to build stuff most of us can only daydream about creating, and when you explain even the most esoteric concepts to me, I feel like I sort of *get it*. I completely understand that you're concerned about sounding ineloquent because you're nervous, but you shouldn't worry. You've dealt beautifully with so many social situations since we've been together. More than one person has told me they couldn't even tell you were shy at all." Rosa waited to let the words sink in, then concluded by saying, "I'm *very* proud of you. Proud to be yours. Proud to watch you keep raising your goal posts higher." By this point Alice had turned a lovely shade of pink that Rosa yearned to feel against her lips. She kissed the heated skin gently, then murmured, "You're my inspiration… but you knew that already, didn't you?"

Rosa had never kept that a secret. The example Alice set for her every day had become the strongest driving force behind her ongoing recovery from the public shaming and Internet terror campaign. Watching Alice consistently withstand episodes of mental anguish in the pursuit of normalcy, simply because she wanted so badly to feel *content,* had convinced Rosa to do the same. Alice's positive influence was the sole reason she was currently poised to change her life once again, a thought she couldn't dwell on too long lest she tumble into her own personal rabbit hole of imagined doom.

"I love you," Alice whispered, giving her a final, lingering kiss. "I couldn't do this without you."

Rosa shook her head, once. "You could, but I'm so happy you're not."

A knock on Alice's window drew their attention back to Trayvon, who stood next to their pile of luggage and gestured impatiently for them to get out of the car. "At least steal a boat first!" he called through the glass, with a smart-assed grin.

Alice broke into a giggling fit that left her bent at the waist, wiping moisture from her eyes. "Fine, let's go check in."

Rosa got out of the car and joined Trayvon at their pile of bags. She hefted the large one she and Alice had decided to share, then shouldered her extra backpack. When Alice busied herself at the passenger side door too long, checking again to make sure they hadn't left anything behind, Rosa said, "Remember what Dawn told you: every fear you overcome leaves fewer potential ways for your anxiety to ruin a future day."

Alice snorted and finally got out of the car, closing the door behind her. "I know, I know. She says this is good for me, and she's pretty much always right." She grabbed her extra backpack, then paused when Rosa's smartphone rang from its temporary home in her jeans pocket. She pulled it out and looked at the display, a smile instantly breaking out across her face. "It's Bree." She thumbed the speaker button without hesitation. "Hey, Bree! Are you here yet?"

"Hello, sweet Alice." Their friend's voice held a distinct note of satisfaction. "Do me a favor and tell your woman she owes me fifty bucks."

"You just did." Alice giggled and met Rosa's eyes. "But why?"

"Because you answered her phone."

Alice shot her a questioning look, and Rosa offered a sheepish shrug in response. "When she was knocking sense into me last summer, we may have made a bet about where your and my relationship would be a year later..." She raised her volume. "Is that what you're referring to, Bree?"

"I've had my eye on a purchase for months now, waiting for this day." Bree gloated audibly, clearly tickled to have won a wager Rosa had long forgotten. "Anyway, we're a few miles down the road. You guys already there?"

Alice's face lit up at the news of their proximity. "Enid's with you?"

"Hi, Alice!" The cheerful reply elicited simultaneous grins from both Alice and Rosa. "Hey, Rosa! I can't wait to see you two again in person."

"Likewise." Over the past year, Rosa had become surprisingly close to Enid through regular online chats and weekly phone calls, finding her to be an excellent source of objective advice and nonjudgmental support. She'd saved Rosa from doing something stupid to ruin her relationship with Alice more than once. When she and Bree agreed to join them for a mini-reunion at Camp Rewind to celebrate Alice's teaching debut, Rosa had been overjoyed at the opportunity to revisit the fun atmosphere of camp and bask in the glow of friendships that had only grown stronger with time. "Bad news, though...there's a rumor Marcia might hook us up with a private cabin, since Alice is here in a professional capacity."

"Bummer," Enid answered smoothly. "Maybe we'll get an invitation for a slumber party?"

"Slumber party!" Bree said enthusiastically in the background. "I love Camp Rewind!"

Alice turned a deeper shade of red, made worse by Trayvon's knowing leer. She handed the phone to Rosa, who switched off the speaker as they walked closer to the front entrance. Warmed by the way Trayvon looped his arm around Alice's waist and marched them confidently toward the main office, Rosa murmured, "Well, you just managed to embarrass the hell out of my girlfriend."

"Is it terrible to admit I'm glad that's still possible?" Terrible or not, Bree sounded unambiguously gleeful. "She's so cute when she blushes."

"Yes, and she's adorable right now, believe me."

"We'll check you in, Rosa," Alice called over her shoulder. She paused to blow Rosa a kiss, wearing a bashful grin that did little to hide exactly how much she'd secretly enjoyed Bree and Enid's teasing. "So you can finish your call."

Pleased by Alice's unexpected display of confidence, Rosa agreed despite her instinctive urge to stay close. Alice didn't enjoy feeling too clingy, and Rosa knew better than to challenge her instincts. "All right."

"Did we scare her away?"

Rosa snorted at Enid's question, delivered as it was in a voice of pure innocence. "For now." She walked back to the entrance of the camp to get a view of the parking lot. "I'm waiting outside for you two fools to arrive."

"Sweet of you. Now, Rosa," Bree said in a tone that clearly signaled a change in topic. "This morning, I read something rather interesting online. An announcement from a major publisher about an upcoming nonfiction, semi-autobiographical book about public shaming in the Internet age…written by a woman whose bra and panties I once picked up off the floor?"

Rosa rolled her eyes at Bree's typical instinct to veer into the inappropriate. "That's me."

"Wow, a book?" Enid's surprise made it clear that Bree hadn't yet shared the news. "That's great, Rosa. Congratulations."

"Thank you." Rosa endured a renewed torrent of her own worries as she considered the floodgates she was likely to reopen by venturing back into public life. "I'm hoping it'll help people gain a better appreciation for how the whole situation felt from my perspective, but I'm also worried it might be the stupidest decision I've ever made."

"More stupid than saving an explicit video of yourself showing both your naked pussy *and* your easily identifiable face to an inherently insecure 'cloud' storage location?"

Rosa had to chuckle at the sound of Enid giving Bree a well-deserved smack in reaction to her blunt comment. It had taken her some time, but Rosa could appreciate the humor in the situation when pointed out by a good friend. "Touché."

"Seriously, Rosa, nothing could be as bad as what you've already endured. By publishing this book, you're reclaiming your dignity. Your *voice*." Bree actually sounded a little choked up. "I'm really fucking proud of you, and that's the truth."

Bolstered by the approval, coming as it did from someone whose friendship she valued, Rosa accepted the praise with a quiet murmur of thanks. "I appreciate that."

Enid radiated sympathy. "You're worried the book will stir everything up again?"

"Yes," Rosa said plainly. "I *know* it will, at least a little. But I need to learn how to live my life despite that, if I ever want to regain my confidence and sense of security. And, you know, if I ever want to speak to the issues I care about again. Alice knows what could happen, but she begged me to go ahead and submit the book to my publisher anyway. She thought it was the right call, and I think…" She paused and allowed a wry smile. "I think Alice is a very smart woman."

"You've come a long way since that day you told me you'd rather dump Alice than let her life be ruined by an association with you." Bree turned smug. "See how my excellent advice panned out? Maybe I'm in the wrong profession. I should be a therapist, or at least a life coach, or something."

"You're a real superstar." Rosa fought to keep a straight face as a trio of excited new arrivals emerged from a parked car and began to unload their bags. "But, yes, fine, you were right. Things have been great with Alice. At this point, I trust wholeheartedly that nothing the outside world throws at us will tear us apart. More than that, I realize that I'm our relationship's own worst enemy and, thanks in part to you, have vowed never to give in to my self-destructive instincts again."

Enid spoke up, honey-voiced. "*You* did all that, darling?"

Bree chuffed, her pleasure obvious even over the spotty reception. "No big thing."

"It was *both* of you, actually." Rosa stepped aside to let the small group of exuberant campers walk past her toward the main office, then broke into a sunny grin when a familiar sedan pulled into the lot and parked. "But your contributions aside, I have to hand it to Alice. She's stronger than I could have ever imagined. More importantly, I love her like I never knew was possible. She makes me want to be strong, like her. She makes me brave."

"That's wonderful." The driver's side door of Bree's car swung open and its owner emerged. She broke into a smirk as she ended their call and opened her arms in greeting. "Now get over here and give me a hug, you sappy dope."

Rosa went. It was true—she *was* a sappy dope.

But also a happy one.

❖

Later that night, in a secluded clearing of trees well away from the bonfire around which most of the camp partied, Alice stood within her close circle of friends—Rosa, Trayvon, Bree, Enid, and Jamal—and lit a joint that she quickly passed to the right. Trayvon grinned at her and took a drag, then passed it along to Jamal, who eyed their surroundings nervously as he followed suit.

"Jamal, relax." Trayvon reassured him as he gestured at the impressively tall redwoods that encircled them. "Who's going to bust us out here?"

"I'm not worried about Marcia," Jamal said, and exhaled a massive lungful of smoke while handing the joint to Bree. "It's the snakes, man. Woods are full of 'em."

Outwardly calm, Rosa turned to stare at Alice with wide eyes. "I forgot."

Giggling on the inside only, Alice wrapped her arm around Rosa and pulled her into a sheltering embrace. "I'll protect you," she murmured, kissing Rosa's cheek. "Don't worry."

Rosa accepted the joint from Enid so she could take a long, desperate puff. "He said the S-word. Of course I'm worried."

Alice took the next hit, a big one, and stretched to press her mouth against Rosa's as she blindly passed the smoldering joint off to Trayvon. Employing a trick Rosa had taught her almost exactly one year ago, in a spot not terribly distant from where they were standing now, she gifted Rosa's lungs with smoke from her own. She smiled as she backed away, unsurprised when Bree felt the need to offer a suggestive comment.

"If you two aren't looking for anyone to crash your slumber party, you might want to cut that shit out." Bree paused to suck on the end of the joint, then held it out so Enid could do the same. "Some of us get turned on watching women kiss each other."

Heavy-lidded already, Enid raised a hand and flashed a crooked grin. "Guilty."

"And then there are those who crave a more masculine display," Trayvon remarked, and gave Alice a playful pinch on her elbow. He shot Jamal a sideways look. "You get many men here looking to hook up with other guys?"

"From time to time," Jamal said lightly. He took a casual draw from the joint as it continued its circuit around the group, the threat of snakes apparently forgotten in the wake of Trayvon's question. "When I'm lucky."

Enid's eyebrow popped as she glanced between the two men. "Yowza."

Jamal and Trayvon both tried and failed to suppress eager smiles as they not-so-surreptitiously looked each other over. Jamal shrugged, then turned mildly self-conscious eyes to Alice, as though checking her reaction. "I'm down for some fun is all I'm saying. Whatever shape it happens to take."

Pleasantly buzzed, Alice showered Jamal with a beaming grin and all the approval in her heart. "I can't claim firsthand knowledge, but rumor has it that Trayvon provides *excellent* fun."

Trayvon bumped Alice's fist with his, then pantomimed the act of slipping her imaginary cash from his pocket. The entire group laughed, Alice loudest of all. Loose and happy from the pot, surrounded by good-natured allies, she barely remembered the persistent anxiety she'd had to battle whenever she allowed her mind to drift to thoughts of actually trying to teach this class. After the following afternoon, all the anticipation would end, and she could take pride in having achieved yet another difficult accomplishment. She knew in her heart that everything would most likely turn out well, that she'd do just fine, but now that she was surrounded by her friends, it was easier to focus on the present instead of worrying about what might come to pass.

Jamal rolled his shoulders and, lips still curled from joining in the group's laughter, said, "I'm glad to gather firsthand knowledge about Trayvon's fun factor, if invited to do so."

Trayvon glanced at Alice as though seeking permission. Alice laughed. "Go. Just make sure you're there for my class tomorrow. Ten o'clock sharp. Nine thirty would be better, since you're a major part of my moral-support team."

Trayvon nodded, looking like an eager puppy. "Nine thirty it is, at the latest."

"I'll make sure he's there on time." Jamal threw an arm around Trayvon's shoulders and drew him closer so they could tussle playfully. "You know I can't miss your class. I'll be there at nine to start setting up."

"Have fun, you guys." Rosa watched with an amused expression as their friends ambled away from the group in search of private time.

"Good," Bree said, straining to hold in the massive hit she'd just taken. She passed the joint to Enid. "More for us."

Rosa turned to Alice with an almost scandalized expression. "Did you know Jamal was into guys?"

"Sure." She and Jamal had formed a close friendship after a year's worth of trading emails, to the point where they'd become wonderfully honest with one another. He was probably her best friend, after Rosa, with Trayvon trailing only slightly behind. She wasn't sure whether her two favorite men would hit it off for longer than a single night of covert pleasure, but she couldn't help but feel tickled by the impromptu connection. "He's into a lot of things."

"Just like our girl Rosa." Bree gave Rosa a playful punch, always ready with a lighthearted jibe. "At least, that's what they say online."

Rosa took a hit from the dwindling joint and very slowly, very deliberately, passed her exhalation to Alice while pulling their bodies flush. When they separated to breathe, she looked into Alice's eyes and said, "Actually, I'm mostly into Alice these days."

"I'll bet," Enid chirped in a goofy, slightly slurred voice. "*Into* her, get it?"

Bree glanced down at Enid, rolled her eyes with undisguised affection, and waved away the roach Alice tried to offer them. "I think my lady friend has hit her limit."

Enid turned to shoot a mock glare at Bree, but ended up stumbling into her embrace instead. "All right, yeah," she finally agreed, somewhat haughtily, from within the strong circle of Bree's arms. "I may be a little stoned."

Alice dissolved into quiet laughter and chided her. "Lightweight." Enid's defeated shrug and Bree's nod of agreement helped her find the confidence to keep the teasing going. "So much for that slumber-party idea."

Rosa snickered. "Oh, I don't know. Enid looks about ten minutes away from a good, hard slumber to me."

Groaning in disappointment, Enid gazed up into Bree's eyes with a beseeching pout. "But I *really* wanted to have an orgasm tonight."

Bree clicked on her flashlight and waved to Rosa and Alice as she walked away arm in arm with her lover. "If you can stay awake until we get to your bunk, I promise to get you off."

"But what if I can't reciprocate?" Enid yawned.

"Then you'll owe me one." Bree hastened their pace. "Come on. Let's sing to stay awake."

Alice shared a grin with Rosa when their friends broke into song—two different ones, from the sound of it—as they trudged off toward the women's sleeping cabin. Rosa took Alice's hand and raised it to her mouth, kissing gently, then smiled against her knuckles. "What about us? Sex or sleep? Your choice."

Not for the first time—not even for the hundredth—an exuberant wave of happiness crashed over Alice and carried her away. All the trials she'd faced during the past twelve months—from her mother's icy reaction to her disclosure of her new relationship, to her father's embarrassed silence, to the eight hellish weeks early on when Rosa had nearly fallen apart under an onslaught of renewed vitriol following the publication of that essay about her article—seemed almost trivial in light of the constant joy Rosa brought to her life. Bar none, their relationship was the best thing that had ever happened to Alice. It was their one-year anniversary, they were back in the place where they'd first met, and she had a much higher tolerance than Enid, along with a pressing desire to physically reconnect.

"I'm not tired yet. Want to go back to our cabin?"

Rosa led her away from the clearing by the hand. "I thought you'd never ask."

Unlike their last stay at Camp Rewind, they had relative privacy this time around, albeit not total solitude. Their modest accommodations were located amidst the other counselors' lodgings, in a small cabin that sat directly behind the cozy abode of Marcia, the head counselor. Even though they had the room to themselves, the screen windows and close proximity to their neighbors meant that camp hadn't lost any of its thrilling, clandestine appeal. Taking care to walk gingerly, Alice followed Rosa into their cabin and winced when the screen door squeaked upon closing. Rosa turned to her with an apologetic cringe, then whispered "Shh!" for good effect. Alice bit her lip in an effort not to dissolve into noisy giggles.

Rosa gathered her into a familiar embrace and walked Alice backward to the bed. She whispered into her ear, "You have to be *very* quiet for me, Al, no matter what happens. No matter what I do."

A shiver swept through Alice's body, triggering a rush of wetness to stain her panties. Her laughter died in her throat. "What are you planning to do?"

Sharp teeth nipped Alice's earlobe. "*Everything.*" Rosa's breath was fire.

Alice trembled even harder when the backs of her thighs hit the mattress. She sat down on instinct. "What if I can't stay quiet?"

"Then I'll have to put my hand over your mouth," Rosa murmured while doing exactly that, a brief demonstration meant to entice. "Or use your panties as a gag. I'll bet they're soaking wet, aren't they?"

Alice nodded. No point in lying or playing coy. "I'll try to be good."

Rosa yanked Alice's T-shirt off over her head, then pressed on her shoulders until Alice lay flat on her back. "You're *always* good, baby. You know that." She planted her knee between Alice's thighs and unbuttoned, then unzipped her jeans, shoving herself firmly against the steamy juncture of the parted legs before she peeled the denim away from Alice's heated flesh. She sat back after she'd stripped Alice to her bra and panties, and stared down with dark, glittering eyes that made Alice squirm in anticipation. After a moment, Rosa yanked on the cups of Alice's bra so her breasts spilled out over the top, then kissed Alice's stomach reverently as she knelt on the floor between her legs. "Go on, sweetheart. Pull your panties out of the way so I can taste."

Alice was positive Rosa could see the large wet spot on her panties even in the near darkness and flushed at the thought. Even if she *couldn't* see it, Rosa surely smelled her arousal. Turned on by the idea of Rosa's eyes on her, especially when they could be heard by anyone passing by, Alice gathered the sodden material in her hand and yanked it to the side. She startled when, seconds later, a *click* announced the sudden appearance of a small, bright beam of light that Rosa had aimed directly at her exposed pussy. As Alice watched in shock, Rosa bent, pink tongue spotlighted against the darkness, to give her shiny, swollen labia a drawn-out lick. Alice gasped loudly, then clapped her hand over her mouth to muffle the sound.

"As much as I adore making love to you in the dark," Rosa murmured, "what I like even better is being able to watch your pretty, wet pussy react to my touch." Aiming the flashlight deftly, she ran her tongue up Alice's labia, over and over, spreading her juices around until a shiny trail connected her top lip to the turgid clit. Rosa moaned, low and needy, then whispered, "And making *you* watch." She lowered her face and laved the swollen clit languidly, putting on a show clearly intended for Alice's benefit. After some time, as Alice's chest heaved with increasingly ferocious desire, Rosa pulled away completely. Before Alice could protest, the beam of light shifted to reveal Rosa positioned near her entrance, two fingers at the ready. "Look while I put my fingers inside you."

Alice's thighs wobbled when Rosa brought her hand between them, rubbing her opening for only a second before angling her wrist to slide the two fingers deep inside. Alice fell back against the mattress and slapped both of her hands over her mouth, trying not to scream in pleasure or yell out her praise for Rosa's sexual ingenuity. The light moved away from Rosa's busy hand for a moment, then returned after she'd stuffed a pillow they'd brought from their newly rented, shared apartment beneath Alice's hips. The minor adjustment allowed Alice to very clearly see Rosa's fingers as they fucked her in the slow, driving rhythm she liked best.

After a minute or so, Rosa paused to offer her the handle of the flashlight. "Take this. Keep it pointed on my face until I make you come." She shone the light up from beneath her chin as though prepared to tell a spooky tale around the campfire, until Alice gathered the presence of mind to snatch it away. Once she was in the spotlight, Rosa wrapped her newly freed hand around Alice's thigh and lowered her mouth to lap suggestively at the swollen clit. "Remember, be *very* quiet. We don't want anyone else to know what you're letting me do to you."

Alice held the flashlight on Rosa's face with a shaking hand, biting her other wrist to keep from crying out. Rosa was so incredibly beautiful, quite literally the girl of her dreams, and the sight of her enthusiastically delivering pleasure would never get old. As though reading her mind, Rosa shot her a saucy wink and buried her face in Alice's wetness, fingers pumping harder while her thumb slid down to glide over Alice's slick anus. Determined to stay silent, Alice moved the hand not occupied with the flashlight down to further expose her clit to the rapidly fluttering tongue that batted against it, then caught the back of Rosa's head so she could more easily roll her hips against her talented mouth. She kept the beam of light trained on Rosa the entire time, transfixed by the lewd imagery as well as the reality that she was fucking Rosa Salazar's beautiful face, one year later, in the place where the two of them first became *us*.

Alice threw back her head and came with a muffled groan, not entirely silent, but probably not loud enough to draw an investigation from Marcia, either. She twined her hand in Rosa's long, dark locks until she'd finished twitching against her tongue and around her fingers, only letting go when she sensed that Rosa needed the fresh air. Rosa crawled up to lie beside her and folded Alice into an intimate embrace that made both of them sigh in unison.

Needing a moment to recover from her staggering climax, Alice kissed lips tinged with her own flavor and patted the center of Rosa's chest. "How is it that the sex only gets better and better?"

Rosa tickled the base of her spine, drawing lazy patterns with her blunt fingernails. "Well, you know what they say about practice."

Alice grinned and took Rosa's nipple between her teeth, then bit down. Rosa's swift inhalation hinted at the intensity of her body's reaction to the simple touch. "It's fun?"

"In this case, *very* fun." Rosa stroked her hair as Alice suckled her nipple. "I love you, Alice."

Alice lifted her head and found Rosa's gaze in the dark. "I love you, too."

"Thanks for sticking with me this year." Rosa reached for her hand and laced their fingers together. "I know it hasn't always been easy."

Alice chuckled. "For you, either. That horrible lunch with my mother would have driven a lesser woman away."

"Nah," Rosa said. "I've dealt with far worse than your mom. At least she didn't threaten to gut me and leave me for dead."

"Not out loud, at least." Alice laughed along with Rosa, even though they knew she was only half-joking. As much as Alice had endured in order to be with Rosa, she wasn't the only one who'd made sacrifices. Rosa's willingness to put up with Alice's continued attempts to maintain a civil relationship with her parents all but confirmed that theirs was true love. Keenly aware of the many ways Rosa had improved her life, Alice brightened when the most exciting idea about how to celebrate their anniversary occurred to her. She slid her free hand between Rosa's legs and teasingly stroked her labia as she launched into the pitch. "So…what do you think about borrowing a paddleboat tomorrow night during the bonfire? We could go back and find that boathouse—"

"Seriously?" Rosa squirmed beneath the fingers currently painting wet circles around her swollen clit. "We'll get caught. Again."

"Not if we don't fall asleep this time."

Rosa's breathing picked up when Alice moved down to penetrate her using three slim fingers, then stretch her open in a way she knew would make Rosa even wetter. "But what about the snake?"

"That snake is long gone, honey. It was a year ago. I'm sure he's moved on. You should, too."

Rosa's eyes slipped shut. She set her jaw and rode Alice's fingers with an expression of deep concentration. "We barely lived down our first attempt at grand theft paddleboat...and it's not like we don't have a private room this time..."

Alice propped herself up on her elbow, driving harder into Rosa while using her thumb to stroke the sensitive clit her hand naturally bumped against. "It'll be a fun way to celebrate teaching my first class, not to mention our one-year anniversary. Don't you think?" When Rosa didn't answer immediately, too caught up in the pleasure of her fingers, Alice said, hopefully, "You know, I'm kind of like a camp employee this time around. I'm probably allowed to use a boat, even at night. I'm sure it'd be fine."

Rosa tipped her head back and her mouth fell open, but no sound emerged. She gripped Alice's hand tighter, as though the anchor she was providing might prevent Rosa from being swept away. Shuddering, Rosa whispered, "Does that mean you'll run the idea past Marcia?"

With a resigned sigh, Alice gave up on the admittedly risky plan. "Never mind. You're right. Not a smart idea."

Rosa rippled in pleasure, then again in surrender. She groaned, spread her legs wider, and lifted her hips to meet Alice's increasingly demanding thrusts. "All right," she gasped, a little more loudly than Alice had expected. Her next words came out a decibel lower. "We'll borrow a boat."

Overcome with guilt brought on by the realization that she had once again talked Rosa into a foolish plan that could easily come back to bite them both in the ass, Alice shook her head without slowing the rhythm of her hand. "No, I'm sure you're probably—"

"Alice!" Rosa whimpered, half moan, half plea. "We're stealing the boat. Why not, right? Camp Rewind is all about taking risks." She contracted around Alice's fingers, further wetting her hand, and quickened the motion of her urgent hips. Though Alice could feel that she was on the edge of orgasm, Rosa still managed to bite out, "The last one I took here paid off a thousandfold. I'm…willing…to take… another…oh, *fuck*, I'm gonna come."

Alice closed her eyes and buried her face in Rosa's neck, holding on tight for the ride.

Like always, with Rosa, it was one well worth taking.

About the Author

Meghan O'Brien is the author of multiple lesbian romance and erotic novels, including *Infinite Loop*, *The Three*, *Thirteen Hours*, *Battle Scars*, *Wild*, *The Night Off*, *The Muse*, and the novella *Delayed Gratification: The Honeymoon*, all from Bold Strokes Books. She is also the author of a veritable cornucopia of dirty stories, published both online and in various print anthologies. She lives in Northern California with her wife Angie, their son, and a house full of animal companions.

Books Available From Bold Strokes Books

Camp Rewind by Meghan O'Brien. A summer camp for grown-ups becomes the site of an unlikely romance between a shy, introverted divorcee and one of the Internet's most infamous cultural critics—who attends undercover. (978-1-62639-793-4)

Cross Purposes by Gina L. Dartt. In pursuit of a lost Acadian treasure, three women must work out not only the clues, but also the complicated tangle of emotion and attraction developing between them. (978-1-62639-713-2)

Imperfect Truth by C.A. Popovich. Can an imperfect truth stand in the way of love? (978-1-62639-787-3)

Life in Death by M. Ullrich. Sometimes the devastating end is your only chance for a new beginning. (978-1-62639-773-6)

Love on Liberty by MJ Williamz. Hearts collide when politics clash. (978-1-62639-639-5)

Serious Potential by Maggie Cummings. Pro golfer Tracy Allen plans to forget her ex during a visit to Bay West, a lesbian condo community in NYC, but when she meets Dr. Jennifer Betsy, she gets more than she bargained for. (978-1-62639-633-3)

Taste by Kris Bryant. Accomplished chef Taryn has walked away from her promising career in the city's top restaurant to devote her life to her six-year-old daughter and is content until Ki Blake comes along. (978-1-62639-718-7)

The Second Wave by Jean Copeland. Can star-crossed lovers have a second chance after decades apart, or does the love of a lifetime only happen once? (978-1-62639-830-6)

Valley of Fire by Missouri Vaun. Taken captive in a desert outpost after their small aircraft is hijacked, Ava and her captivating passenger discover things about each other and themselves that will change them both forever. (978-1-62639-496-4)

Basic Training of the Heart by Jaycie Morrison. In 1944, socialite Elizabeth Carlton joins the Women's Army Corps to escape family expectations and love's disappointments. Can Sergeant Gale Rains get her through Basic Training with their hearts intact? (978-1-62639-818-4)

Believing in Blue by Maggie Morton. Growing up gay in a small town has been hard, but it can't compare to the next challenge Wren—with her new, sky-blue wings—faces: saving two entire worlds. (978-1-62639-691-3)

Coils by Barbara Ann Wright. A modern young woman follows her aunt into the Greek Underworld and makes a pact with Medusa to win her freedom by killing a hero of legend. (978-1-62639-598-5)

Courting the Countess by Jenny Frame. When relationship-phobic Lady Henrietta Knight starts to care about housekeeper Annie Brannigan and her daughter, can she overcome her fears and promise Annie the forever that she demands? (978-1-62639-785-9)

Dapper by Jenny Frame. Amelia Honey meets the mysterious Byron De Brek and is faced with her darkest fantasies, but will her strict moral upbringing stop her from exploring what she truly wants? (978-1-62639-898-6)

Delayed Gratification: The Honeymoon by Meghan O'Brien. A dream European honeymoon turns into a winter storm nightmare involving a delayed flight, a ditched rental car, and eventually, a surprisingly happy ending. (978-1-62639-766-8)

For Money or Love by Heather Blackmore. Jessica Spaulding must choose between ignoring the truth to keep everything she has, and doing the right thing only to lose it all—including the woman she loves. (978-1-62639-756-9)

Hooked by Jaime Maddox. With the help of sexy Detective Mac Calabrese, Dr. Jessica Benson is working hard to overcome her past, but they may not be enough to stop a murderer. (978-1-62639-689-0)

Lands End by Jackie D. Public relations superstar Amy Kline is dealing with a media nightmare, and the last thing she expects is for restaurateur Lena Michaels to change everything, but she will. (978-1-62639-739-2)